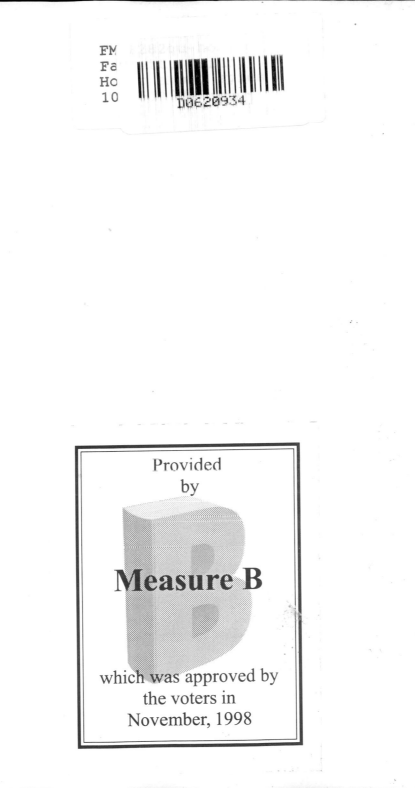

Provided
by

Measure B

which was approved by
the voters in
November, 1998

Honor Among Spies

Also by Quinn Fawcett

A Tom Doherty Associates Book  New York

Honor Among Spies

Spies

QUINN FAWCETT

HONOR AMONG SPIES

Copyright © 2004 by Quinn Fawcett

This book is printed on acid-free paper.

A Forge Book
Published by Tom Doherty Associates, LLC
175 Fifth Avenue
New York, NY 10010

www.tor.com

Forge® is a registered trademark of Tom Doherty Associates, LLC.

ISBN 0-312-87644-0
EAN 978-0312-87644-9

First Edition: May 2004

Printed in the United States of America

0 9 8 7 6 5 4 3 2 1

To Bone and Maestro . . .
lost souls of the French Quarter

Honor Among Spies

IT WAS no great task for a man to disappear on Jamaica.

This wasn't to say in the physical sense, though that, too, presented no insurmountable difficulties. European expatriates, fleeing deeds committed before, during, or after World War II, had from time to time come to the island with the express intent of modifying their identities or leaving them behind altogether. As far as was generally known, no Nazi war criminals had ever fled here. But wars sometimes made criminals of men nonetheless, even those with essentially ethical natures.

Criminal. Ian Fleming, basking in the dazzling sun and succulent humidity of the afternoon on his verandah, considered the word. It didn't, he decided almost too quickly, apply to him. The acts he had committed following the war weren't ones he cherished in his memories, but they also weren't crimes. He had been one of "Churchill's Boys," a select and highly covert group appointed by the prime minister to hunt and dispatch those Nazis who'd escaped their righteous punishments in the war's aftermath.

Such had been the PM's justification for the secret operation, which had actually started out as a program of wartime assassinations but was carried over past 1945 and the war's end. Even though Churchill didn't at present occupy the office of prime minister, it was presumed by many in the British intelligence field that the great war commander would resume his post sometime soon. Fleming, though he was no longer a part of that community, agreed with the assessment. So it was that Churchill's Boys had proceeded with their work, operating under spy chiefs that the once and—likely—future PM had personally appointed.

Fleming's rationalization for taking part in it was even simpler. He had followed his orders. He had done his duty.

During the war he had worked for the Department of Naval Intelligence. He made a successful career of being a spy. It allowed him to bring to bear all his personal assets, his organizational talents, his derring-do in beguiling and outfoxing the enemy. However, during that clandestine postwar operation he had been transformed, gradually but inevitably, into something that didn't sit well with his basic nature. He had become an assassin. The body count rose. The faces of the former Nazis he and his colleagues had erased from existence still bobbed to the surface in his memory from time to time.

But Jamaica was a fine place to lose oneself. The past couldn't be altered, but with a certain amount of determination it could be effectively outrun.

Ian Fleming was a fine specimen of an Englishman. Nearing forty, his physique remained lean and toned. He was long-legged and agile. His handsome appearance, manners, and proper education had time and again proven themselves valuable assets. He was most certainly not sliding toward middle-aged decrepitude.

He had fulfilled a longtime dream when he started construction on the tropical island hideaway of his home. The house, of course, remained a work in progress, a task that didn't daunt him in the least. He was devoted to Goldeneye. He had lifted the title of his home with a mild sense of irony from a wartime operation against the Germans in Spain.

The house had two stories. The luxuriant verandah he was currently lounging upon faced the aquamarine splendor of the Caribbean. His property included a private cove a short distance down a greenery-festooned pathway. The beach's white sands glimmered mirage-like in the brilliant afternoon sun. Only a private drive led to his front yard. His home had no telephone, no electricity. All was bucolic and serene.

In London presently, where he spent the bulk of his year, early

February was gripping the United Kingdom in its icy claws. Fleming had suffered his last winter in the nation of his birth. He had made it clear to his employers, Kemsley Newspapers, that for the winter months he would be *here*, on Jamaica, wallowing in the sumptuous heat. He'd earned a good enough name as a journalist that his employers did not object to his somewhat eccentric conditions. Recently he had bolstered his reputation by penning that exposé of the unethical doings of one Lord Dale Hemmingford, which had caused more than a minor stir.

Fleming, laid out on his cushioned lounge in a swimsuit and green floral shirt, sipped with deliberate ease at his gin and tonic. He planned later to visit his private beach, to take a refreshing dip in those inviting jewel-colored waters. In them swam chalk bass, cardinalfish, those eye-catching royal gramma with their yellow and bright purple bodies, and a host of other sea creatures. Such plans merely filled out the hours of these hedonistic days. He felt no urgency. The present was placid.

The past, however, had arrived twenty minutes ago in the physical form of the blue airmail envelope that Isaiah Hines, Fleming's houseman, had delivered on a tray. Fleming had yet to open it, to even touch it. It sat on the three-legged rattan table alongside his lounge.

He had noted the name above the return address in the left-hand corner. The sight of it had given him serious pause.

Next to the letter was a sterling silver cigarette case, gleaming brightly in the sunlight. He reached for this instead. Opening the cover, he saw, as he always did, the engraving. *My dearest Ian . . . Eternally yours . . . Nora.*

It had been some weeks since the wretched death of Nora Blair DeYoung. Murder, it had been. The immediacy of the tragedy had already receded in Fleming's heart and mind. The pain had taken root at a safer, lower level, well beneath his surface, where he was able to face it in manly fashion. Nora had been both his betrayer and his lover. He had silently forgiven her the wrongs she did him. He had also admitted—alas, only to himself, since Nora was gone—the depth of feeling he'd had for the woman.

He slipped a Players from the case, snapped shut the lid, and lit the cigarette with his gold lighter. He was putting off the inevitable. He was trying to delude himself that if he sat here sunning himself long enough, the envelope would simply vanish. Or, failing that miracle, the name above the return address would drop or gain a mere letter or two, changing it into something else. Someone else. Anyone else.

This wasn't the sort of hesitant behavior he normally indulged in. Fleming prided himself on his ability to face matters in a forthright manner. Life as a government agent had taught him to confront unpleasant facts on an almost daily basis. He had been toughened by his years. Still . . . there was that *name.*

Prescott W. Quick.

If there were two or more Prescott W. Quicks in the world, it was highly unlikely one of those counterparts would be writing to Fleming. There was only one man in his past with that name. By Scot, he thought he even recognized the penmanship. Prescott had always had a flamboyant way of drawing his cursive *Q*'s. It was pointless to be stalling like this. Open the blasted letter and have done with it.

Despite this self-admonishment, Fleming drew coolly on his cigarette, alternating now and then with a studied sip from his gin and tonic.

Prescott W. Quick had, of course, also been one of Churchill's Boys, Fleming's associate in that bloody postwar mission that convinced him, Fleming, to leave behind the spy game forever.

Resentment at this intrusion bubbled up in his chest. This offense wasn't well placed, and he knew it. Did Prescott know that Fleming had taken great pains to bury this portion of his personal history? Unlikely. Fleming had resigned and withdrawn, intending to make his break with governmental work clean and absolute. He didn't want tangible reminders of the rather abhorrent deeds he had committed. He certainly didn't wish to have a chummy correspondence with any of his former fellow assassins. What point would there be to a friendship of that nature? Would he and his bygone colleagues sit about the parlor and reminisce over brandies about those ex-Nazis the PM had been unable to suffer to live? Should they congratulate themselves on seeing justice done, despite the fact that those men—former German officers or not—had not had the luxury of pleading their cases in a lawful Allied court?

He was still loath to open the letter, no matter that only by reading the missive could he ascertain why Prescott was contacting him after so long a spell of silence.

He sighed and glanced up into the sky. There was a ghostly bone-white crescent of the moon visible behind a few gossamer wisps of cloud. The sun burned its welcome heat onto him. He had never objected to Jamaica's sultry, sweat-inducing humidity as other European visitors to the island often did. He had endured one too many English winters. He had picked the site of his tropical retreat wisely.

And now his sanctuary was being rudely intruded upon.

At last he snatched up the blue envelope. The return address was in the States, namely New Orleans in the state of Louisiana. Fleming had passed through the colorful city before. It was a curious place, particularly its celebrated French Quarter—aptly named, since its ambience was decidedly more European than American. The street number next to the Dauphine Street address indicated, if his memory served, that it was indeed within the confines of the Quarter.

"Sah?"

Fleming glanced up, realizing he'd been gazing a prolonged moment at the face of the envelope, even as his innate military instincts had let him hear Isaiah Hines slip quietly out onto the verandah. Isaiah was hovering a deferential two steps away. He wore a short-sleeved khaki-colored shirt and white linen trousers. The tall Negro houseman was as lean as Fleming and, if anything, even firmer in his build. His muscles were sinewy and taut. His natural dark flesh tone was diluted by some European ancestry. He was well spoken and efficient in his duties. His manner betrayed the formal education he'd had, above what was normal for one of Jamaica's native inhabitants. He was roughly five years Fleming's junior.

"Yes, Isaiah?"

"If you'd care for another, sah?" The houseman indicated the empty glass atop the rattan stand. Fleming hadn't realized he'd drained it. "Or perhaps something to eat?"

"Food?" Fleming offered his butler-cook a wry smile. "Oh, I should think not. I don't appear to be burning up much energy dawdling away the hours in this chair. I shall instead simply look forward to supper. Do you have any thoughts on the menu?"

Isaiah brightened perceptibly at the mention of dinner. During the weeks of his painful mourning over Nora, Fleming had shown a marked disinterest in food, enough to worry his houseman visibly. Isaiah, however, was too polished a servant to have displayed these sentiments overtly.

"I had the notion of attempting chowder, sah," Isaiah said with just a trace of pride.

"Splendid." Fleming often permitted his houseman a certain freedom in the planning of the meals. Chowder had been one of Cesar Holiday's—Isaiah's predecessor, who had also died tragically—best dishes.

"Perhaps to go with the lobster I had thoughts of thawing from the cold storage," Isaiah added.

"I believe there's something of the clairvoyant in you, Isaiah. One of your sumptuous lobster dinners was what I'd had in mind." Fleming now grinned outright. "For the moment, however, yes, another libation sounds appropriate."

Isaiah whipped away the empty glass, returned a fresh, adroitly mixed gin and tonic a moment later, then once more crept silently from the verandah.

Leaving Fleming to gaze again at Prescott W. Quick's letter. The pointlessness of his stalling at last overcame him.

"Rot," he muttered aloud and brusquely tore open the envelope. As he tugged free the enclosed stationery, something slid loose from the folded sheets of creamy white paper. He picked it from where it landed on his lap. It was a photograph.

It was of a nude female—naked, at least from the waist up. It was no candid French snapshot, however. The woman was quite obviously dead. She was laid out on bare dusty floorboards, her arms twisted at odd angles. Her eyes were wide, and her hair—so radiantly blond as to be platinum—lay fanned about her skull. Her features might have been attractive were they not currently locked in a sickening rictus that bared her white teeth. She looked to be no older than twenty.

Her throat had been cut. Or, more aptly, her head had been nearly hacked off. The neck bone was plainly visible at the heart of the massive fatal wound.

All this was, of course, sufficiently gruesome. However, one final item added a dash of the truly macabre to the already potent ingredients of horror. Lying between the young woman's breasts was a cross composed of what appeared to be slender animal bones with black feathers tied to them by red thread.

Fleming studied the photo for a long grisly moment, automatically forcing aside his emotional reactions. He didn't know this girl. But evidently Prescott W. Quick had seen fit to include this snapshot with his letter.

With steady hands and a grim cast to his eyes, Fleming gathered the photo and letter and went into the house, to his lounge.

Chapter 2

THE TWO sheets of creamy white, densely written stationery bore this letterhead: FROM THE DESK OF PRESCOTT W. QUICK, FINDER OF LOST FORTUNES.

Fleming studied this curiosity a moment, but there was no further information beyond the same Rue Dauphine address as on the envelope's face. Perhaps the letter itself would give some clue as to what his former colleague was presently doing for employment. Evidently he, too, had retired from the spy business. There had certainly been no "Finder of Lost Fortunes" bureau at Whitehall during Fleming's stint there.

His lounge was a large chamber with earthen-toned carpeting that nearly duplicated the rich wood hue of the wainscoting. Its furnishings were comfortable and spread out, allowing a good deal of breathing space. Tasteful yet relaxed. That was Goldeneye's basic character. He had settled into an armchair, having brought along his drink as an afterthought. He read:

Dear Mr. Ian Fleming,

At the peril of flattering myself, I think it safe that you may recall my name. If not, this epistle shall likely be of little or no interest to you. As you have doubtlessly by now noted, enclosed is a photograph, one of a series, that recently came into my possession. The unfortunate young lady's identity is known to me. However, to give this ghastly murder meaning, beyond its obvious ability to horrify, I must first provide some details.

I resigned from my official duties shortly after, as I later discovered, you yourself did. Resettlement to the city of New Orleans suited me, as I had visited the charming burg several times previously. My current trade is a somewhat peculiar one. I am a private detective, modeling myself with admitted whimsy on the fictitious Sherlock Holmes, a literary character who brought me much delight in my youth. I restrict myself to essentially harmless cases, commissions I can often resolve with a spot of legal research without troubling myself to leave the comfortable confines of my home.

The enclosed photograph and several like it were delivered anonymously to me during what started as a rather mundane appointment, though I shall for the time being withhold the names of the parties involved. A man suspected his new son-in-law of an illicit romantic liaison. He named the hours the lad was unaccountably absent from his job and home, the address where he said he was spending these interludes, and even the name of the suspected female party. Though I would normally refrain from this sort of physical investigation, it seemed frankly an effortless means to earn my payment.

I shall truncate this tale before it grows tedious. The woman in the photograph I have sent you is my client's daughter, not the son-in-law's mistress. The mistress, sadly, was quite real. However, it is that mistress's identity which is the truly shocking aspect of this already appalling case. Her name, when I first learned it from my client, did not register. It was only upon espying her when the son-in-law paid one of his routine calls at her home that I made the mental connection. Her name (this at least I must reveal to you) is Faith Ullrich, and she is the veritable image of her father. His, too, is a name I feel secure you shall remember: Wallace Ullrich.

Fleming nearly started in his armchair, but his natural cool-headed tendencies kept his equilibrium for him. He was quite absorbed, despite his initial misgivings, in Prescott W. Quick's strange letter. His immediate tranquil surroundings had seemed to recede as he read the pages. Now, at the mention of Wallace Ullrich, the present retreated even further...and the past advanced grimly. It was too bad that the past had chosen this balmy idyllic day to pay so intrusive a visit on him.

Wallace Ullrich was another name from the secret roster of Churchill's Boys.

Neither I nor the police know for certain who is responsible for the hideous murder of the young lady in the photograph. Faith Ullrich and the son-in-law have both vanished. The cross of chicken bones and feathers, which appears in the photograph, was discovered along with the body and makes for a very disturbing clue, suggesting as it does the involvement of some sort of occult ritual. The press has understandably made a great hullabaloo of it, and the public outcry is substantial. Naturally I have cooperated with the local constabulary and turned over the series of prints I received anonymously... all but the one I have sent you. I also withheld, though my conscience troubles me over it, the brief scrawled note that accompanied the package of gruesome photographs. It reads thus:

sins of our fathers
we know what you've done, Quick

Could this information aid the police in their probes? I cannot answer. The message fills me with an old dread. "Sins of our fathers." It might be that we are those fathers, my dear Ian. I am at a loss as to how I should act. I have put

away my preceding years, those particular years you may recall we had in common. I had stowed them rudely in my
mind's attic, with no desire to ever brush away the cobwebs
and unseal the rusted locks. I do not wish to lose the refuge
of forgetfulness.

I did not know whom else to turn to, and so I have im-
posed this horrid dilemma on you. You have my apologies
even as I ask your aid. I always regarded you highly, dear
Ian, though you may not have suspected the esteem in
which I held you. I ask only that you contact me. You shall
find an easier job of it than I had of unearthing your whereabouts. Any communication from you would be most welcome. Until then, I remain . . .

Respectfully yours

The signature prominently displayed Prescott's embellished
cursive *Q*. Fleming stared another long moment at the frightful
photo of the murdered girl. Solemnly he tucked everything back
inside the blue airmail envelope and laid it on the stand nearby
his chair. He lit another Players and tapped the first ash tip into a
brass ashtray.

Well, this certainly put a crimp in his afternoon of idle indul-
gence.

It was, of course, far too disturbing to ignore. Prescott was obviously reluctant to contact him, had even apologized contritely
in the letter for doing so. It seemed his former colleague had followed a route not dissimilar to Fleming's—retirement from service, withdrawal to an exotic locale, the dogged mental effort to
elude an unpleasant past. Fleming realized he shouldn't be surprised by this. Surely his conscience wasn't the only one per-
turbed by the deeds he and his fellows had committed following
the war. In fact, Prescott seemed wounded rather deeply.

Deliberately he called up a picture of Prescott W. Quick. He had been a lanky figure of a man, over six feet tall, gangly of limb but not at all awkward in his movements. He had dark reddish hair and almost gaunt features, which were rescued from outright homeliness by his dazzling long-lashed hazel eyes and the fetching grin he could summon at an instant's notice. He had been something of a lady's man, despite his unconventional appearance. This went some distance toward verifying one of Fleming's pet theories: Good looks were no match for confident charm. Prescott was also highly intelligent, with a mind created to absorb the most minute facts. He had been a career intelligence man when Fleming knew him, intent on spending his years in that community.

Apparently that same ruthless postwar operation had changed his mind for him.

Fleming had never imagined there was anything like a close camaraderie between them. Oh, there was that natural bond of men engaged shoulder to shoulder in a perilous activity; such attachments were inevitable. But evidently Prescott had admired him to an unsuspected degree. It was a curious thing to discover now, years after their association. Fleming chuckled dryly to himself. Well, he was no reader of minds after all.

What, then, to do about Prescott's petition for help? There was a quandary.

The first and most enticing option was, naturally, to overlook it altogether. From the apologetic tone of the letter it was likely Prescott would understand this impulse. Had this strange situation been reversed, Prescott might well decide to act—or refrain from acting—in a like manner.

His former colleague was disinclined to involve the local authorities of New Orleans in the full breadth of the matter. That made perfect sense. There was the not inconsiderable fact of the Official Secrets Act to take into account. Like all those involved in clandestine operations, Prescott was forbidden to disclose any aspect of the intelligence missions he'd participated in. That *sins of the fathers* message would reveal much more information than was prudent.

Why, however, hadn't he thought to contact Whitehall, the seat of the British Secret Service? This situation would surely be of interest to that body. Fleming believed he could answer that himself. Prescott had cut his ties. He had divorced himself utterly from his past. Contacting Whitehall might seem the equivalent of ripping open an old wound. So he'd turned to Fleming instead, his old associate who had resigned from service even before he did so.

There was sense to it. And yet Fleming remained averse to making even a show of lending a hand.

If Prescott fancied himself a private detective—"Finder of Lost Fortunes" indeed!—he should have the mettle to go solve this puzzle himself. The obvious suspects in the girl's murder were this unnamed son-in-law and Faith Ullrich. An affair was afoot, after all. Passions running high. Snap irrevocable decisions being made. The mistress and the husband conspiring to kill the wife, then vanishing. It was ludicrously pat.

Still, that chicken bone cross. It hinted at *vodun*, a practice certainly not unfamiliar to the island of Jamaica.

And why the photographs? This might prove to be a niggling detail in the end. Perhaps a guilty conscience was to blame. If these two were amateur murderers, their behavior was likely to be quite erratic. They might well have sent the photos to Prescott themselves.

Faith Ullrich, the spitting image of her father, Wallace? Fleming had no reason to trust implicitly Prescott's memory. The man might simply be mistaken, his recollections overheated and jumbled by the violence of the episode he had unwittingly waded into. Yes, plausible.

But the note . . . *we know what you've done, Quick*. That was undeniably disquieting.

He had to consider the possibility of duplicity. He had been lied to before, led on, beguiled. Sir William Potter, Nora Blair DeYoung. Both had cozened and used him. Though instinct told him to take Prescott at his word, he must keep the potentiality of chicanery in mind. However, there could be no obvious means of fabricating that photograph. It was, decidedly, of a dead woman.

Surely Prescott was withholding further facts on the matter. It was likely he would wait until Fleming made contact before revealing whatever else he knew of the case, such as the identities of the family members of the brutally murdered girl.

Which returned him inevitably to his original predicament. Respond to Prescott's appeal or ignore it.

He lit yet another cigarette and finished his gin and tonic with slow deliberate sips. Through the louvers of the lounge's unglassed windows he could hear the warm emerald waves crashing languidly upon the white sands of his cove. He had planned to spend some while in those waters, losing himself in the gentle currents and communing with the mostly innocuous sea life of the Caribbean.

Yet he had made his decision. As unpleasant as his dilemma appeared, he would face it without further vacillating. There was nothing to gain in delay.

He stubbed out his Players, set down his empty glass, and levered himself upward from his plush armchair. Isaiah, alert to his movements, appeared in the doorway of the lounge.

"I shall need some stationery and a fountain pen," Fleming announced to his houseman.

Chapter 3

IN THE end Fleming composed a rather neutrally worded return letter. Afterward, he was able to return to his normal daily routines, languorous though they might be.

On a deeper mental level, however, his curiosity would not be quelled. It was perhaps his journalistic instincts that had been aroused. Prescott's letter—to say nothing of that photograph of the dead woman—had piqued his interest. He wanted to know more, even as he instinctively withdrew from involving himself directly in the matter by agreeing to aid his former colleague.

Fleming settled on a compromise between these conflicting impulses.

He had been spending far too much time at the house these past weeks. Granted, he'd needed that period of retreat from the world at large. It had permitted him an interval of seemly mourning for Nora. Now, however, he felt something more like his old self. And his old self was no hermit.

"Isaiah, may I presume the auto has a reasonably full tank of petrol?"

"It does indeed, sah," answered his houseman from the foot of the stairs as Fleming descended the flight from his bedroom. "I took a look at the engine only yesterday morning. All is in order."

"Good fellow."

It was an hour before noon. Fleming was dressed in his white linen suit, the breezy fabric suitable for the sweltering midday. He had completed the ensemble with a cool satin shirt of regal purple and a comfortable pair of sandals.

"Does the house require any urgent items? I shall be going

into Kingston and could visit our dear friend Henry Long while I'm there."

Isaiah lifted a dark rueful brow. Henry Long, who operated a well-stocked chandlery in the city—and did a fine side trade in information—was far too calculating a businessman to be named a friend by anyone Fleming knew.

"Nothing critical, sah," said Isaiah. "The house's supplies are adequate presently. But if you happen to be passing Mistah Long's anyway . . ." From a shirt pocket he extracted a pencil and note pad. As he quickly wrote a few lines, he asked, "Shall I pack a lunch for your excursion?"

Fleming shook his head, taking the small sheet of paper Isaiah offered. "I'll find a meal if I desire one. In any case I shall return for dinner."

"Very good, sah."

Isaiah held open the front door as Fleming stepped out. A late morning breeze frisked the trees. Fleming's 1935 Lagonda Rapier sat in its customary place at the terminus of the short drive that led to his tucked-away home. Its polished blue-green body gleamed, almost mimicking the enticing hues of the Caribbean's warm waters. He treasured the auto. Driving was something of a passion for him, and ownership of this fine vehicle was the perfect complement to the general rustic luxury of his house. He had made a superb refuge for himself here on Jamaica. Though he took satisfaction from his current occupation as a journalist, the day would eventually come when he would retire altogether from the newspaper business. From then until he was prepared to lie in his grave, regardless of what subsequent trade he took up, he would dwell yearlong on his island.

The Rapier wore its canvas hood, which kept stray leaves from dropping into it and birds from roosting in its cushions. He undid the metal snaps along the top edge of the windshield and around the seats, then stowed the canopy in the auto's trunk. He climbed inside with a small smile of anticipation, slotting the key and engaging the ignition.

The motor came alive with a gratifying masculine growl. He let it rev a moment. Isaiah, naturally, had been true to his word. The mechanical pitch was as perfect as a conscientiously tuned harp.

He put the car in gear and turned down the packed earth of his drive, seeking out the coastal road.

The letter he had penned to Prescott W. Quick three days ago, which Isaiah had posted for him, contained little beyond acknowledgment of his former colleague's message. Fleming offered reserved sympathies for the man's plight. As Prescott had been careful to, he made no direct reference to that common past when they'd both been Churchill's Boys. He had made no clear offer of help and felt no repentance for the omission. Prescott was in no position to demand or even expect anything of him. Fortunately, from the tone of the man's original letter, he seemed wholly aware of that fact.

It had been a bit of an unsettling experience writing that letter, opening even a small door onto his best-forgotten past. He certainly hadn't done the craven thing, which would have been to ignore Prescott's missive entirely. But neither had he allowed himself to become entangled in the man's problems. Jamaica was remote, far from New Orleans and whatever storm may or may not have been brewing there.

Still, curiosity prickled at Fleming, enough to send him into Kingston today, rather than simply letting the matter lie.

He pushed the Rapier toward speeds that might have been less than safe for another driver. He, however, knew how to handle a machine, this one in particular. He performed no outright dangerous feats but enjoyed the whistle of the wind as it raced past the windshield and tousled his dark hair.

Traffic was thin on the coast road. He dodged past a puttering saloon car and a mule-driven cart laden with a cluster of wooden barrels, careful to slow when passing the latter; mules could react violently to an automobile whipping past. It felt decidedly good to be figuratively stretching his legs in this manner. Even if this wasn't a pure pleasure jaunt, he still enjoyed the passing tropical scenery.

It was a fairly long drive into Kingston from his home, which lay outside the village of Oracabessa. Still, he made good time.

He slowed to a quite moderate pace as he broached Kingston's limits. The capital city was teeming in comparison to the not so overpopulated countryside. Jamaica's European influence—some native citizens might say "dominance"—was most manifest here, in the number of white faces, in the shops and hotels that catered to visitors from abroad. Further evidence was readily found in the examples of Continental architecture that reared here and there among the pastel-painted structures and rather humble abodes of the indigenous populace.

Though it smacked somewhat of hypocrisy, Fleming occasionally thought that this fine tropical sanctuary had been at least mildly spoiled by the arrival of the European. Jamaican culture was not an aggressive one and not prepared to repel the might of the French and English. A certain degree of unrest resulted. Still, it was a friction that Fleming in no way held himself accountable for. He, after all, lived a quite peaceful life far from this flurry. He provided livelihoods for Isaiah Hines and his sister Ruth and the other local artisans he occasionally had come to the house. His conscience was decidedly clean on the matter.

He wended his way through the narrow streets, dodging taxis, bicycles, carts, an omnibus, and a wide array of pedestrians. Negro children scampered about. Women hauled vegetables and other wares to the marketplaces. Men whitewashed walls, erected their vending stands, and ran errands for their employers. The city was its own swirling ecological system. As always when he visited, Fleming thanked the heavens he hadn't chosen to live here.

He at last pulled up to a squat gray building, its blinds drawn as usual over its windows. He entered the newspaper office, whose nondescript exterior belied the tumult within.

The front office area of this branch of Kemsley Newspapers was its usual riot of scuttling clerks and correspondents. The wide pool of news desks was alive with the staccato chugging of numerous typewriters. Sheets of paper were torn from rollers, replaced by fresh ones. Voices yelped into telephones.

Fleming was recognized and greeted by several of the staff members. He returned these hails with a nod and a warm smile as he crossed to the far side of the cluster of desks, finally settling beside the one nearest a pebbled-glass door. Behind that door was the office of Merlin Powell, Fleming's editor.

He knew this was somewhat risky, approaching Powell for a favor. If his editor suspected that he was presently caught up in some sort of intrigue, he would be on Fleming like a shark scenting blood in the water. That recent trip to San Francisco with Nora Blair DeYoung had—in the course of an adventure that had grown more complex and dangerous at every turn—eventually produced a fine feature story from Fleming.

"Miss Chestnut, is our Mr. Powell in at the moment?" He leaned a hip on a cluttered desk and smiled.

"Oh! Mr. Fleming, why, I, er . . ." Sarah Chestnut was mid-twenties, with dark hair and long bangs and with a figure that had all the proper feminine curves. However, the flustered air she radiated when engaged in anything but her job detracted fatally from her basic attractiveness. A shame, Fleming had always thought. Her fingers hovered above the keys of her typewriter as she tried vainly to meet his gaze.

"Why, oh, yes, he is, Mr. Fleming." She wore a skirt and blouse of matching dull brown and a choker of pearls.

"Thank you so much, Miss Chestnut," he said. "And may I add how very enchanting you appear today." The flirtatious words came almost automatically. No one in this office, so far as he knew, had ever made a successful advance toward Sarah Chestnut, but that made the game all the more engrossing. This was, he realized suddenly, the first overture—offhand as it was— toward any woman that he'd made since Nora's sad demise. He must indeed be healing.

Before he could push off from the desk, a finger tapped his right shoulder smartly.

"Fleming," said Merlin Powell behind him, "I do hope this means you've decided to report for work."

A moment later he found himself in Powell's office. The chamber was large, but one felt mentally squeezed by it nonetheless, owing to the tall metal filing cabinets occupying every available inch of the walls.

Powell wedged himself behind a desk infinitely more cluttered than Miss Chestnut's, while Fleming took a facing hardback chair. An overhead ceiling fan revolved its blades in its tireless unavailing attempt to beat back the heat and humidity that the editor so loathed. Fleming had wondered from time to time why the large man had accepted this appointment to Jamaica. A posting in chilly old England would surely suit his temperament better. Perhaps he had a wide streak of self-sacrifice of which Fleming was unaware, a proud fealty to Kemsley Newspapers. Perhaps he'd been packed off to the island as some form of punishment.

Such speculations hardly mattered at the moment. Fleming faced his editor squarely.

"As truly lovely as it is to see your handsome features," Fleming began, "I must at this time contritely admit I've not come here today to report for work, as you put it. Instead, I wish to ask a—"

Powell waved rather gruffly in his direction. "Oh, for the love of St. Peter, Fleming. I never actually imagined you were here on official business. You're a lost cause."

"I thank you, sir."

Powell folded his hands among the litter of file folders and notebook pages atop his desk. His body was large and square, his face roughly congruent to these dimensions. He wore a beige shirt that was inevitably damp beneath the arms.

"I merely wanted to inform you that the worst of the Hemmingford business has evidently died away," said the editor in a level tone. "He's ceased, for the moment anyway, to make those appalling squawks about bringing litigation against everyone involved in that scandalous story we printed."

Fleming nodded. "That is good news," he said sincerely.

Lord Dale Hemmingford, the powerful British industrialist, had taken rather severe umbrage at the feature Fleming had filed with Kemsley Newspapers. The formidable white-maned magnate had found himself quite publicly implicated in his involvement with one Reginald P. Jessup, a career American criminal and the man who had murdered Nora Blair DeYoung. Fleming had acted out of a sense of revenge and justice—and then, frankly, put the entire matter behind himself. In the past weeks he hadn't given Lord Hemmingford many complete thoughts.

Powell continued, "Our Mason Caldwell"—the newspaper's lawyer—"tells me Hemmingford had no luck whatever trying to foist the matter on the courts. It seems the storm has passed. For the paper at any rate. I'm not so confident about you. Hemmingford has surely learned how to hold a grudge during however many centuries that ancient vulture has lived. He is likely still quite thirsty for your blood. I recommend you remain vigilant."

Fleming favored his editor with a cool smile. "Shall I quake in fear on an hourly basis with the thought that Lord Hemmingford might stretch out his mighty arm across the Atlantic and swat me off the face of the planet? I should think not. However, I appreciate your cautioning—and your concern. It's most decent."

Powell seemed to have no ready retort to being thanked. As a substitute he grunted noncommittally.

"Very well," he said brusquely. "Now, then. What actually brings you here today?"

"The hope that you'll grant your employee a favor."

Powell's heavy shoulders shrugged. "Well, you can always hope."

"I wonder if you might make use of your contacts in Whitehall on my behalf."

"What? Whitehall? Again?" The editor frowned. "It wasn't too long ago you had me delving into the files of the British Secret Service, Fleming. To confirm or deny the credentials of two British agents—" His eyes clouded a moment as he retrieved the names. "Davenport and Stahl."

"Correct," said Fleming, impressed by the man's ready memory.

"As I also recall, you never satisfactorily divulged your reasons for wanting that information."

Powell was circling, looking for the scent. If he suspected Fleming of being on the trail of a newsworthy story, he would want to sink his claws into it for the good of Kemsley Newspapers. Fleming would need to be careful.

He tried a quick counteroffensive. "I understand that feature I filed concerning Lord Hemmingford boosted sales for this paper . . . substantially."

Powell drummed his fingers. Finally he said, "I see. You believe I *owe* you. Very well." His drumming fingers abruptly acquired a pencil. "Tell me the information you're seeking this time."

Fleming, a bit surprised he'd won the editor over so swiftly, leaned forward in his chair. "Quick, Prescott W. Quick, is the name. He's retired from MI-5, sometime during the past few years."

Powell made quick jottings on a pad of yellow lined paper. "And you wish to know what about this man?"

"If he actually is retired," Fleming said. His military training had left deep impressions on him. He had to consider the possibility that Prescott was misrepresenting himself. Retired, was he? Fleming would prefer to have the fact confirmed by an outside source. Powell's Whitehall spies—whoever they were—had proven themselves effective when he'd inquired about Davenport and Stahl.

"Is that all?" asked Powell.

"If he is retired, I'd like to know what the circumstances were. Willing retirement—or otherwise."

"I see." More jotting.

"Mr. Quick is allegedly currently residing in New Orleans."

Powell's lips worked. "New Orleans."

"Yes. It's a city in the United States."

"Is it now?" Powell said drolly, laying down his pencil. "I hadn't heard the French had let it go."

"May I trust that this will all be handled discreetly?"

Powell regarded him flatly a moment. "No, Fleming, of course not. We mean to shout it from the roof of Buckingham Palace. Oh, do begone with you. If you wish to check back here later today, I may have your answers for you."

Fleming rose from his chair. "It's most kind of you."

"Yes, it is," Powell said levelly, already reaching for the phone atop his paper-strewn desk. "And more one thing, Fleming."

"That is?"

"I no longer *owe* you."

Fleming closed the pebbled-glass door behind him as he exited.

Chapter 4

WHILE POWELL turned the clandestine wheels of his spying machinery, Fleming stopped in at Henry Long's chandlery a short distance from the newspaper office.

The supply house was large and dark, its thick wooden walls blocking out the bright morning light. The shadowy interior, filled with a bewildering cornucopia of steel and brass items, gave one the sense that the place was a world unto itself.

The uncontested ruler of that world of nautical, automotive, and general supplies sat at his usual place behind the front counter. Henry Long seemed as large and dark as his establishment. His eyes, behind the preposterously small lenses of the spectacles he always wore, regarded Fleming with cool assessment as he approached the counter. It was as if the chandlery's proprietor were already calculating potential profit and loss.

"Henry, do you keep it so dogged dim in here so that your customers must grope about in the same half-blind manner you do?" Henry's shoddy eyesight was an old topic of banter between them.

"Ah, Mistah Fleming," Henry's low voice came grumbling from his large body. "I recognize your voice. Come closer, sah." He lifted a hand from the counter and made as if to fumble in Fleming's direction, like a blind man looking to confirm another's presence by touch.

Fleming chuckled at the display. "Perhaps I can simply give you some money for goods, Henry." He removed Isaiah's list from his shirt pocket. "Add a set of spark plugs to that, won't you."

"Is your Rapier ailing then, sah?"

Fleming nearly bristled at the comment. "Quite the contrary. However, precaution is prudent." Henry's own vehicle was a rather shabby 1933 Aston Martin tourer, which likely never achieved any more speed than a donkey at a halfhearted trot. Still, Henry was quite entitled to a bit of revenge for Fleming's remark about his vision.

Henry had wrested himself off his perch behind the counter, gone through his cluttered aisles filling the items on the list, and returned with all neatly packaged by the time Fleming had smoked a cigarette.

"It's a pleasure to have you back, Mistah Fleming," Henry said, squinting happily at the notes Fleming had piled on his countertop.

Fleming frowned mildly at the dark-skinned man, wondering if this was some further bit of badinage. "Back, Henry?"

The chandlery's owner gave him a guileless look. "Yes. Back on the island."

"I returned early last month, Henry. I've even been to visit you since, if you recall. It's a hair too late to welcome me—"

"I meant back from your recent trip to the United States. The city of San Francisco."

Fleming blinked. "Henry, how in God's name do you know about that?"

"My goal is to remain informed. Thank you, sah. Do come again."

Fleming decided to simply let it go. Henry Long was a wily party, after all, with mysterious depths of information from which to draw. He left the chandlery shaking his head in some amusement.

To use up more time, he ordered a cup of coffee at a sidewalk café that seemed intent on re-creating the ambience of the Left Bank. The white-jacketed waiter even spoke in a somewhat labored French accent. However, the surrounding afternoon street scene—that of black men hauling crates of clucking chickens, to say nothing of the smells of mule droppings—made it frightfully apparent that this was not *Paree*.

He idled some while here, willing to expend the bulk of his day in Kingston waiting for Merlin Powell to tap his Whitehall contacts, rather than making a return trip to the city tomorrow.

It was somewhat disturbing that his editor had those contacts, that any civilian agency had even the smallest unauthorized access to information guarded by the British Secret Service. But then England was no longer on a wartime footing, and perhaps security had uncinched just a bit. At any rate the situation was benefiting Fleming, so he wouldn't complain.

He knew he was doing the right thing checking up on Prescott in this fashion. He still had no intention of involving himself deeper in the man's supposed troubles; but if the situation were to alter in some unforeseen manner, Fleming would at least be armed with some certain knowledge about his former colleague. That showed prudence and sensibility, qualities that Fleming possessed in just the right quantities.

It was nearly two hours since he'd left Powell when he drove back to the newspaper office. With his package of goods from the chandlery sitting in the left-hand passenger seat, he took the precaution of retrieving the canvas hood from the Rapier's trunk and buttoning it neatly over the auto's interior.

When a moment later he rapped on his editor's office door, a curt voice said, "Come."

Powell appeared not to have moved from his chair. Still wedged behind his desk, the ceiling fan whirling above and the damp stains having grown beneath the arms of his beige shirt, his eyes rose as Fleming resumed his seat in the facing hardback chair.

"Well?" Fleming asked when Powell remained silent.

"Well, indeed," his editor breathed. "You realize, Fleming, that each time I make use of these particular contacts, I am using up a favor of my own."

"For which you have my undying appreciation."

"I'd rather you didn't burden me with your gratitude."

"As you like."

Powell turned his gaze toward the disordered surface of his desk, rummaging among papers. "Very well. Prescott Wainwright Quick. Former MI-5 field agent. The specifics of his activities while in service I cannot say. I should add that I cannot say because my contacts have rather limited access to information."

That, Fleming thought, was in its way something of a relief.

His editor went on, "However, he is legitimately retired. Apparently retirement was indeed the man's own decision. Yet his general profile makes note that he was developing something of a drinking problem toward the end of his career. One might guess that he was encouraged to resign, but that's mere speculation, and I'll let you draw your own conclusions."

Powell had finished. Fleming nodded.

"Again I thank you—" he began, rising from his seat.

"Are you onto something here, Fleming?"

He resettled himself into the chair. Yes, of course. The endgame still had to be played.

"I can't imagine what you mean."

"I imagine you can," Powell returned levelly. "Are you going off on some new story? After several years in the journalism game, I would guess you'd realize that this newspaper is supposed to dole out your assignments. We locate newsworthy stories and then send a reporter to investigate. It's something of a time-honored tradition."

"And a fine tradition it is," Fleming said impassively.

"Don't be cheeky. Do me the courtesy of answering my question. Is this the start of some story you intend to pursue on your own? If so, Kemsley Newspapers wants—nay, deserves—to be involved. We are, after all, your employers."

Fleming folded his hands in his lap. In his most sincere tones he said, "I assure you, there is no story brewing. I asked this favor for strictly personal reasons—else I would not call it a favor. My job is important to me. Not only is it my livelihood, but it gives me my legitimate place in the world, as a man, as a contributor to society at large. I would not shirk my duties as a journalist nor attempt subterfuge with you." Which, in the main, was true.

Evidently his sincerity rang true enough. Powell nodded slowly, swallowing both his disappointment and suspicion that Fleming was up to something vaguely underhanded.

"Very well," he repeated.

Fleming at last excused himself from the editor's office.

As HE HAD promised Isaiah, he returned to the house for dinner, a meal of tangy stew and steaming biscuits, followed by hot sugary pudding in a brandy sauce for dessert.

"Your correspondence is waiting in the lounge, sah," said Isaiah, clearing the dishes as Fleming stood from the table.

The sun beyond his lounge's louvers was nearly brushing the line of the ocean. Isaiah had already lit the lamps, bathing the room in that peculiar wavering light so different from the harsh steady glare of electricity.

Fleming settled into his plush armchair, noting the small collection of envelopes atop the adjacent wood stand, next to the hammered brass ashtray. His houseman appeared an instant later to deliver the cognac he had requested.

"I shall tidy up the kitchen, sah. Then, if I may depart . . . ?"

Fleming lifted the pear-shaped snifter, playing the cognac's inviting scent beneath his nose. "Of course, Isaiah. It's nearly past your hour as it is. Have you urgent plans for the evening?" Normally he didn't pry into his employee's private doings, but he and Isaiah seemed to be slowly fostering a fairly close association, something that might have been called friendship were their stations not so different.

For the first time Fleming could recall, Isaiah appeared suddenly pensive, as though caught off guard by the casual inquiry.

"I . . . well, sah—" He fumbled in uncharacteristic embarrassment. "I've promised to meet . . . with someone."

A tryst, then! Fleming hid the smile that tried to creep out onto his features. The "someone" Isaiah was meeting was likely not his elder sister Ruth, who saw to the laundering of Fleming's clothes.

"Off with you then, man. I shall lock up the house tonight." Fleming made a wave of dismissal.

His visit to Merlin Powell had been fruitful enough. He now had some hard facts about Prescott, even if they only essentially confirmed what his bygone colleague had alleged about himself in that letter. Prescott W. Quick had retired from his duties at Whitehall. He was no longer an active spy. Whatever he was currently up to, it was an independent activity.

Fleming took a slow sip of his drink, and a fine drop it was, then picked up the pile of letters from his stand. There were four, quite a number to arrive all on the same day. Evidently the outside world hadn't forgotten about him here on Jamaica. There was something comforting about that.

He glanced at the faces of the envelopes. Three were expected missives from his various relations. He would reply to them in due time. The fourth bore no return address. His own name and address were rather scrawled in awkward block letters, the sort of printing one might expect from a child.

It was far too soon for Prescott to be responding to Fleming's return letter. Besides, the somewhat aloof wording he had used in replying to his former colleague virtually guaranteed that Prescott wouldn't bother him a second time.

Not hesitating this time, he tore open the envelope and picked out the lone sheet of paper. Along with it, however, came a photograph.

The man had blondish hair trimmed in severe fashion. He was not elderly. He wore a collared shirt of pale blue. And that was the entire extent of what could be deduced from Fleming's study.

What remained was an analysis of the horrors that could be visited upon the human face by a heavy bladed instrument, likely an axe.

It had been chopped at at least four times, crosscutting blows of great strength, hewing through flesh and bone, scattering teeth and laying wide open the head. There were exposed tendons, fractured bits of skull, brain matter, and of course vast quantities of blood. The body was laid out on a floor, this one tiled in a scuffed red-and-black diamond pattern, but nothing else of the surrounding scene could be viewed in the close-up snapshot.

Nothing save the chicken bone cross—black feathers tied to it by red thread—that lay immediately beside the butchered head.

Finally he turned his attention to the accompanying letter. It looked to have been ripped carelessly from a notebook. The brief writing matched the scrawl of his name and address on the envelope. The words were these:

the Ghost of Christmas Past sends greetings
keep your damned nose out of it, Fleming

It said nothing more.

He tucked the note back into the envelope and set it aside. He remained mentally and emotionally composed. Finishing his cognac leisurely, he wondered if Prescott might be able to send him a reproduction of the note he himself had received. Comparison of the writing of the two messages might prove interesting.

Chapter 5

THE POSTMARK, imprinted atop the numerous stamps necessary to get the letter to the island, showed that it had originated in New Orleans. The blurry date indicated it had been posted only a few days after Prescott had sent his letter. If Faith Ullrich and her paramour—the unnamed son-in-law—were behind this, then they had remained at large within the city limits, following the wife's gruesome murder, and following this second brutal killing. They also evidently had some means of spying on Prescott's outgoing correspondence. How else could they have known he'd written to Fleming?

This was detective work, not entirely the sort of discipline Fleming had once excelled in, but not altogether removed from the particulars of the intelligence field either. Still, it was more an affair for Prescott W. Quick, Finder of Lost Fortunes, wasn't it? Or the police force of New Orleans, who had the proper apparatus for delving into such matters.

Yet now Fleming had reasons of his own to be reluctant about bringing in the authorities. That melodramatic *Ghost of Christmas Past* comment. That he didn't like. It was far too similar to the *sins of the fathers* message Prescott had received. Someone was attempting to stir up the settled dust of history. As yet, this unknown party seemed only to be using the information as a warning. *Keep your damned nose out of it, Fleming.* That was certainly clear enough. But what if something more diabolical followed, such as blackmail?

He had no clue as to who the man in the picture might be. It certainly wasn't Prescott. And what sense did it make to send such a thing to Fleming? It was, however, certainly intriguing in a morbid sort of way. . . .

He spent much of that evening ensconced in his lounge, study-ing Prescott's letter, the grisly photos of the murdered girl and man, and the brief message he himself had received. He guessed that whoever had penned the message had used whichever hand he or she was unaccustomed to writing with; that would account for the awful scrawl and was also a means of disguising the owner's true script. Eventually he went off to bed, his mind still digesting the situation.

The following day Fleming was already awake, dressed, shaved, and sitting in the same armchair when his houseman arrived. Birds were trilling and chirping away quite happily this daybreak, raising a melodic bedlam in the trees encircling the house. Accompanying this was the inevitable crowing of a number of cocks and the insistent barking of at least three dogs.

Early risings were a sign of strong character—or so his days in the military had apparently propagandized him into believing. This was perhaps his most ingrained habit. It mattered little what late hours he kept; if he failed to wake on his own, Isaiah had standing orders to rouse him no later than 7:00 A.M.

In the lounge Fleming stared again intently at the message he'd received. *Keep your damned nose out of it.* The theatrical warn-ing, conversely, was impelling him into action. He knew full well he would now need to take active steps in this matter.

ISAIAH HINES SHOWED silent concern, checking in on his em-ployer as often as he thought he could properly do so. The En-glishman had seemed quite recovered from whatever unfortunate incident had occurred during his recent visit to the United States. Isaiah, not privy to the details, had of course made no attempts to pry. Now, sadly, the man appeared to be brooding anew. There he sat, planted in his armchair in the lounge, waving off whatever offers of food or drink his houseman made. He appeared to be in a black study over one or another of the airmail letters he'd received recently. Perhaps a family member was struck ill. Perhaps any number of possibilities. Isaiah cared about his employer's well-being, more so than for anyone he'd previously served. Ian Fleming was a genuinely decent and honorable man, something of a rare find among Jamaica's European inhabitants.

FLEMING WAS PERIPHERALLY aware of Isaiah's anxious hovering. As always, he appreciated the concern. But he couldn't spare his attention from this present matter to assuage his houseman's apprehension. He was busy pondering and rejecting and repondering potential courses of action.

His aversion toward involvement in the matter remained, but yesterday's note had decidedly personalized things. He could, if he chose, take exception to the fact that Prescott had evidently involved him in this unpleasant business, but at this stage such thoughts were only counterproductive, and Fleming was too coolheaded to be sidetracked by superfluous emotions. He needed only to call on his training. In his heyday he had outshone many of his fellows with his peculiar talent of matching lucid thinking to bold endeavors. It made for a potent combination.

Fleming eventually emerged from the lounge. His decisions made, he found himself suddenly with an appetite. He drank several cups of Isaiah's fine coffee and had a spot of breakfast— hard-boiled eggs, a grapefruit half, bacon, toast with marmalade.

"Ah, that was splendid, Isaiah. Thank you." Fleming dabbed his mouth with the patterned cloth napkin and stood up from the table. "I shall be off with the auto again today."

Fleming tucked a slip of paper into his shirt pocket that bore Prescott W. Quick's Dauphine Street address in New Orleans.

"Cheerio then, Isaiah." His houseman opened the front door and nodded a mannerly bow as his employer stepped out into the morning heat. Isaiah's eyes, their cast still worried, followed Fleming a moment before the door closed between them.

The true swelter of the day hadn't yet begun. Presently the air was relatively mild. The incoming doctor's wind had yet to blow. This daily phenomenon, which occurred at nine o'clock each morning, was the correlative of the undertaker's wind, that outgoing breeze that blew at six every evening. These natural cycles kept the atmosphere over Jamaica from growing stale.

It was a short drive this time, not into Kingston but Oracabessa, the nearest village.

Oracabessa was typical of small local townships. Located on the coast, it had a slovenly but productive fleet of fishing vessels, many patched and repatched but providing livelihoods for men and their families. Houses and commercial buildings were mostly slapped-together affairs of timber and tin. A few ramshackle vehicles were in evidence.

The inhabitants were a generally hardworking lot. Fleming's face was known here. After all, he employed local laborers at wages perhaps more decent than most Europeans offered.

He guided the Rapier up the unpaved main street, raising a modest cloud of dust. The village looked vaguely deserted, owing to the number of men and boys currently out on the waters casting nets. Here and there women were seeing to their daily chores while smaller children romped about in the heavy humidity. Insects buzzed about as Fleming braked his auto nearby the unoccupied hitching post in front of the pastel-painted facade of Lucas's General Emporium.

Something like a cinematic Wild West saloon, the slat-board structure was fronted by a raised plank sidewalk, upon which rested a pair of rocking chairs.

One of these rattan-framed seats was filled with the paunchy figure of Lucas Toomey himself. Lucas was ebony-skinned, shoulders and forearms corded with muscle that was betrayed by the middle-aged spread of his waist. In recent years he had inherited this establishment from his father. His left eye was concealed behind a leather eye patch threaded with dirty white string. Fleming had heard that he'd lost the eye during his youthful days as a prize-fighter.

Lucas offered a rather bucktoothed grin as Fleming stepped from the Rapier.

"Hullo dere, Mistah Fleming."

"Good morning, Lucas," he said, stepping onto the sun-baked porch, which gave an acknowledging creak underfoot.

"What bring you to our leetle corner of de world today, sah?"

"The use of your telephone."

"You'll find it inside."

"Thank you, Lucas." He stepped past as the General Emporium's proprietor resumed the methodical rocking he'd been engaged in when Fleming had arrived.

The store's interior was unlit but not as murky as Henry Long's chandlery. Lucas stocked a fair assortment of general goods, but the merchandise wasn't, in the main, of the best quality—which made perfect sense, since his regular customers did not have a great deal of money to throw about. Poverty was hardly uncommon on the island.

Fleming moved through the empty aisles to the wall-mounted telephone at the rear of the establishment. It wasn't enclosed in a booth but was merely bolted to the chipped lime-green plaster. Fleming lifted the receiver.

It took some minutes of speaking to the operator, then slotting numerous coins and listening to the tinny clicks and pops of the overseas connection. Following a brief exchange with the New Orleans operator, during which he consulted the slip of paper in his shirt pocket, Fleming counted the ringings of Prescott's home telephone.

The line engaged on the fourth ring.

"Mr. Quick's office," said a female voice, American, perhaps a Negress. Apparently Prescott operated his business from his home.

"Good morning," Fleming said, trying to remember the precise time difference between Jamaica and the city and deducing that it must still be in the early morning there. "Is Mr. Quick in presently?"

"He is," said the well-modulated voice. "However, he is busy at the moment. Do you want to speak to him?"

"I do. My name is Ian Fleming."

"Hold the line, please."

A hand muffled the far mouthpiece for a moment. Then came a brief fumbling as the receiver changed hands.

"Ian? My word, is it truly you?" Prescott sounded agitated but quite pleased by the call. "I must say, I didn't entirely expect to hear from you after receiving your letter. Again, old fellow, I must apologize for the awful intrusion—. But wait. It is you, isn't it? Ian?"

"Indeed, Prescott," he said, leaning a shoulder against the chipped plaster wall. "It is."

"Ah, that's jolly fine, then. What with all the curious goings-on of late I wouldn't have been utterly surprised if someone weren't calling *pretending* to be you. How are you, Ian?"

"Quite well, Prescott. And you?"

"Fine, fine."

Abruptly an awkward silence filled the line. The memories that Prescott's letter had stirred up were magnified now by the immediate presence of the lanky-limbed hazel-eyed man's voice. And memories of those bygone activities in which they'd engaged together weren't especially pleasant.

Prescott cleared his throat. "Fine," he now muttered, making it bitter. "Such an insipid word. I imagine it's perfectly plain that I am not fine, Ian. Nor is anything about this horrendous situation."

"I'm sorry for the troubles in which you—we—seem to be embroiled," Fleming said.

"*We?*" Prescott managed something like a chortle. "Well, I appreciate your show of solidarity, dear chap, particularly for someone you've not heard from for so prolonged—"

"I said we, Prescott, and I meant it. There have been further developments in the . . . situation." Fleming proceeded to tell his former colleague of the photograph and the brief scrawled message he'd received in yesterday's mail.

"Ghost of Christmas Past?" Prescott said. "Well, they've read their Dickens at any rate. Or perhaps they only saw the film. I say, who starred in that? I believe it was Reginald Owen in the role of Ebenezer. Ah, bloody hell, I'm blathering. Ian! This is a most disturbing turn. How did these blighters know where to contact you? Oh. It's my blunder, isn't it? Damn! They somehow tracked my letter to you. Blast! I've involved you further than was ever my aim. I swear to you, Ian. I didn't intend this!"

It was tumbling forth in a verbal cascade. Prescott sounded quite distraught now. Fleming thought of the drinking problem mentioned in the man's MI-5 file and wondered if he was presently under the influence.

"Calm yourself, Prescott. What's done is done," Fleming said, trying to level off the man's emotions. Cool heads were needed here, not hysterics. "We must address this crisis together—if crisis it is."

"There's a dead young lady whose head was nearly lopped off, Ian. And now another equally brutalized corpse. We've both received messages that point toward a past I think we would both prefer undisturbed. And Wallace Ullrich's daughter, Faith, is mixed up in the affair. I think it safe to call this a crisis!" Prescott's voice nearly broke at this last.

Fleming had to put him on track. He required as much information about the situation as Prescott had.

"Let's take those particulars individually, shall we? Have you any suspicion who the man in my photo might be?"

"Nothing comes to mind," said Prescott, "though perhaps it would help if I saw the picture."

"Has such a murder occurred there in New Orleans in the past few days?"

"If it has, the press knows nothing of it. And they would snatch up this item eagerly, what with the froth the first murder has brought about—"

"The murdered girl, then," Fleming said, cutting him off. "Who is she?"

Prescott let out a long whistling breath. "Her name is Angelina. Angelina Marquette. She was married to Gerard Marquette this past October. She comes from a society family. Rather old money. Her maiden name is Dours. She's been buried under the name of Marquette. So her headstone reads. Do you think that is appropriate? Seeing as how her husband is a chief suspect in her murder. Of course, we don't actually inter people here in New Orleans. The city lies atop swampland. Nothing remains below ground. A true burial would have the inauspicious effect of floating the casket right back up to the surface in fairly short order. No, can't have that. No, instead, mortal remains are entombed *above* ground where—"

Again the man had lost his tenuous control of himself. "Prescott," Fleming said sharply, now growing annoyed. "Damn it, man, have you forgotten your military discipline entirely?"

It was unpleasant to resort to such berating tactics, but it had the desired effect. Prescott cut short his gibbering, cleared his throat again, and said in the cool, steely voice that Fleming recalled from their mutual days in the service, "Quite right, Ian. Allow me to continue. Angelina Marquette. Her father is Edmund Dours, a retired investor. Comfortably monied. Serves on several community councils. A well-placed society family. Angelina has two surviving brothers, both older, both in the service, Navy. They've naturally been given leave to return to New Orleans during this unhappy time."

"What alerted this Edmund Dours to the suspicion that his new son-in-law was engaged in an illicit liaison?" asked Fleming, fairly certain now that Prescott would respond without any agitated digressions.

So he did. "Edmund Dours came to me—what would it be?—nearly a fortnight ago. He's a rather elderly figure but with the bearing of a tiger. He wouldn't say explicitly what had tipped him off. Only that he had misgivings about Gerard Marquette's fidelity. When he delineated his suspicions, however, naming the hours the young man was absent from both home and work, the female party he suspected him of visiting, *and* that woman's address . . . it was clear he had done a good spot of investigating on his own. Evidently he only wanted an outside party to confirm what he likely already knew."

"And so you made these confirmations?"

"I did," said Prescott. "As I indicated in my letter, it didn't seem much of a task."

"Why did Edmund Dours choose you to probe into the matter?"

"Again, he wouldn't say." Prescott made a sound midway between a grunt and a chuckle. "I believe he picked my name randomly from the telephone directory. Had he made the least inquiries about my practice, he would've known I don't normally engage in the more traditional activities of a private detective. Shadowing people and taking covert snapshots and the like. I prefer the purity of deduction."

"Yes," said Fleming somewhat ruefully. "Much like your beloved Sherlock Holmes."

Now Prescott did sniff out a small self-deprecating laugh. "Indeed. Rather silly in the end, isn't it? Finder of Lost Fortunes. I tell you truly, Ian, I don't believe I ever expected to be taken seriously when I started this practice. It was more whimsy than anything . . . or perhaps merely a desire to reinvent myself as something other than—other than—"

An assassin, Fleming filled in silently. Yes, he certainly understood that motivation.

But back to the matter at hand. "So, you visually substantiated the affair that this Gerard Marquette was having? You saw him and his mistress together?"

"Yes," said Prescott. "I made use of a nearby gallery—pardon, balcony. It's a bit of local nomenclature. I hid myself upon it, above and opposite the street door of the lady in question. Faith Ullrich. Young Mr. Marquette appeared dutifully at the appointed hour and was let into the house by Miss Ullrich herself. That, of course, was when I first set eyes upon her. Even from across the street her similarity to her father, our old colleague Wallace, was astounding. The same shade of mahogany hair, the fair complexion, same curve to the jaw and slope to the nose, the firm cheekbones, the confident set of the eyes. I say, Ian, the likeness was more than a bit startling."

"You photographed this woman?" Fleming asked. Though the description sounded rather like Wallace Ullrich as he remembered him, he wouldn't simply take Prescott at his word.

"Oh, yes. I was snapping away like mad from my perch. A short while later I took further, decidedly more risqué photos. From my position I had a good view into Faith Ullrich's bedroom, where the drapes stood only half drawn. When she and Mr. Marquette adjourned to the upstairs, well . . . I felt more than a little like a voyeur. Frankly, the display was distasteful in the extreme. I witnessed—and photographed—acts I rather wish I hadn't."

Fleming nodded in the store's dim quiet. "What do you know of Faith Ullrich?"

"I knew nothing at the time," said Prescott. "But I've since learned a small amount from the probes the police have made following her and Gerard Marquette's disappearance. She's twenty-six, four years older than her adulterous paramour. Unmarried. She seems to have no relations whatever."

"And what of Wallace Ullrich—since you seem convinced she is his daughter?" Fleming hadn't known Wallace well and was certainly unaware the man had a daughter. In truth he hadn't known too terribly much about any of Churchill's Boys, despite the close contact he'd had with some during that post-war operation—and such was how he had preferred it.

"I should say no living relations, then," Prescott amended.

"Living?" Fleming blinked. "Then Wallace is—"

"Oh, quite dead. One year ago. You hadn't heard? Well, I only found out by chance myself. An old acquaintance from Whitehall passing through the city told me the news."

For some reason Fleming found this revelation disquieting. "Do you know how he died?"

Prescott sighed grimly. "By his own hand, I was told. Foul business, that. Left no note. Slit his own throat, ear to ear. You might think, being an experienced military man, he would have picked a better means."

Fleming shook his head. "Ghastly."

"Indeed."

"But," he said, turning his thoughts back to the moment, "do you have any proof that this Faith is his daughter, beyond the family resemblance?"

"If you'd seen the woman, Ian, you wouldn't be asking for further proof. But, as it happens, yes, the police have confirmed that Wallace Ullrich was her father. Her mother died when she was an infant."

"What of that curious cross of bones and feathers that appeared with Angelina Marquette's corpse?" Fleming asked. And beside the savaged head of the blond man, he added silently.

"Naturally it's an intriguing article," Prescott said. "Points toward some sort of . . . of voodoo involvement. But there is no other apparent link. Practitioners of voodoo don't behead women."

"No, not as a rule. What do the police think of it?"

"It is being looked into, of course, though trying to locate modern devotees of the religion is difficult here. They tend to keep to themselves, to understate it dramatically."

Fleming pressed his lips together into a solemn line for a

moment, then said, "So. Edmund Dours hires you to investigate Gerard Marquette, recently married to his daughter Angelina. You verify that the man is having an affair with Faith Ullrich. Sometime after, Angelina is murdered. Marquette and his mistress vanish. And you receive that package containing photos of the dead woman, along with that note."

"Yes," Prescott said to his summation.

"And all this occurs in the space of . . . ?"

"Less than a single week," the private detective finished. "After which I contacted you, for the reasons I mentioned."

"And I subsequently receive a warning message, evidently written by the same party, along with a photograph of a new, as yet unidentified body."

"Yes," said Prescott, meekly this time. "Dreadfully sorry about that."

Fleming felt the bridge of his nose beginning to throb, where a metal plate had been implanted following a sporting accident in his youth. The pain was the usual precursor to one of his celebrated migraines.

"Well, there's nothing for it, then," he said.

"Nothing? Well, I suppose you're quite correct, Ian. I can't ask the police for their aid without revealing the fact that I've retained that note. Withholding evidence isn't a crime looked upon lightly. I suppose I shall simply . . . simply have to . . ." Prescott's voice trailed off sadly.

"Prescott," Fleming said, "I mean to say that I see no alternative for myself in this matter. There are some vague unpleasant eventualities I'm prepared to live with"—such as Lord Dale Hemmingford's lingering rancor—"and others I simply can't let lie. I shall make arrangements as soon as possible to come to New Orleans."

There was a gasp at the far end of the line. Then Prescott fairly erupted, "That's marvelous, old boy! I'm delighted, truly, *delighted*! I say, I'm certainly glad now that I chose to contact—"

"Yes, Prescott, yes," said Fleming, not sharing the man's giddiness. "We shall see if we can't bring this business to some satisfactory ending. I'll contact you when I reach your city. Farewell."

He set the receiver back onto its cradle, then rubbed at the bridge of his nose. His headache was already overtaking him.

Chapter 6

ISAIAH HINES was once again boxed into that disagreeable impasse where the irresistible force of his concern for his employer met the immovable object of the detachment of his station. It wasn't a pleasant state.

The Englishman had returned from his morning errand several hours ago and announced rather stonily that tomorrow he would be leaving—again—for the United States for some indefinite period. He said something about the city of New Orleans and visiting an old friend . . . though the word "friend" came out a bit sardonically. Then he had taken himself off into the lounge, where Isaiah quickly delivered him a brandy.

Ian Fleming didn't display his moods overtly, but Isaiah was perceptive. He had been in the Englishman's employ for only a relatively brief period, but his esteem for his employer magnified his sense that something was not right.

It was too soon to be traveling again. Too soon! The man was only scarcely back from his last excursion, the one that had taken him to San Francisco, where some obvious misadventure had occurred. Isaiah suspected that a woman had been involved—specifically the woman who had stayed briefly at the house before the two of them flew off together to the States. Nora Blair De-Young, her name had been. An attractive white woman with her red hair in becoming ringlets. She hadn't returned from San Francisco, only Fleming. Had it been a soured romance or something more drastic?

Isaiah didn't know and, not being the gossip that some servants were, didn't wish to know merely as a means of alleviating his curiosity. But the Englishman had reappeared at the house something of a broken man—or at least one who'd undergone some serious misfortune. Drawing on internal reserves, Fleming had recovered. Isaiah had been delighted to see the man regain himself.

And now? *Now* some other mischief was afoot. His employer had received unpleasant tidings in the mail. Surely whatever news it was was responsible for this new and sudden departure from Jamaica. New Orleans? Did the Englishman have family there? Was one of them ill, perhaps terminally? It was a grievous thought.

As Fleming's houseman, his actions were restricted. The dictums of service did not permit personal meddling in the private affairs of one's employer. Isaiah had been in service many years and had conducted himself quite properly throughout. It wouldn't do, not at all, to go against the grain now.

If only he didn't so genuinely care about the Englishman's well-being . . .

Yes, much easier this present predicament would be if the man were more typical of the island's European invaders—pontifical, utterly indifferent to his native staff, blithely unaware of anyone else's feelings or beliefs or opinions. The self-important British. The supercilious French.

Fleming, however, was atypical, and Isaiah knew it, and thereby was helpless to the fondness that had germinated in him for his employer.

Isaiah, while brooding over the matter, broiled swordfish for dinner. He also tossed a robust salad of crisp lettuce, tomatoes, diced cucumber, avocado, and whatever other suitable vegetables were at hand. His movements were rather manic. Occasionally he muttered to himself.

UPSTAIRS, PACKING, FLEMING was in little better humor. His headache by now had more or less receded. He wasn't pleased with the results of his telephone call to Prescott W. Quick. He wasn't especially sanguine about allying himself with the man, whose manner during their exchange had been less than clearheaded. Plainly he wasn't the same cool, lucid individual Fleming remembered. It was entirely possible Prescott's drinking problem was quite real.

In many respects Prescott was Fleming's double. They were both of respectable English families, both well educated. They shared an appreciation of women and fine living. Both men had been successful intelligence agents. Prescott had once been a man of forthright action, an able decision maker with a clarity of purpose something like that of a well-oiled machine. Now, from the wild fumblings of his speech patterns, he seemed more a rambling wreck of a man, thoroughly unnerved by this present crisis.

Perhaps Prescott was a *faulty* double . . . a version of Fleming that had gone astray in recent years.

Fleming brusquely tossed several clean and pressed shirts into the suitcase that lay open on his bed, dismissing these metaphysical thoughts. He wasn't anticipating with any great pleasure partnering himself with a former colleague from the not-so-good old days, a man he could well have done without seeing again for the remainder of his lifetime. He didn't dislike Prescott, per se. But the man was uncomfortable living proof of a particular segment of Fleming's past.

He chose more items from his drawers, nearly at random. This was certainly no pleasure trip he was set to undertake. Using the telephone in Lucas's store a second time, he had secured his flight, which was scheduled for early tomorrow morning. A hop to Miami, Florida, then a skip to New Orleans, Louisiana.

What had decided it for him was Prescott's show of proof that Faith Ullrich was in fact Wallace Ullrich's daughter. The police had confirmed this, he'd said. Without that element Fleming wouldn't feel currently compelled to make this journey. Even with the dead girl—Angelina Marquette—the unnamed dead man and the cryptic warning messages both Prescott and he had received . . . no, even these factors wouldn't be sufficient impetus to force him into action.

But with Faith Ullrich, the daughter of yet another of Churchill's Boys, mixed up in the affair, Fleming *had* to involve himself. And likely, before this was over, he would need to involve MI-5 as well. Now there was an unpleasant thought. It was quite bad enough having the past scratching in so animated a fashion at the lid of its coffin, but to reawaken matters further by contacting Whitehall with this imbroglio—that was something almost beyond the pale.

It was far too implausible to be coincidence. His experience with the duplicitous Nora Blair DeYoung had taught him that there were no fanciful flukes of fate in life. Actually she had *re*-taught him that fundamental lesson. Many of the lies she had told him were founded on the acceptance of coincidence. And for a while, to his chagrin, he had been duped into believing what he should have known instantly were untruths.

It would not happen again.

Ghost of Christmas Past. Sins of our fathers. Our fathers. *Our.* It was a significant pronoun. Faith Ullrich might well have an insider's knowledge of the doings of Churchill's Boys. Wallace, of course, had been bound by the ironclad conditions of the Official Secrets Act, forbidden—as they all were—to divulge any information about their clandestine postwar operation, or any other classified activities, for that matter.

Yet secrets could conceivably pass between a father and his daughter. Quite conceivably. And if Faith, an adulteress, was making use of this information for sinister reasons, then she had to be stopped. She and her confederate, this Gerard Marquette character. And whoever else might be lurking in the wings. Two grisly murders had already been committed. Faith and Marquette were the logical suspects. Fleming had received a message evidently meant to frighten him off the matter.

If Faith Ullrich was loose with damning knowledge of the activities of Churchill's Boys, she was a walking time bomb.

He finished his packing rather apathetically. In the morning he would rise, shower, shave, and be off, leaving the Lagonda Rapier with Isaiah when he arrived at the airport in Kingston. He included among his things the revolver he'd kept for some while in the house. It was an Enfield Mk II, a .38. He had a carrying permit for it, should the customs officials in Miami offer him any difficulties.

He made his way downstairs when his houseman rang the bell. Dinner. He wasn't particularly hungry, but food would be necessary to store up his strength for tomorrow's journey. He retained more than enough military discipline to force himself to eat.

It was, predictably, a sumptuous meal, and as Fleming tucked in, his appetite came readily to life. The fish was quite delicate, apparently broiled in a choice white wine. He ate a fine helping, then started in on the hearty salad, which he topped with a dash or two of the tangy dressing Isaiah had prepared.

The tall black butler appeared somewhat flustered, though only Fleming's growing familiarity with the man's normal bearing alerted him. The corners of Isaiah's mouth were pinched, and his eyes beneath his dark brows made sharp darting movements.

"Is something troubling you, Isaiah?"

He froze for a heartbeat in the act of clearing Fleming's salad plate. A look of acute inexplicable guilt passed briefly over his features, as if he'd just been asked if he had been pilfering his employer's liquor.

He recovered quickly and smoothly, however. "No, sah. I am quite well."

Plainly, though, he *was* upset. Yet Fleming understood, at least as well as Isaiah did, the limitations of rank that separated them. It simply wasn't decorous to get too personally involved with one's house staff. Etiquette forbade it.

But etiquette had its place.

Fleming remained at the cleared table. He picked a Players from his engraved silver cigarette case and lit it, blowing out a thoughtful stream of smoke.

"I would think you'd be pleased to have me out from underfoot for a while," he said with studied joviality.

Isaiah, pausing at the connecting door into the kitchen, looked back gravely into the smartly appointed dining room where Fleming took his meals. The walls here were a creamy beige, warmed by the room's lamplight.

"I have no need, sah, for any sort of holiday from you." It might have been an attempt at banter, such as Fleming and Henry Long engaged in, but it wasn't. Isaiah's tone was much too somber.

"You'll have the chance to polish your chess game while I'm away," Fleming tried again. "You can concoct a few more of those diabolic knight forks of yours." Isaiah had proven himself an adroit player. The few times they had played, they had divided the victories evenly.

"Yes, sah." The houseman remained at the doorway into the kitchen. His right hand was winding itself slowly and tightly into a pale yellow wiping cloth.

Fleming frowned. He set his elbows on the teak surface of the table and leaned forward. "Isaiah, if you're unhappy with some aspect of your current position in this house, I should like to address it before I leave. I wish no surprises when I return."

This, at least, was relatively safe ground. He was speaking to Isaiah as an employer, though hoping to sound out the man's troubles more from a motive of friendly concern.

"Mistah Fleming," Isaiah said formally, drawing up his shoulders, "I am, I assure you, perfectly content with my post. If my performance is unsatisfactory, however, it is of course your prerogative to relieve—"

Fleming stabbed out his cigarette in a seashell-pink ceramic ashtray.

"For the love of God, Isaiah," he said, giving up the pretense. It was time to bring this tournament of protocol to an end. "I'm asking after your welfare, man. You've been a splendid employee. You've, frankly, served above and beyond the call. I have no quarrels whatever with your efficiency. You appear troubled. I am inquiring as to what is behind your distress. There. That's the breadth and length of it."

It had been an unseemly display, and he knew it. Isaiah blinked back at him a moment, caught quite off guard by the demonstration.

"Sah . . ." he began in a soft, uncertain tone, "I—" He gathered a nervous breath. "I am concerned for your well-being." He nearly flinched at his own words, but he had committed himself now. "Your . . . state . . . upon returning recently from the United States was, ah, disconsolate. I felt worry. When you reclaimed yourself, it was a relief. To me. Now, er, now it seems that some other matter has disturbed your life's balance, and I—I am once more *concerned*—" He cut himself off abruptly, clenching his teeth as though he had overstepped himself.

The Englishman had folded his hands quietly on the tabletop. As he regarded Isaiah, a smile curled his lips.

"Isaiah," Fleming said gently, "your concern is most thoughtful. I thank you for it."

The smile finally reached his eyes and softened their somewhat melancholy cast.

"Isaiah," he now said in a more genuinely cheerful voice, "why don't you unearth that chessboard again? If you're disposed, I should like a game to while away these final hours of mine on the island. Bring it into the lounge, there's a good man. We shall open a bottle of respectable Scotch, and I will regale you with the sad tale of Miss Nora Blair DeYoung. Is that agreeable?"

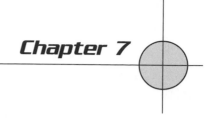

Chapter 7

THE DOUGLAS DC-3 grumbled over the wide blue-gray sheet of Lake Pontchartrain, dipping at last under the cloud cover and allowing a glimpse of the lakefront. Numerous U.S. military installations had been based along the strip during the war, including, interestingly enough, a German POW camp. Beyond, the city of New Orleans flashed past, still rather distant.

Then the airstrip of Moisant Airport came into view. The airplane, twin props spinning, banked gracefully and a few moments later touched down in a stately landing that barely rocked Fleming in his maroon-cushioned seat.

Miami had been a smooth stopover. He had handed over his passport to the mannerly customs official, declared his Enfield revolver, and answered a brief battery of routine questions. There was time, after having his passport stamped, for a spot of coffee and a visit to the currency exchange window before embarking on his connecting flight to New Orleans. The cost of this journey was coming out of his own pocket. No sense in even trying to beguile expenses and another ticket from Merlin Powell, as he had done for his ill-fated excursion to San Francisco. Fleming had no intention of returning to Jamaica with a story for Kemsley Newspapers. Whatever happened in New Orleans would remain forever buried there. He hoped.

Fleming collected his suitcase. The airport was rather busy, though he couldn't tell at a glance if more people were arriving at or departing from the city.

He felt rested. Last night's unprecedented informal interlude with Isaiah Hines had been markedly pleasant. For that time the two men had shucked virtually all the strictures of their differing races and social standings. They played numerous games of chess and drank off a fair amount of one of Fleming's superior bottles of Scotch. Fleming, as promised, had recounted the tragic narrative of the death of Nora. He questioned now his impulse in divulging most—but certainly not all—of the details of that misfortune. He had felt keenly the curious need to unburden himself, to share with the man, who by rights he should call a friend, some portion of what he had endured. Isaiah had listened solemnly, accepting the Englishman's words, nodding in sincere sympathy.

The experience had felt purging. Servant or not, Isaiah Hines had demonstrated a genuine thoughtfulness for Fleming's welfare. It was truly touching.

Today, however, beneath the cloud-smeared light of late afternoon in this foreign territory, he was in a different frame of mind. He felt neither melancholic nor anxious. He was instead in a state of sure readiness for—for . . . well, whatever was to come. It was, of course, his military training asserting itself, clearing his mind of the trip wires of disruptive feelings. Whatever misgivings he had about this visit to Prescott W. Quick and the disinterring of the past were immaterial. He was primed.

His .38 had a holster. Stepping briefly into a stall in a public lavatory, he slid the pistol into a comfortable position at the small of his back, beneath the warm black coat he was wearing. The weight and mild pressure against his spine were familiar, reassuring.

Isaiah had prepared a smart breakfast for him this morning before accompanying him on the drive into Kingston. The houseman's deportment had reverted to its normal state of studied deference. He had treated Fleming with flawless, proper courtesy, with no obvious hint of the previous night's informality. Nonetheless, Fleming sensed a subtle change in the man, a hint of awareness that they had bridged a social and racial chasm between them. He had made a comrade of Isaiah, and that link would likely endure. It was, he judged, a fine thing, etiquette be damned.

There were, of course, taxis waiting in a predatory queue

outside the terminal. Fleming surveyed these a moment, eyes sharp, senses alert in that general manner of readiness that had preceded every military action he'd ever undertaken.

The lead cabbie hopped out of his vehicle as Fleming approached, suitcase in hand. The air was almost crisp, with a prelude of rain in those fleecy gray overhanging clouds. New Orleans, he knew, had long, humid summers that rivaled Jamaica's year-round clime. This, however, was early February, and winter's mild teeth marks still indented the air. Hardly the stuff of an English winter, however, for which Fleming was grateful. Even San Francisco had been far too chilly for his tastes.

"Get'cha bag for you, sir?" asked the cabdriver in a somewhat groveling effort at formality, hindered by his lax local accent. He was middle-aged, with a rounded stomach and short, thick limbs. His dark hair was dense and cropped. His jowls sported at least two days' worth of unchecked stubble.

Fleming nodded, letting himself into the back of the taxi while the driver placed his luggage in the trunk, then squeezed himself behind the wheel. The vehicle seemed in relatively good repair, with one obvious dent in the passenger door that had scraped away a patch of the cab's orange finish. The taxi's engine fired immediately as the stumpy driver turned the key and nudged the accelerator.

As was fated to happen whenever Fleming found himself in the transposed traffic patterns of the Colonies, he winced as they swung onto what was patently the *wrong* side of the road and sped off.

"Which hotel is yours, sir?" asked the driver, who himself was steering inappropriately from the auto's left side.

Fleming lit a cigarette, regarding the man's chunky skull from behind. There was some shading to the cabdriver's tone he didn't like, some hint of disdain beneath his aggressively civil manner. He is taking me for an easy mark, Fleming thought coolly. Someone to prey upon.

"I've booked no hotel, driver," he said, which was true. He hadn't planned on making arrangements until he'd conferred in person with Prescott.

"Well, lettin' it go a bit late, ain't'cha, sir?" Fleming caught a quick glint of an exploitative grin in the rearview mirror.

"What, pray tell, do you mean by that?" He blew out a steady plume of cigarette smoke.

"Carnival an' all, sir," said the driver with a note of incredulity. "Fat Tuesday's a-comin'."

Fleming allowed a few seconds of silence, then said, "Perhaps you'd care to put that into the king's English, driver."

"Uh," the stocky man fumbled, "y'know, sir, Mardi Gras. On the twenty-first this month."

Mardi Gras? Oh, dear Lord, thought Fleming. As though New Orleans weren't decadent enough in its normal state. Adding that infamous festival of debauchery, if only as background dressing, might indeed complicate matters. Why hadn't Prescott made mention of it? In his agitated state he had likely simply forgotten to.

The taxi had wound its way out of the lanes immediately circumscribing the airport. They idled at a crossing.

"To the French Quarter, driver." Fleming recited the Dauphine Street address. "I've not come for merrymaking, and I've not come for sightseeing, rest assured. So, pray, don't dawdle or deviate from the most linear route, which, let me mention, I'm quite familiar with. Let us away."

There was a certain sport in couching one's rebuffs in that stiff English of the homeland, which Americans were either so charmed or intimidated by. The cabdriver said not another word until they had reached Fleming's destination, moving the taxi at a steady speed and making no departures whatever from the long roadway that connected the airport in the suburb of Kenner to the city's old pulsing heart, the French Quarter.

HE HAD LAST seen the city during that prolonged wild goose chase that Sir William Potter had sent him on. Repugnant business, that; not worth reliving in his memory.

New Orleans—and the French Quarter in particular—oozed with a sense of history. Or as much history as any part of the States could have accumulated in its brief lifetime. Fleming judged that this nation was effectively still in its swaddling clothes, its status as a world power notwithstanding. Yet only Mother Russia was now a match for this youthful juggernaut of a country. If he were to be utterly honest with himself, he would have to concede that England, owing to its vast losses during the war, was now relegated to a lesser ranking in global magnitude. Still, his homeland was steeped in *centuries* of history. No corner of this callow nation could hope to boast as much. History in a sense equaled strength. History spoke of durability and fortitude.

He shook off these pointless thoughts. The cabbie had let him off at the curb in front of Prescott W. Quick's home—and office, as attested to by the small gold-on-black placard that swayed in the breeze from its two hooks above the doorway.

FINDER OF LOST FORTUNES.

So it read beneath the man's name. Where Fleming, upon encountering this title in Prescott's letterhead, had found it initially curious and amusing, now he thought it somewhat disturbing. It had an air of frivolity that seemed quite inappropriate in the face of this current crisis. Men were supposed to put away childish things. Prescott, following his retirement from the very adult duty of being a spy, had apparently taken those childish things out of storage for another go-round. It boded ill.

Fleming might have telephoned his former colleague from the airport but hadn't troubled to. Prescott would be in or he wouldn't. If the latter, Fleming would make an appointment with that well-spoken secretary of his, then go and secure lodgings. Hopefully that cabdriver's dire warning about having let it go too late would prove to be an exaggeration. Surely a room would be available somewhere. Wending through the Quarter's quaint, narrow one-way streets, though, it had certainly seemed the place was more active than the last time he'd visited. Mardi Gras was looming. It would arrive in—what?—just under two weeks. With luck this affair would be concluded before then.

Suitcase in hand, he studied for a moment the wood-framed, olive trimmed with white, two-storied abode of Prescott W. Quick. A wrought-iron terrace hung before the European guillotine windows of the upper floor. Ivy crawled among the scrolling metal curlicues. The house was recessed several feet from the street, fronted by a similarly ornate gated iron fence, upon which hung a small red mailbox. A small garden of jasmine and willowy ferns was split by a swept-clean pathway of red and yellow bricks. This track led to two cement steps and the house's front door. A baroque brass knocker was set in the center of the dark lacquered wood. Lacy white curtains masked the two ground-floor windows.

These curtains didn't stir as Fleming unlatched the gate. With a sense of inexorable moment he approached the door, lifted the heavy knocker molded to look like a lion's head, and thumped the door twice. He remained coolheaded and primed for action. He shifted his weight minutely to assure himself his Enfield remained securely holstered at the small of his back.

The door was opened almost immediately by a dark-skinned woman in an immaculately white dress that was tied with a checkered apron. She looked to be in her mid-twenties, her dark coiled hair bound up in a scarlet head scarf that seemed at once functional and ornamental. Her cheekbones were high and rather elegant. Her eyes above them were sharp. It was quite an attractive secretary Prescott had chosen for himself, if indeed this was the same woman he'd spoken to during yesterday's call from Jamaica.

"May I help you?" she asked. Her tone was sure and even, with just the proper level of civility. Yes, this was she.

"Good afternoon," he said with equal courtesy. "My name is Ian Fleming. If I'm not mistaken, we spoke yesterday, long distance . . ."

Her keen eyes scrutinized him closely for a scant second, as if she were corroborating his face with some mental file; impossible, naturally, since they had never met before. "Yes, of course, Mr. Fleming. Won't you step in? Mr. Quick's been expecting you."

Too long he had been accustomed to hearing blacks speak only in the musical patois of Jamaica, he realized. Even Isaiah, with his superior education, carried traces of the pidgin in his speech. This Negress, however, was decidedly eloquent. She held the door as he stepped into the house's mahogany-trimmed vestibule.

"If you'd like to wait in Mr. Quick's office?" She gestured toward a high open doorway. "I can take your bag if you'd like," she added.

"No need, thank you," Fleming said, stepping into the house's large front room. Its ceiling was quite high, the light fixture in its center a flamboyant brass affair with glowing multiple bulbs inside carefully cut glass housings. Ah, in the land of the idolatrous electric light once again, he thought with a silent sigh.

He set his suitcase on the thick nap of the blue and purple carpet. Prescott's office was well kept, a rather no-nonsense layout of comfortable furnishings. Fleming realized he had half expected the office to be as fanciful as the man's self-appointed title. But there was nothing whimsical about the setting—no antique pistols mounted on the beige-painted walls, no deerstalker cap left jauntily on the corner hat rack, nor any other impish tribute to the fictional Sherlock Holmes upon whom Prescott had based his practice. There was a large, orderly desk with a telephone sitting on one corner, two chairs of upholstered leather before it, and a wall of bookshelves with every inch devoted to stolid thick-bound volumes that were probably of some legal nature. Next to a soot-free fireplace stood a serving cart upon which sat a bottle of fine-looking port and several glasses.

This Fleming eyed a moment, thinking an aperitif would not be unwelcome just now, and wondering further if this ready supply of spirits was another indication of Prescott's supposed drinking problem. He hadn't eaten during his flight, forgoing the not especially appetizing meals the comely stewardesses tried to tempt him with. The breakfast Isaiah had prepared had been hardy, but he was again due for some food.

He would confer with Prescott, he decided, then take himself off to find a room and dinner. Restaurants, he knew, were plentiful in New Orleans, a city as famous for its cuisine as it was for its jazz.

Fleming heard footsteps descending from the house's upper level and turned. The stairway, curiously, hadn't been located near the front door as seemed logical. Instead, it was evidently set farther back on the premises. Hard-soled shoes moved swiftly down a hallway. There was a pause for a brief verbal exchange. Then into the office came the rangy figure of Prescott W. Quick.

"Ian!" the narrow-faced man fairly crowed. He shut the tall varnished office door behind him, marched across the intervening stretch of carpet and grasped Fleming's hand firmly, pumping it enthusiastically. "Ah, my dear dear chap, how pleasing to see you in the flesh. My, you've kept yourself in fine repair, haven't you? The years scarcely show on you!"

It was a quite boisterous display, but Fleming bore it good-naturedly, returning Prescott's handshake and smiling.

It was obvious even at a glance that the few intervening years since Fleming had last seen him had changed the man. His long-lashed hazel eyes remained as dazzling as ever, and he'd taken on no noticeable weight. However, gray marked his temples heavily, contrasting starkly with the natural dark red of his hair. That hair also seemed to be beating a hasty retreat from his forehead, leaving a last lonely forelock where his sharp widow's peak had once been.

His gaunt, somewhat homely features now sported deep parallel etchings about his mouth. The flesh sagged in reddened pouches beneath his eyes. He didn't look entirely healthy, and Fleming was reminded of his whimsical thought that Prescott was his own faulty twin.

But all that was banished by the radiant grin he turned on Fleming; and yes, the fetching quality of that smile was still quite present, heralding the allure and magnetism that Prescott had used to entice many a female. He wore a dark gray suit and black tie, the garment cut so as not to overaccentuate his lankiness.

"Prescott, you look well," Fleming half lied, at last loosening his hand from the man's eager grip.

"Poppycock," he retorted cheerfully. "Entropy is waiting for all of us. It's merely tapped me on the shoulder first. Still, I imagine I've a few worthwhile years left in these bones. Do sit. I—ah! Port. A dram, yes? If memory serves, you were no teetotaler, Ian. Really, had you contacted me, I could have come to collect you from Moisant."

Fleming settled into one of the leather chairs in front of the desk. He unbuttoned his black coat. "When I spoke to you, I hadn't yet made my arrangements. It wasn't difficult to find a taxi. Thank you, Prescott." He took the small tulip-shaped glass that his former colleague offered. Waiting until the man had taken the adjacent chair with his own glass, he said, "Chin-chin."

Prescott echoed the toast, taking a sip of the port, which was indeed a fine drop.

Fleming had been undeniably disturbed by his initial contact with this man. Prescott's letter, that simple communication from someone out of a past best left neglected, had been unsettling. Speaking to Prescott yesterday on the telephone had had much the same effect. Now, strangely, sitting here in the man's actual presence, Fleming felt quite composed. No upsetting images of their days as Churchill's Boys came gushing from the vault of his memory. He was here to deal with this crisis involving Faith Ullrich and

Gerard Marquette and the murdered girl, Angelina. He remained focused squarely on that.

Prescott had lapsed into a sudden silence. It was the same sort of awkward hesitation that had marked their telephone conversation of yesterday. He was gazing uncomfortably into his glass, brow furrowed, seeming to be mentally fishing with some desperation for words to puncture the uneasy pause. His buoyant spirit appeared all but evaporated.

He's feeling it, Fleming thought. The past. Their shared . . . what was it? Guilt perhaps. Perhaps even dishonor. For the deeds they had committed in the name of duty.

Fleming bent to unbuckle his suitcase. Reaching into an inner pocket of the bag, he produced the envelope he had received two days ago. In it he had included the photograph Prescott had sent earlier.

"Might I see the message you received?" Fleming asked.

Prescott started slightly in his chair. "Yes, yes, of course," he said in a distracted murmur, pushing himself to his feet and stepping around his large desk. From a deep drawer he came up with another envelope and passed it over.

It took only an instant to confirm what Fleming already knew. The childish scrawl of the two messages was the same. Prescott's was even written on a matching sheet of carelessly ripped notebook paper. He handed both to his former colleague.

Prescott examined them. His hazel eyes, Fleming saw for the first time, were quite bloodshot. An expression of sharp uneasiness washed over his lined features.

"Yes," he muttered again. "We've the same pen pal, decidedly."

"Decidedly," Fleming agreed. He took another swallow of port. "And the same photographer, I should say." He held up the two grisly snapshots.

Prescott blanched noticeably. With a slightly trembling hand he took the photos, gazing with revulsion at the blond man's hacked-apart head.

"What remains," said Fleming darkly, "is to determine what we should do about all of this."

Prescott dropped back into his chair with a labored sigh.

"I'm afraid matters have grown somewhat more complicated, old fellow. I've only just learned from my contacts on the police force that the Red Dwarf has been brought in to lead the investigation."

"I beg your pardon?"

"Inspector Everett McCorkle. He's something of an eccentric but has a reputation for getting excellent results. He's said to be keener than a bloodhound."

"And he is referred to as the Red Dwarf why?"

"Oh, he's not called that to his face, I assure you," said Prescott. "His formidable stature does not, I'm afraid, extend to his physical dimensions. However, he might well beat us to the punch in tracking down Faith Ullrich and Gerard Marquette."

Fleming brooded on that. Not only a gruesome mystery to solve, but now apparently they had some stiff competition in the matter. That made it a race.

"We can't have it, Ian. We can't allow it." Prescott's voice was suddenly quite brittle. "Our . . . past—it can't become known. *Cannot.* Not merely because these fiends evidently hold crucial information about our postwar operation that would threaten England's national security. No. Worse than that and much more personal . . . I won't have myself publicly named an assassin. An executioner. The shame is too vast. Our secrets must remain secrets."

The hurt and remorse and fear were at that moment all there to be read nakedly on Prescott's face. How frail he looked, thought Fleming. How shattered by his past. Fleming understood.

"Prescott, we shall make certain what is buried stays buried."

It was a promise he had no authority to make, but speaking it to his former colleague now was much like promising it to himself— or to his own dark, fragmented reflection.

Chapter 8

IT WAS patently useless to try to reconstruct the features of the mutilated male in the photograph, but Prescott studied the picture a long moment nonetheless, his bloodshot eyes small and helpless. He gulped the last of his port. So much worse was this picture than the one of the dead girl, Angelina Marquette, who after all had only had her head nearly lopped off. The murderer or murderers hadn't taken the extra measure of butchering her entire face. But she had been stripped bare, Fleming recalled. This fellow was still clothed.

"I tell you, Ian," Prescott finally managed in a tiny voice, "it frightens me. It *sickens* me. I've encountered nothing like this since I took up this profession. Oh, there has been the occasional spot of unpleasantness, to be sure, I'm something of a criminal investigator, after all . . . but nothing, absolutely nothing of this magnitude. I haven't been witness to these sorts of atrocities since—since—"

The old days. But it was needless for either man to complete the sentence.

"I should say I do not intend to report receiving this photograph and message to the police," Fleming said after a pause. "We must resolve this independently of the authorities."

"Yes. Of course . . ." Prescott looked at this moment quite sickly. "I—I don't wish to be engaged in this on my own. I require counsel." He turned a rather beseeching gaze on Fleming.

Prescott wanted him to solve this problem for him, Fleming thought with quiet fatalism. Blast. He needed a partner in this, even one in as shaky a condition as this man. He didn't wish to be boxed into playing the role of leader . . . or nursemaid.

"Have you any idea, Prescott, any at all, who this man might be?" Fleming didn't expect anything like a useful response.

Surprisingly Prescott straightened in his seat, his long-lashed eyes taking on a thoughtful cast.

"My surest guess, by dint of deduction, is that it is one of Edmund Dours's sons. You'll recall he has two boys in the Navy, both home on leave. Doubtless they're both acutely interested in locating their sister's killer. It's reasonable to assume they've done a bit of probing on their own. Perhaps one or the other of them ran afoul of our miscreants."

Fleming blinked, then took the photo back from Prescott. Militarily cut blond hair, visible where the skull wasn't split open. Quite blond, in fact. Youngish, as attested to by the firmness of what remained of the desecrated features. Male. Angelina had had remarkably fair hair, so blond it was platinum. The facts fit well.

"That's a sound bit of reasoning, Prescott," he said sincerely.

Prescott gave a tiny shrug. "I've not completely lost my talents, old boy. It's only that I never expected to be caught up in something of this nature. I was quite prepared to go to my grave without ever again wallowing about in this kind of bloodshed and mayhem."

"I understand that." An image of Nora Blair DeYoung, her head staved in by a fireplace poker, came utterly unbidden to mind. Coolly he pushed it away. "Well, it's easily enough found out," he continued. "Contact this Edmund Dours—"

"—and ask him if one of his sons has turned up with his face axed into quarters? Or eighths. Or however it's currently divided." His voice was threatening to quiver once more, even laced as it now was with sarcasm.

"Are you still in contact with Mr. Dours?" Fleming asked. Prescott *had* to get hold of himself, no matter how unnerving the present situation. Fleming required as much information as the man had to give.

"I am no longer engaged by Mr. Dours. I was hired to investigate his son-in-law's suspected infidelity. I resolved that matter. However, as you've gathered, things have since become a hair more drastic. It's currently a police matter."

Fleming leaned forward in his chair, meeting Prescott's gaze levelly. "And we both have reasons for wishing to withhold certain aspects of this case from the police. Think of those charming messages we've both received." *Sins of our fathers. Ghost of Christmas Past.* "I wouldn't like to explain either of them."

Prescott grunted. "Bloody can of worms, that." A rather American expression; then again, the man had been living as a native in the States for some while now.

"Very well. Our first action should be to determine if your theory as to this man's identity"—he waved the photograph—"is correct." Fleming was careful not to speak in commands or even employ a tone of order giving. Too easily, he felt sure, Prescott would fall meekly into line behind him, quite content to let Fleming lead this operation. "What is your view? Do you hear me, Prescott?"

"Blast it, Ian, of course I do." His right hand bunched itself into a fist and thumped the arm of his chair soundly. "I am not, however, constrained to *like* any of this."

This produced a faint smile of sympathy from Fleming.

Prescott gathered a deep breath, nodding thoughtfully. "There's been no mention of a fresh murder of this sort in the local press, and the newspapers would most certainly make banner headlines of it, just as with Angelina's murder. It is possible the body has not yet been discovered—wherever it is. Or the police have found it and are keeping mum."

"That would require the cooperation of the remaining members of the Dours family, would it not?" This presumed that it was indeed one of the Dours sons in the photo, Fleming thought.

"It would." A mildly crinkled corner of Prescott's mouth curled upward. "However, the local constabulary can be quite . . .

persuasive. Perhaps they have convinced Edmund Dours that their investigations will meet with greater success if they hold at bay any further public outcry."

Fleming absorbed this. "Interesting. Where was Angelina Marquette's body discovered?"

"The pictures I received weren't, I'm afraid, much help. You can see by the photographic angles used that little is to be garnered about the settings of these homicides. Her violated corpse was found by a watchman in an unused storage shed along the riverfront. So my police contacts were kind enough to tell me."

Fleming tasted something unpleasant at the back of his throat. He drank off the remainder of his port. "Violated?" he asked quietly.

Prescott got up to refill their glasses. "Yes. Though it appalls me to say it. She had been stripped bare for a purpose."

Fleming accepted the replenished glass. Repulsive or not, it was a clue. One of the perpetrators—if indeed there were more than one—was male. Gerard Marquette? Ravishing his own wife before nearly decapitating her? He remained the star suspect. He and Faith Ullrich, who had been established as his mistress.

"Might your contacts have means of verifying if one of Edmund Dours's sons has of late turned up missing . . . or murdered?"

"Any respectable private investigator has police contacts, Ian. But getting them to divulge information about this case may prove impossible from this point onward. Everett McCorkle—the Red Dwarf I mentioned earlier—runs a tight ship. He's rather harsh with those with loose lips. As far as the coppers are concerned, this is a covert operation."

"Would you have any idea what this McCorkle makes of the chicken bone cross found with Angelina's body?" asked Fleming.

"No firsthand knowledge, no. But I am led to understand that the Red Dwarf is a thorough chap in his methods. I think it safe to say that he shan't neglect the voodoo-like overtones of Angelina's murder—whether that bone cross truly signifies anything or not. It does certainly resemble a classic occult fetish." Prescott nodded grimly. "Once this second body turns up—if it hasn't already—with yet another such article on the scene, I imagine he will probe deeply into the local voodoo community."

Fleming said, "You mentioned when we spoke on the telephone that that community is rather clandestine."

Prescott lifted his shoulders. "Like all religions, it is in part a commercial enterprise. Christians peddle dispensations. Some voodoo practitioners sell powders and charms and elixirs for every ailment and need you could imagine. However, there are those of the true faith, the genuine adherents. *They* are harder to find. But they exist."

Fleming nodded. Such authentic practitioners certainly existed on Jamaica.

"Is there any indication that either Gerard Marquette or Faith Ullrich mingles with this local community?"

"As far as I've heard," said Prescott, "none whatever. But it would be difficult to know with certainty."

"It will put a crimp in things," Fleming said, "if Inspector Mc-Corkle prevents you entirely from making use of your police contacts."

"True. I, too, am always in favor of knowing how the competition is faring." Downing a good part of his second glass of port, Prescott appeared more centered than before. Perhaps his old military instincts were finally asserting themselves. "However, other avenues of information exist. This is a curious city, Ian. More of a hamlet in some respects. A great deal of village gossip flying about. People rub elbows on a daily basis, particularly here in the Vieux Carré. They inevitably get into each other's business. Edmund Dours lives here in the French Quarter, on Ursulines Street. There's quite an unofficial network of information out there, if one only knows the proper code words."

Fleming's curiosity was piqued by this tangent. "And they are?" he asked.

"Hah! I fear they'd mean little coming from you, old boy. You're newly arrived. No one knows your face. No one in the trusted circle has vouched for you."

"May I take it that you are a member in good standing within this circle?"

Prescott's smile was much more genuine this time. "Two years I've lived here, Ian. Nearly three, actually. I purchased this house with the bulk of my life's savings and sank the rest into my practice. Rather do or die it was, now that I consider it. However, during that time I've fairly established myself among the natives. I'm what they call a *stand-up guy*." He even managed to speak this last in a passably flat American accent.

"Are you now?" Fleming said with a smile of his own, sipping off a small part of the fine port.

Prescott, downing a more generous swallow, now appeared quite pleased with himself. "Oh, indeed."

"Are you then suggesting that we tap into this clandestine network of rumormongers to procure what information we desire?" Prescott at last was contributing, Fleming thought, pleased. Perhaps as a partner this man wouldn't prove a consummate waste.

"That is my suggestion, old bean. I recommend we call upon the Bourbon Street Irregulars."

WHITE MEN, THE Queen judged, did not appreciate mystery. This was comical since they themselves were mysteries, albeit of the least intriguing variety. Whites were puzzles not interesting enough to bother solving, what with their unimpassioned manners and their anemic religions.

Every so often, though, something interesting *did* occur in the white world.

Cleopatra had been a queen long ago, and she was one now. In her present incarnation she was, in the opinion of the men permitted to view her face, as desirable as her ancient namesake was reputed to have been. And like that woman, she, too, was a ruler.

She had many cats in her home, all breeds and colors, and when she moved about, it was with unmistakable feline grace. Her gaze—eyes almost jade in color gazing from that timelessly sublime face—was as inscrutable and penetrating as any cat's.

At the moment she had human company in her home, beyond the presence of her regular servants and bodyguards. She received her visitor in her parlor, a room whose windows had long since been walled over. Light came from a few strategically placed candles, which burned only bright enough to hint at her shape when she sat on her throne, a high-backed chair with arms carved in the image of ravens. It was always warm to the point of clamminess in here, even in winter, as if her very presence provided a kind of erotic heat. Every man who entered felt it. Dark red silk hung everywhere in the room.

"The discovery of the second body will cause more trouble than the first, my Queen."

Her visitor stood a respectful distance from her seat on the dais. His head remained bowed, and the weak candlelight shone across his hairless skull. Several of her cats were circling this man.

"We can expect reprisals," Cleopatra pronounced. Lacquered nails tapped an arm of the chair. Her fingers were narrow and elegant.

"Undoubtedly, my Queen," said Hush, who had not spoken above that rasping whisper since a white policeman had beaten and throttled him at the age of fifteen. Hush was her principal intermediary with the outside world, though she of course had many other sources of contact—spies, informants, a veritable web that connected to every corner of the city of New Orleans. There were greater places of power on this earth . . . but none greater here in these United States. New Orleans pulsed with an otherworldly beat the whites would never understand.

"We must be prepared for what must follow," the Queen said. A fine crescent of bright teeth shone briefly from her dusky face. "Go now."

Hush, head still bowed, backed from her parlor.

Chapter 9

NIGHT WAS falling beyond the front office's lacy curtains. Fleming declined to join Prescott in another glass of port. "It's time I located a room for myself," he announced. "Do you recommend a nearby hotel?"

Prescott looked upon him utterly aghast. "Hotel? Are you mad, Ian? I shan't hear of it. I had planned all along to billet you here, man. My house is comfortably spacious. I've a suitable guest quarters. *Here* is where you will stay. I will brook no argument."

Plainly, by his stern expression, he wouldn't. Fleming shrugged. Prescott obviously retained enough innate English propriety that any contradiction would only deteriorate swiftly into a fearsome battle of manners.

"That's most kind, Prescott. Thank you." Frankly, Fleming hadn't been looking forward to his search for lodgings. His flight from Jamaica, with its inevitable accompanying time change, was at last catching up to him. The glasses of rich port on an essentially empty stomach also likely hadn't been the wisest of actions.

"I should also be delighted if you'd permit me to take you out for a fine French Quarter dinner," his former colleague—and current partner—continued.

A dinner companion? Indeed, why not? Fleming had been dining alone unconscionably often of late. Such hermitage could not be good for the spirit.

"That sounds splendid, Prescott. First, though, where may I wash up?"

The guest room was on the upper level, toward the rear. The house was larger than it had appeared from the street, occupying a long, if somewhat narrow, plot. Everything looked to be in good repair, Prescott's furnishings tasteful without being garish. The room into which Fleming was ushered was quite inviting. A bed layered in quilts and downy covers dominated the space. There was a tall, dark-paneled wardrobe against the wall, where he could store the scant items of apparel he'd brought with him. The door to a bathroom was in the corner. It all looked extremely cozy.

"This is marvelous, Prescott."

He was lingering in the doorway. "There's a staunch tradition of hospitality in the American South, Ian. I daren't transgress that law. No, truly, I'm pleased to have you under my roof. If you've need of anything, call for Martha."

Fleming turned an eye toward him. "That's the young lady who answered my knock earlier?"

"That is she." Prescott nodded, smiling. "Martha Andry. Secretary, cook, maid. My keeper, if you would. She's quartered at the rear of the house. I would be thoroughly at sea without her. She's been in my employ since I opened my practice. Well, meet you downstairs in ten minutes, dear chap." He slipped away toward his own bedroom, located at the front of the house.

Fleming quickly emptied his suitcase. He changed into a pair of charcoal-colored slacks and a stiffly collared white shirt and tie. The bathroom where he washed up was tiled in radiantly white hexagons, the fixtures twinkling brass, and the sink and tub black, green-veined marble.

He adjusted his holstered Enfield revolver and slipped on his warm black coat once more. Carrying a gun had once been second nature; now, as familiar and comforting as the weight at the small of his back was, he was also aware of the odd sense of dislocation it brought him. It was a bit like coming loose in time, tumbling backward into a past when traveling without a weapon would have been unthinkable.

Meeting Prescott in the mahogany-trimmed vestibule downstairs, he saw the man had traded his dark gray suit for a more elegant black one, adding a red vest with a gold pocket watch for jaunty effect. His receding hair was neatly combed. His secretary, Martha, was straightening the shoulders of his coat with short efficient tugs. They were speaking in quiet amiable tones when Fleming entered.

"Well," said Prescott, "I believe we look presentable enough. Thank you, Martha. We shall return in an hour or two. Don't trouble yourself burning the midnight oil if we're longer. Get yourself off to bed, there's a good lass. Well, Ian, shall we?"

The temperature had dipped since the falling of night, but it was still nothing that Fleming could rightfully call brisk. Dark clouds remained swollen above the city but as yet hadn't delivered the rain they had seemed to promise earlier.

On foot they turned off Dauphine Street and came upon Bourbon, that fabled avenue, one block later. While much of the French Quarter—or the Vieux Carré, as it was also known—appeared to be residential, Bourbon Street was devoted to restaurants and taverns and other pleasure spots. The sidewalks were more crowded than earlier in the day. There was a mood of festivity in the air.

"Mardi Gras approacheth, Ian," Prescott pronounced, seeming now to be in quite good spirits. "Time for the God-fearing to relieve themselves of all their wicked impulses."

Fleming, picking his way along the sidewalk stones, furrowed his brow. "How is that, Prescott?"

"Lent, my boy."

"Lent?"

Prescott turned reproachful hazel eyes on him. "Come, come. The forty days preceding Easter Sunday. A time of atonement and self-deprivation. Fasting, the temporary surrendering of one's more ignoble habits, that sort of twaddle."

"I am aware of the nature of Lent. What, pray tell, has it to do with this Mardi Gras gala?"

Prescott barked out a hearty laugh as they made their way further along Bourbon. Some among their fellow pedestrians were dressed in curious attire, ensembles that might be called costumes. Most seemed to be in a festive humor. Music sounded from some of the open doorways they passed, the lively conflicting tempos of American jazz.

"Mardi Gras, Ian. Shrove Tuesday. The Tuesday immediately before Ash Wednesday, when our Lord rode an ass into Jerusalem, if you care to subscribe to that sort of thing. Mardi Gras marks the final day before the inauguration of Lent. Last chance for the true Christian to make merry, what?"

Fleming shook his head with a puzzled smile. "I wasn't aware this peculiar holiday had any meaning at all. Or if I suspected it, I had no clue as to what it might be in celebration of."

"Ah, Ian," Prescott said expansively, "this is New Orleans, a city that requires only the flimsiest of excuses to lose itself in revelry. Fat Tuesday merely happens to be our best justification. I do truly adore the place. Ah, here we are. I believe you'll be satisfied with this establishment. I've had the luxury of sampling the Quarter's finest restaurants during my time here. This one isn't as grandiose as some, but its board of fare is extraordinary. Come now, in with you."

It seemed as much a club as a restaurant. A dais draped with colorful bunting was set in one corner, upon which a piano, double bass, and drums combo was currently thumping and tinkling out a brisk, adroitly mixed rhythm. The musicians, all black, wore white dinner jackets and what appeared to be stovepipe hats. They traded the measures of the song among themselves, patently improvising whole passages, keeping the cadence alive and coherent by some expert sleight-of-hand. They were, of course, the only blacks in the place. The segregationist American South would have it no other way.

Linen-topped tables were spread all across the wide floor. Roughly half were occupied, but it was enough to keep the staff moving at a steady clockwork pace. The decor was gracious but hardly oppressive. The fronds of large ferns lolled from their massive black urns along the walls. Romanesque pillars supported the ceiling here and there.

Prescott was immediately recognized by the maître d', a short, prim, moon-faced man in black tie who stepped around from his oak pulpit inside the restaurant's front doors. He hailed Prescott with what was either sincere warmth or well-polished faux cordiality.

"We haven't seen you in weeks, Mr. Quick," said the maître d', adopting an amicably chiding tone. "We were beginning to feel snubbed."

"There, there, Elwood. Don't burst into tears. It would be unseemly. Elwood, make the acquaintance of an old dear confederate of mine, Mr. Ian Fleming. He'll be visiting me for a while."

The maître d' made a mannerly bow in Fleming's direction. "Then you come well recommended by the company you keep, sir. Welcome."

Fleming returned him a friendly smile.

"Did you wish to bask in the entertainment this evening, Mr. Quick?"

"It's fine music, Elwood, truly. But I think something a bit away from the commotion."

"Easily done, sir." The short man spun and marched them to a table in a relatively sequestered corner of the dining area. The aromas lacing the air were savory, and Fleming's appetite sharpened further. The maître d' returned to his post, and a waiter in a starched white shirt and dark trousers appeared immediately in his stead, proffering leather-bound menus and clearing the extraneous place settings from the table. Prescott ordered a drink, though Fleming settled for a glass of grapefruit juice. They settled in to study the menu, with which Prescott was indeed familiar. Normally Fleming would have perused the selections leisurely, but by now he was fairly crying out for sustenance and accepted Prescott's recommendations without contention. The man had been something of an epicure in the old days, he recalled. There was no reason to think that had changed.

Prescott sipped at his whiskey, tapping a toe to the spirited music at the far end of the room. Fleming lit a cigarette, casting casually about to ensure that their table was beyond likely earshot of any of the restaurant's other patrons.

"Prescott, there's something else about this matter we must address," he said quietly.

The lanky man turned a bemused gaze on him. "Ian, are we to chart strategies through dinner as well?"

"There's a point I was reluctant to bring up at your office."

Prescott's brows rose slightly above his hazel eyes. "And that is?"

"The business of the evident interception of your outgoing mail." Which was how Fleming's location in Jamaica must have fallen into the hands of whoever had sent him that brief scrawled message and photo.

"Ah. Yes. I've given that some thought. I normally place my correspondence in the box upon my gate. You may have noticed it. The postal carrier collects it from there. Apparently some party—surely one of the devils involved in this—meddled with my mail. Hence, that letter you received. I've since had Martha carry my missives directly to the post office where—"

"Have you considered the possibility of a quisling?" Fleming asked, tone low and level.

It was a term from the war. "An informer?" Prescott said, voice dropping as well.

Fleming nodded, breathing out a wreath of bluish smoke. "An insider is the likeliest suspect in such matters, as you well know. Someone nearby and trusted." He gazed steadily and meaningfully at his dinner companion.

Prescott's lips abruptly tightened. His features became a hard mask. "You mean . . . Martha."

Obviously the thought was a distasteful one to him. "Consider it, Prescott."

"I have given that theory as much consideration as it deserves, Ian," he said icily, "in the space of time between your utterance of it and my current reply. Which is this: shit. Purely and simply. You are speaking without any—*any*—knowledge of the lady in question. This is no keen insight of yours, let me assure you. It's misguided finger-pointing. Terribly misguided. You do not know Martha. She is an outstandingly fine individual. Honest, hardworking, dependable. More loyal than any other person I've ever had the pleasure to know. To attempt to label her as a quisling is a greater effrontery than you can begin to imagine. I do not expect an apology from you, since you've not had the delight of getting to know her as I have. But you will drop this subject, and you shall not introduce it again. Is that clear?" Cold fire now blazed in Prescott's eyes.

Fleming coolly blew out another stream of smoke. "Very well, Prescott. The matter is closed."

The pouched flesh beneath Prescott's left eye twitched a moment, as though with a muscular tic; then he drew a long centering breath. "Good," he said slowly. His right hand, which had bunched into a fist, spread itself on the tabletop's white linen. "Ah, here come the appetizers. Battered oysters in white sauce. I promised you a fine meal, Ian. Let's enjoy it."

Chapter 10

WHETHER OR not Prescott would consider the prospect of Martha being on the wrong side of this, Fleming had to give the theory its due. Prescott was apparently quite dependent upon his secretary-maid. His trust in her was implicit. It would be no great feat for her—who had easy access to all of Prescott's things—to have noted Fleming's address upon the envelope containing Prescott's letter to him. She might well have read the contents of that letter. He *had* to suspect her. His logical military instincts demanded it.

Still, Fleming wondered how he himself would respond to a similar accusation against Isaiah Hines. He would keep his suspicions silent for the time being.

Following the sumptuous meal, Prescott suggested they step out for a proper drink, with no hint of their earlier friction. Fleming agreed, in the back of his mind alert to further signs that the man had troubles with alcohol. He wasn't sanguine about aligning himself with an inebriate. Of course, Fleming himself was no teetotaler, as Prescott had observed. But neither did he have a weakness for drink, merely a taste for it. Perhaps this was another example of the similarity of the two men—similarity to a point, after which they had apparently diverged. One man remained whole; the other had . . . crumbled.

Yet how deep a flaw was it that separated them? They had experienced very similar pressures in the lives they'd both led. Prescott seemed to have reached a breaking point. How close was Fleming to his? Though he would argue otherwise, it was perhaps not much further away than a hearty nudge. Even the thought was uncomfortable.

They entered a rather smoky tavern where yet another trio of able musicians worked through an uninterrupted sequence of jazz and ragtime standards.

It was a lively spot, the clientele mostly young, some of the more attractive ladies dancing racy shimmies before the stage. There was a dartboard upon one wall and a billiards table of dark green felt tucked away in an alcove toward the rear. A number of men stood about the table, observing the proceedings somberly and exchanging murmured comments at each move the two players made.

He and Prescott made their way through the jostling bodies to the bar. Its surface had suffered numerous nicks and scrapes. The bartender was a burly-looking man with a thick black beard, who was tending to his clients with marked speed and efficiency. Tacked up behind the bar was a yellowed headline proclaiming V-J Day. Prescott ordered another whiskey; Fleming, a gin and tonic, neat.

"Chin-chin," he said as they tapped glasses.

The billiards match was proceeding solemnly, Fleming could see. Of course, it wasn't proper billiards. The balls were the wrong color, and there were far too many on the table. Whatever culture the Americans conscripted from their onetime motherland, he reminded himself drolly, was inevitably warped or bastardized or otherwise transformed into something larger, louder, and more frenetic.

"This place has always put me in mind of that wonderfully disreputable public house in—where was it?—Salisbury. Do you recollect that, Ian?" Prescott chuckled a moment into his whiskey glass. "You, I, and Samuel Litchfield, I believe. Yes. Great hulking Sam, with that horse-face of his. We were all bound for the coast somewhere. We stopped off at that pub—at your insistence if I recall, old boy. Wasn't there some business with you and that serving maid . . .?"

Fleming shrugged in turn. "Modesty and taste forbid me recalling it too clearly."

"Ah," Prescott sighed, "the frivolities of youth. Hah. In truth it was a few scant years ago, wasn't it? Seems more a lifetime." The incident, somewhat cloudy in his memory, had in fact been only a handful of years ago, Fleming thought. During the war. Before he and Prescott and Wallace Ullrich and the others had formed ranks as Churchill's Boys. Fleming didn't mind if Prescott rambled on in this nostalgic vein, as long as he refrained from *that* uncomfortable topic.

He took a swallow of his cocktail, just as a round of formal applause sprang up from the tavern's rear alcove. The group gathered about the felt-topped pool table was apparently lauding the game's finale. The winner appeared to be the younger of the two contestants, a somewhat scruffy-looking fellow in his twenties with dark wiry stubble along his jaw. He wore dungarees, a leather jacket with a matted fleece collar, and a black cloth cap. He was quite lean, even compared to Prescott, virtually emaciated, with narrow limbs, a pinched torso, and a face that bordered on the skeletal. He was grinning proudly, bowing with exaggerated ceremony to his audience.

The second player was older by a good two decades or so. His skin was bronzed in a way that suggested mixed Spanish blood rather than Negro. He was clean-shaven with fairly handsome features, solidly built but not especially tall. His wavy hair was absorbently dark, so black it seemed bluish. His eyes were steady and deep-set. He was dressed in attire nearly as casual as his opponent's, though his appeared to be in better repair. He wore a composed air about himself, and his movements as he congratulated his competitor and went to hang his cue stick on a wall-mounted rack were both fluid and economical, a hybrid of those of a dancer and a boxer.

Prescott glanced toward the hubbub, his eyes lighting in recognition. He turned back toward Fleming with a sly smile. "Now, this is fortuitous. Come, Ian, I'll make introductions. It will only cost us a couple of drinks."

Fleming dutifully followed Prescott into the rear nook.

The winning player, the young man in the leather jacket, turned sharply on the balls of his feet at Prescott's approach. His white-toothed grin hitched briefly on his stubbly features, then recognition lit his eyes, which were a fawn-like brown.

"Hey there, Mr. Quick. What's bringin' you out among the riffraff tonight, huh?" He offered his hand, which Prescott shook without hesitation.

"I see you finally bested your arch-nemesis, Slim. Good show, that."

"Aw, c'mon now. I've beat Chopper plenty of times. Old man's stick ain't what it was, y'know."

"I like to throw the kid a victory every once in a while," said the older contestant, stepping up alongside. "Keeps him from getting too despondent. Today's youth aren't as resilient as they were in my day."

The younger man (Slim, was it? Odd name.) turned a droll look on his companion. "An' when was that, Chopper ol' buddy? In caveman times?" The exchange had the sound of long-playing banter.

The older fellow (Chopper? An even more bizarre name.) also shook Prescott's hand while making a swift furtive study of Fleming standing to the right and slightly behind. There was something like professional calculation in that brief glance. Fleming wondered what the man did for a living.

"Gentlemen," said Prescott to the pair, "perhaps you would allow me to buy you both a refreshment."

Slim, who as yet hadn't seemed to even notice Fleming's presence, grinned anew. "Yeah, 'nother grog would do me right."

"Rum it is," Prescott said, evidently quite at ease consorting with this rabble-like duo. "And, Chopper, it's still whiskey, is it?"

"Kentucky," said the bronze-skinned man. His deep-set eyes flickered once more over Fleming.

As a group they nudged and sidled their way back toward the

bar. "Buck," Prescott called to the black-bearded bartender and placed the order, securing fresh glasses for himself and Fleming as well.

The gaunt one named Slim at last turned a flat, vaguely insolent look on Fleming. "Hey, Mr. Quick, who's your sidekick? 'Nother private dick?"

At that moment it occurred to Fleming that these two must be members of the Bourbon Street Irregulars, that semiunderground network of gossip handlers, informal scouts, and quasi-ne'er-do-wells that Prescott had spoken of so glibly earlier. He proposed to use tavern toughs such as *these* to aid them in the investigation? Once more it boded ill.

The bartender delivered their drinks. Slim snatched his off the scarred wood, licking his lips thirstily. The one called Chopper picked up his whiskey glass thoughtfully but didn't raise it to his lips. Both men's cocktails were loaded with ice, another American eccentricity.

Slim made to take a hasty swallow of his rum, but Chopper gave him a soft subtle jab in the ribs with his elbow.

"Thanks for the round, Mr. Quick. We'll be happy to drink it when we know whose company we're keeping." The gaze he gave Fleming was deceptively blank.

"Ah, gentlemen, you're quite correct. Do forgive my lapse. This is Mr. Ian Fleming, a man I've known for a desperate number of years who is visiting me for a time from the tropics, where he currently resides. Mr. Fleming is a member of the press but is presently on hiatus. He is not here to scrounge about for a story. Instead, he's come to aid me . . . in a case."

It was rather more information than Fleming would have wished to have revealed to complete strangers, particularly a pair as shady looking as this. But it was necessary to trust Prescott at least to some degree; otherwise he might as well not be partnering with the man at all.

"The press, huh?" Slim wedged a Lucky Strike into a corner

of his mouth and lit it with a scratched Zippo lighter. "Newspapers? Radio? Or do you do them reels they show 'fore the cartoon
at the movies?"

"I'm a newspaper journalist." Fleming didn't especially care
for the lad's rather impudent tone, which straddled the line between jocularity and rudeness.

"Hey, you're an English guy, too, ain't'cha? Are you a famous
reporter? I mean, I never heard'a you, but, well, you might be.
Are you?"

"You'll have to forgive Slim, Mr. Fleming," said Chopper,
leaning an elbow on the bar. "He only reads the funnies. Big
words give him a headache."

"Can it, old-timer."

Neither of the two spoke in that twangy manner of the Deep
South. The lad's accent might belong to New York, though Chopper's neutral tones were impossible to place. Apparently Prescott
wasn't New Orleans' only transplanted resident.

"Gentlemen," Prescott said quietly, voice only just audible
above the spirited clamor of the band and the appreciative hoots
and hollers from the crowd. "Perhaps, if you're not otherwise
engaged, we might discuss a bit of business. As I mentioned, I
am presently at work upon a case, and Mr. Fleming is aiding
me."

"If there's more'n a dime in it, I'll consider it," said Slim immediately, dragging on his cigarette. "I don't mind bustin' my
hump on the docks, but it ain't payin' enough. I'm sick'a comin'
up short."

The thought that this stick-limbed, starved-looking lad of
twenty-four or twenty-five tackled the heavy labors of a dockworker was frankly laughable to Fleming. He couldn't weigh
much more than nine stone and appeared to have less muscle on
his bones than a rooster.

Chopper gave an impartial grunt. "We'll listen to what you've got to say, Mr. Quick, as always. You've thrown some good jobs our way in the past."

Fleming lifted his fresh gin and tonic to his lips, studying the twosome of Slim and Chopper over the brim and wondering if this situation wasn't already degenerating into something unmanageable.

Chapter 11

FLEMING SINCERELY hoped that Slim and Chopper hadn't been christened with their names. The thought that parents could inflict such cruelty on helpless babes was unsettling.

At a table in as quiet a corner as they could find in the saloon, Prescott told the two men what services he required. Both appeared to recognize the name of Edmund Dours immediately. What Prescott wanted, he explained, was information on that man's two sons, naval men, said to be currently home on leave.

Fleming noted with approval that Prescott betrayed nothing untoward. That Angelina had been murdered was public knowledge. However, Prescott gave no hint whatever that one or the other of Edmund Dours's male offspring might possibly be among the dead as well. It was the kind of slippery negotiation one was compelled to employ when dealing with underworld types such as these.

"Underworld," Fleming knew, might well be overstating it. But if these men weren't gangsters, they certainly weren't lawmen either.

Slim finally dropped his Lucky Strike to the floor, grinding it under the heel of his boot and saying, "'Kay, Mr. Quick. It sounds reasonable." He shot a glance at his confederate. Chopper made an almost imperceptible movement of his eyes that apparently signaled agreement. "Yeah. But look—I don't know 'bout my pal here, but I gotta have somethin' up front. I know we don't usually do it this way, but even just a fin, Mr. Quick, that'd do me okay."

The lad seemed more than a tad uncomfortable talking about the state of his finances, as if the matter were one of some shame. He lowered his eyes and folded his hands on the table. The knuckles of his right were scarred, some of the wounds purplish and relatively recent, others old pale stripes.

"It's no burden, Slim," Prescott said in a quite gentle tone. "I've paid in advance for your services in the past." He picked out two bills, fast and neatly, without revealing the full contents of his billfold. "A fiver then. For each of you." He set the American notes on the tabletop.

Slim pocketed his swiftly with a few mumbled words of thanks. Chopper, however, picked up his whiskey glass instead, taking a measured swallow before saying, "You don't need to front me, Mr. Quick."

Prescott cleared his throat, then shot his hazel eyes covertly at Slim and back to Chopper. Fleming caught the movement, as did the mid-forties, wavy-haired man. Slim remained oblivious, draining off the last of his rum with downcast eyes.

"But to keep it equitable," Chopper continued smoothly, tucking the bill into the heavy denim coat he wore, "I'll take it."

Fleming realized that the man meant to slip the five dollars to his younger—and evidently more needy—accomplice later.

"Fine, gentlemen, fine. Contact me in the usual manner. I would wish you luck, but I know you don't need it."

Slim and Chopper nodded in unison, then stood and slipped out the saloon's front door. It was by now fairly late, the evening having long since given way to true night.

"What a curious pair," Fleming said, not sure now whether to be disturbed or amused by the two men.

"They're quite reliable, I assure you."

"I accept your assurance."

Prescott cocked an eye at his somewhat distant tone. "Are you troubled by my making that payment in advance? They shan't simply abscond with the money. Those two are men of business, whatever else you might wish to call them. They know they can earn the occasional fee by doing footwork for me."

Fleming waved this off. "No, no, Prescott. The ten dollars

doesn't bother me. They just seem rather . . . eccentric." And what, he wondered silently, are you doing fraternizing with such types?

Prescott chuckled amiably. "Ah, Ian, this isn't Regent's Park. It's the French Quarter, a close-knit, rather jammed-together habitat where all walks of life have come to roost. You have the wealthy and the indigent, the violent and the passive, the aristocratic and the proletarian. It is here that I've chosen to make my home. I have a house, I have a practice that earns me my daily keep. I do not look down upon others. I have made myself a part of this community. One meets all kinds here. And if one dares to think oneself a genuine denizen of the Quarter, one accepts the wide-ranging characteristics of one's neighbors. It's that simple."

Fleming nodded at this oration. "Very well, Prescott. I shan't contradict your philosophy. Nor did I mean to. I am merely curious about those two."

"Understandable, then. What did you wish to know about them?"

He hardly knew where to begin, but since Prescott was making the offer, he would avail himself. "Slim and Chopper? Those names first of all. I do hope those are monikers."

"Naturally," said Prescott with a curling smile of amusement.

"I see. Slim, then. Presumably he goes under the title because of his rather gaunt physique. Does he truly work at the docks along the river?" That river, of course, was the wide and far-reaching Mississippi, the chief river of the North American continent, which curved past one of the long borders of the French Quarter on its way to emptying itself into the Gulf of Mexico. The waterway carried a great deal of shipping traffic, and New Orleans' docks and warehouses remained busy year-round.

"He does," Prescott said. "Slim is a scrappy fellow, rest assured. Much stronger and tougher than he might first appear, though he sat out the war owing to a heart murmur, of all things. Has a bit of a bad temper, however. Seems unsatisfied to remain a penurious workingman for the rest of his life. He gets himself into a fair number of brawls, I'm afraid. Still, when he's on a job for me, he's always behaved himself."

Fleming recalled the lad's scarred knuckles and nodded. "Well, Chopper, then. I admit I rather cringe at the thought of how he might have earned that appellation."

Prescott laughed again. "There, I fear, you have me. He's lived here in the Quarter for a good number of years. As far as I know, he's always gone by that name. Nicknames aren't uncommon here. Gamblers, for instance, often use them."

So did draft dodgers and hired killers, Fleming thought wryly. "What does he do when he's not being engaged by you?"

"I don't know that Chopper has anything like steady employment. I've certainly never known him to have a job. So far as I'm aware, he has a fat little nest egg stored away somewhere and lives predominantly off of that. I'm not even certain why he allows himself to be hired out by me, if the money isn't a crucial factor. He was a screen actor, you see. Yes, a genuine Hollywood type, though I don't believe I ever saw any of his films. He played numerous supporting roles and the like, from what I've gathered from rumor. However, his ethnicity was apparently a detriment. He has a fair dose of Portuguese blood in him. The studio heads would never have permitted him to be a leading man. So one day he simply disappeared from the scene and resurfaced here." Prescott paused to take a swallow of his whiskey. "Sounds a bit outlandish, doesn't it? Yes, one hears quite a few peculiar tales here. Normally a personal history like that I would discount as embroidered or outright false. But Chopper has proven himself an honorable man. I wouldn't believe that he would lie."

Fleming nodded. "Well, I was merely curious. Thank you for shedding some light."

"No bother, dear chap." Prescott drained his glass in one final gulp, swaying slightly in his chair as he did. He fished his gold pocket watch from the fob on his sporty red vest. "However, the hour is—oh, dear—rather late. I think we've accomplished all we can on your first day here. Shall we call it a night?"

"Indeed," said Fleming, leaving the last half of his drink untouched and standing along with Prescott.

THEY WENDED THEIR way on foot back toward Dauphine Street, encountering only a few other late revelers, till even these thinned and there was no one else about.

At least until Fleming felt a familiar prescient tingle. His senses, which fortunately hadn't been too dulled by the modest amount of alcohol he'd had this evening, sharpened suddenly. His steps slowed.

"Wait . . ." he said quietly.

Prescott, on the other hand, had indulged more liberally. He was maintaining a composed front, but it was evident that walking a straight line required an effort. He swung a quizzical glance at Fleming.

It was not, of course, any unnatural gift of perception that was alerting Fleming. No doubt he had heard or seen something at the periphery of his senses, something that scarcely registered consciously but that had tripped an alarm nonetheless. In the field he had benefited from these "intuitions" more than once.

He managed a seemingly casual glance behind them, catching just a hint of movement half a block back—as of someone withdrawing quickly into a doorway. He couldn't be certain, however; the motion might well have been a gate or a shutter swinging. Still, now that his guard was up, he did not relax it.

"What is it, dear chap?" Prescott said far too loudly.

"I believe we're being followed. Lower your voice."

"Balderd—" Prescott started, dismissing Fleming's worries with inebriated good cheer, but he caught himself almost instantly and reconsidered. Quietly he asked, "What shall we do?"

"We continue on ahead. To the corner. Act as though I've just told a joke."

Prescott let out a reasonably convincing laugh as they walked onward. Fleming was able to scan a good deal of the street behind with a few subtle turns of his head. Again he noticed movement— just as ill defined but definitely not a trick of the eyes—this time behind and on the other side of the street.

At the corner they turned. Once around, Fleming stepped tightly up against the wall, pulling Prescott with him. The lanky Englishman was trembling.

"Bloody hell, what is this!" It was a stifled hiss, thick with agitation.

Fleming's hand disappeared beneath his coat to grip the Enfield in its holster. His other hand waved harshly at Prescott for silence. He listened hard, hearing . . . footsteps? Yes. Two sets of footfalls, coming rapidly now down the street off of which they had just turned. Soft-soled shoes: If he hadn't been listening specifically for them, he would have missed the sound. He drew back an extra step, crouching slightly as he planted his stance, tensing. The Enfield slipped smoothly into his hand. The closest streetlamps wavered a pale light over the vicinity. They were far from Bourbon Street's rather gaudy illumination.

The pair came sliding around the corner, meaning to be stealthy, using the shadows to full effect.

The Enfield's bore was no more than three feet from the nearer man's head when they both froze to a halt.

"A moment of your time, gentlemen, if you would."

They were both blacks, adults, male. Their clothes, too, were dark, mingling them further with the night. Details were nearly impossible to pick out.

Before Fleming could begin to study them or say anything more; the closer of the two disappeared below the level of the revolver. The move was fantastically fast, akin to the speed at which a flea could jump, but what followed was much more impressive. Fleming had no time to appreciate the maneuver, however, much less put up a defense. The Negro pivoted out of his crouch without a pause, an arm as hard as timber flashing upward to catch Fleming just above the wrist.

He didn't entirely lose his grip on the pistol, but the blow crushed his hand against the nearby stucco wall, and for a full heartbeat his fingers would not respond. It was all the time the pair required. Both men whirled sharply about and bolted, separating immediately.

"That one's yours!" Fleming called to Prescott without looking back, pointing off at the Negro who was dashing back up the street at high speed.

Blast. Fleming's long legs carried him after his own quarry, who had peeled off in the opposite direction, sprinting down the middle of the deserted street. He moved like a cheetah, limbs flashing, sparing no backward glance. Fleming put on his best burst of speed, but it was apparent before he'd covered half a block that it was hopeless. He kept at it regardless, calling on every iota of strength and every memory of his athletic youth, all to no avail.

An auto—a great white tank of a thing—appeared suddenly at the next intersection, tires shrieking as it slewed to a stop. The rear door flew wide, and the black youth dived for the interior like a torpedo seeking its target. The engine gunned, and the car hurtled away.

It had been a Studebaker. White body, whitewall tires—all immaculate. A scrupulously cared-for car. Of course he had automatically looked for the plate, only to see it smeared liberally with something—grease or mud—so as to make it utterly illegible. Interesting that this was the only part of the auto to be so dirtied. He'd been unable to get even a glimpse of the driver.

Fleming's heart was performing a painful tattoo in his chest. He holstered his Enfield as he tried to regain his breath. He flexed his hand, wrist tingling at the bone where he had been struck. It was a pity the sight of the revolver hadn't cowed their pursuers-turned-pursuees. If one wasn't willing to fire a gun—and he hadn't been, not without better cause—then it was bad form to draw it. His bluff had been called. This annoyed the gambler in him.

He retraced his steps, seeing Prescott lurching unsteadily back toward the same corner. Fleming was winded, but Prescott appeared absolutely ruined. His wheezing could be heard from several yards off, and his face, when he finally approached, was the red of a spoiled tomato. He was urgently loosening his tie. He put a hand to the wall and heaved hoarse breaths.

"No luck?" Fleming ventured.

Eventually Prescott straightened, blotting beads of sweat from his brow with a handkerchief. "Like trying to overtake bloody Jesse Owens. Who were they?"

"How on earth should I know?" Fleming felt a stab of misplaced irritation.

"Perhaps they were merely robbers."

"Do you believe that?"

"I believe I should like to sit down, very soon. Come. My house is only another two streets." Prescott staggered forward.

Truly this was a man in decline, thought Fleming, keeping alert to their surroundings. Once Prescott had been an impressive physical specimen. Now evidently age and drink had conspired to strip him of every vestige of youthful vitality.

"Mine jumped into an automobile," Prescott said as they made their way. "He was some distance ahead, but I saw. A white car . . ."

"A Studebaker?"

"Why, yes, I believe so."

It must have picked up Fleming's man first, then swung about to collect the other. Or else there were two such cars. In either case it spoke of an organized effort. Not simple street robbers, then.

"I want nothing of this said to Martha," Prescott said before they climbed the steps to his front door. "She worries enough about me as it is."

"Very well." Presuming she didn't already know about the incident, Fleming added silently.

Despite Prescott's earlier orders, Martha was indeed waiting up. She came into the vestibule to collect their coats when they entered the house. Fleming retained his, wishing to keep his holstered .38 concealed. Prescott chided her with mock sternness for remaining awake till this ungodly hour, which the young black woman countered by asking her employer just how many whiskeys he'd had that night. It was indeed a lax relationship they shared, even more permissive than that which Fleming and Isaiah Hines had.

Fleming bid them both good night and made his way upstairs to the guest quarters.

As he made himself ready to sleep, he heard the sudden grumble of thunder overhead. A moment later rain began a soft patter on the roof, which soon became a heavy drumming. The day's promised downpour was finally arriving.

HE CAME AWAKE sharply, alert. Listening. Hearing . . .

Footsteps, on the stairs. He snatched his watch off the night table and squinted furiously. He had been asleep some two hours. The rain had passed.

The footsteps went by his door, along the upper hall. Their owner was male, judging by the slight creaks his weight elicited. An instant later Prescott's bedroom door opened, then closed. Then silence.

Not an intruder. This was Prescott himself, then. Fleming was sure of it. Well, it was the man's house, after all. He had the run of it. Perhaps he required a final nightcap before sleep, if he were as heavy a drinker as he seemed to be.

But no . . .

This was Prescott returning from his nocturnal visit to the quarters at the rear of the house. A visit to Martha, the potential quisling in this. At that instant Fleming knew it, surely and intuitively, according to honed instincts that had seen him through a war and beyond.

No mere servant, she. No. Martha might indeed be Prescott's keeper, as he had asserted earlier. She was also his lover.

Chapter 12

"GOOD MORNING, Mr. Fleming. Would you like to start the day with a cup of tea?"

It was Martha, who emerged from the rear kitchen wearing a dress as immaculately white as yesterday's and another head scarf, this one a festive orange color. It was nearly seven o'clock, and Fleming was shaved and dressed. Prescott wasn't yet about.

"Coffee would be my preference, if you don't mind."

"My pleasure." She turned to leave Fleming in the broad downstairs hallway.

"Actually," he called on a sudden impulse, "you wouldn't have any chicory, would you? I understand that's a New Orleans favorite." He had always made a point of sampling the local fare wherever he traveled.

Martha turned back and wrinkled her pretty little nose. "Chicory? I've probably got some around somewhere. Are you sure you want *that* instead of real coffee? Chicory is a ground-up, roasted root. Not too pleasant. It's what the Johnny Rebs drank when the coffee disappeared, along with most of the food."

Another myth exploded, thought Fleming. "Coffee, then. Please." He wandered into a cozily furnished drawing room.

She really was quite a comely young woman, with her high cheekbones and sharp eyes. How, Fleming wondered distantly, had her liaison with Prescott started?

Racial relations in the American South, Fleming knew, were even more strained than those on Jamaica. A romance between a white man and a Negress? Wasn't that something akin to playing with fire? Apparently Prescott and Martha were keeping their courtship secret. Fleming tried to remind himself that he had no actual proof of the affair, just the inconclusive sound of footsteps on the stairs last night and that bolt of intuition that had struck him so deeply. But part of what had made him so successful a spy was reliance on those subconscious connections that bypassed the forebrain and, in his case, had always—well, *almost* always—proven themselves correct.

He made himself comfortable in a deep armchair. The drawing room was paneled in soft beige woods, with a sumptuous carpet underfoot. A grandfather clock that looked to be quite the antique swung its pendulum at a mollifying tempo in one corner.

Martha delivered him his coffee there. She had included a plate of cookies, which appeared to be chock-full of nuts of some variety, and the morning newspaper.

"Most kind of you, Martha."

"You're welcome, Mr. Fleming. Mr. Quick usually rises at around eight. If you want anything else, like breakfast, just let me know."

He was grossly tempted to question the woman, of course. In fact, it was most likely that he would eventually need to grill her in some capacity. Prescott might be positive of her loyalties, but the man's romantic—or at least amorous—involvement with her brought his judgment into sharp question. Fleming was not similarly biased. As long as Martha's allegiance remained dubious, the opposition had a potential informant right here in this house.

I am back in the spy game, he thought with pragmatic resignation, taking a first sip of what turned out to be an excellent spot of coffee and picking up the local newspaper.

The paper was something of a rag, he judged with his journalistic eye after scanning a few of its lead features. The gossipy antics of provincial celebrities and politicians weren't the sort of copy that would have passed muster with Kemsley Newspapers. Still, it made for amusing reading. New Orleans politics, he recalled, were notoriously corrupt. Yes, there had been that one truly infamous governor of Louisiana some years ago, who had been assassinated. Huey Long. Popularly known as the Kingfish. (Did everyone here live under a nickname?) Despite the gangster-like tactics he was credited with employing during his tenure, the man was still celebrated by many. Curious.

On the front page he also found a column beneath the heading ARRESTS, alongside which was a file photo of a bushy-haired man with ostentatious sideburns. He was identified as Inspector Everett McCorkle.

Fleming poured another cup of rich coffee from the silver pot Martha had left and focused on the article. Inspector McCorkle, it read, recently assigned to the Angelina Marquette murder case, had stepped up police efforts to solve this most ghastly crime. Though he refused to comment specifically, it was presumed that the citywide arrests of the past few days that he'd ordered tied in directly to the investigation. Those arrests, listed chronologically, spelled out the twelve police raids in forty-eight hours that had resulted in thirty-one prisoners. All were from among the city's Negro population, though no other details were provided. Nowhere was there any mention of a second body surfacing, a male with his face hacked to bits. Perhaps it hadn't yet been discovered. Or perhaps the news was being carefully withheld.

Prescott had said the Red Dwarf ran a tight ship. Apparently he wasn't one for speaking to the press either. Fleming returned to the photograph. He looked to be roughly age forty. There was a decided smarminess about the man's expression, a haughty amusement. Here, then, was their competition, the individual he and Prescott had to beat out before Faith Ullrich and Gerard Marquette (along with the information Faith evidently possessed concerning Churchill's Boys) fell into police hands.

Arrests among New Orleans' black citizens, though—why? Were those bone and feather crosses leading the police into the city's so-called voodoo community? Were Faith and Marquette actually connected to that circle?

Fleming poured another cup of coffee. He even found himself nibbling a few of Martha's cookies.

Eventually he discovered a bit of international news. The dateline of the article, picked up from some larger news service, was Seoul. The situation in Korea, that seemingly minor spit of land extending itself from Southeast Asia, was looking bleak. There the Russians and the Americans—using North and South Korea as proxies, of course—were squaring off on their respective sides of the thirty-eighth parallel. It was an uneasy sort of truce-stalemate, and in Fleming's judgment it wouldn't last. What it might lead to, however, was anybody's guess.

At that moment Prescott entered the drawing room. The man appeared only half awake, eyes thoroughly bloodshot, features bleary. He was blinking at Fleming as if trying to ascertain what this unfamiliar man was doing in his house.

"Why, good morning to you, Prescott."

"Morning," he said, tasting the word and finding it sour. "I tell you truly, Ian, I can no longer even remotely imagine how I managed to rise to the blatting of a bugle every morning."

Martha materialized with a fresh pot of coffee and another cup and saucer. They made no greetings to each other, but Fleming noted the subtle familiarity of body language between them.

Prescott was wearing a deep purple smoking jacket with quilted blue lapels and slippers on his feet. He poured himself coffee, adding a mound of sugar, then wandered idly around behind Fleming's armchair to see what he was reading.

"Korea," he grunted. "The next hot spot, wouldn't you say? War with the Russians is in the offing if we're not careful. Yes, the great Communist menace. Our onetime allies. Never trusted them, of course. No thinking man did. Not with that bloody nonaggression pact they made with Hitler." Prescott crossed the carpet to plant himself on a plush settee. "Well, now the masquerade's done with, it seems. We've got a mighty empire on the far side of the globe fanatically dedicated to the eradication of capitalism. Which in the Free World's mind translates as the eradication of democracy."

"You seem to have some misgivings about the matter," Fleming said, folding the paper and laying it on the low table in the middle of the room.

Prescott sipped his coffee. "It's not clear-cut, old boy. I don't like this new war because it's not a proper war. No one will declare anything. It's all posturing and politics and threats and counterthreats and espionage. No proper battles are fought. There's value in that, I suppose. The world is weary of war, isn't it? Nobody wishes to see their sons marching off again. Still, this is amounting to a prolonged standoff. And if war were to come, what then? Bloody atomic bombs. Would make the Blitz seem like a church picnic."

By now Prescott had had time to absorb a useful amount of coffee. Fleming turned back to the article on McCorkle and handed over the paper.

Prescott's bloodshot eyes narrowed as he read. "What the devil is he up to?" he finally said.

"Looking for axe-wielding voodoo cultists, perhaps."

"Or leading everyone a merry chase. From what I gather of his reputation, you never can be certain with the Red Dwarf."

They brooded on that in silence a moment.

"Prescott," Fleming said finally, "I should like you to print another batch of those photos you took of Faith Ullrich and Gerard Marquette the night you did that spot of"—he nearly said "spying"—"surveillance for Edmund Dours. You said you've retained the negatives."

Prescott nodded. "Already done so. Actually I meant to show them to you yesterday, but it must have slipped my mind. Come, old boy. They're in my office."

Once inside, with the office door closed, Prescott dipped into a drawer of his large desk, retrieving a manila envelope. His expression was grave as he handed it over.

"Keep in mind, these are quite candid. And quite distasteful."
Fleming took the packet and seated himself again in one of
the leather chairs facing the desk. "Don't fear, Prescott. I am over
eighteen and not especially delicate."

"Very well. But you've been warned." Prescott moved toward
the fireplace. The serving cart of yesterday was still there. He
picked a handsome meerschaum pipe from its neat wood stand
atop the mantel, fiddled briefly with it, and put it back.

Fleming undid the envelope's catch and drew out a thick stack
of photographs. They were black and white, the texture of the
film a bit grainy but each shot well focused. Prescott must have
had a steady hand that night.

"The house is on St. Philip Street," Prescott provided. "I'll
take you there for a look, if you like."

First there was simply a picture of that house, sitting at one
corner of an intersection, outer walls supported by heavy beams.
Its ground-floor windows were shuttered. A terrace wrapped both
visible faces of the house some fourteen or fifteen feet above
street level, braced by flanged metal columns. The guillotine
windows of the upper story were not shuttered.

Prescott said, "My police contacts told me that Faith Ullrich
left behind the bulk of her belongings when she fled, presumably
in the company of Gerard Marquette. She had been leasing the
house for the past ten months, evidently since shortly after her father's suicide, which occurred back in England."

Fleming flipped to the next photograph, seeing a dark human-
shaped smear against the house wall, which must be Gerard Marquette hurrying toward his mistress's front door. There were no
details of the man to be seen.

Next the door stood open, the house's interior light silhouet-
ting two figures who had to be Faith Ullrich and her paramour.
She stood in profile, and yes, there was some familiarity to the
firm cheekbones, curving jaw, and sloping nose. But again there
were no definitive details. She was wearing a diaphanous gown.

Marquette was dressed in a business suit. Faith was several inches taller than he.

Prescott had gotten two more snapshots of the pair retreating inside the house. Marquette had dark hair and a rather slight physique. Faith, from what Fleming could discern, had a nicely proportioned figure.

Fleming noted the steep angle of the shot. "Where were you when you took these?"

"The building on the adjacent corner, currently unoccupied. I know the gentleman who owns it. He hired me to do what amounted to a dash of legal research into property rights. He's been rather exaggeratedly grateful ever since. He made loan of the building's key to me. I made use of its terrace."

"Fine bit of reconnaissance, that," Fleming said with some approval. "You secured a good vantage. It appears to have paid handsomely."

"Yes," Prescott said sourly. "Handsomely indeed. Keep looking, Ian. You've not yet reached the more charming chapters of this sordid tale."

The remaining photographs had been shot levelly, not at the previous downward angle. Prescott had indeed had a fine view into the upper-story boudoir, whose drapes were only partially drawn.

Here were Faith and Gerard Marquette apparently just having entered the bedroom. They had drinks in hand. Marquette's back was toward the window, his slender body blocking the camera's view of the woman. From Prescott's angle much of the chamber was visible, including the bed and an ornate vanity table.

The following three or four shots were of the pair talking, drinking, laughing, making themselves comfortable. Marquette was loosening his tie. A clear unimpeded shot of Faith Ullrich finally materialized in the stack, and this Fleming studied carefully a moment. The light in the bedroom was much better than it had been below. Faith was a remarkably attractive woman, but it wasn't this trait that commanded his attention.

He scrutinized the face. Her complexion was fair, even creamy. She had long dark tresses that might indeed be that special shade of mahogany that Wallace Ullrich's hair had been. Clearer now were the firmness of the cheekbones, the curve of the jaw, and the appealing slope of the nose. What was most telling, however, was the confident cast of the eyes, distinct and unmistakable even at this distance. The set of those eyes was supremely self-assured, a gaze that swept everything fearlessly, like a lighthouse's glaring beam, and assessed and judged any who fell under it. Those were indeed Wallace's eyes. In this photo she was gazing with a kind of libidinous mirth at Gerard Marquette.

In the next she was helping him remove his clothes.

Faith Ullrich, Wallace's daughter—no sense in trying to repudiate the verifying evidence—grinned as she stripped the man bare. She seemed well in charge of the procedure. Marquette's body was revealed in stages. It was willowy indeed. He wasn't skeletal, as, say, that Slim character was; that lad at least gave one the impression there was some vigor about his scrawny hide. Marquette's slight frame instead appeared . . . dainty. He wore an air of softness about himself, especially now that he'd been divested of his masculine apparel.

His clean-shaven features were nearly as delicate as his body. His face's angles lacked any manly firmness. His chin was slight, his cheeks rounded, his eyes wide and inoffensive. He looked, if anything, something like a fair-faced child of ten or eleven years, without yet any of the explicit distinctions of gender.

This silent mental observation soon became quite ironic as Fleming continued through the stack.

Faith, still wearing her gauzy gown, had seated Marquette at her vanity table. The next snapshots were less focused than the previous, as though Prescott's hands had suddenly lost their steadiness. Still, Fleming could perceive that Faith was applying cosmetics to the nude man's face.

When he had stood and turned from the table, he had been quite made up. What was probably red lipstick outlined his mouth. That was surely rouge upon his cheeks and mascara ringing his wide eyes. The process had clearly very much aroused him, evident now that he was unknowingly facing the camera. Fleming shifted a bit uncomfortably in the leather chair.

"As is said in the States, Ian," came Prescott's voice from near the fireplace, "I told you so."

Fleming ignored the comment and pressed onward.

Gerard Marquette's metamorphosis wasn't yet complete. Faith, still grinning lustfully, set about re-dressing the man. Not in his business suit again, no, of course not; why should the perversions cease now? Soon he was sporting a complex array of rather whorish feminine undergarments. The depraved ensemble fit him quite well.

The pictures went in and out of focus from here on through the remainder of the thick stack, as Prescott reacted violently to the warped acts of debauchery that followed this initial outfitting.

Faith Ullrich at last discarded her gown, revealing a body that was among the most exquisite Fleming had ever seen. But it was hardly a stimulating sight as she proceeded to engage in acts nearly too salacious to contemplate with the transformed Gerard Marquette. Implements whose uses Fleming would rather have not seen demonstrated were brought into play. The variety of unnatural deeds was staggering. So, too, were the mentalities that could have conceived of such untold degeneracy.

The activities seemed to cut themselves off mercifully before they reached whatever repugnant finale was in store. The last two snaps were merely of Marquette—refurbished as a male once more—exiting the house and Faith closing the front door.

Fleming dropped the photographs back into the manila envelope, wiping his fingertips against the legs of his trousers. It had been something of a soiling experience. But at least he had been thoroughly satisfied as to Faith Ullrich's lineage. Yes, she was undoubtedly the daughter of that former member of Churchill's Boys.

"After a point I couldn't continue," said Prescott, wandering over from the safe distance where he'd been standing throughout and taking the adjacent leather chair. "I took far too many of those dreadful photos as it was. Two and a half bloody rolls of film. It was like being under a spell. Too horrifying to look at, too appalling to turn away. Anyway, it was certainly unequivocal proof of Marquette's faithlessness to his wife, Angelina. That was what Edmund Dours hired me to secure."

Fleming lit a cigarette and drew in the soothing smoke. "What was Mr. Dours's reaction to this . . . evidence?"

Prescott shrugged. "I never discovered. I handed over the photographs the following morning and counted myself lucky to be away from such deviation. A day later I received those pictures of Angelina Marquette's corpse. And that damned message. Soon after, I contacted you." He still sounded rather contrite about this last, still regretful of involving his former colleague in what had turned into a grisly predicament.

Fleming puffed meditatively on his Players a moment, coolly distancing himself from his understandable emotional reactions to the profane snapshots of Faith Ullrich and Gerard Marquette at play.

"Do you think those two might be dabblers in—shall we say—occult practices?" Fleming asked.

"Voodoo, you mean, of course. Did they fashion those crosses of feathers and bones that have appeared in the photographs of both bodies—is that what you're asking?"

"Yes," said Fleming.

"Would you put it past them?" Prescott countered grimly.

Fleming glanced at the envelope. "No," he finally said. "Do you truly think those two are the murderers, then? Of Angelina?

Of that as yet unidentified young man who might well be one of Edmund Dours's sons?"

Prescott stared gloomily off at his bookshelves for a lengthy interval. At last he turned his bloodshot hazel eyes toward Fleming. "I imagine that people capable of those acts in those photographs are quite capable of any deviant deed."

Fleming blew out a long plume of smoke. "So do I."

Chapter 13

PRESCOTT RESISTED the idea of breakfast, but after some insistence by Martha—acting something like a chiding wife, Fleming noted—he changed out of his lounging attire and came downstairs again to the dining room to eat.

Savory cooking aromas were emanating from the kitchen as Prescott and Fleming seated themselves at a dining table of blond lacquered wood. A hand-painted vase filled with gardenias was the centerpiece. Martha brought the food through the kitchen's connecting swinging door. Prescott's portions looked quite wholesome—half a cantaloupe, toast, a bowl of thick vegetable soup, a glass of tomato juice. Fleming was treated to some livelier fare—spicy sausages, scrambled eggs mixed with diced fried onions, flapjacks with hot maple syrup, and a bowl of what he discovered was grits. Only this last dish was rather bland, with the consistency of wallpaper paste and what he imagined might be its flavor as well. But a few pats of butter and a generous dose of syrup brightened up this, too. He dined with some relish.

Prescott ate dutifully also, having resigned himself to the sensible feeding of his body. More than once during the meal, though, he eyed Fleming's food covetously. They finished with another round of coffee.

"How shall we make use of this day?" Fleming asked when Martha had cleared the plates.

Prescott pursed his lips in thought a moment. "It's likely we will have some word from Slim and Chopper before the day's through."

"So soon?"

"Oh, yes. They're really quite efficient and reliable, those two.

However, I believe we could best use these daylight hours by putting out the word that we're interested in the present whereabouts of Faith Ullrich and Gerard Marquette."

At this Fleming frowned. He was pleased to see Prescott voicing an opinion on the matter. It was an indication that he still saw himself as a partner in this, not a subordinate willing to lay the entire matter in Fleming's lap. However, this tactic didn't seem particularly sound.

"I'm not sure I agree, Prescott. Our chief concern in this is keeping certain details of this case secret from the police. If we announce that we're on the hunt for Faith and Marquette, we will essentially be declaring publicly our involvement in this affair. That surely will eventually call some attention from the authorities."

"Come, come, dear chap. I wasn't proposing printing our intentions in the newspaper or shouting them out on street corners. I don't believe you yet fully grasp the nature of that clandestine network I've referred to before. You've only met two of the envoys from that particular underworld—Chopper and Slim. There are others. There is a veritable rumor mill at work in the French Quarter, and since matters have so far remained within these boundaries, we would be foolish not to use what facilities are at the ready. We won't be carelessly tipping our hand, I assure you. Not if we conduct our operation properly. And, as I've said, I know the code words."

Fleming wasn't precisely dubious about the existence of this clandestine informational network. Prescott was certainly swearing by it. He had decided to reserve any permanent judgment until those two Bourbon Street Irregulars—Slim and Chopper— either delivered news of Edmund Dours's sons or failed to do so. In the meantime he would go along. In theory Prescott was quite right: Why not use what facilities were available?

He retrieved his Enfield from his room before they ventured out. He was dressed in brown wool trousers and a beige shirt but had traded his warm black coat of yesterday for a lighter tan jacket, which still neatly concealed his holster at the small of his back.

Off they went, Prescott making farewells to Martha and promising to be back by dinnertime. Again the dynamics between them were much like those of a husband and wife.

Stepping onto the street, Fleming was of course on the alert, picking out every movement, noting doorways and niches along the street that could conceivably conceal a person. There were no white Studebakers in evidence. Prescott, at his side, was making a similar scan as they moved off, though his moves were noticeably more nervous.

Seeing the French Quarter on foot, in the full light of day, was much different from experiencing it at night. Their surroundings were a veritable feast for the eyes. The Quarter's architecture was enchanting, a kind of storybook land where the most improbable of creatures might dwell. Fleming didn't relax his vigilance, but neither was he blind to the pleasures of this environment.

The style of construction was decidedly old European, such as might be found in a French or Spanish village where time moved at a lackadaisical pace, perhaps even in a counterclockwise direction. Doorways were narrow and often shuttered. Brick, mortar, and stone accounted for many of the building walls. Roofs were canted, sporting brickwork chimneys and ornate cornices. Windows were tall and also narrow. There seemed to be nothing above three levels.

Nothing appeared newly built either. Everywhere there was the sense of age; not a history of manifold centuries, no, but a kind of genteel venerability. Flowers and shrubs were in evidence everywhere, bursting from gated front yards, ivies and ferns dangling languorously from those fanciful wrought-iron terraces that were so common.

In addition to that sense of age, there was also the prevailing impression that much of the French Quarter was in the process of long decay. Here and there gray mortar had crumbled from walls. Sidewalk stones were fractured. At one place, somewhat alarmingly, brackish water appeared to be bubbling freely from the ground. Prescott mentioned casually that New Orleans actually lay *below* sea level by several feet.

Fleming, somewhat dismayed, said, "People must spend a fair amount of time bailing out their cellars."

Prescott laughed. His earlier anxiousness was evaporating. "They would, but there are no cellars here. New Orleans is a rather tenuous crust of stone and metal atop swampland that would just as soon swallow the city whole."

The general moldering of the scene was rather quaint, however, only adding to the cheerfully languid atmosphere.

A few automobiles crept along the single-direction lanes. A horse-drawn wagon—with wooden sides and a bed filled with scrap metal, the transport reminiscent of Jamaica—went clattering noisily past. Fleming noted the street signs, the rich sounds of the decidedly non-American names: Burgundy, Chartres, Dumaine, Decatur.

Prescott took it upon himself to point out many of the sights. As they entered Jackson Square Prescott rattled off brief histories of the cathedral, with its towering steeple that stood taller than anything else in the Quarter; of the Cabildo, the onetime seat of the city's colonial government; and of the Pontalba Buildings, two ranks of rather majestic apartment buildings that overlooked the square. Jackson Square itself was a sunken pedestrian promenade that circled a small but immaculately kept park in its center. A good deal of activity was occurring in the square.

"It's a bit like a circus, isn't it?" Prescott remarked as they made their way along the walkway.

"It is indeed."

The square milled with a wide variety of people. A Negro bootblack was doing a brisk business at one corner. One burly fellow was hauling a massive block of ice on a herculean shoulder toward a restaurant's service alleyway. Others appeared to be merely idling, enjoying the afternoon's relative warmth. They ranged from the lower classes and common laborers to well-off types like Prescott himself and even a few who were likely residents of those regal apartments that abutted the square at either side. Fleming saw a juggler keeping four orange balls in continuous looping motion.

While they strolled through this human menagerie, Prescott paused a few times to speak to individuals who were plainly natives.

Fleming hung back, but his sharp hearing picked up much of what was said. One exchange, between Prescott and a sandy-haired chap wearing a spattered cook's apron and smoking a dark Turkish cigarette nearby a diner's refuse barrels, went thus:

"Good afternoon to you, Curt."

"Hey, Mr. Quick, how'yuh?"

A moment of idle pleasantries, then:

"Curt, I'm putting my ear to the ground."

"Uh-oh. Somebody's in trouble." The man grinned, revealing several gaps in his upper front teeth. "Who yuh after?"

"Two people, probably keeping company. Faith Ullrich and Gerard Marquette are the names." Prescott described each briefly, providing easily remembered highlights—Faith's attractiveness and long mahogany-colored hair, Marquette's slight physique. "They don't wish to be found."

"Who doen? Ain't nobody I know who ain't on the run from somethin'. 'Cept you, of course, Mr. Quick. You're too respect'ble for that."

"Decent of you to say, Curt. Naturally there's a modest fee for any information."

"Natch'ly." Curt pitched the stub of his cigarette into one of the barrels. "I'll peel an eyelid, casual-like. I sure ain't got nothin' better to do with my time." With a nod he went back inside the diner.

That seemed to be all there was to it. As they made a long circuit of the Quarter's streets, Prescott repeated a version of this dialogue a number of times. He spoke to an assortment of characters, male and female, all of whom recognized and greeted him pleasantly. Occasionally one of them eyed Fleming, lingering on the periphery, with some suspicion, but Prescott assuaged this with a few simple words. "He's with me." That seemed enough of an explanation.

These contacts all appeared to be of the working class—busboys, bartenders, street sweepers, cabdrivers, grocers. Fleming thought he was beginning to understand. These were indeed Bourbon Street Irregulars . . . but this wasn't any sort of organized network. These people who worked and sometimes lived in the French Quarter were merely in key positions to absorb gossip, to eavesdrop, to invisibly observe. They were fixtures here and likely went largely ignored by the general populace. Yet word passed easily among them, so rapidly in fact that when Prescott stepped into a cluttered little meat market, the gray-haired, sharp-eyed butcher behind the counter had already heard his spiel secondhand and promised to be on the lookout for the fugitive couple.

"Ah," Prescott said, appearing quite satisfied. "I believe that should do nicely."

"And you're confident none of these people will slip word to the police, inadvertently or otherwise, that you're searching for our pair of suspected murderers?" asked Fleming as they turned back toward Dauphine Street and home.

"I pay a fair price for information when I need it. Saves me the bother of pounding the pavement, as they say, myself. There's a sort of conspiracy of silence in constant effect here. These people don't tell tales out of school. They don't run to the police when something is afoot because there's no percentage in it. I've made my reputation among this crowd by remaining honest and equitable."

Fleming kept his lingering doubts to himself. He had, after all, partnered himself with Prescott because the man had an insider's knowledge of this territory.

As they continued homeward, Fleming thought he detected, at some distance, the tattoo of drums and the sounds of a crowd.

"Prescott, do my ears fail me, or do I hear native drums beating somewhere in the bush?"

"I told you, Ian. Mardi Gras approaches. It's surely one of those raucous parades that crop up this time of year. Likely it's off on Rampart Street or beyond. Frankly I don't pay much heed. I adore this city, but Fat Tuesday might be said to be more trouble than it's worth. Or perhaps I'm simply too old to frolic as once I did."

It was deep into the afternoon by now. More clouds had scudded in overhead, but these didn't appear to promise any further rain. The temperature, however, was beginning to dip, the intermittent breeze growing steadier and chilly.

"I'll take you past Faith Ullrich's house, if you like," Prescott said.

"Yes."

It sat on a corner of St. Philip Street, evidently empty, looking much as it had in the surveillance photos. Fleming noted the colors—yellow stucco walls supported by heavy beams painted a deep kelly green. An eye-catching combination but hardly remarkable in the setting of the Quarter, where color schemes tended toward the exotic. They didn't linger but moved on past.

In that house's upper-story bedroom Faith Ullrich and Gerard Marquette had engaged in those abominable acts. Both creatures were murder suspects, twice over. For all Fleming knew there might be another murder afoot this very moment.

And yet those murders weren't the primary worry in this situation, were they? No. It was those scrawled messages both he and Prescott had received, those allusions to their mutual buried past. A past that Faith Ullrich, Wallace Ullrich's daughter, might well have intimate knowledge of.

He and Prescott were involved in this muddle because of *that*, because of the crucial importance of leaving those secrets undisturbed. It was a matter of national security. MI-5 certainly wouldn't be pleased if the facts of that particular postwar operation saw light. The situation had to be squelched. Now. Before the police unearthed too much. And if Prescott's assessment of Inspector McCorkle was correct, they were in a tight race with that so-called Red Dwarf.

National security. Was even that passably noble cause the root of their, his and Prescott's, motivation in tackling this? No. Be fair, man, he told himself. Be honest. It is to cover up our own unclean participation in that mission as two of Churchill's Boys that is compelling us so desperately.

As they rounded the corner onto Dauphine Street, Prescott came to an abrupt halt. Fleming, too, checked his stride. The house was half a block distant, and at first glance he could see nothing out of the ordinary. Then he noticed: The door with its baroque brass knocker stood wide.

He looked sidelong at Prescott. His lined face was set suddenly in a fierce cast, hazel eyes sharply focused. His lanky body was coiled. He gave his right arm a quick snap, and as if by magic a tiny ivory-handled derringer appeared in his hand. Fleming had had no idea the man was carrying it.

"Prescott—" he began, meaning to caution him against overreacting. An opened front door could be explained any number of ways. Besides, Martha was surely in the house.

But Prescott had transformed into a man of action. "Let's move," he said tightly, coolly, darting forward at a crouch, keeping near the house fronts as he approached his abode.

Fleming followed, naturally, though he didn't yet draw his own pistol. Here, then, was something of the Prescott W. Quick he remembered—decisive, primed, swift to action but always collected.

They closed on the house's front fence. The gate, too, was

opened. There was no movement behind the lacy curtains of Prescott's office nor within what could be seen of the vestibule.

"Are you armed?" Prescott asked in a sharp hiss over his shoulder as they hunched at one end of the ornate fence.

"I am."

"Then cover my movements." At that he sprang, pouncing toward the open gate. Fleming put his hand beneath his tan jacket, once more closing it over his .38's grip but not drawing the gun. The situation didn't yet seem to warrant the risk of bringing it out in full daylight, for the neighbors or casual passersby to see.

Prescott meanwhile was charging the short brick pathway toward the front door. The gold-on-black placard swayed in the wind above it. FINDER OF LOST FORTUNES.

He leapt quite agilely up the two cement steps and across the threshold, staying low, the derringer raised in front of him. The nimbleness of his movements belied his age. Fleming watched keenly as he disappeared into the house. Had some foul play occurred while they were out? It was certainly possible.

He waited. After a full minute, with nothing to be seen, he crept toward the gate. He had heard no shots being fired, but neither had Prescott reemerged.

He remained hunkered, planning to allow Prescott another thirty seconds before he at last drew his pistol and followed him inside. At that instant the man did appear in the front doorway, standing erect, the derringer evidently returned to its sleeve holster. He beckoned Fleming within with a wave of his hand.

Inside the mahogany-trimmed vestibule he said, "It's all right. Martha had a bit of trouble a few moments ago. Come, she's in the drawing room."

Prescott led him down the hallway. "I'm going to fetch her some tea. Keep her occupied a moment, won't you?" He still appeared composed, but there was a tic beneath his left eye.

Fleming entered the drawing room. Martha was seated on the plush settee, hands folded across her checkered apron. Her orange head scarf was absent, revealing a thatch of dark kinky hair. She appeared to be in the act of calming herself, drawing slow deep breaths. She looked up.

"Mr. Fleming." Her voice was toneless.

"Martha, are you quite well?" He stepped around the settee to face her.

"Yes. Yes, I am." She inhaled and released another long breath. "I was going out to get the mail from the box. I saw someone out there looking like they were fiddling with it."

Fleming's brows lifted. "Who was it?"

"A white lady. Long blond hair, not too tall, wearing big dark glasses and a long coat. Gray it was—no, more beige. She had the collar turned up. I couldn't see much of her face at all."

"What did you do?"

"I saw her when I'd opened the front door just a crack. She didn't see me. But she was poking around the box, and that's Mr. Quick's mail, and nobody fools with Mr. Quick's property." She said this evenly, with some conviction. "So I ran back to the kitchen, grabbed my big butcher's knife, ran back, and came storming out. I yelled at her—didn't care that she was white— yelled for her to get herself out of that box, there wasn't anything of hers in it. I had that knife, but I kept it hid behind my leg where she couldn't see it. Then I marched down to the gate, and she started backing away fast. She looked scared, from what I could see of her face. So I let her have a little peek at the knife, and that did it. She turned tail and bolted. That's all that happened. I'm all right."

Fleming assimilated this report, still standing before the settee. "How old was this woman?"

"I can only guess. But she looked to be around twenty or twenty-five. Had a good figure from what I could tell what with that long coat she had on."

It was a concise, neat accounting, well detailed, uncluttered by hysterics. Martha was apparently levelheaded in a crisis.

The alternate possibility was, of course, that she had fabricated the story. There was no proof that any of this had occurred, beyond her word. A strange blond-haired woman meddling with Prescott's mailbox . . . it might only be a means of diverting suspicion from herself—a rather clever and effective means, at that.

Still another alternative was that this had been Faith Ullrich in disguise, her mahogany-colored hair concealed beneath a wig.

Prescott bustled into the drawing room at that moment, bearing a cup of steaming pekoe. He knelt before the settee, passing Martha the bone china cup and clasping her free hand protectively. His own hands were now trembling. He cooed soft soothing words to her, though she herself remained quite poised.

After a moment he turned to eye Fleming over his shoulder. "Seems things are heating up a bit."

"So it would appear," Fleming said neutrally, excusing himself from the room, leaving Prescott to comfort his lover.

Chapter 14

AFTER MARTHA was well settled, Fleming followed Prescott into his office. The man was plainly upset and exerting a tenuous control over himself.

"I find it most disagreeable, Ian," he said, chewing out the words darkly, "that this case is intruding on my household."

Fleming could sense Prescott's potent anger thrumming just beneath the surface. "Indeed. Things were quite personal enough as they were. But to have it enter one's personal *affairs* . . ."

Prescott didn't rise to Fleming's somewhat subtle bait; he didn't seem to notice it, actually. Well, if he wanted to pretend his liaison with Martha was a secret, so be it.

"We should assemble what information we can on Faith Ullrich and Gerard Marquette," Fleming said, trying to focus the man. "The police will have better resources than we, but we must compete as best we can."

"Yes," Prescott grunted offhandedly. Then he shook his head and said more concisely, "Yes. Of course. We should be able to put something together from my files."

Prescott collected general news items and had retained a newspaper clipping of Marquette's recent October marriage to Angelina Dours. The local paper had made quite a fuss over it, devoting a full three columns of print to the event. The reception was held in City Park, a large woody preserve, one end of which abutted Lake Pontchartrain. There was an accompanying photo of the great open-air canopies and swarms of well-dressed guests. The caption read: LOVE BENEATH THE DUELING OAKS.

"What in heaven's name does that mean?" Fleming asked. He

had drawn one of the leather chairs up against the front of the desk.

Prescott glanced up from behind that desk. His eyes peered above a pair of horn-rimmed reading glasses. "Ah. Just what you might imagine it means. The Dueling Oaks. A place where disputes were settled, back at the start of the 1800s. Two men would come together over some matter of honor—or something less noble—and resolve things with the aid of rapiers or shotguns. Duels were quite common here, once upon a time. Actually today it's a lovely stretch of greenery. There's even a golf course out there somewhere, if you're still partial to that Scotsman's game."

Gerard Marquette came from a local family, a clan of molasses manufacturers who owned a plant in New Orleans East. They were well-off but certainly not wealthy—and definitely not as well placed in local society as the Dours family.

"Did he marry her for her money?" Fleming wondered aloud to Prescott, dotting the question mark of that same query on the paper before him. They were both making notations on sheets of Prescott's creamy white stationery and passing them back and forth between themselves. That drawing up dossiers on the enemy was an activity from the old days was something neither man needed to remark upon.

Prescott paused, fountain pen in hand. He looked thoughtful a moment. "It's conjecturally possible."

"Well, yes, Mr. Holmes, it is that," Fleming countered drolly. "I was curious if you had an opinion."

Prescott mused a while longer. "No, I don't believe it was so. Angelina wasn't the sole heir to the family fortune. With the passing of Edmund Dours the estate would be divided among her and her two elder brothers. It would make for a tidy measure, certainly, but nothing significantly greater than what Marquette would have eventually come into himself, upon inheriting his family's enterprise. He could have sold off the concern and counted himself a relatively prosperous man. He has no siblings.

He's the direct heir to the molasses empire, as it were. It would all be his. Besides—"

"—why wed Angelina mercenarily, then murder her four months later?" Fleming finished. "Yes, you're quite correct."

It was by this give-and-take, this notating of facts and speculations, that a fairly clear picture of Gerard Marquette emerged—or as clear as they could make it.

The twenty-two-year-old Marquette was a sexual deviant. That was conclusive from Prescott's photos. In Faith Ullrich he had evidently found an accomplice, a woman willing, even eager, to engage with him in those deeds of carnal depravity that assuaged God knew what dark, unwholesome corner of his psyche. His perversions certainly seemed deep-seated, not the sort of thing one merely toyed with whimsically. No, one needed to be utterly dedicated to perform such aberrant acts.

Faith Ullrich fulfilled Gerard Marquette's base needs. It was doubtful that Angelina Dours had as well. The notion that Marquette had *two* such women in his life stretched all probability. Marquette had taken Faith as his mistress. They had concocted a plan to eliminate Angelina. Why? So that he and Faith could marry? Why would the sanctity of marriage mean anything to a pair like that? And why send evidence of the murder to Prescott, a private investigator whose only involvement had been to confirm an affair that Edmund Dours had seemed quite sure of beforehand?

Fleming pondered much of this out loud.

Prescott nodded. "Yes. The theory holds water nicely up to a point. Then leaks spring out everywhere. The affair, the murder. Classic scenarios. Then—voodoo trinkets and utter muddle!"

They had even less concrete information about Faith Ullrich. Yet here they had a key clue that the New Orleans police couldn't possibly have. Yes, the police had established that Faith was the daughter of one Wallace Ullrich; they likely had even learned about the man's suicide last year. What they didn't know, couldn't know, was that Wallace, along with Prescott and Fleming, had been one of Churchill's Boys. That postwar operation was utterly secret, and no amount of digging, no tapping of any imaginable source, could uncover it.

"Marquette and Angelina lived on St. Charles Avenue," said Prescott, "during their brief four-month marriage. It's a fair distance from the Quarter. In the Garden District."

"And there's another quandary. Angelina Dours's body, so you said, was discovered in a shed nearby a warehouse along the river. Why would Marquette bring her all the way down here to decapitate—or kill her elsewhere and haul her corpse to the river? Where's the sense?"

Prescott tapped a moment with the nib of his pen. "I don't believe she was murdered somewhere else and then brought to that shed. Marquette, perhaps with Faith in tow, may have bundled Angelina into the shed where—you might recall—she was violated before being nearly beheaded. Perhaps he wanted someplace quiet and out of the way to perform his ghastly deed."

Fleming silently hoped that the foul acts had occurred in that sequence. If Marquette had violated his wife *after*—. It was nearly too distasteful to contemplate.

"I see no obvious point where either of these characters could connect to the practice of voodoo rituals," he said.

"Nor do I," Prescott agreed. "Yet . . . those murders, they nearly *feel* that way, don't they? The grotesque violence of them, those damned idolatrous crosses. It's all like some form of pagan murderous rite."

"Such as a human sacrifice?" Fleming had learned a thing or two about *vodun* from living on Jamaica. "Aren't you confusing voodoo practitioners with the ancient Aztecs?"

Prescott turned a flat gaze on him. "Perhaps this is some bastardized brand of voodoo. These are the States, after all, Ian. Nothing reaches these shores without being modified to fit the American character."

Yes, in these United States all was bigger, faster, louder. "So I had noticed."

Prescott said thoughtfully, "There was once a great slave uprising on Santo Domingo, the island we now call Haiti. In the late 1700s this was. Toussaint L'Ouverture led it against the white plantation owners. It was a veritable bloodbath. Half a million blacks revolting, destroying plantations, slaughtering some two thousand white islanders. There was a vast voodoo ceremony— demented dancing, the drinking of animal blood, that sort of thing. Shiploads of survivors came to New Orleans afterward."

Fleming was nonplussed. "Are you theorizing that Gerard Marquette is descended from these people?"

Prescott shook his head sharply. "No, no, old boy. The Marquette family came from the state of Virginia in the early 1800s. What I am saying is that voodoo—as a cultural touchstone, as a theology, if you deign to call it such—is embedded in the culture of New Orleans. Marie Laveau was this city's most illustrious *voodooienne*. High priestess, if you will. She made a going concern out of the religion, selling charms and potions."

"I see nothing inherently murderous about that," Fleming observed.

"It was an enterprise, to be sure. But she had many true believers. Some linger today. My speculation is that Marquette and perhaps Faith Ullrich as well may have gotten themselves involved somehow in this modern heathen sect."

"So they would have accomplices," Fleming said, thinking of the blond-haired woman Martha had claimed was meddling with Prescott's mailbox earlier. This presumed, of course, that that woman hadn't been Faith herself in disguise—and that the blond even existed and wasn't instead an invention of Martha's. Then there were also the two black men of last night and the white Studebaker.

"It's entirely possible. They had to have been introduced into the circle somehow. Perhaps they only got a taste of it and liked the flavor—and subsequently moved on into their own aberrant version of the cult. There's the grisly murder of the young man we suspect to be one of Edmund Dours's sons to consider also. His head was hacked to bits, likely with an axe. That would take a strong man. Does Gerard Marquette strike you as a particularly manly and muscular fellow?"

"Quite the opposite," said Fleming.

"I concur." Prescott removed his reading glasses, his lined features still thoughtful. "So, an accessory to the crime, unless of course Angelina and the young man were both drugged prior to their deaths. But let us suppose an abetter exists for the moment."

"Why a single accomplice?" Fleming asked, falling now almost automatically into the tempo of this theorizing. It was again a familiar process. One began with a hypothesis and built, testing it for veracity as one went. He had started many an espionage operation thus.

"Indeed. Why only one?"

"Why not a ring of them?" Fleming pressed. "Faith and Marquette might have a veritable gang of confederates about them."

"Yes. Possible. We might even do well to work from that assumption."

"Makes the odds a bit more daunting."

"Ian, I don't recall percentages ever disheartening you in the past."

"How nice that you remember me so fondly."

A shy sort of smile pulled at Prescott's mouth. "Actually . . . I always very much admired your derring-do. I was more a stickler for regulations. Levelheaded but not terribly bold. I tended to err on the side of caution. You, though, you went crashing in where angels feared to tread."

"Sometimes blundering in, I must confess."

"Still. A fine career you made for yourself. Your service to the Crown was exemplary. It was my abiding admiration for your talents that prompted me to contact you in the first place."

"Yes, yes, Prescott, let us not rehash that," Fleming said, dismissing the subject before it entirely sidetracked their efforts. "We can suppose, for the moment anyway, that Faith and Marquette have surrounded themselves with a crew willing to aid them in these murders. Perhaps they, too, are involved in this subcult of distorted voodoo you seem eager to believe exists. Very well. Faith Ullrich, as evinced by the messages we've both received, has some knowledge of her father's—and also our—postwar activities. What do she and her cohort, Marquette, plan to do with this information? Blackmail the two of us?"

Prescott sighed grimly. "Yes, it all comes down to that, doesn't it?"

"It does," agreed Fleming. Quite a bloody impasse it was. Would they have to wait for Faith and Marquette's next move to hope to divine the pair's intentions? Would that mean the hacking up of yet another body?

The abrupt jangling of the telephone on the corner of Prescott's desk interrupted the silence that had descended.

Prescott shook himself and snatched up the receiver. "Prescott W. Quick speaking. Yes? Ah. Good." He hung up and eyed Fleming across the desktop. "As promised, we've received word. Slim and Chopper are ready to make their report. Shall we away? Not too early, do you think, for a tipple or two?"

Chapter 15

THE SALOON they entered was a rather seedy warren away from the general hubbub of Bourbon Street. This one was on a street called Conti and was serving a clientele of laborers, who were swilling cold American beer at an alarming rate. They were a vociferous lot, calling out loud toasts and friendly off-color insults with equal abandon.

"Where are your Irregulars?" Fleming asked, taking in the scene.

"Follow the sound of the clicking pool balls, my dear chap. Chopper and Slim seem to have a mania about the game. I could never get into the spirit of it myself, I'm afraid. But I was quite the cricketer in school, so I can excuse anyone's pointless sporting obsession."

There was indeed a felt-topped table at the tavern's rear, lying below a lighting fixture that had only a single bulb functioning at full strength. A pair of vague male shapes was wandering about the table, cue sticks in hand.

Prescott moved first toward the bar, where he immediately caught the eye of the bartender, who looked to be the physical equal of any of his brawny customers.

Before Fleming reached the rail he was already pouring Prescott's whiskey—further testimony that Prescott was a widely known figure in the French Quarter, not that Fleming required any more proof. "What's your buddy havin', Mr. Quick?" the bartender asked in a deep baritone.

"Gin and tonic, neat," Fleming provided.

"'Nother Brit, huh?" The husky man lifted a black bushy eyebrow.

"British, yes," Fleming said.

The bartender mixed his drink. "I got my ass saved by the RAF over the Channel once durin' the war. Ev'ry Brit who walks in here gets his first on the house. My way of sayin' thanks."

"I'm glad we could be of service," Fleming said, taking the cocktail and offering a smile.

"You, however, Mr. Quick," the bartender said wryly, turning, "used up your first one a long time ago."

"I did indeed, Frank," said Prescott amiably. He laid a bill on the bar top. "Do keep the change of that."

They moved away from the rowdy pack up front and toward the saloon's dimly lit rear. Slim's unshaven skeletal face was shadowed by the brim of his black cloth cap as he bent over the table into the circle of anemic light to make his shot. His features were tight with concentration. Standing at the far side of the table was Chopper, watching impassively.

Prescott and Fleming waited at the periphery until Slim had made his play. Two of the balls—one white, one black—plunked into two separate pockets on the table.

Fleming looked to see if this was a winning move in the match. He didn't wish to loiter about until the game was done before this pair gave their report. However, a glance at Slim's surly curling lip and brief four-lettered summation of his shot told the story.

"What'd you use top english for?" Chopper asked. "With bottom english you would've drawn the cue ball back from the pocket, nice and neat. Instead, you sent it into the corner."

"Thanks a lot, old man," Slim said through gritted teeth. "I saw it happen."

"Just trying to generously provide you with some pointers."

"*After* the shot, I notice."

"Why would you have listened to your opponent if I'd told you before?" Chopper said guilelessly. "Hello, Mr. Quick, Mr. Fleming." His deep-set eyes noted them across the pool table.

Slim, still wearing his familiar dungarees and worn leather

jacket with the matted fleece collar, hung his cue stick on the wall rack with some disgust. "Yeah, howdy."

"Good evening, gentlemen," said Prescott, pausing for a healthy swallow from his cocktail glass. "You said you've some news for us."

Chopper and Slim traded a glance. It looked like a reflexive move, as if the pair never operated independently.

"We do," said Chopper, motioning Prescott and Fleming toward the corner farthest from the front of the saloon. There was a ledge along one pressed sawdust wall where these Irregulars had left their drinks sitting. Slim snatched up his, took a gulp, then lit a Lucky Strike. By the light of his scratched Zippo Fleming noticed for the first time that tonight the scrawny lad was wearing a string of shiny beads about his neck. The baubles looked quite out of place against his scruffy apparel. Must be something to do with Mardi Gras, Fleming concluded.

The four of them settled into the ill-lit corner.

"Edmund Dours's two boys—named Martin and Elliot—got into town a week, week and a half ago," Chopper said, pausing for a pull on his glass of Kentucky whiskey.

"They're home on leave from the Navy, all right," said Slim. "Hardship leave." He fixed Prescott, then Fleming, with a steady gaze.

"Indeed?" Prescott said neutrally.

"Indeedy."

"The boys are staying at the Dours family home on Ursulines," Chopper continued. "Only . . ."

"Only, Elliot's there and little Marty ain't," Slim said.

Chopper lifted a hand. "That we don't know, Mr. Quick. We don't know for sure."

"Naw, we don't, Mr. Quick. Can't give you a hunnert percent on it. Elliot we both eyeballed stepping out the front door." A physical description followed: tall, trim, handsome-ish, blond-haired. "Got the skinny on who he was from a guy whitewashin' a wall 'cross the street from the place. He knows from the housemaid. Elliot's the older one, twenty-eight. Martin's twenty-five."

"Why don't you believe Martin Dours is at the house?" Prescott asked, his tone remaining noncommittal, giving away nothing. Fleming nodded in silent approval.

" 'Cause I sent him a telegram," said Slim.

"How clever of you," Prescott said.

"Actually Slim here borrowed a coat from a porter we know at a hotel." Chopper eyed his confederate with his own nod of approval. "Dummied up a telegram for Mr. Martin Dours and went and rang the bell. Asked if he was in. Housemaid said he was . . . but said it—"

"—like she was lyin' through her teeth," Slim interjected.

"Yes," said Chopper. "Slim said the telegram had to be signed for by the recipient, or it couldn't be handed over. It was a nice bit of acting. Very believable." Fleming recalled Prescott's telling him that this man had once been a screen actor. "Raised something of a stink, didn't you?"

"Damn right I did," Slim said proudly, taking another swallow of his rum.

"Yes. Well, the housemaid couldn't produce Martin Dours. Edmund Dours was eventually called to the scene. Slim says he didn't look well—"

"Like he'd got himself kicked in the gut sometime recent."

"—and when Slim tried raising a ruckus again, the old man simply closed the door on him."

Prescott turned his hazel eyes on Fleming for a moment. "Interesting," he finally said.

"Yeah, downright *rivetin'*," said Slim. There seemed to be something further on the lad's mind.

"Well, I believe I owe you gentlemen the rest of your money." Prescott picked a few notes from his billfold and passed them to the two Bourbon Street Irregulars. The cash quickly disappeared into their respective pockets.

"I see your glasses are getting low," Prescott said. "Perhaps you'll permit me to buy you a round before Mr. Fleming and I must be off."

"Something else that's interesting," Chopper said in that flat, almost staccato voice of his.

Prescott paused in withdrawing from their corner huddle. Fleming eyed the pair with renewed wariness.

"Maybe mighty interestin'," put in Slim.

"And that would be?" asked Prescott.

Chopper said, "Word is going around that you're looking for two people."

"A dame name of Faith Ullrich an' a fella named Gerard Marquette. That's what we find interestin'."

"Mostly because Gerard Marquette got married to Angelina *Dours* this past fall," Chopper said. "I always read the society page."

"Which makes her Angelina Marquette," Slim continued. "Or *made* her, anyway. She's the gal the papers say what got iced down by the river."

The pair were now both gazing levelly at Prescott, waiting. For what Fleming was unsure.

"If there's somethin' bigger goin' on here, Mr. Quick," Slim said, "we're wonderin' why you ain't tapped us for it yet. That's all."

To this Prescott only chuckled. He drained his whiskey and set the glass on the ledge. "Gentlemen, I have put the word out, yes. Just a general call for anyone wishing to earn a bit of money to keep a watchful eye out for that aforementioned duo. If I have need of something more specific, rest assured I shall call upon you. Frankly"—this he said with sudden sincerity—"I vastly prefer dealing with you over some of the less responsible characters in the Quarter."

" 'Preciate the vote of confidence, Mr. Quick." Slim grinned around the stub of his Lucky Strike.

"Yes, thank you," said Chopper. "Get in touch if you need us."

"I will do so, most assuredly."

After Prescott had bought the two their promised fresh drinks and he and Fleming had exited the saloon, Fleming asked, "What was all that about, there at the end?"

"Ah," said Prescott, "the hurt feelings, you mean? Those two wanting to be *in on it*, whatever it might be. Professional pride, dear fellow. I told you, that pair is quite reliable and efficient. I can't recall, in fact, that they've ever failed me. They see themselves as . . . well . . . freelance secret agents, you might say. If something juicy is afoot, they want to have a hand in it." He chuckled. "Also I'm sure Slim already needs more money. That lad seems to have a rough time of holding onto a nickel."

Fleming nodded as they strolled along Conti Street, away from the river. "Interesting what they had to say about Edmund Dours's two sons."

"Yes. We should take as our hypothesis that Martin is the unfortunate victim in that photograph you received. Poor boy. I wonder what he did to get himself so brutally terminated."

Dusk was settling over the Quarter. The air was now quite brisk, but Fleming had changed back into his warmer black coat. Above, the rising moon was lost behind thickening strands of cloud.

"Perhaps he went poking about where he wasn't welcome," Fleming observed dryly.

Prescott chuckled yet again, though this time it was a bit strained; it was, after all, not a humorous matter. "Yes. Likely. We should exercise caution."

"I have been exercising it." Fleming felt the weight of his Enfield revolver beneath the coat.

"Yes. I also."

Prescott gave his right arm a small stretch, as though testing the flexing muscles that would drop the ivory-butted derringer neatly into his palm. Sleeve guns had been in use while Fleming and Prescott were in service, but those weapons had been tubular things, firing .32 cartridges and meant for use at extremely close range. Prescott's rig was more the sort of thing the archetypal riverboat gambler would carry.

"I don't know about you, Ian, but I'm not yet ready for supper. I should like another drink first. And perhaps another after that. Would you care to join me?"

HUSH KNEW FEAR in the presence of the Queen. But that was just and proper, for to not feel such appropriate awe would be an insult to the woman.

She was, of course, more than merely a woman, more than the sum of flesh and bone and thought. She was spirit beyond the innate spirituality of all human creatures. She was magic. She was *obeah*.

Hush was a heavy, forbidding man and a strong one, his shaven head lending him an even greater air of menace. As a teenager he had gotten into an altercation with a policeman for no better reason than that the white uniformed devil had dispersed him and a group of friends from loitering on a street corner, saying, "Move along there, niggers." It had been the last straw in a young life fraught with similar—and usually worse—indignities. Hush had gone mad with rage that moment, and the policeman required the help of two others before wrestling the boy to the ground, where he was pummeled, kicked, and finally choked to within a few gasps of his life.

It was a short time after this incident, during the inevitable sentence he served for "assaulting the law," that he first learned of the Queen's existence. A pair of her agents in the jail recruited him, telling him just enough tantalizing secrets of her clandestine dominion to lure him in. He pledged himself, and he learned self-control and discipline. Such traits were needed to provide the Queen useful service. It would be some years more, after her benevolence provided the money that paid for his education, that he actually met her. By then she had been built up in his mind as a figure of legendary proportions. Seeing her in the flesh had not disappointed him in the least.

He did not fear the whites. He hadn't feared them even as a fifteen-year-old boy when he felt his own life being strangled from him. He did, however, acknowledge that they ruled the visible, material world . . . the world white men mistakenly believed to be the *real*—and therefore more important—world.

But Queen Cleopatra ruled where they did not, at least as far as the city of New Orleans was concerned.

Hush climbed the steps to her house. The quiet street on which she lived was well kept—neat gardens, the surrounding homes painted and in good repair, unlike so many other streets in the city's black slums. The vicinity was also, he knew, well guarded. He felt unseen eyes watching in a night softened by the street's lamps.

He was put through the normal preparatory routine before being admitted to the Queen. He never carried a gun but always submitted to the search of his person by the house's sentinels. He was not put out by this procedure. The Queen's safety was paramount.

Eventually he found himself inside the candlelit chamber that gleamed darkly with red silk. The veils hung over the windowless walls, stirred here and there by the wandering movements of the many cats that inhabited this sacred place. The Queen was there, of course, atop her high-backed throne. She was merely a suggestion of a female shape. She wore white, and she was thin, but little else could be seen of her. Even so, she exuded a sense of age and wisdom and beauty and elegance that was palpable. To say nothing of the aura of sexuality that seemed to broil about her.

Hush bowed his hairless head. He wore a dark suit, one more expensive than most blacks in the city could hope to afford. As always the chamber was warm, almost clammy with heat, but he did not sweat. It was impossible not to desire Cleopatra, but she was as beyond him as any goddess, and he was content to be her supplicant . . . which allowed him to be near enough to feel her heat.

"Tell me of them," said the Queen. Her voice was cool and assured—the purr of a lover and the authoritative tone of a monarch, all at once.

"Two white men," Hush answered, voice raspy and barely audible in his permanently damaged throat. Still, he was always certain she heard his every word. "One lives here. The other is visiting from somewhere else. They are Englishmen, both."

"This second," Cleopatra said, a fingernail tapping the throne's arm, carved to resemble a raven, "he comes from . . . an island."

Hush's large brown eyes were the only expressive feature in his otherwise heavy, almost leaden face. But in the Queen's presence even those eyes didn't dare stir in unseemly fashion.

"An island? England, do you mean, my Queen?" he ventured.

"No." Her tone remained steady. She did not censure. Hush could only imagine how terrible it would be to be castigated by this woman.

"Where then, my Queen?"

One of the cats brushed his pantleg, but he didn't flinch. He had visited here many times; he was used to the animals.

She shifted slightly in her chair, which sat atop the dais in the room's center. "Somewhere . . . closer to all our hearts. Nearer to the truth of all things. Jamaica. He comes from Jamaica."

An Englishman from Jamaica? Hush accepted this immediately. Queen Cleopatra was the ultimate reliable authority. Her eyes and ears were many places. Her knowing ran deep beneath the veneer of the perceptible world. It wasn't merely that she sat at the center of a network of spies throughout the city. He knew of that, of course. He was a part of that same network. But her powers, like the woman herself, were greater than the sum of their components.

"What do you wish to do with this Englishman from Jamaica, my Queen?" he asked. "Him and the other white man."

Again one of the cats brushed against him. For the briefest instant, though, he imagined that the Queen's next words rose from *it*, not from the dimly seen throne several steps away.

"We must deal with them both."

Chapter 16

IT WAS difficult to draw Prescott away from the bars or to even bridle the rate of his drinking once he had truly begun, and after a few pointed efforts Fleming stopped trying. He surrendered himself to simply keeping an eye on the man and waiting until he finally tired or the need for food lured him back to the house. The alcohol had at first buoyed Prescott; now it appeared to be finally dragging him down. It was by now well past dinnertime.

They were back on Bourbon Street, which tonight was quite lively indeed. Jazz seemed to blare everywhere, and there were people literally dancing in the street. Many wore strands of colorful beads, such as Slim had been sporting earlier.

Fleming was drinking at a quite moderate pace. Breakfast had been some while ago.

There was a fine variety of good-looking women about, however, which made the task of chaperoning Prescott a bit more agreeable.

"Ah jus' *love* y'all's ache cents!" squealed one young thing who had stopped to chat.

"Yours is quite enchanting as well, my dear," Fleming said suavely. Prescott was busily attacking a fresh whiskey, ignoring them both. Not the behavior of a casual drinker, Fleming took the time to note.

She giggled loudly, seeming delighted by the idea. "Ah never think of me as hayvin' an ache-cent!"

"Were it any thicker, young lady, I might require a translator." They were standing at the bar. The club's floor was crowded.

She had soft brown hair, twirled up into one of those configurations that defied physical logic. Still, she was most attractive, radiating that effortless vigor of the young. She was evidently unescorted.

"Ah'll bet you don't hayve anything like Mardi Gras in England."

"We prefer to restrict ourselves to Guy Fawkes Day and New Year's Eve," said Fleming, picking out two cigarettes from his case and offering her one. "That is as boisterous as we permit ourselves to become."

She accepted the cigarette and his light. "Well, stick around, an' you'll see some sights to remember!"

"I've no doubt." His gaze lingered on her eyes momentarily.

She allowed the look. Some of her giggly schoolgirlness evaporated. "Mah name is Jennifer."

"Ian."

"Ah come into the city every Carnival. Is . . . this your first?"

He widened his eyes in amused shock. "Is it so obvious?"

"Now, nuthin' to be ashamed of."

"Why, thank you. As it happens, however, I am here for reasons other than pleasure."

"Well," she sighed, "that's a real shame."

"Perhaps next Carnival."

"Ah'll keep mah eye out. Thanks for the cigarette."

With that she slid off into the crowd, Fleming chuckling quietly after. Flirtation was often harmless; was just as often rewarding, even as only a rehearsal for more serious interactions. He turned his attention back to Prescott.

Prescott had been in good spirits earlier. It seemed that initial phase was passing. At the moment he was fairly slumped against the bar, his features growing swiftly bleary. These were the rapidly revolving stages of intoxication as experienced by the chronic drinker, Fleming judged. Soon Prescott would start to slide into insensibility.

"The UN shall name MacArthur to lead the fight," said

Prescott, apropos of nothing, speaking with the overly precise enunciation of one who is truly inebriated.

"Are you speaking again of Korea, Prescott?" Fleming asked, realizing the man was picking up their conversation from that morning. Better to humor him, so as to eventually steer him toward home.

Prescott slumped onto a stool that became suddenly vacant. He had ordered yet another whiskey while Fleming was talking to the young lady. Now he took a fearsome swallow from it.

"Mark my words," he said, hazel-eyed gaze not quite focusing on Fleming. "And MacArthur won't be content to leave the battle in Korea, either. Oh, these are grievous times. It's not like the days when we had Hirohito and the Nazis"—he pronounced the word "Nah-zees"—"clear-cut lines, one knew who was who, the enemy was there, right *there* across the battle lines! It's all become so bloody ambivalent!"

He was working himself into something of a froth. Fleming eyed him apprehensively—this, the man he was supposed to be relying on as a partner.

"Feeling nostalgic toward the war?" Fleming asked wryly, attempting to lighten the mood.

Apparently it was the wrong tactic. Prescott's eyes narrowed. "The war, yes. The war made sense. Good versus evil. The crushing of a diabolic fascist regime that was seeking to conquer the world! How could it be any more unambiguous? It's . . . it's what followed—. What we did. What—. After the war, yes. That's when the lines started to blur. And blur and blur and—"

To Fleming's dismay Prescott's eyes were filling with tears. Feeling a sharp pang of embarrassment at being witness to the display, Fleming nonetheless had no vast experience at consoling an adult male in such a state.

"Prescott, it's time we made for your home—"

Prescott's hands were suddenly trembling violently. His lean features, which now looked truly haggard, contorted themselves as he fought back the sobs trying to erupt from his chest. His moist eyes brimmed with internal torment.

"It—it was all so damnably *indistinct*! After the war. All of us, our merry little band! Skulking about liquidating those men. Assassinations, they were! It wasn't war any longer. No. No, we were sent off to—to carry out *murder*! God. God—damn—it! I lost myself, Ian. I tell you the absolute truth. I was a lost man. My humanity, my heart, my *honor*! I lost those dear things. I lost them each time we . . . we Churchill's Boys"—this he spat out—"dispatched another one on our list. We—we—we—I—I—I—"

"Prescott, keep still!" Fleming hissed. It was one thing to be a drunken spectacle—and yes, a number of people were glancing their way—but whimpering aloud about information guarded under the Official Secrets Act was simply not cricket.

Fortunately this nightclub was an energetic hot spot, with an inevitable jazz trio playing atop a constricted corner stage. The noise covered much of Prescott's ramblings, which now broke down into stifled weeping. He put a hand over his face, turning away, leaning heavily on the bar.

Patrons wandered freely in and out of the narrow French doors that opened directly onto Bourbon Street's sidewalk. The sense of overall revelry was sharper in the air than Fleming recalled it being only last evening. Mardi Gras was indeed looming ever nearer. Here and there were revelers already in costume. One curvaceous female wore a complex Arabian headdress and layers of undulating silk veils. Another young woman was dressed as an American Indian squaw. There was a man done up as a pirate, another masquerading as a Chinese coolie.

Fleming was reaching for Prescott's arm when he felt eyes suddenly upon himself, not for the first time that evening. He paused, lighting a fresh cigarette as he turned, and picked through the faces of the crowd as casually as possible.

And saw, abruptly, large dark glasses and blond hair.

Which wasn't in and of itself disturbing, of course; the fact of the woman wearing sunglasses at night didn't especially cause her to stand out in *this* crowd. But the eyes behind those glasses were fixed on him. That he could feel. And she matched, generally, the description Martha had given of the woman she'd professed was attempting to meddle with Prescott's mailbox that afternoon.

He didn't have a clear view of her. She was some distance across the open area, nearby the doors, and there were numerous jostling bodies in the way. The dark lenses of her glasses were large—also as Martha had described them—and her face appeared to be heavily made up. As the crowd milled and shifted, he even caught sight of the knee-length beige coat she wore with the collar turned up, hiding her throat and jawline. He saw that she was several inches shorter than Faith Ullrich, which immediately invalidated his theory that this could be her in disguise.

He turned, stubbing out his cigarette. Prescott had lapsed into a grave silence, staring doggedly at nothing, his hands locked around his latest whiskey.

"Prescott."

No response.

"Prescott, I'll be back in a moment. Stay here. Stay quiet."

Still nothing, which Fleming hoped signified that the man was done with his unseemly emotional display. At any rate Fleming didn't have the time to nursemaid him. He made his way down the bar. He caught the eye of the bartender and asked if he wouldn't mind doing what he could to keep Prescott here until he returned.

The cheerful bartender nodded. "I'll take care of Mr. Quick. Wouldn't want him walking the streets in the shape he's in anyway."

Fleming edged toward the nightclub's front, using the crowd for cover now. Peeking carefully through the intervening bodies, he saw that the blond-haired woman was still there. She was looking about in some urgency, apparently having lost him—if indeed she'd truly been spying on him in the first place. He ducked low and moved onward.

Slipping through a thick eddy of revelers, he darted suddenly and sharply toward the spot where she was standing. Or had been.

She had spotted him and was swiftly backpedaling, spinning now, the tails of her long beige coat twirling, and bolting out the nearest of the doors. Her shoulder jostled someone sharply, who cursed as his cocktail glass tumbled to the ground. Then she was out, fleeing down Bourbon Street.

Fleming leapt after her. He still hadn't gotten anything like a good look at her face, just those large sunglasses and a flash of bright lipstick. But obviously she *had* been spying on him. It was more than enough to warrant pursuit.

She looked to be a svelte woman, but she was doing some impressive broken field running at the moment, already a half block distant by the time he stepped past the cursing man and cleared the doorway. He broke into a run himself, his athletic legs carrying him swiftly and easily. It was getting through the swarming celebrants filling the street and sidewalks that proved difficult, though. He was made to dodge and sidestep every few strides, unable to work himself up to a decent speed. The blond woman, however, was knocking unwitting bystanders aside quite carelessly in her mad dash.

She was maintaining her lead as she came to the intersection of Bourbon and Toulouse streets. Here, though, the random patterns of the crowd were thinner. Once Fleming reached this area, he would have a good chance of overtaking her. He ducked past a figure wearing a black cloak and a highwayman's mask, aiming to slip past a last knot of wandering bodies into the clear.

A strong hand, however, seized the back of his coat's collar and yanked him to an abrupt startling halt. His feet went out from beneath him as stitches tore across the collar. Thoroughly off balance, he crashed gracelessly to the pavement.

It had been the cloaked man. Fleming scrabbled to get a foot underneath himself, struggling to turn, to work a hand around under the coat to his revolver. But the powerful hand was still gripping his collar, jerking him about as he tried desperately to regain his footing.

Suddenly he was whirled around, the crowded street pitching crazily. People were gaping at the scene, uncertain if it was some sort of act or not. Fleming couldn't even draw a breath to shout for help.

He was now facing his assailant, a tall, muscular male with tanned flesh and a nasty sneer on his face beneath the black satin mask. His hair—a wig?—was quite long and pulled back into a single braid. He looked to be in his thirties.

That was all the time Fleming had for his study of the man, who continued to grip him fiercely by the collar, lifting him now so that his toes dangled above the ground. The fellow was strong as an ox and apparently quite unconcerned about anything his captive could do to break the hold. Fleming groped urgently again for his .38, but his position was too awkward. He was helpless.

He remained in that helpless dangling state for no more than three seconds—just long enough for the masked man's other hand to come flashing out of the cloak's folds. A bottle was in his grip.

"Way done tol' yo', *mon ami*, to keep yo' dame nose out of it," the man said in a harsh gravelly voice just as the bottle collided with and shattered against Fleming's left temple. After that there was blackness.

THAT BLACKNESS LASTED only about a minute. Fleming swam hard against it, rebounding from the physical shock and struggling back through the pain toward consciousness. When his eyes opened, he was surrounded by a gaggle of ogling revelers. The big masked man wasn't among them.

He was laid out on his back. He rolled onto a hip and sat upright, pain as bad as any of his worst migraines roaring through his
skull. He put his hands to his head, wincing. He felt dampness at
his left temple. Yes, where the bottle had struck. He was unsur-
prised when the palm came away slick with red.

"You're gonna hafta get to the hospital, fella."

"Why'd that big guy hit you?"

"Somebody get a cop!"

They stood about him in an unbroken circle, more onlookers
crowding inward to get a peek at the commotion. It was far more
attention than he wanted. Fleming picked a handkerchief from
his coat pocket and pressed it to his wound. He didn't know how
badly his scalp had been opened. It didn't feel as though he had a
concussion. Mopping gingerly at the injury, he found that the
bleeding was already stanching itself. Just a scratch, then. He'd
been quite fortunate.

"Where did the man go?" he asked, at last able to get his feet
underneath himself. Hands reached down to pull him upward.

"Took off like a bat outta hell down Toulouse," someone said,
pointing toward the street.

"You're gonna need to go the hospital," another repeated.

"Somebody find a cop!"

Neither of these last two was a good idea. Fleming definitely
didn't want the police involved. That would only eventually lead
to a long interrogation, where he would be asked questions he decidedly didn't wish to answer.

"No need, no need," he said firmly, standing unassisted now.
Bourbon Street swayed a bit around him, but he was steady
enough. He looked about. The masked man was indeed gone,
and of course there was no sign of the blond-haired woman.

"We gotta get a policeman here!" said the same insistent on-
looker, evidently quite fixated on the notion.

Fleming drew himself fully erect, straightening his coat, dusting off the sleeves. He gave no sign of the pain throbbing through his head.

"I *am* a policeman," he said with a kind of icy dignity and pushed himself suddenly through the gawking circle.

Voices called after him as he strode away, but no one followed. He had to get away from the scene of the incident as quickly as possible. Keeping the handkerchief pressed to his temple, he marched back toward the nightclub where he'd left Prescott. His feet wobbled somewhat alarmingly beneath him.

"Ah, Ian, how pleasant to see you. Wait. You've been away awhile, haven't you? What is happening here?" Prescott hadn't moved from his barstool but looked to have had at least one more whiskey since Fleming had absented himself. Just as obviously, in that time his mood had rotated once more. In any case he was now decidedly drunk.

Fleming gripped the man's elbow.

"Come, Prescott," he said through gritted teeth, a fresh pulse of pain lancing his skull with his every heartbeat. "We must go home now."

The bartender was edging their way with a look of sharp concern.

"Very well, very well." Prescott offered a slovenly smile. "But—just one more, I should think, before—"

"No, Prescott. *Now.*" He intensified his grip on the elbow.

Prescott's face cleared suddenly. The new merry twinkle vanished from his long-lashed hazel eyes. "Oh. Something's happened. Ian, I believe you're injured. Yes"—he pushed away his nearly empty whiskey glass—"yes, let's away. Martha will tend to you if you're hurt."

Fleming had to help him off the stool. Together they fairly staggered from the club.

Chapter 17

MARTHA PRESSED a cup of black coffee into Prescott's hands. He was still muttering, "Ian, Ian, what happened to you? Oh, my dear friend, you've been hurt." He was in a pathetic state.

Fleming could barely bite down on his exasperation. They were alike, he and Prescott. Englishmen, former spies. Yes. But Prescott was flawed, perhaps catastrophically so. At the moment Fleming felt not a shred of sympathy. Who, after all, was to blame for Prescott's faults?

After a few minutes of calm, soothing assurances, Martha left Prescott in the drawing room. She led Fleming into the kitchen at the rear of the house. It appeared clean and well stocked.

"I would guess that hurts," she said, looking at his head.

The handkerchief he was still holding to his scalp was damp with his blood. "Quite correct." Actually, excruciating was more the word.

She laid a pair of aspirins on his palm, then handed him a glass of water.

"A trip to the hospital would be wise," she said. They were at the sink. She motioned him onto a stool. She dipped a cloth in a basin of hot water and started dabbing in a delicate circle around his injury. "I don't have anything stronger for pain."

"Circumstances dictate that I avoid hospitals." He swallowed the aspirin.

Her lips pressed briefly into a tight thin line. "Okay. I'll do what I can. I'll dress this. I can even sew it if you want. But I'm no doctor, and I can't tell how bad you're really hurt. You understand that, Mr. Fleming?"

"I do. A bandage will do." He remained still as she worked,

washing away the blood that was already crusting about the wound.

"Time for the iodine. I'm sorry, Mr. Fleming, but this is going to sting. No way around it. Got to get that cut clean before I dress it." She dampened a corner of her cloth with the contents of a small opaque bottle.

"I appreciate this, Martha."

She sniffed sharply. "You're a guest in Mr. Quick's house. That puts you under my care. But I wouldn't mind knowing what the hell's going on here, if you'll pardon my language. That blond lady fooling with the mailbox, you coming in looking like you've been in a barroom brawl. Things are getting out of hand. I don't poke, and I don't pry, but I'd like to have a clue about what's happening."

From her tone it was clear that she didn't actually expect her wishes to be answered.

Nonetheless, the reply that left Fleming's lips was terse: "I suggest you ask your employer. When he *sobers up*."

She continued working without a pause, and Fleming instantly regretted the comment. His anger was toward Prescott, not his secret paramour.

Finally she said, "Mr. Quick is a troubled man." She spoke levelly; the combination of well-modulated speech and plain speaking was effective. "More so than even you might've guessed. He's wounded. In his heart, not his body. When he first hired me on, almost three years ago now, I thought he might actually be crazy. I almost quit, even though he's never been cruel to me in any way. He was trying to put this PI practice of his together, and he didn't have the first idea what he was doing. He'd get sauced up almost every night and sometimes go on crying jags."

She finished cleaning out Fleming's wound and started gingerly applying a bandage. She was proving a very effective nurse.

"But gradually, over time," Martha went on, "he pulled himself together. His practice became successful, and that seemed to make him very happy. I know he used to work for the British government, doing something hush-hush. I don't know the details. I'm guessing—guessing, mind you, he hasn't told me anything—that you used to, too. Maybe you still do. It's none of my business. But whatever happened to him in the old days hurt him badly. He suffers. But he's rebuilt himself, Mr. Fleming, and he's become as fine a man as any I've met, and I'm proud to know him. I just wanted you to know the facts before you made any real judgments."

She finished taping the neat gauze bandage across his temple. "There. Won't even spoil your good looks."

He managed a smile at that. "You're most kind, Martha."

"Just doing my job, Mr. Fleming." She turned and headed for the drawing room.

FLEMING FOLLOWED SOME while later, going up to change first and giving Prescott some time to resettle. The collar of Fleming's coat was nearly ripped free. He examined his bandage in the lavatory's mirror. There was a dot of blood at its center, but it didn't look at all bad. If anyone asked, he could easily concoct some story to account for it. Already the pain in his head was becoming manageable. When he finally returned to the drawing room, Prescott was being coerced into eating by the barbed admonitions of Martha.

There was more coffee and a tray of cold cuts and rye bread. He helped himself to a sandwich, finding himself quite famished despite the upheaval of the night. His headache retreated further.

Prescott chewed his own sandwich docilely. His eyes were slowly focusing themselves. Even a man with a fairly strong constitution could only drink so hard for so long. A few more years of such tippling, Fleming judged, and Prescott would lose whatever lingering youthful stamina he currently retained.

Nonetheless, Prescott now appeared to be returning to some level of sensibility.

Looking around the drawing room at Fleming and Martha, he muttered, "I see I've been . . . excessive . . . again." He sounded contrite, even disgusted with himself.

"Don't fret, Mr. Quick, you're among friends." Martha refilled his coffee cup.

He nodded morosely to himself. Fleming finished the last bite of his pastrami sandwich and lit a cigarette, settling into the deep armchair.

Prescott cleared his throat, his eyes fixed to the floor. "I am sorry, Ian. Sorry for you to have witnessed me in such a state. It's truly shameful. Honestly, though, I don't behave in this manner very often anymore. There was a time—. But that's neither here nor there. I wish to apologize."

Martha was stacking dishes atop the tray. She turned, seeming to want to lay a comforting hand on Prescott but making no move toward him. "Mr. Quick, don't carry on so. You'll get yourself upset. Like you said, you don't do this often any—"

"Yes, Martha, yes." He gave the woman a melancholy little smile. "But our good Mr. Fleming here doesn't know that. What he sees is a blundering drunkard who can't exert a mature control over himself."

Fleming felt no great urge to contradict the man just now.

With a lingering look of deep, barely concealed tenderness, Martha finished collecting the dishes and left the room. The antique grandfather clock ticked in its corner, marking the lengthening silence.

"Prescott," Fleming finally said as gently as he could, "I will not remain joined to an active alcoholic. That spells simple disaster, for both of us. If need be, I will simply go this alone." Martha's words earlier had softened his anger somewhat, but this issue still had to be addressed squarely.

Prescott released a long sigh, nodding. "Very well."

"Meaning?" Fleming pressed.

Prescott lifted his eyes from the floor. They brimmed now with a steely tenacity. "Meaning I shall refrain from all spirits until the conclusion of this. If you could find a Bible in this house, I would swear upon it. But I will give an oath with more substance." He seemed then to gather every tattered bit of his dignity he could find. "I pledge to you upon the blood I have spilled in this life of mine, upon every corpse I ever made of a living, breathing being, upon the deeds I carried out in the unspoken name of king and country. If I fail, may I *drown* in that blood."

Despite himself, Fleming was affected. It was a powerful invocation, for of course Fleming, too, had participated in those selfsame deeds.

"Very well," he finally said

"Meaning?" asked Prescott, with just a dash of wryness.

It provoked a small smile from Fleming. "Meaning I accept your word." And I will hold you to it, he added silently.

"You're injured, Ian. I believe I've been babbling on about that. I've no idea if you've explained to me what happened yet or not. If you'd be so good, I would like to know what's befallen you."

Fleming drew on his cigarette, meeting Prescott's eyes levelly. "Are you lucid enough to understand what I'm saying?" He didn't pad the question.

Prescott wasn't put out. "Yes. I've regained enough of my wits. My memory leaves off at that club on Bourbon Street. Whatever occurred must have followed after that point."

"It did." Fleming ground out the cigarette's butt and proceeded to explain what had happened. Prescott nodded along to Fleming's narrative, determinedly focused.

"Fascinating," he said at last. "Two more players in our drama. And one that fits Martha's description of the woman from this afternoon. This does give us some new elements to work with." His brow crinkled in thought.

"Yes." And, Fleming had to admit, the blond-haired woman's appearance did corroborate Martha's account.

"That one in the black cloak," said Prescott. "He must also be one of that circle around Faith and Marquette, just as we postulated earlier. Yes, a coterie of accomplices. And you say he was a muscular fellow? Perhaps he's the very one that took an axe to Angelina Marquette and Martin Dours." Prescott seemed to be gathering himself before Fleming's eyes, drawing energy and clarity from the act of collating these new facts. That was good.

"It's possible," Fleming said. "His accent was quite curious, though. When he said I'd been told to keep my damned nose out it—"

"—which corresponds to what you received in that message." *Ghost of Christmas Past.* "Of course. But his enunciation. His accent. Very thick. It actually sounded . . . almost French. *Mon ami,* he said. Yet, at the same time, it was a very American dialect, very southern. That distinctive twang one hears everywhere down here."

"Indeed?" Prescott's brows lifted. "The man must be a Cajun."

"Cajun?" Fleming had only heard the word applied to food.

"Acadians. Really, Ian, history is such an engrossing subject. You might want to devote an hour or two to it someday. Nova Scotia, it was. French colonists. They were run out by our own British troops in the mid-1700s. For some reason they chose southern Louisiana as their new homeland. Many settled here. They're an odd lot, quite insular in their ways, distrustful of outsiders—and for good cause. Attempts have been made to extricate them from here as well. Many live in the backwoods, among the swamps and bayous. They speak a strange patois. A mixture of English, Spanish, German, Indian, Negro and, yes, French idioms. Makes for a potent accent."

It was a quite lucid historical sermon, without any slurrings or hitches in his speech. Yes, Fleming decided. Prescott was coherent enough.

"Well, whatever his ancestral origins, we should make some sort of effort to locate him." He touched his temple softly with his fingertips. It was swelling into a hard little knot.

"Looking for a spot of revenge?"

"I wouldn't mind it, no. But that's not the point. This man may be a suspect the police know nothing about. We must take advantage of that. Bear in mind, we are attempting to keep ahead of the authorities on this. If they round up Faith Ullrich and Gerard Marquette and whoever else is involved before we determine and undo whatever it is this murderous cabal means to do with the information they have about our pasts . . . all of this will likely have been for naught."

Prescott nodded. "Yes, I am aware. It's a race. It's a matter of honor."

Fleming frowned. "Honor? How so?"

Bloodshot hazel eyes gazed back at him. "Well, dear chap, I don't entirely know your feelings about the situation, but I am quite affronted by all this. I am not proud of the deeds I undertook following the war. Hah. That's a decided understatement. *But* I did those things out of a sense of duty— duty to the military code I was raised under, to the prime minister, to the Crown. I must not allow further harm to come from what has already occurred. What if . . ."

Fleming watched a pained expression pass over Prescott's features.

"What if," he continued, "it's not blackmail? What if Faith and Marquette decide to tell the world about the existence of Churchill's Boys? Release it to the press? Think of the repercussions, the tarnishing of the Crown, the great dishonor that would follow. I don't wish to live out the remainder of my days being thought of by the world at large as an executioner." Prescott shook his head sharply. "No. I won't have it. I won't have my honor further pulverized. I'll see these fiends destroyed before that."

Fleming blinked at this clearly and coldly pronounced diatribe. Prescott was obviously passionate about the matter.

The bloody history of Churchill's Boys released to the public . . . ? It was a dreadful thought.

"Very well, Prescott. But how shall we go about finding the man who gave me this rude bump on my head? I'm afraid I don't have much of a description, beyond his large physical dimensions. All I saw of his face beneath that mask was a rather unpleasant sneer."

Prescott had a swallow of coffee. "Well, it's better than nothing at all. A large Cajun loose in the Quarter? That might be all the profile we require."

The long-limbed man climbed from the settee with some effort.

"However, there's another matter I must deal with beforehand. Martha. I am going to temporarily relocate her. These devils—whoever they are—obviously know where I live. Now, with this assault on you, there is finally violence directed at a resident of this house. I want Martha out of any potential harm. It's something I should have done at the start, but frankly I dreaded the thought of being separated from her. Afraid I would . . . crumble. Selfish of me. Unconscionably so."

Fleming stood as well. "It is for the best, Prescott," he said. Even with the blond-haired woman's appearance tonight, there was still no clear-cut reason to trust Martha fully. She might still be a quisling. Best indeed to have her out of the house.

"Yes. Now, if you'll excuse me, I must go tell Martha she will be spending an indefinite period in a hotel room. She won't be pleased. If you hear raised voices over the next half hour or so, don't be bothered." Prescott exited the room.

Chapter 18

FLEMING TOOK a quick morning bath in the guest quarters' black marble tub. Prescott had made a poignant point yesterday. Their past *had* to remain buried—and not merely because they both fervently wished their actions as Churchill's Boys to stay secret. More was at stake. If word leaked out, the repercussions could be grave indeed. Perhaps catastrophic. A less than ethical top secret British intelligence operation would be uncovered. There would be scandal. There would be international backlash. Diplomacy would suffer. England—poor, miserable England, still struggling to regain its collective footing in the war's aftermath—would be sullied, its honor besmirched.

It could not be allowed to happen.

Fleming shaved, dressed, and went downstairs.

A great upheaval had erupted last night when Prescott told Martha that he was going to relocate her to safer ground temporarily. Martha had fairly raised the roof in protest. Fleming, in his room, did his level best not to overhear, but a few snatches reached his ears nevertheless.

Martha insisted repeatedly that she would not leave him, not now, not in what was obviously his time of dire need. The two remained at clamorous loggerheads for an hour, all told. It was another hour before Martha had unwillingly packed her things and Prescott, who had made her hotel arrangements, escorted her outside and into a taxi he had called for.

Though it was early, Fleming found Prescott in his office, leafing studiously through the dossiers they had produced yesterday on Faith Ullrich and Gerard Marquette. He was wearing his horn rimmed reading glasses. The eyes behind them were of cou bloodshot, but he appeared admirably focused. Fleming hoped his resolve of last night—to remain sober—was at least temporarily heartfelt.

"Did the ghostly echo of a bugle rouse you out of bed with the sunrise?" Fleming asked. The silver coffeepot sat on the desktop. He filled a cup. The brew was almost caustically strong, as if Prescott had guessed wildly when adding the ground beans.

Prescott grunted ruefully. "Yes, perhaps my military habits are reasserting themselves, given the present stimuli of these circumstances."

"How did it fare with Martha last night?" Fleming asked, then instantly thought better of it. He already knew the answer, after all.

Prescott slumped a bit in his chair, as if weighted down. "It was worse than I'd imagined."

Fleming checked himself this time before he made some thoughtless comment about such conflicts being inevitable between lovers. Prescott still thought his relationship with Martha a secret; let him keep believing so.

Prescott nodded to the telephone on the corner of his desk. "I phoned my police contacts this morning. As I feared, no one will let slip a word now that Inspector McCorkle has the reins of things. Men must tremble in his presence."

"Someone may yet provide us some helpful information," Fleming said, not especially believing it. He eyed the pages of stationery. "Did you think of something we neglected to add?"

"No, no. Merely meditating. Reading between the lines, as it were. I've been reconsidering a particular point. I think today we would do well to make contact—or in my case, renew contact— with Edmund Dours. This all started with him, after all. He would still be in touch with the police, particularly if his son Martin has now turned up dead, too. He'll have access to information—"

Fleming lifted a hand to stop him. "Yes. Still in contact with the police. Too close contact, I should think. We absolutely don't want the authorities to know we're pursuing the matter."

"I realize that." Prescott took a swallow of his own coffee. "But Edmund Dours could be a fount of knowledge. If we could find a way to tap into him, learn what the police know . . ." He trailed off pensively.

It was a valid point, and Fleming considered it. His nature cried out for action to be taken, but he had to temper such impulses with rationality. They had to move cautiously. There was too much at risk.

Then a thought occurred. At the same instant Prescott shot him a sharp look.

"We could try making contact with the other son—Elliot Dours!" Fleming said emphatically.

Prescott nodded with a slow curling smile as he removed his reading glasses. "The precise thought just struck me as well." He chuckled. "Seems we're getting in tune, doesn't it? How shall we go about it?"

It was nearly as chancy as contacting Edmund Dours, Fleming realized. If the father was cooperating with the police in their efforts to find his child's—children's, likely—murderers, then this son, Elliot, was surely caught up in matters also. Yet there was some elusive niggling intuition tugging at the edge of Fleming's mind, telling him certainly—even without any positive proof—that *this* was the course to pursue. Find the son. Get him to divulge what he knew of the police's endeavors to solve these crimes. That would give Fleming and Prescott a significant advantage in this race. And they needed every handicap they could find.

They emptied the coffeepot as they discussed it.

Prescott said, "You'll recall we postulated that Martin Dours got himself murdered because he was delving into his sister's death on his own. Elliot might be making independent investigations as well."

"Then we'd better locate him before someone takes an axe to him." Fleming stood.

They bustled out into the morning. Birds were chirping obliviously in the nearby greenery, thoroughly unconcerned with these dire human matters. The day was starting out cloudless and relatively warm. Prescott was dressed in his black suit. Fleming wore khaki trousers and his tan jacket. The presence of his Enfield revolver beneath it was by now not in the least disconcerting.

They turned off Dauphine onto Ursulines Street and started toward the river. Prescott, of course, knew the address of the Dours family house.

There was a modest amount of foot and auto traffic through the French Quarter this morning. At a corner, where Chartres Street crossed Ursulines, they halted. There was a white building on one corner with a vast forward court that appeared to be a convent. Prescott nodded further up the street.

"That three-story brick pile there, that's the one."

It was a handsome abode, with a wide oak door set above two marble steps. A rococo gas lamp was fixed above the entrance.

"Rather brazen of that unkempt Slim character to go knocking on such a door pretending to have a wire for Martin Dours," Fleming observed.

"Yes. Slim can be quite the bold one."

They had devised a reasonably sound plan. Prescott was to call on Edmund Dours, in the guise of a strict visit of sympathy. Since Prescott had been involved in the case early on, it wouldn't be entirely out of place for him to pay this commiserating visit to the grieving father. And with some luck—perhaps with a great deal of it—he could arrange to meet later with Elliot Dours or at least learn something about the young naval man's movements.

Fleming left Prescott at the corner, peeling off to find his way to a Decatur Street café where they would rendezvous when this was done. He would have liked a more active role in this venture but settled for what fate had dealt him.

He sat at a window table in the unpretentious eatery, with its bare floorboards and dusty light fixtures. His waitress was a sleepy-faced girl with bangs and freckled cheeks who could have passed herself off easily as a sixteen-year-old. Fleming smoked a cigarette while he waited for his order to arrive.

He touched the swelling at his left temple, which was still quite tender but no longer throbbing. In fact, his sleep had been rather free of pain. He had applied a fresh bandage from a first aid kit he found after his bath.

When breakfast arrived, he dug in with some appetite, speculating uselessly on what progress Prescott was making. It had so far been half an hour, which meant he had at least gotten past the front door.

One thing Fleming had learned last night, unmistakably, was that the opposition knew he was in town. That big masked man, the Cajun, had quoted that scrawled message he'd received at his home on Jamaica. *Keep your damned nose out of it, Fleming.* He chewed wistfully at a strip of bacon, sopping up the remainder of his eggs with a triangle of toast. Nothing would have suited him better than staying far, far away from this imbroglio. But the situation had dictated otherwise. He was caught in this, and that was that. Resolving the matter was the only recourse.

He kept an eye on sun-dappled Decatur Street beyond the café's windows. A U.S. military jeep went rolling past, carrying a pair of servicemen in their olive drab uniforms. Across the lane an aged, humpbacked white man was sweeping the sidewalk with dreary methodical swings of his broom.

The Mississippi River was just a short distance beyond Decatur, across an intervening area of gravel and concrete that was split by railway tracks. The river's large warehouses were visible above the nearby rooftops. He heard the blast of a ship's horn.

At that moment Prescott came into view, hurrying along the sidewalk, making for the café's door. His features were set in an intense cast somewhere between dismay and eagerness. A moment

more and he had swung through the door and was approaching
Fleming's table, drawing short excited breaths.

He pulled up a chair as Fleming hunched forward, intent and
curious. "I take it your mission produced some interesting news
for us?"

"Oh, it has. Yes." The drowsy-faced waitress appeared at his
elbow. "Ah. Coffee, please. Two sugars. No, make that three.
Thank you."

Fleming waited until she had slipped away. "Well?"

Prescott was making efforts to slow his breathing. At last he
said, "Martin Dours is, I believe, quite dead."

"You're certain? Chopper and Slim were unable to confirm it."

"Well, I can't produce the body either, Ian. But my suspicion is
a bit more solid than the fact that Martin wouldn't come to the
door to sign for that bogus telegram." His coffee arrived, and he
took a hasty gulp. "Edmund Dours received me, as you've probably guessed by now. We went into his study. He's a shattered
man. Barely resembles the person I dealt with only—what?—two
or three weeks ago. He looks to have aged a decade, and he was
already an elderly man. Before, he had the bearing of a jungle
cat—alert, predatory, animated. Now he's a shell. It was quite an
unsettling sight."

"Couldn't the death of his daughter account for that?"

"Yes, of course it could. But Edmund, when I first met him,
struck me as a very decisive man. Unwilling to lie back and let
events overtake him. When he suspected his new son-in-law of infidelity, he took swift action, engaging me to uncover the facts.
Angelina's murder was surely a horrendous blow. But"—Prescott's
fingers drummed the tabletop—"he was made of hard stuff. Her
death would have spurred him into action. He would have taken
every conceivable step to find her killers. However, if one adds
the murder of another one of his children—Martin—it might
have been enough to tip him off the mental edge. Too much

tragedy. Sufficient to break him utterly. Which was the state I found him in."

Fleming considered. It was a thin bit of supposition. "Is that the full basis of your theory?"

Prescott shook his head as he swallowed more coffee. "No. I casually mentioned that I'd heard that his sons were in the city and that I hoped they were proving to be of some comfort to him in this most grievous hour. It was a rather cheap ploy. I mentioned them by name. Elliot and Martin. Edmund was sitting across from me, sort of huddled in his chair, a palsied, brittle old man. When I uttered Martin's name, his shivering worsened significantly. His mouth worked, but no sounds emerged. An expression of devastation came over his pruned features. I had struck the nerve. Yes. I am satisfied that Martin Dours also has come to a sticky end and that his murder is being kept out of the press, likely at the urging of Inspector Everett McCorkle and the police, who want to avoid any further public outcry at these atrocities." He gulped more coffee. "We can only wonder what progress the Red Dwarf has made in this case."

"I'd rather not wonder," Fleming said. "I would prefer to know concretely. That was the purpose of this particular mission. Did you glean any idea how we might covertly contact Elliot Dours?"

Prescott nodded. "Actually, it was the housemaid who tipped me off. A rather skittish little thing. After a sufficient amount of time sitting in that gloomy study with Edmund Dours, I expressed my final sympathies and excused myself. By then he seemed scarcely aware of my presence. The maid appeared to see me out. I told her I had hoped to communicate my commiserations to Elliot and Martin as well but that both boys seemed to be out at the moment. Again at the mention of Martin Dours I received something like the reaction of the father. The housemaid fairly cringed. But she told me that Elliot would be home by lunchtime."

"Yes, but where is he now?" pressed Fleming.

"That's where I'm taking you, old boy, now that I've reported and caught my breath. I'm afraid I ran the distance from the Dours residence, and my once nimble body is no longer accustomed to it. Let's get this bill paid and be off. Waitress!"

NEW ORLEANS HAD a wealth of exotic-sounding street names—Desaix, Cadiz, Desire, Montegut—reflecting a lavish gumbo of locales. The French Quarter might be the white heart of the city, where a white man's blood beat fastest and hottest, but there were other realms, where other forces ruled.

Hush had a room on one of these streets. It was kept scrupulously neat. Its furnishings were decidedly modest, though the man earned exceptional money for a member of his race in these southern reaches. That wherewithal was reflected chiefly in the number of books he owned. Two of his walls were stocked floor to water-stained ceiling with thick volumes. He owned no fiction titles. These were all studious tomes, filled with the musty incantations of white law. Hush had been sent to school in the North, his tuition paid by the organization that possessed him body and soul. His was not indentured servitude. He wasn't working toward his personal emancipation. He worked for the Queen. He was dedicated to her and to all she represented.

If necessary, he would willingly die in her service.

Another amenity that spoke of Hush's financial fortitude was the private telephone installed in his room. He had been placing and receiving calls since late last night.

What Queen Cleopatra had foretold had, of course, come to be.

The police were harassing those most visible areas of what they would call the "voodoo community." It had begun only a few days ago. Such persecutions weren't uncommon. In fact, the mistreatment of blacks by whites was an activity embedded in the very foundations of this country . . . a home of the free that had gotten an early taste for slavery, which it had never, in all truth, fully abolished. Just as white men still yearned for the sweet taboo of black women, so, too, did the police act as their ancestral slave-owning ilk had.

However, these past few days the harassments had been *very* forceful, far beyond the norm.

A small shop on Carondelet Street had been summarily closed by the Board of Health. The place sold potions and baubles of no real value, mostly to curious white customers. The same day, a man who made a modest living pretending to tell fortunes by casting bones and burning eye-watering incense had been arrested on a purely fictitious assault charge; the man was seventy-one years old. About town similar incidents were occurring.

Raids, false arrests, seizures of goods. All aimed at blacks that dealt publicly in so-called occult arts, though in virtually every case so far these practitioners were merely charlatans cashing in on the mystique of their ebony skin and the gullibility of white people. Mumbo jumbo was a viable commodity.

It was the two butchered bodies, of course, that had started all this. And those bone and feather crosses . . .

The Queen had many contacts besides him, Hush knew. She even had eyes, it was said, that could see into the workings of the police. That was a most impressive feat. Hush did not believe this was merely a matter of bribery and agents. Cleopatra, if not omniscient, had vision beyond that granted to beings of mere base flesh. She had warned of the Blood Red Devil, the one called Inspector Everett McCorkle. He was the one behind this sudden campaign of terrorization.

Hush's telephone had rung throughout the night and continued to do so now in the daytime. No one in the rooming house ever complained of the noise. He had not slept. He was not tired. He sat by the phone and recorded the information as it arrived, writing it in a notebook in his painstakingly neat hand.

Hush was left-handed. As a boy in school, malevolent nuns—representing a god of vast guilt and suffering—had spanked that hand endlessly, but he had never been able to create anything with his right beyond a near-illegible scrawl.

He would meet again with the Queen soon. *Then* these white tormentors would feel the reverberations of their actions.

Chapter 19

CAFÉ DU Monde was large and charmingly appointed, the savory aroma of what Prescott said were *beignets*—local pastries of some sort—pervading the air. It sat several blocks down Decatur Street, across from Jackson Square, and had indoor and outdoor seating. The exterior section lay beneath a large canvas awning. There were enough tables and chairs, within and without, to accommodate a veritable host of guests.

As picturesque as it appeared, Fleming judged it was also one of those irresistible tourist stopovers, much like Big Ben or the Empire State Building—quite eye-catching but nonetheless at least slightly spoiled by the constant gawking attention poured onto them. Certainly Café du Monde wasn't as imposing as these other sights, but still there were a number of obvious out-of-towners festooning the place.

Fleming neatly ejected the thought. He and Prescott were here to locate Elliot Dours, who the Dourses' housemaid said had come here to meet someone. Prescott had been fortunate to glean that chance tidbit of information, as Edmund Dours had been useful only in semiconfirming the death of his son Martin.

They had a fair idea of what Elliot looked like from Slim and Chopper's earlier reconnaissance of the Dours house. Twenty-eight years old, tall, trim, rather handsome in a square-faced sort of way, with his light blond hair cut in military fashion.

As they came to the café, Fleming and Prescott both nonchalantly scanned the crowd. The interior was visible from the sidewalk through a series of tall windows. Nobody remotely matching the likeness was indoors. Most of the patrons were outside anyway, owing to the clement morning weather.

They slowed, walking in a blasé manner along one edge of the exterior seating area, which was separated from the sidewalk by a low iron fence.

"Have you got him?" asked Fleming in a soft murmur.

"Chap in the blue blazer? Yes. I do believe that's our lad."

He was seated alone in the center beneath the broad awning. He fit the description perfectly—hair, features, build. Noting him from the corner of his eye, Fleming saw he appeared quite restive. His fingers were drumming the small round table expectantly. He glanced at his watch and toward the sidewalk repeatedly. Yes, a man waiting on an urgent appointment.

"Who do you imagine he's waiting for?" Prescott asked quietly as they turned at a corner support for the awning.

"I think it might prove worthwhile to sit and find out. What's your view? Approach him now or wait and watch?"

"Surveillance would be my choice."

Fleming nodded. "Mine as well." It seemed particularly sound as he hadn't yet devised any prudent scheme of how to accost Elliot Dours. One couldn't simply stroll up and ask what he knew of the police investigations into the murders of his sister and younger brother. Whatever tack they chose would need to be decidedly artful.

They came around the rear and entered the café's exterior seating area, picking a table on the periphery that left them a good view of their quarry. A young waiter in a long white apron materialized almost immediately. Fleming reluctantly ordered another coffee, though by now he'd had his fill of it. Prescott, not interested in food at this hour, ordered the same.

They settled in to wait and watch. It was a fairly familiar scenario for both of them. The intelligence work they had engaged in during their careers hadn't all been dashing heroics and heart-pounding excitement, not by half. As in any military undertaking there had been a vast amount of physical inactivity, much of that consumed in planning and coordination, the rest occupied by this particular vacant exercise: waiting. Watching to see what happened. It could be maddening. But Fleming retained more than enough levelheaded patience to bear it out. He could only wonder if Prescott would remain as determinedly focused.

Elliot Dours, despite being a military man himself, was demonstrating no such patient composure. He continued to drum the table, fidgeting like a child in church. Fleming stayed alert, ready to move if the man decided he could wait no longer for his appointment.

Across Decatur and the gracious common of Jackson Square the minutes were being marked on the giant clock face that adorned the front of the imposing cathedral. Ten minutes. Twelve, Fifteen.

He and Prescott spoke intermittently, only enough to give the appearance of two men enjoying a morning cup of coffee together. Actually, the brew was quite good, mixed as it was with hot milk, though Fleming only sipped at his. "Café au lait," Prescott informed him, one more indication that New Orleans had a more European essence than American.

Eighteen minutes had elapsed since they had sat. At twenty-two minutes Elliot, who had been waiting who knew how long so far, was tapping his foot manically, shooting angry looks at his wristwatch every thirty seconds. It seemed unlikely he would be able to sit still much longer. Fleming nudged Prescott, telling him quietly to make it arly to pursue the man when he bolted.

As it happened, Elliot Dours did not dash off. At that moment a rather stout figure ambled casually into the maze of tables that was the outdoor seating section. He had a newspaper folded beneath one arm and was puffing leisurely on a briar pipe. He wore a dark business suit, somewhat the worse for wear, offset discordantly by a yellow rose tucked into his buttonhole. His hair was mousy brown and thinning, and he sported a thick mustache whose ends were waxed, the two points lying across his doughy cheeks. He looked to be in his late forties.

That newspaper and pipe, Fleming concluded, were someone's

overblown notion of an identification signal. Perhaps the rose as well. Yes, Elliot had been told to rendezvous at Café du Monde with a man sporting these overt accessories. It was a kind of vaudevillian version of an undercover operation.

Elliot leapt to his feet as the man sauntered up to his table. He seized the plump man's sleeve and fairly dragged him into a chair. This new arrival shook off Elliot's hand indignantly. A waiter approached the table but scampered off when Elliot spun and hissed at him.

"Oh, dear Lord," Prescott said softly. "That's Manfred Rexroth."

Fleming shot him a questioning glance. They were too far away to hear what Elliot was saying as he leaned toward the man and spoke in what looked to be tight, furious whispers. Moving nearer to eavesdrop didn't seem prudent.

"Rexroth," Prescott quietly explained, keeping the pair furtively in sight. "He works for another local private investigator, named Harry Braniff. My competition, if you would. Rexroth does a good deal of his legwork. Braniff is a rather smug and ineffectual creature. He has an office outside the Quarter, in the Faubourg Marigny. That way." He nodded down Decatur Street in the direction they had come. "He tends to prey on the unsuspecting, inflating his credentials and abilities, not to mention his bill, whenever he can get away with it. I'm pleased to say I've lost very little business to him these past few years—and likely stolen a fair amount from him. Our young Mr. Dours must have picked him out of the telephone directory to make independent inquiries into the unhappy events that have befallen his family. I should make an effort not to be seen by Rexroth." Prescott ducked his head, though the man wasn't looking their way.

Fleming acknowledged this with a curt nod, straining uselessly to overhear the conversation three tables away. Elliot Dours's demeanor was growing more irate by the second. He was waving a finger sharply in front of Manfred Rexroth's puddy nose, above the briar pipe. The portly man tried to bat the hand aside, but this only made Elliot angrier. The display was starting to draw attention from the adjacent tables. Rexroth was now looking about nervously.

A moment later Elliot, having reached the limit of his thin patience, stood once more and seized the man's lapels, hauling Rexroth forcefully to his feet. He gave a high yelp of surprise and fear, his pipe and newspaper falling to the ground. Elliot Dours was evidently quite physically fit. Fleming had no doubt he could pummel Rexroth unconscious with no more than two well-thrown punches, and the situation appeared to be escalating toward just such an end.

"Think you can swindle me, you worthless flimflammer?" Elliot shouted, now shaking Rexroth like an overstuffed rag doll. "You and that Braniff bastard take our money, then you don't deliver! And you let my brother—my brother—" What followed was a sort of animal screech of pure rage. Elliot cocked a fist, teeth bared in his squarish face. Rexroth was wide-eyed with terror, struggling vainly to break free.

Fleming was already up and moving. A great hullabaloo was going up from the café's patrons. In another instant someone would start shouting for the police. Fleming vaulted agilely over a chair, dodged another intervening table, and caught Elliot's elbow just before he could land his first blow.

Prescott had reacted at the same instant; apparently he, too, had remained alert during their vigil. He ducked around the far side to wrest Rexroth's quaking body from Elliot's grip. The stout frightened man nearly stumbled as he came free.

Prescott spat, "Get the hell out of here, Rexroth, before this fellow gives you what you doubtlessly deserve!"

Rexroth, sputtering mindlessly, left his pipe and paper, turned about and scuttled away on his stumpy legs. He crossed Decatur, nearly getting himself flattened by a fast-moving Ford in the process, and disappeared through Jackson Square.

Fleming restrained Elliot Dours from pursuing, locking the man's arms behind him securely—at least for a moment; then Elliot abruptly broke the hold with a powerful pivot of his upper body and rounded, face lit with hot fury.

"Couple more of Braniff's henchmen, huh?" He bared his teeth again.

"We've nothing to do with Harry Braniff," Prescott said with great indignation.

Fleming said in a mollifying tone, "He's correct. We're not in Braniff's employ. We are, however, in a position to help you. We're after the same thing you are—a murderer or pair of murderers. If you'll come with us, we are prepared to aid you."

The surrounding tables were still in chaos, and yes, someone was at last raising a call for the police.

Elliot's eyes—an almost pastel blue but currently alive with choler—darted back and forth between Fleming and Prescott.

"You don't have much time to decide," said Fleming.

The naval man's brow furrowed. He was considering.

"Why should I trust you?"

"Because we give you our word," Prescott said, simply, levelly. And evidently convincingly.

Elliot Dours nodded sharply, once. "Let's go."

The trio hastened from the café. Prescott urgently flagged a passing taxi to the curb, and they piled hurriedly inside, Elliot pressed between them on the backseat something like a prisoner.

The cabbie, at Prescott's urging and the promise of a hefty tip, sped them off.

Chapter 20

PRESCOTT MADE good his promise and gave the cabdriver, who handled his taxi with a kind of reckless grace, a lavish gratuity. They had gone from Café du Monde—and what could have become an unwanted encounter with the police—to this hotel lobby in something like ninety seconds, or so it seemed.

"What is this?" asked Elliot, clenching his right fist repeatedly, apparently disappointed he hadn't had the chance to lay it into Manfred Rexroth's pudgy face.

"A place for quiet conversation," Prescott said, urging the naval man in through the doors. Fleming, following, didn't see the hotel's name, but obviously it was a posh affair. Fixtures gleamed, and prismatic light spilled from grand chandeliers. They crossed an expanse of royally lush carpeting, passing the busy front desk and entering a lounge where all was relatively peaceful.

A lad in the uniform of the hotel appeared as they seated themselves—Elliot reluctantly—at a cluster of chairs, which were arranged to face each other. "Something from the bar, gentlemen?"

Fleming saw Prescott begin to answer automatically, then check himself and say, "A ginger ale, George." Apparently Prescott had visited here before. "Mr. Dours?"

Elliot Dours, still hostilely uncertain about all this and not liking it, merely glared back.

"Make it three ginger ales." The boy vanished.

"Right," said Elliot with finality. "Who the hell are you?"

At that Prescott produced a business card.

"Finder of Lost Fortunes?" Elliot snapped after a glance.

"What the hell's that mean? Are you another private dick, because if you are—"

"Yes, Mr. Dours, I am a private investigator. This is Mr. Ian Fleming, and he is not, though we are engaged in this effort together."

Fleming kept his face blandly neutral as Elliot turned to frown his way.

Prescott continued, "I should point out right now that I am not attempting to persuade you to hire my services. I want no fee from you, now or ever. Mr. Fleming and I have reasons of our own to be interested in this . . . matter. I would be most drastically obliged if you would give us leave to humbly explain ourselves in detail."

It was the sort of forceful courtesy that only the English could manage—or perhaps the Japanese.

The American pursed his lips a moment, then nodded. "Okay. I've come this far."

The ginger ales arrived, the boy setting the glasses atop the low table at the center of the cluster. No one touched his drink. They sat isolated on their island, away from the few other patrons in the lounge.

Fleming lit a Players. He and Prescott sat on either side of Elliot Dours, leaving the man caught in the crossfire of their gazes. He still appeared angry and impatient, but apparently he was going to listen.

Fleming gave Prescott a shallow nod, indicating he should start things off.

"I am the private detective your father contracted to make a surveillance of Gerard Marquette. And of his mistress, Miss Faith Ullrich."

Elliot stiffened, fist clenching again. "Yes. Marquette. I was home for the wedding. That soft little man. More a mouse than a man, really. He seemed . . . so harmless. And Angelina"—a rubbery ghostly smile flickered over his lips—"she seemed to love him so much. I'd never seen her happier. She was a woeful thing when she was young. Gloomy little kid. Something of an ugly duckling frankly." The smile vanished utterly. "She blossomed as an adult. Became a startling beauty. Do you think Marquette and that Ullrich bitch killed her?"

Prescott didn't wince at the forthright question. This was a time to tell the truth, after all—or as much of it as was judicious.

"They are our primary suspects, yes."

Elliot nodded. "Police think so, too."

Fleming drew on his cigarette, regarding the blond-haired man. "We've been making investigations of our own, Mr. Quick and I. Independent of the authorities. I presume you've been trying to do the same—engaging this Harry Braniff character?"

Again Elliot tensed. "He's a cheat. He's useless. Martin and I hired him on the sly. Didn't want our father to know. Look, how can I be sure you two are on the level, that you're not looking for an angle? Braniff's eyes lit up with dollar signs when he learned who we were. Dours. In this city that means money. Our family's very rich in its way. How can I believe that you two aren't somehow after a piece of that money?"

His tone had shifted as he spoke. His final question was less an accusative inquiry than a plea. He *wanted* to believe in their trustworthiness.

He's on the verge of surrendering all hope, Fleming realized. He has lost his sister, his brother. He has been swindled by Braniff. He's run out of allies. Soon he will fall to utter ruin, like his father.

Prescott said gently, "I could produce my detective's license. But you know as well as I do that credentials carry no telling weight. I've given you our solemn word that we are sincere. That, too, under the circumstances, you might rightfully discount. I tell you that we are seeking the killers of your sister." Prescott eyed the man closely, pausing before adding, "And of your brother."

Elliot's eyes went wide at that. His face lost some color.

"The only means of convincing you of our honesty," Prescott went on in the same soft voice, "may be to tell you why Mr. Fleming and I have taken an interest in the matter."

From his chair Fleming shot a dire look at Prescott, who returned it with a slight turn of his head and a subtle lifting of his brows, as though to ask: What else can we do?

It was perilous. Dreadfully perilous. A tip of ash fell unnoticed from Fleming's cigarette to the carpet. He could intervene now, cut short all of this. But then Elliot Dours would slip through their fingers. They needed him. He was a source of crucial information.

The long silence was growing heavier and more ominous by the second. Elliot was staring at Prescott perplexedly, waiting for him to continue. Fleming debated silently, coolly.

It was the only item they had to offer Elliot, he finally decided. A bargaining chip. We reveal our secrets; he tells us what he knows of the police investigation.

It was Fleming who broke the lengthy pause.

"You are in the Navy, Mr. Dours?"

The pastel blue eyes shifted. "I am. Career. My seventh year."

"I served during the war. Royal Navy, of course."

"What does that have to—"

"What ship do you serve on, Mr. Dours? Where is she currently docked? What's her complement? What's her rate of fuel consumption? What waters does she patrol? What—"

"Hey!" Elliot fairly barked, looking quite dismayed at this sudden battery. Prescott merely looked on. "Mr.—what was your name? Fleming? Look, Fleming, your questions are way out of order." His shoulders were drawn up to full attention, perhaps unconsciously. "What gives you the gall? What on earth would make you think I'd begin to answer any of those questions? You say you were a naval man. Well, what kind of idiot Navy man would ask questions like that? What sort of Navy do you Brits have anyway?"

Fleming ground his cigarette butt into the table's ashtray and looked at Elliot squarely.

"The secrets we bear aren't always our own, are they?" he said. "There are subjects we remain silent on because we are honor-bound to do so. Do you understand that?"

Elliot's lips twisted. "Of course I do."

Fleming drew in a long breath. Here things would be most perilous indeed. He would have to proceed prudently.

"Mr. Quick is a former military man as well. We both worked for British intelligence during and after the war. We've both since retired from that community. But we are obliged to maintain certain secrets. Bound by duty, bound by the strictures of the Official Secrets Act."

Fleming paused, letting Elliot absorb that fully.

Then he went on, "Somehow—we don't know precisely how—some top secret information has gotten loose. It directly affects Mr. Quick and myself. We have good reason to suspect that Faith Ullrich has hold of this information. What she and her likely accomplice, Gerard Marquette, intend to do with it we don't know. Whatever is being planned, we very much wish to stop it before it happens. Therefore we have taken it upon ourselves to delve into this business, in the hope of finding Ullrich and Marquette before the police do. The nature of the information in question is so delicate that we don't want even the authorities to have access to it. We must defuse the bomb first, so to speak. Then you, your father, and the police can do what you like with that murderous duo."

It was, Fleming thought, a satisfying explanation. He had revealed just enough, without violating the code of silence he and Prescott were constrained to follow. He hoped it was adequate to sway this man.

Elliot sat in wordless deliberation a moment. What he asked, however, was quite unexpected.

"How do I know you two aren't in cahoots with Ullrich and Marquette?"

Fleming blinked, surprised and even affronted at the suggestion. It was Prescott who stepped in smoothly now.

"That's a fair question, Mr. Dours. Let me answer it with another one. If we were the opposition, why wouldn't we have killed you—say, in the back of that taxi a short while ago? Kill you . . . as has been done to your sister, Angelina, and your brother, Martin."

Elliot suddenly sagged, as though the question had punctured him. It took a while longer for him to lift his head, eyeing the two of them.

"How do you know about my brother?" A shivery wire of grief now threaded his voice.

"We have been investigating, as we've said," Prescott said. "In truth, we don't *know*. We have surmised. We believe his murder was even more brutal than that of your sister. You alone now can confirm, finally, if he is actually dead."

Fleming, tense in his chair, waited.

At last Elliot breathed, "Yes. True. He's dead. They found his body on the floor of a bathroom in an abandoned house on Touro Street. His poor mutilated body." He seemed to have no energy left now for anger. Sorrow tugged at his square, firm features.

"How was it discovered?" Fleming asked. The ploy had succeeded; they had revealed their reasons for involving themselves in this, and now he was divulging what he knew. We have become his new allies, his new hope, Fleming thought.

"There's this police detective working the case," said Elliot. "This weird little red-haired guy. McCorkle. He said the police received an anonymous tip. They went in and found Martin."

Prescott asked, "When was the last time you saw your brother alive?"

"Five days ago. He said he was going out for a drink, and did I want to join him? I declined. Damn me. It might not have happened if—" Elliot bit into his lower lip, then went on, "Three days before that we'd gone to see Harry Braniff. We told him about Angelina and everything else we knew. He listened, then made these grand promises that he and his agents would get to the bottom of it all. He said he could find that Ullrich whore and that pansy Marquette. I saw those photos my father said you took, Mr. Quick. I thought I was going to vomit. Braniff said he'd find them. Martin and I were at the end of our wits. The police hadn't come up with Angelina's killers. We wanted this thing solved. We wanted some revenge. Braniff said he'd deliver. He collected a fat retainer from us. Then, so far as I know, he did nothing. I was told to meet with that fellow you saw at Café du Monde. Braniff had telephoned, set up the meeting. Made it sound like cloak-and-dagger stuff. Made it sound also like that butterball with the waxed mustache would have some concrete news. He didn't. He was trying to play patty-cake with me. You should've let me slug him, Mr. Fleming. You should've."

"That fellow's name is Manfred Rexroth," said Prescott. "He works for Harry Braniff. Incidentally, he is Braniff's *only* employee. There is no phalanx of agents working for that charlatan. If you want, when this is over, I'll provide you with Mr. Rexroth's home address. And Mr. Braniff's, if you like, though you could just as easily pay him a call at his office."

Elliot somehow managed to sniff out a small laugh at that. "That's nice of you."

"Why did you choose Braniff in the first place?" asked Fleming. "You were, I presume, born here. Weren't you aware of the man's less than estimable reputation?"

Elliot shifted a bit uncomfortably in his chair. "I've been in the Navy the past *seven* years, Mr. Fleming. Besides, I've never had to hire a private dick before. I didn't know anything about it. Neither did Martin. Braniff's name was the first in the phone book. Damn it. It was a stupid move."

"An understandable one," Prescott said gently. "One could appreciate your impatience with the police." More intently he asked, "What progress have they made in this case?"

"Well, they haven't found Ullrich and Marquette yet," Elliot said sourly.

"Yes. Can you give us some specifics? Mr. Fleming and I have made a few strides, which I'll be happy to tell you about. We would like to discover if the efforts of the police can add to our own headway."

Frustration now joined the sorrow on Elliot's face. "It doesn't boil down to much in the end. That McCorkle fellow I mentioned has been around the house a few times. I'm told he's some kind of wizard as a detective, but you couldn't tell by what he's done so far. He doesn't promise things the way Braniff did. But he hasn't produced anything I'd call worthwhile yet either. He's been arresting coloreds right and left, but I'm not sure there's any rhyme or reason to it. Martin said it was like McCorkle was going after these folks just to look busy." He whacked his knee with his fist, but it was a weak, tired blow. "It's damned infuriating."

"I'm sure it is," Fleming said. "Does he believe Ullrich and Marquette are at large in the French Quarter?"

"McCorkle doesn't know. They're making inquiries. He keeps saying that. *Making inquiries.* What the hell are he and the cops doing—going house to house ringing doorbells? Ullrich and Marquette in the Quarter? That's a maddening thought. Those two right under our noses. Enough to make you—make you—" He bared his teeth.

"What have the police uncovered about Faith Ullrich?" Fleming pressed, hoping that this newfound source of information would furnish them with something useful. "Her background. What she's been doing here in New Orleans. Do they have any idea?"

Elliot's feral grin faded quickly. He sat almost dazed a moment, then said, "You couldn't spare a cigarette, could you? Hey, thanks. Got a light?"

Fleming snapped shut the engraved case Nora had given him and lit Elliot's cigarette with his gold lighter.

"Thanks. I gave these up years ago, but what the hell, huh? Anyway. Ullrich. Yes, McCorkle did some digging. She came to the city close to a year ago, rented a house on St. Philip Street here in the Quarter. She had money when she arrived, enough to pay off the first four months in rent right off the bat. She's English. Her father died just before she came over. Suicide. Maybe he left her a nest egg. Anyway, she hasn't had to work a job of any sort since she arrived. She's unmarried. Twenty-six years old. Educated."

Fleming nodded, though this was nothing they didn't know. Again he hoped this man had something valuable to say.

"Does McCorkle know anything about her habits? What she did socially, recreationally?"

A shudder went through Elliot as he drew intently on the cigarette, stifling a cough as he did so but obviously relishing the tobacco's flavor. "I guess you've seen those pictures Mr. Quick took through her bedroom window. Her and Marquette . . . together. McCorkle's seen them, too, of course. I guess *that's* what that perverted slut did with her spare time."

"What was Inspector McCorkle's reaction to those photographs?" Prescott now asked.

Elliot waved his hand. "You can't tell much from that guy. Strange little man, I swear. Fusses with his clothes a lot. Wears this ridiculous straw hat with an orange band around it. He said it was obvious from those pictures that Ullrich and Marquette are sexual degenerates. No argument here. He also said that that alone didn't make them homicide suspects. It was them disappearing together after Angelina's . . . murder . . . that did it."

This was going nowhere, Fleming thought. "Does McCorkle think they were part of . . . a group of some sort?"

Elliot frowned. "What kind of group?"

Fleming groped, "Of like-minded individuals, perhaps."

"What, like a society of sex perverts?"

"Possibly. Or any organization at all. Perhaps a religious cult?"

"You're talking about those chicken bones and candles and feathers and crosses and garbage that the cops who first searched her house found?" asked Elliot.

Peripherally Fleming saw Prescott's lanky body stiffen suddenly. Quietly, gravely, Fleming said, "Yes. All that."

"Didn't know you knew about that stuff." Elliot shrugged, taking a final long puff from the cigarette and grinding it out in the ashtray. "Yes. It was all in a trunk in Ullrich's bedroom. When this McCorkle guy got assigned to the case, he made a big deal out of it. See, items just like those were at both murder scenes."

Chicken bones in the shape of crosses. Black feathers tied to them by red thread. Neither Fleming nor Prescott interrupted.

"That's McCorkle's big push, see," Elliot continued. "He seems to think it all ultimately ties into some—I don't know— some circle of voodoo witch doctors or something. Even though McCorkle says it's probably Marquette and Ullrich who did the killings, he's going after anybody in the city he can find with any . . . I guess you'd say *affiliations* with this kooky nonsense. It's crazy, if you ask me. We've got two prime suspects, and he's wasting time and police manpower waging war against these local Negroes who don't do any more harm than the Gypsy lady at your typical carnival. Why's he doing that, do you suppose?"

Chapter 21

IT WAS nearing noon by the time Elliot Dours left the lounge. He had to get back to Ursulines Street for lunch, he said. He had promised his father. Edmund Dours, understandably, wasn't a well man these days. He required the company of this last vestige of his immediate family. Elliot and one of the Dourses' longtime housemaids were now keeping the old man under nearly constant watch, working in shifts.

"You'll keep me informed of your progress," Elliot said upon leaving. Not a question; a directive.

He had cooperated. Fleming and Prescott were now in his debt. It was one more complication.

The hotel they had come to was on Bienville Street. It was something of a walk back to Dauphine Street, but Fleming was glad for it. It gave him time to digest what they had learned from the naval man, though of course he remained especially alert whenever they were out of doors. That white Studebaker wasn't forgotten. Prescott, too, was mulling the new information.

"Well, Mr. Holmes," Fleming finally said, attempting a droll tone, "it seems your deductions are becoming realities."

Prescott snorted ruefully. "I suppose I'm better at this game than I imagined. Or fortune has favored me. It may be that I am the most underqualified private investigator in the world, you know."

"More so than Harry Braniff?"

"Hah. Point taken. Well, this confirms that at least Faith Ullrich is involved in some brand of voodoo, now doesn't it?"

They crossed Bourbon, which at this hour was conducting itself with workaday propriety, without hint of its saucier nighttime personality.

"That trunkload of bones and feathers and whatnot found in her bedroom certainly makes it appear so," said Fleming. Unless she merely collected such paraphernalia as a hobby, he added silently. "It also seems your capable Inspector Everett McCorkle is pursuing that line of the investigation most vigorously."

"McCorkle's attack, though, from what Elliot was saying," mused Prescott, "it sounds rather widespread, doesn't it? As if he's overturning an entire anthill to find a particular ant."

Fleming nodded. "Whereas we have some knowledge of this murderous cult's likely membership—Faith Ullrich and Gerard Marquette, of course. But also the Cajun and the blond-haired woman. McCorkle may know nothing about these."

"Yet," sighed Prescott as they at last turned onto Dauphine Street, "we still don't know what they plan to do with that information Faith evidently gathered from her father."

The history of Churchill's Boys. Damn Wallace Ullrich for revealing the details of that operation to his daughter, Fleming thought darkly.

"True," he admitted aloud. "But at least we have the shape of the enemy now. It may be we are a nose ahead of our competitors—the New Orleans police." It came out a trifle smug.

He had immediate reason to regret any hint of self-satisfaction, though. As Prescott's house came into view, so, too, did the figures of the two uniformed policemen who were standing at that house's gate, apparently waiting.

Fleming and Prescott exchanged guarded glances, but they had already been seen by the officers. Wordlessly and without hurrying their pace, they proceeded to the gate. Fleming noted the police cruiser parked at the curb.

"Which one's Quick?" asked one of the policeman.

"I am *Mr.* Quick," Prescott pronounced with the sort of subtle imperious dignity for which the English accent was invented.

"You got a name, Mac?" This was the second officer, addressing Fleming. Both men were on the burly side; their hefty leather belts were festooned with the tools of their trade—holster, pistol, handcuffs. Both wore that air of vague menace that American policemen were issued along with their uniforms.

After a moment Fleming said blandly, "I do."

When nothing followed, the first policeman said in a kind of twangy growl, "Don't be a wise ass, feller."

"My name is Ian Fleming."

"Swell." He opened the police car's rear door. "Okay, in with both y'all."

"Are we under arrest?" asked Fleming.

"I'll let you know when you are."

It was evident shorthand for *Cooperate or you* will *be arrested*.

No other obvious course available, Fleming and Prescott climbed inside.

FLEMING HAD EXPECTED that the police cruiser would ferry them to a precinct house or similar official locale. When it didn't, he was unsure whether to feel relief or a greater trepidation.

After a brisk ride out of the French Quarter they had come off Esplanade Avenue and were now inside City Park, following serpentine lanes through the greenery. Tall oaks quickly blocked off any view of the surrounding city. It wasn't so grand as the preserves London boasted within its limits, but it was apparently fairly sizable. Few other cars were about, but hikers and picnickers were visible here and there. Fleming and Prescott hadn't traded a word during the journey; the officers sitting beyond the mesh screen that bisected the car were also silent.

Finally they turned down a cul-de-sac. A stately black-topped Oldsmobile was parked at the end.

Here, then, thought Fleming coolly, was a site for mischief if ever there was.

The officers stepped out and opened the cruiser's rear doors. The air was fresher here than in the Quarter, washed as it was through the park's abundant foliage, and Fleming drew it deep into his lungs. This cul-de-sac was quite isolated, nothing in immediate view but the two autos. Casually stretching, he mindfully noted the position of every player on the scene. Neither he nor Prescott had been frisked, implying that this was indeed not an arrest. It also meant the two policemen weren't the only ones present who were armed.

A classically attired chauffeur was attending the Oldsmobile. He came around to open its rear door now. The action was performed with some great ceremony. Both officers drew their broad shoulders straight.

With the self-conscious stateliness of royalty, out stepped the individual Fleming and Prescott had evidently been brought here to meet. The figure was male, in his forties. He stood no taller than five feet five. He had close-set eyes and wore a flamboyantly cut brown suit. Atop his head was a broad-brimmed straw hat with a colorful orange band. Beneath it he sported a great bush of curly red hair—much brighter than Prescott's—and full sideburns. He remained a few yards off, seeming to automatically adopt the sort of pose familiar from bronze statues of dead generals.

One of the policemen approached, spoke briefly in a reverential whisper, and retreated. Fleming certainly knew enough not to tip their hand by speaking out of turn. However, this man who could only be the fabled Red Dwarf also made no move to initiate conversation. He stood there studying his two visitors as one might observe fish behind glass, his eyes picking over them leisurely. The grainy photo Fleming had seen in the local newspaper hadn't done the man credit. Despite his diminutive proportions, it was plain he was larger than life.

It was Prescott who finally said, "Well, I presume you know who we are. At this stage identifying yourself to your guests would only be tasteful."

A strange humming sound rose from the little man at this. It took Fleming a moment to recognize it as laughter.

"Ah, Mr. Quick, you're nobody's fool. You're also an adequate PI, so my identity is no secret to you. However, I will give your friend here the benefit of the doubt. I'm Everett McCorkle, Mr. Fleming."

"Mr. McCorkle," said Fleming by way of a greeting.

"It's Inspector, of course. But you very likely knew that. Looks like you bumped your noodle." He nodded to the bandage at Fleming's temple.

Fleming's face betrayed nothing. Whatever cat and mouse the Red Dwarf had in mind, he and Prescott could only wait it out. The two officers were now standing a short distance off, on either side of the group. They looked uncomfortably like sentries. Fleming heard a raven's urgent caw from the enclosing trees.

McCorkle's close-set eyes shifted to Prescott. "I rang you several times this morning. You weren't in?"

"I wasn't," Prescott answered. He, too, was wearing a stoic front.

"Most successful PIs keep office hours. Don't you have a secretary?"

"I do." It was the same bland intonation Fleming had used earlier.

It produced another weird humming laugh from McCorkle. It seemed to drone in the man's throat.

"Mr. Quick, I might think you were being . . . recalcitrant." The notion appeared to amuse the inspector.

Prescott blinked innocent hazel eyes. "Nothing is further from my intentions, I assure you, Inspector."

"Ah, then you're going to be cooperative."

"I should quite like to know to what I am lending my cooperation," Prescott parried.

"To the investigation, of course."

"Of course."

McCorkle removed his straw hat to fiddle unhurriedly with the orange band that wrapped it. Odd apparel for a man high in the ranks of the police, Fleming thought. This Red Dwarf certainly did seem to be an eccentric, just as Prescott had said. He also represented a great threat, in that if he was successful in resolving these murders, he might also uncover the information that Faith Ullrich possessed. That information could be trusted to no one, not even the police.

"You received photos of Angelina Marquette in the mail, Mr. Quick. Photographs of her corpse. Well?"

"Well?" Prescott echoed. "Are you asking a question, Inspector? Of course I received the photographs. I handed those photographs over to the police. I have been quite thoroughly questioned on the entire matter, which, if you're curious, you'll no doubt find in your own records. Are you now reopening that same interrogation?"

"Would you lend your cooperation if I did?" McCorkle set the hat back atop his head, adjusting it several times so that it sat just so upon his red curls.

"Yes," said Prescott, simply and levelly.

The inspector nodded leisurely, then moved his gaze back to Fleming.

"I wonder what help you might be, Mr. Fleming."

"I don't understand, Inspector." Which was at least partially true. McCorkle seemed to be doing nothing so much as fishing here, sounding out the two English ex-spies—or perhaps toying with them. Toward what end, Fleming waited to see.

"This is a dangerous case," McCorkle said.

"Mr. Fleming is not a private investigator, Inspector," Prescott interjected. "He is a friend of mine from days when the world was a little less weary. He is here in New Orleans strictly to visit me."

"Funny time to come calling."

"The arrangements were made before this unfortunate business with Angelina Marquette cropped up."

"Yet you didn't cancel the visit."

Prescott said, with a hint of impatience, "I thought the police would have resolved the matter by the time he arrived."

McCorkle treated them to another laugh-hum. Then his features settled into a serious cast.

"Gentlemen . . ." He put his fists to his hips, another "monument" pose, one that should have looked laughable on someone of such small stature; yet, oddly, he bore it effectively. "I said this is a dangerous case. I mean that. Mr. Quick, you received those photos. Obviously the killer or killers have some interest in you. Don't get me wrong. I'm convinced—as is the rest of the department—that you're completely innocent in this. However, innocence has never stopped a bullet . . . or in this case—well, you saw that photo of Mrs. Marquette."

Fleming recalled the glimpse of neck bone in that grotesque picture of the nearly decapitated woman.

"My men and I are doing everything we can to wrap this up," Inspector McCorkle continued. "I have reason to believe that . . . the occult may be involved." He spoke this last in something of an ominous stage whisper.

"I see," said Prescott dubiously.

"I doubt it, Mr. Quick. You don't know these people. You're not from these parts, not by a long shot. There are evil forces at work. Always at work. Death might take a holiday, but the devil never does. He works through the misguided, the desperate, the heretical. We've got plenty of those types in supply here. We've got crazy Negroes that think they can find salvation by drinking a dog's blood. You can't imagine what these people are capable of . . . the stories that don't get told in the light of day, the things that never turn up in the newspaper. A dangerous breed of people. They brought their crazy African ways here with them, long ago, and they've never let them go. Not completely. They pay lip service to God, and they do it convincingly—and I'll even allow as how some *do* believe. But"—McCorkle's close-set eyes burned suddenly with a kind of cold fire—"those niggrahs are savages at heart."

Fleming said nothing, but it was Prescott's silence that was somehow more poignant. Fleming glanced at him sidelong. His features were absolutely steely now; yet still they communicated a look that mixed contempt with shock.

It was apparently lost on the Red Dwarf. He continued, "Now, Mr. Quick, I can certainly understand your anxiety about this situation. You were, after all, singled out to receive those photos— God knows why. But be assured, we *will* solve this. However, I can also understand how you, being a capable private investigator, might take a notion to having a crack at this case yourself. You might even have called in the help of an old friend."

Whatever else the little man knew, Fleming thought, he had no knowledge of the letter that had arrived at Fleming's home in Jamaica. It was that, not Prescott's call for help, which had brought him here.

McCorkle dropped his arms, then languidly picked some bit of invisible lint from his sleeve. "All this is to say that I trust you both will refrain from taking any unauthorized actions. It is, I promise, only your welfare I have in mind."

"Most kind, Inspector," Fleming finally provided, seeing that Prescott was still staring disgustedly.

McCorkle turned and stepped back into the black-topped Oldsmobile. The policemen moved in from either side and herded Fleming and Prescott into the cruiser's rear. The ride home was as silent as the outgoing trip.

FLEMING SAID, "How much, we must ask ourselves, does he know?"

Prescott closed the house's front door behind them. He was shaking his head, still in dismay. "Did you hear? Such . . . malice. Such filthy, ignorant malice. I can never grow accustomed to it, Ian. Hatred based upon the gradations of fleshy pigment. It's this sort of vile thinking that has led to those WHITES ONLY signs you see all about. Slavery may belong to a page of history, but it's not forgotten. Its legacy is not difficult to find."

He was thinking of Martha, of course, thought Fleming. His racially forbidden lover.

Fleming sympathized, but there were more pressing issues. "Yes, Prescott. But we have, I think, just been blatantly warned off this matter by the police. Therefore, this Red Dwarf knows something of our activities. We must decide if we're to surrender here or push onward."

Chapter 22

IT DID not, in the end, amount to much of a debate. They *had* to press onward. The stakes in this were appallingly high. He and Prescott couldn't simply fold their cards now that the game was growing uncomfortably hot.

"How does McCorkle know we are making an independent investigation?" Prescott asked. They were sitting in his office chairs. The morning's coffee cups remained on the desk. Martha's absence was already apparent.

"He doesn't." Fleming puffed coolly on a Players. "At least, I would wager he doesn't. His mode of attack was hardly direct. He was likely hoping one or the other of us would provide him something concrete through a verbal indiscretion. You've seen interrogations, Prescott. You know the procedures."

Eyes that were no longer bloodshot, yet that were now heavy with unwanted memory, turned on Fleming. Both men had participated in their share of interrogations—as the inquisitors.

"I do know those *procedures*, Ian." His gaze shifted across the room to where the serving cart still sat, the bottle of port atop it. He sighed and looked pointedly away. "Yet I also wonder how the Red Dwarf knew of your visit."

"The police watching the house?" Fleming theorized aloud.

"Those weren't police that fled in the white Studebaker."

But Fleming was already dismissing his own hypothesis. "I should think someone simply must have leaked word to the authorities about my presence." By now he knew far better than to suggest that Martha might have had a hand in it. Besides, he was virtually convinced of her innocence himself, since the blond-haired woman had proven to be no fabrication.

"Who, then, do you suppose?" Prescott looked pensive.

"One of your Irregulars, I would say. We haven't made any great secret of my presence here."

"But, Ian, I've assured you of the Quarter's blanket of silence regarding the police—"

"Honor among thieves, Prescott? Come, come. And yes, I do gather that your Bourbon Street Irregulars aren't in truth *thieves*. At least not in any serious manner. But we've made ourselves conspicuous by putting out the word about Marquette and Faith Ullrich—regardless of your assurances. Someone has obviously talked. Now our race with Inspector McCorkle is even tighter. Who can find the murderers first?"

Prescott nodded somberly. Then he planted his palms on his chair's arms and levered himself decisively to his feet. "That is as good an argument as I require that we must *act*. We must move quicker. We know of the Cajun. McCorkle may not. That Cajun would no doubt stand out better in a crowd than the blond-haired woman. I suggest we aim toward him. I further suggest that Slim and Chopper will find him more swiftly than you and I."

Fleming stood as well, grinding his cigarette's end into the ashtray. "And if it's Slim and Chopper who talked to the police?"

Prescott bit back some immediate retort, then said, "You're correct, of course. There is the possibility. But I judge it very slight. If we do nothing but second-guess ourselves, *nothing* is what we shall end up doing."

It was a resolute tone, and Fleming was pleased by it. Here at least was the voice of this man as he had once been, his former self—determined, resourceful.

"In that case, Prescott, I will leave you to locate your Irregulars."

"Have you some pressing appointment of your own?"

"I thought it might prove interesting to pay a visit to this Harry Braniff character. We have an idea of what the police are doing. Braniff is the only other person who, ostensibly, has been investigating this case. I should like to discover if he's learned anything useful."

Prescott shook his head, saying, "I doubt very much he'll have anything. You heard Elliot. Braniff delivered nothing. And I know his reputation. He's a crook. But go on, if you wish. Give me a moment, I shall write down his address."

As Prescott went around his desk to consult a directory, Fleming saw those hazel eyes straying once more toward the bottle of port. He said nothing as Prescott passed him a slip of paper. The man would either make good his oath of alcoholic abstinence or he would fail. That the latter might mean disaster was only one more potential pitfall in this.

They parted outside the house, Prescott turning one way down Dauphine, Fleming the other.

The Faubourg Marigny lay just beyond Esplanade Avenue, which was a broad two-direction street split by a charming grassy median, upon which stood a file of stately oaks. Large, almost mansion-like houses abutted the roadway. It was humorously disconcerting crossing that thoroughfare on foot, needing to glance both ways for traffic, so accustomed had Fleming become to the Quarter's quaintly narrow one-way lanes in so short a time. Somehow he managed to get himself safely across.

This neighborhood was immediately and markedly different from the Quarter. Its streets wound and bent, crossing each other in a fashion more random than the normal grid patterns of American cities. It looked more modern and in generally better repair than the French Quarter, and yet, lacking that overall sense of long crumbling decay, it was also less charming.

The day had warmed even further, belying the two preceding chilly nights. This was certainly better than the ruthless bite of English winters.

Glancing about at street signs and following the directions Prescott had provided, he soon found Frenchman Street, a lazy stretch fronted by shops and houses. The workaday folk going about their business here were less exotic than the denizens of the Quarter.

Harry Braniff's office was a squat little storefront wedged beside a grocery. Dusty blinds were drawn over the windows, but the sign on the door was flipped to OPEN. Across the pebbled glass of that door read this legend in baroque gold script: HAROLD BRANIFF, LICENSED INVESTIGATOR.

Fleming turned the knob. Immediately he was struck by a smell of mildewing paper. He had entered a cramped little reception area. Cardboard boxes lined walls that needed fresh paint. A countertop with no one behind it split the small chamber in two, adding to the sense of constriction. A bell sat atop it, nearby a telephone.

Fleming stepped forward to slap the bell. From the room's rear a portly mustachioed man in a shabby dark suit emerged, offering an ingratiating smile as he came up to the other side of the counter. "Yes, s—"

Manfred Rexroth recognized him then. The artificial smile froze on his lips.

"Oh. You."

"Yes. I." Fleming fixed him with a steady gaze. "I'm the one that kept you out of harm's way this morning at Café du Monde. Do you recall?"

The stout man was still wearing the yellow rose in his buttonhole. He tried smiling again, with better sincerity, but his doughy face hadn't been made to wear the expression naturally.

"Of course I do," he said. "Wasn't that Prescott Quick who was with you? That fellow I was meeting with was being unreasonable. Very unreasonable. I couldn't tell you why he got into such a snit. Thank you for intervening. I'm indebted to you, naturally."

"Indebted?" Fleming gave Rexroth a somewhat steely smile of his own. "I like that. I also like a man who pays his debts."

Rexroth squirmed a bit at that. Trying to exert some control over the situation, he said, "Is there some business you'd like to conduct with us?"

"Us," Fleming said in a cool tone. "The rest of that plural includes, I presume, Mr. Harry Braniff?"

"Of course." The man's eyes were starting to dart about nervously, as they had at the café that morning when Elliot Dours had nearly assaulted him.

"Is Mr. Braniff in presently?"

"No." A tremble in his voice. It wasn't a lie, though, Fleming judged.

Very well, he thought. He planted his hands on the countertop, leaning forward. He reared above Rexroth by something near to half a foot, much of that owing to the man's poor posture.

"Perhaps you can help me."

"Yes. Perhaps." Obviously the idea wasn't especially agreeable to him, but just as obviously Fleming had him rather intimidated. It seemed a good idea to increase the pressure.

"It was Elliot Dours with whom you were meeting at Café du Monde this morning."

Rexroth swallowed. "I'm sorry, but I can't reveal the names of clients. I—"

"You haven't revealed his name, I've just said it, Elliot Dours. Who, along with his brother, Martin Dours, engaged Harry Braniff's services. And you, Mr. Rexroth, work for Harry Braniff."

The invocation of his name further unsettled the man. He suddenly seemed keenly aware that he and Fleming were quite alone here. He retreated a few inches from the counter.

"And who might you be, sir?" The tremble in his voice was worsening.

Fleming said blandly, "I work with Mr. Sherlock Holmes. My name is Dr. John Watson."

Rexroth attempted an amused chuckle at that, but it was far more disastrous than his smile had been.

"I want to know what you and Mr. Braniff have uncovered re-garding the case that Elliot and Martin Dours brought to you."

Rexroth actually gasped. For a moment his apprehension vanished, and he gave Fleming a deeply offended look. Rallying his courage, he said, "Now look! Whoever you are—you can't come barging in here like—like—" His hands made inarticulate pinwheels in the air. "It's outrageous! I can call the police—" One of those hands moved toward the telephone sitting on the counter.

"Pick up that phone," Fleming said darkly. "Please. Be my guest. Ring for the police. How long would you estimate before they arrive?"

Rexroth's hand went immobile above the receiver.

This was almost too easy, thought Fleming. Simple bullying. He hadn't planned on this tactic when he'd set out for this office. Truthfully he hadn't known what approach he planned to use to coax what he wanted from Harry Braniff. But Braniff wasn't here. Fate instead had presented him with this easily menaced fellow. One would be unwise not to make use of this happenstance.

Fleming turned, stepped to the door, turned the sign to CLOSED, and flipped the lock. Returning to the counter, he found Rexroth gaping, aghast that this situation had turned so unpleasant and po-tentially perilous in so short a time.

"Mr. Rexroth," he said in that same ominous tone, "you will divulge all you know. You will not equivocate or otherwise with-hold information. When we are finished here, I shall go on my way. Is that clear?"

He ran a hand through his thinning, mousy brown hair. "Yes. Y-yes, Mr., Mr.—"

"Doctor," said Fleming. "Doctor Watson." He silently admit-ted he was rather enjoying this. Braniff, after all, had defrauded Elliot and Martin Dours, two men seeking only the rightful retri-bution for their sister's murder. They had deserved better. And this Manfred Rexroth here was Braniff's lackey.

"Okay. All right. Yes." He cleared his throat. "Elliot and Martin

Dours came here, oh, a week ago. Their sister had been killed, you see—"

"Do spare me the preliminaries. I am acquainted with the case itself. I want to know what you and Braniff have uncovered concerning it."

"Right." Rexroth licked his lips, apparently calling the facts to his memory. "Well, the Dours brothers told us who the suspects were. A Miss Faith Ullrich and—. Oh, but you must know all that, too. Anyway. Mr. Braniff has, well, friends in the police department. He contacted them to see what they knew, since they were already investigating the case. Usually that's no bother. They do Mr. Braniff favors, and he returns them."

It sounded a dubious relationship. Did Braniff kick back a portion of his inflated fees to these "friends" on the police force, saving himself the fuss of actually making his own investigations? It was more than plausible. But Fleming said nothing.

Rexroth continued, "Well, all of a sudden everybody's lips were buttoned on this. It was strange. Mr. Braniff tried every policeman he knew and got nothing. Then a day later one of the detectives showed up here. He's a man named McCorkle, I think. I guess he takes on the big cases, the really nasty murder investigations and whatnot. He's supposed to be good. The best. But he came here alone—"

"Were you here?" Fleming asked.

"No. Actually, I'm not usually here in the office. But Mr. Braniff wanted this afternoon off for some reason, so I'm covering. Anyway. He told me later that McCorkle said to lay off. Just lay completely off the case."

"Did Inspector McCorkle tell him why?"

Rexroth shook his head. "But when somebody like him says to back away, you do it."

Fleming let out a breath. "And that's what you did. You abandoned the case, then and there. Somehow, though, it seems Mr. Braniff failed to inform Elliot and Martin Dours that he was no longer pursuing the matter. He also neglected to return to them their retainer."

The plump man swallowed again. "Y-yes. That's true." Then he blundered on into a whining explanation, "But—but it's Mr. Braniff's business. I work *for* him. I just do what he says. What else can I do? I'm an employee. I don't—I can't—it's not my—"

Fleming lifted a hand and was rewarded with immediate silence.

"If Mr. Elliot Dours wishes to reclaim the money he has wasted here, that's his affair. I have what I wanted. You've been most cooperative, Mr. Rexroth. I thank you for your time."

He turned, undid the lock with a sharp snap, and pulled open the door, eager to be away from the office's atmosphere of decomposing paper and the odious presence of Braniff's toady.

Behind him Rexroth called in a quivering voice that was also thick with relief that the episode was over, "Anytime, Dr. Watson!"

Chapter 23

THE QUEEN's blood was tropical, and it ran hot. The sweltering rhythms of her island homeland beat still in her veins. In childhood—for she *had* had a childhood, despite the semidivine status so many believed her to possess—she had known desperate poverty and all that it entailed: hunger, sickness, degradation. She had survived these things, and she would never know their like again, no matter what course her life took from here. No matter even if all she had caused to be built was sacked and burned. She would go on.

However, what she had created—the organization whose foundation she was—was precious to her. It was also immensely profitable. She was much more than its clandestine figurehead, though its parts could function for a time without her. She provided a central pivot for it, an anchor. The adoration that she absorbed from those around her was a congealing element.

Trouble was afoot in the city. This was nothing new. The white men were causing it. This, too, was nothing novel. The whites had magnanimously surrendered their sacred right to own black slaves (though it had taken this nation's bloodiest war to bring that about), but they had done so grudgingly, insincerely. Since they could no longer legally possess the Negro as one did a head of cattle, they instead kept him stripped of dignity, so as to make him less than human. It was an ongoing process.

Presently a peculiar campaign of persecution was under way, and it was beginning to find victims among Cleopatra's people.

At the moment Cleopatra was behaving in a most un-Queenly manner. There were many telephones in the house, the lines separate, all a part of the informational web that spun outward from her and across the city. She herself did not deign to speak through the instrument, but anything genuinely urgent was relayed to her. It was Corinne, the house servant who was in charge of these communications, who had brought her the latest bulletin in what was gearing up to be a veritable war.

The Queen was not taking the news well. She had gone into her parlor, which, as well as being sealed from the view of the outside world, was also virtually soundproof. She was stalking furiously about the chamber. She did not move like a cat now; rather, like an enraged lioness in a cage. Her cats had in fact fled to the corners, unnerved by this uncharacteristic display of temper from their mistress.

Cleopatra was spitting out curses as she paced. Not curses such as the people who venerated her so feared but simple vulgarities—coarse, curt, and to the point.

This was the price of carelessness. Two of her agents, men who had been in her employ for years, had been arrested on purely spurious charges less than an hour ago and were currently being interrogated by the police. They would, of course, say nothing to their captors, and just as certainly they would be treated brutally—kept from using the bathroom, questioned repetitively for hours on end, denied water, coffee, cigarettes, and whatever other simple comforts the white monsters would think to withhold. Very likely they would be treated to more serious physical abuse as well. The men would divulge no names, no locations, but they would suffer for their allegiance to the Queen.

In chess a queen needed pawns as a vanguard. So, too, did the Queen require active agents.

It was, in the end, a business, and she was the head of that enterprise. Many of the activities of this citywide business she had founded were, strictly, illegal, but the laws that said so belonged to the white world. Gambling and whoring were not in and of themselves immoral. Puritan ethics forbade such things, but most whites weren't Puritans. Not by any stretch of the imagination.

Cleopatra whipped her long-fingered hands through the air, clawing at an enemy that wasn't there but catching the long veils of red silk that hung about the chamber. A cat hissed its fear from a corner. She wore a loose-fitting lounging robe that was trimmed with sable. She spat more curses.

She had foreseen this. Those two bodies . . . the nearly headless woman, the mutilated man, both white. Here now was the backlash of those murders.

The Blood Red Devil. That was the name she'd given to Inspector McCorkle, who, her informants within the police department had told her, was now heading the murder investigations. Then those very useful—and very well paid—informants had abruptly gone mute.

Her two agents currently in police custody were key to the floating dice games that ran in perpetuity in a particular district of the city. Those games were now suspended; no money was coming in from them. Both men were also devotees of the magic many said she embodied. They had slipped up, despite the warnings she had ordered to be issued throughout the organization. The police had netted them—not because of the branch of the gambling syndicate they operated, but because of the religion they practiced.

"It's a goddamn crusade!" the Queen cried vehemently.

She spun to a halt, the hem of her robe twirling. Her chest rose and fell, her ageless features distorted by her rage. Her jade eyes blazed. No one would call her beautiful at the moment. She gathered herself, drawing on the adamantine will that had built the empire she ruled. She went to the parlor's door.

"Corinne," she at last called, her voice smoothly modulated once more.

The heavyset woman appeared immediately.

"Contact Hush," Cleopatra ordered. "It's time our enemy truly understood what prices must be paid. We will deal with the two Englishmen at last."

PRESCOTT PUT TOGETHER a bachelor-like meal of sandwiches from last night's cold cuts. He seemed quite lost in his own kitchen, searching cupboards with a bewildered air. His attempt to brew coffee afterward was relatively successful, though he left a remarkable mess in his wake.

They took their coffees into Prescott's office. Fleming recounted his visit to Harry Braniff's place of business. Prescott chuckled. Evening was darkening the city beyond the lacy curtains. They lounged in the leather chairs.

"I would say Manfred Rexroth got what he deserved, but I imagine he deserves far worse."

"I merely gave him a fright," Fleming said, though it had felt good to take some positive action. "Still, I wonder at what he said regarding McCorkle—about the Red Dwarf ordering Braniff off the investigation."

"We had a similar experience, you'll recall."

"I do. But why is McCorkle making such efforts?"

Prescott said, "I've found that the police do not always appreciate the activities of private investigators. Likely the Red Dwarf merely wants the field cleared."

"Yes. Likely." Fleming nodded. "And you? Did you ferret out Slim and Chopper?"

"That pair does not keep office hours. They are easier to find by night. However, I did locate Slim at the river. He agreed to corral Chopper and meet with us tonight." Prescott frowned. "I also made the usual rounds, checking with the other various Irregulars to see if anyone had any useful information."

"And learned?" Fleming sensed the news would not be good.

"Nothing of Faith and Marquette. Those two, of course, may not be in the Quarter at all. This is a sizable city, with many warrens in which to hide. However"—Prescott's gaze sharpened—"I do have information on someone described by several individuals as a sleek-figured, blond-haired woman wearing dark glasses and a long coat."

Fleming's brows rose. "Indeed?"

"The Irregulars are a veritable army of unnoticed eyes and ears, as you surely know by now. Presently they are tuned to Faith Ullrich and Gerard Marquette, in hope of collecting some reward money. However, they see what they see and hear what they hear."

"Yes, understood," Fleming said.

"Apparently the blond-haired woman, still unidentified, has been doing some circulating herself. She is making inquiries about the two of us, by name."

Fleming asked levelly, "What sort of inquiries?"

"The sort we don't want made, dear chap." Prescott smiled tiredly now, abruptly looking every bit his age. "She is trying to ascertain what we're up to. Asking around at taverns I frequent. Offering money for information. Essentially, precisely what we are doing. She is trying to use the same covert network of the French Quarter to get a fix on us."

First McCorkle, now this. It was going from bad to worse. "What success has she had?"

"None, I'm told. No one knows this woman. To be trusted within Quarter society one must first have established oneself. One must be a fixed and known quantity. I, over these past few years, have become that. My reputation is firm. I am well liked. This anonymous woman, however, is an absolute outsider as far as the Quarter's denizens are concerned. It is highly unlikely anyone will breach the general code of silence for her, no matter what amount of money she offers as incentive."

"But the fact that she is trolling for information about us is disquieting enough."

"I agree."

Fleming set down his coffee cup on the desk, pushing it away. His eyes turned meaningfully toward the bottle of port.

"Did you want a real drink?" Prescott asked, following his gaze. "I forget I'm still the host here. I'm afraid I won't be joining you. See? My teetotaling resolve has lasted some hours now." He smiled in mock pride, but beneath the expression was something brittle and pained, perhaps lingering mortification over his state of drunkenness from the previous night.

"A glass of port would be marvelous," said Fleming.

Prescott stood and crossed toward the bottle.

"I received a call just before you returned from Braniff's," he said, filling a tulip-shaped glass.

"From one of your Irregulars?"

"No. A call for my services. Which I had to turn aside, of course. I'm afraid my practice has suffered during this adventure." Prescott returned with the glass.

"Not irrevocably, I hope," Fleming said, taking it. It might not be the most sensitive thing he could do—drinking in Prescott's presence—but the man was either going to commit to his temporary sobriety or not.

"I hope not as well. No, don't fret. Ironically, if we resolve this matter, it shall likely be my greatest accomplishment ever as a private detective—and one I also shall never be able to boast about. Drink up, Ian, while I look on longingly. Then it will be near enough time to rendezvous with Slim and Chopper. I have one of those feelings, I'm afraid, one of those grim and grisly intuitions . . . the sort I would get in the old days when something was about to go seriously awry. Or when time was running dangerously short." A perceptible shudder went through his lanky frame. "Do you ever get a feeling like that?"

Answering with blunt honesty, Fleming said, "I've felt it since we began this, Prescott." Then he drained off the glass of port in a single, rather gauche swallow.

Chapter 24

IT WAS another lively night. More revelers milled haphazardly about Bourbon Street, the French Quarter's primary artery. Quite a number now were costumed or masked, as if some freakish mass metamorphosis were occurring, changing ordinary people into wizards, devils, ballerinas, sultans, jesters, and all manner of outlandish borrowed identities. Once more the night was charged with giddy alcoholic festivity, and beneath that merrymaking surface there seemed an essence that was almost decadent, as if the scene had the potential to deteriorate in rapid order into an orgy of absolute excess.

The bar was on St. Ann Street, and Chopper and Slim were huddled inevitably over a game of pool. Prescott earned an incredulous look from the bartender when he ordered a soda water for himself. A rum and some Kentucky whiskey lured the two Irregulars to a corner table. Slim seemed in a foul mood, grumbling over what had been a particularly strenuous day on the docks. He latched on eagerly to the new assignment that Prescott posed, which was the locating of the Cajun who had assaulted Fleming the previous night. Fleming provided as thorough a description as he could. Chopper, the more reserved of the two, considered the proposal thoughtfully.

"That's all the detail you've got? You don't want to tell us what this guy's mixed up in or why you're after him?" Chopper asked these questions quite blandly.

"We're really not at liberty to divulge more," said Prescott. "Do bear in mind, though, that this man is dangerous."

The mid-forties Portuguese half-breed shrugged.

"Aw, c'mon," Slim said impatiently. "They ain't askin' us to

bag him, just spot him. And we've worked offa less before. A big
hulkin' coon-ass wanderin' 'round the Quarter. Hell, how hard
could he be to find?"

Fleming imagined that that off-color "coon-ass" meant "Cajun," but sometimes there was no telling with American lingo.

"He's not going to want to be found, Slim."

"Nobody wants to be found down here, Chopper. That's why
people come here. So what? Let's go find him anyways!"

The duo soon agreed. Slim didn't ask for an advance this time.
Fleming wondered if that meant the lad had temporarily stabi-
lized his finances.

They left the two Irregulars at the bar. Passing through Jackson Square, Prescott accosted the sandy-haired cook with the
missing front teeth once again. Curt was his name, Fleming recalled. After a moment of friendly banter between him and
Prescott, Curt said, "I bumped into that blond dame las' night.
Yuh heard 'bout her? One that's been goin' 'round askin' 'bout
you two?"

"So we've heard," Prescott said. "What did you say to this
young lady?"

Curt's lips peeled back briefly from his gapped teeth in dis-
taste. "Say? Didn't say nothin', Mr. Quick. 'Stead I asked *her*
what the hell business she had pokin' her nose 'round where it
weren't wanted. She tried flashin' cash at me, but I told her to go
jump in the lake." He proceeded to describe the woman in immediately recognizable terms. "Heavy makeup, too. Not, y'know,
done up like a streetwalker or nothin', just thick, so's yuh
couldn't really tell what she looked like 'neath it and those sunglasses she was wearin' at night. Who the hell is this broad, Mr.
Quick?"

"I would be curious to know myself, Curt. I thank you."

"Anytime."

Prescott gave Fleming a grave look as they turned out of the
square. Fleming nodded; yes, it was serious indeed.

The revelers were moving in unpredictable flurries, spilling from the bars and clubs, merging and mingling in the street. Jazz beat beneath the scene, an appropriately chaotic pulse, defining the high-spirited and increasingly drunken steps of the waltz. Disguised, the celebrants obviously felt free of their normal identities—and therefore of the strictures of those lives. As he and Prescott attempted to ford Bourbon Street once more, they found the going exponentially more difficult. Bodies collided carelessly. People danced, twirled, gyrated. Voices lifted.

Fleming was jarred rather roughly by a stumbling figure made up as a toreador. Annoyed, he turned to rebuff the man, who was already being swallowed up by the now quite dense crowd. Before he could say anything, he was bumped hard from behind, which nearly carried him off his feet. Prescott, who was leading the way, appeared to be encountering similar difficulties.

This time Fleming pivoted sharply, coming round with his elbow strategically aimed. One good jolt deserved another.

That elbow was stopped in midswing—stopped, caught, and held in what felt to be a very large and very powerful grip. Instantly Fleming reversed the move, managing to break loose. But he was in a solid ring of bodies now, Prescott cut off from view. These were not costumed revelers. They were men—black men, all of them—dressed as laborers.

Fleming's move for his Enfield was admirably fast and utterly hopeless. The men were so tight about him now that he would have been unable to even raise the pistol. Hands caught him, many hands this time, grasping his arms, locking them at his back. As he was forcefully spun around, yet another hand clapping over his mouth, he came face to face with the individual who had apparently first seized his elbow.

Actually, face to face was imprecise. Fleming found himself nearly crushed against the heavy, broad chest. He thought fleetingly that it was the Cajun; but no. This man was a Negro as well, a large man, perhaps most distinguished by his utterly hairless skull and the look of cold remorselessness he wore. Unlike the others, he was well dressed in a fine suit.

No obvious orders were given, though Fleming had no doubts whatever that this man was in charge; but working as from a single mind, his encircling captors manhandled him helplessly forward. He was unable to move a limb in any effective way, much less raise a call for help past the hand stifling his lips.

Without fuss or useful resistance Fleming was borne away from the costumed throng, their happy caterwauling echoing through the streets.

HE WAS NOT surprised, really, when he was bundled into the back of the immaculately kept white Studebaker with whitewall tires parked a short distance off Bourbon Street. He'd been relieved of his revolver and thoroughly searched for other weapons.

Instantly Prescott was thrust in through the opposite door. Fleming questioned the unexpected surge of relief he felt at seeing his colleague. Surely it would have been better if one of them had escaped this abduction. Still, it was good to find Prescott relatively unharmed, though he appeared quite ruffled.

Two of the black men in laborers' clothes crushed onto the Studebaker's rear seat, one on either side, guarding the doors. A man was already at the wheel, and the engine started immediately. Before the auto pulled away, the heavy hairless individual swung himself into the passenger seat. With that the car swooped away into the street.

The blacks on the backseat were statue-silent, with faces as inexpressive. Fleming didn't need to be told that any attempt to lunge for the door or make some desperate signal for help through the windows would be looked upon unfavorably. The Studebaker was accelerating smoothly, not so fast as to attract undue attention but making rapidly for the border of the Quarter.

Glancing surreptitiously behind, Fleming saw a second Studebaker—this one black but no less pristine—following hard on their bumper. Its front license plate was blurred with streaks of grease. No doubt the balance of their abductors had climbed into this vehicle.

"Are you all right?" Fleming asked Prescott, keeping his tone soft and level.

Prescott, jammed tightly against him on his right, seemed preoccupied trying to draw a full breath. His hazel eyes quivered slightly in their sockets, and his face was wan.

"You should be unharmed, Mr. Quick." The large bald man in the dark blue suit was turning about in his seat, eyes like flint regarding the two white passengers. His voice grated harshly, so faint as to be nearly drowned by the engine and yet, somehow, conveying a stolid authority. "You as well, Mr. Fleming. If either of you is injured, say so."

They remained silent. Plainly it had been meant to demonstrate that the raspy-voiced man knew their identities. And the truth was that Fleming hadn't been unduly mistreated during what was undeniably a *very* professional kidnapping.

Prescott at last seemed to find that crucial swallow of air. Color returned to his cheeks. He gave Fleming a nod, indicating he was indeed all right. For the moment at least.

Fleming automatically noted a passing street sign: St. Claude. It was a wide boulevard, and they were moving down it speedily, sliding through the traffic, hitting every stoplight on the green, as though even this detail had been planned.

After a few minutes they turned off this thoroughfare, onto narrower residential streets. These residences weren't much to look at—ramshackle housing with poorly tarred roofs and peeling paint. Negro children skipped rope on the corners. The pervasive sense of poverty was palpable, the sort of indigence so common on Jamaica. They wended their way further into the slum.

The streets were marked erratically, but Fleming mentally inscribed distinguishing landmarks and street signs when he saw them; not with specific purpose in mind, not with thoughts of retracing his steps at some future point, presuming he survived this episode. It was merely procedure. It was his training. This was what one did in just such a crisis. Though his spying days were over, what he had been taught was not lost.

Throughout their jaunt he had not seen a single police car, though how he would have called attention to himself he didn't know. It was moot now. The Studebaker turned onto yet another street, this one conspicuously different from those through which they'd just passed. Here the houses—though of no different design than the rest—were in fine repair. They stood straight, without garbage in their yards. Their coats of paint were fresh.

The automobile slowed and stopped. Behind, Fleming heard the black Studebaker's brakes, then its doors opening. A rank of the black men took positions along both sides of the white Studebaker.

The hairless man seemed to give another of his silent and unseen orders, and Fleming and Prescott were both drawn out of the car. Fleming's arms were once more efficiently held immobile at his back, but this time he was permitted to move his own feet. He was being led toward one of the houses, indistinguishable from the rest—at least until they reached its gate, where two more black men rose from behind a row of impeccable hedges. Each had a shotgun in hand. Fleming had the distinct sense there were many more such sentries in the vicinity.

The bald one in the dark suit went forward and parleyed. Only the harsh scratchiness of his voice could be heard, not the words. Evidently they were sufficient; Fleming and Prescott were marched up onto the porch. Their escorts disappeared at the same moment new sentinels sprang up—seemingly from nowhere—and maneuvered the two white Englishmen inside. Only the big hairless man came as well.

Inside, Fleming had a glimpse of a foyer, of polished hardwood floors and framed watercolors on the walls; then they moved deeper into the house. He smelled potent incense burning and heard the distinct, plaintive meow of a cat. He didn't struggle against his escorts. He had tested the holds of the two men who held his arms behind him, enough to know that any of the fast escape maneuvers he knew had a low chance of success. Prescott, being similarly ushered at his side, was also putting up no fight.

Then they were through another door, this one giving onto a space as dark as country night. This effect was intensified when the door closed smartly at their backs. At the same instant Fleming felt his arms released.

He flexed his hands, recirculating blood rushing to them, warming them. This place, too, was warm, humidly so, as though the sultry climate of his island home was inexplicably contained within these walls.

And it was not, in fact, pitch black in here. Candles guttered, spattering murky light onto tall veils of red that slowly undulated, but there was no exterior light here, no windows outlined by the outside streetlamps. Looking behind, he could not even detect the frame of the door through which they'd just passed. Their escorts, too, had effectively vanished.

He studied the space. Had they been brought here to be murdered? Would his and Prescott's corpses become photographic subjects, heads defiled by an axe blade, their murder scenes marked by crosses of chicken bones and black feathers?

With a cool effort of will he turned his thoughts away from such fearful wonderings. Desperate situations became truly hopeless only when one let panic take the lead. Fleming wasn't one to fall victim to fear.

His eyes were adjusting to the very weak light. The room's candles had been placed with purpose; they threw limited illumination that was further disrupted by the tapestries of what looked to be red silk that were hung all about. Everything was placed so that what stood at the center of the space remained frustratingly obscure—and yet, manifestly, *this* was the focus of the entire room.

The seat was atop a dais of some sort. It was more than a chair. It seemed a throne—high-backed, broad-armed, intentionally imposing. Even standing in faint silhouette as it was, Fleming could see that it was elaborately carved, the design sensationally baroque. The arms appeared to be shaped as birds.

It was occupied. The figure wore white, and the material seemed to be diaphanous. It draped a narrow body. The figure sat in an attitude of . . . what? Command? Divine detachment? Fleming didn't know. Yet it *did* communicate a startling presence, immobile and silent though it was.

"It"? Hardly. This, he knew with a fundamental certainly, was a woman.

Something brushed Fleming's ankle, the contact so unexpected he started but didn't cry out. Looking downward, he just made out the shape of a long-haired cat the color of cigar ash. It meandered over toward Prescott, who did let out a startled inarticulate gasp when it similarly grazed by him.

The white-clad woman on the throne was studying them. Fleming knew this as surely as if her eyes shot tracers in the dimness. He felt those eyes surveying, weighing, reckoning, judging. He felt . . . exposed.

Again he shook off his own thoughts. This entire scene was calculated. It was manipulated for effect as certainly as a Hollywood melodrama was meant to make American housewives sniffle into their hankies. He would not give in to such theatrics, cleverly contrived though they might be. They had been brought here for a purpose—something, surely, worthy of the efforts that had been made on their behalf. Fleming resolved to stand silent, to bide his time, to show no card, though for all intents and purposes he had been dealt no hand here.

Prescott, however, had evidently settled on a different tack.

"What in God's name is this?" he spat out. "Waste no more of our time, whoever you may be. Get on with it. I demand it!"

It was an astonishing bit of bravado, especially since Fleming was sure Prescott was more frightened than he. He didn't think such an aggressive offensive wise, but it was done. Fleming waited for a response.

The sleek feminine shape shifted on its seat, the movement slight but unmistakably languorous and fluid, sliding its delicate weight from one side to the other. The head—a dark face above the white collar of the gown—tipped a few degrees. The invisible eyes were still inspecting.

"Hush."

Her voice, as silky as the fluttering draperies, carried all throughout the chamber through some trick of acoustics, though she'd spoken with only a soft, unhurried breath. Fleming thought the word an admonishment meant for Prescott, but immediately the large bald man, who had faded from sight, reappeared a reverential distance from the foot of the throne, head bowed. Candlelight shone ghostly across his skull.

"Have you not made our guests feel welcome?" It was a modulated voice, gliding effortlessly through its octaves. The tone was assured, beyond that of someone who merely commanded the present moment. This woman's dominion was much greater, much grander, Fleming thought. Or so she believed, at least.

"I asked if they were unharmed, my Queen," rasped the black man in the dark suit. Hush—of course, his *name*. Appropriate. His manner was abject.

"Well, that's a start," said the woman. Unleashed laughter frolicked somewhere behind her words. There was a powerful sensualness to her that couldn't entirely be accounted for by the tones she employed or her posture in the chair. Fleming found himself wondering at the slender body that gauzy wrap must contain. The very air seemed to be swimming with motes of energy, with a barely latent sexuality that had no proof of itself but for the reaction it was now firing in Fleming's cells.

Sweat came to his forehead and underarms. There was some odor here, perhaps a lingering trace of the incense he'd smelled earlier. Something was pulling powerfully at his senses, widening them, opening a chasm before him and inviting him to jump in. He turned his head sharply on his neck, then back in the opposite direction. He squared his shoulders. This carefully orchestrated setting was influencing him, despite his resolve to remain detached. He would not succumb. He cinched tight his responses, holding them in check with a white-knuckled mental pressure.

Nonetheless, when the woman addressed him directly, he felt her voice purr through his marrow. Hush had once more vanished into the shadows.

"Mr. Fleming."

Whatever else she was, she was mannerly, he thought. No reason not to reciprocate.

"Yes. May I know who addresses me?"

"You *may* . . ." Promises waited behind that, along with more dormant laughter.

"You referred to us as guests," he continued, pleased at the calm stability of his own tone. Prescott, silent now after making his forceful play, anxiously eyed him sidelong. "Then it is incumbent upon you, as host, to provide us with the basic necessities. At the moment your name would do."

At last her laughter came free, cantering out into the open like a wild mare. Her chest rose and fell in the chamber's murk. The laughing notes, carrying once more to every corner, struck like hoofbeats, rhythmic, then slowing. Finally they stopped.

"My name has never been uttered on these shores, Mr. Fleming. Names are mighty things. They put shape to blood and bone. They mark men so that they may be found later."

Another cat rubbed past Fleming's leg. This time he did not flinch.

"However," she added, "that you are guests is quite correct.

Therefore, I will give you the easiest of the titles I wear. I am, Mr. Fleming, Mr. Quick . . . Cleopatra."

Again, appropriate. Hush had addressed her as "my Queen." The tendrils of fear Fleming had felt earlier were evaporated.

"It is a pleasure, then," he said, determined to deal with this woman from a sure footing. Perhaps he was holding some cards after all. And one didn't need every ace in the deck to play a hand.

"And mine, gentlemen." Her hands came together before her, fingers steepling; and though she was little more than a suggestion of feminine form, those fingers were doubtlessly long and exquisite. "You have had our attention for some while now."

"You've been watching us?" This came from Prescott, the question quavering somewhat in his throat.

The two black men who had followed them on Fleming's first night in the city, the white Studebaker in which they'd fled: It had been a surveillance operation, of course.

"We've been watching *you*, Mr. Quick," said the Queen. "If any man was going to act independently in this, we judged it would be you. We were pleased when Mr. Fleming arrived, presumably to aid you. You have a personal stake in this. We have known of your involvement in the murders from the start."

"Involvement . . . ?" Prescott retreated an uneasy—and probably unconscious—half step.

"Why, yes. You received photographs of Angelina Marquette's mistreated corpse."

This Cleopatra, then, decidedly *did* hold cards; and they'd not yet seen the best of them, Fleming would estimate. Prescott's jaw was working silently. He looked confused now, as well as frightened. Fleming cut in, "I confess I still don't understand why you sent those photos."

"I had nothing to do with that girl's murder!" Prescott cried out. Plainly this scene was getting to him, as it was surely meant to. "I was sent those damned photos. I didn't ask for them, I didn't want them. I've wanted nothing to do with this—this evil, nightmarish—*damn* it! God *damn* it to hell!"

He was unraveling. He was a man only tenuously held together under the best of circumstances.

Fleming reached out and closed a hand tightly over his shoulder. His frame trembled. One of the felines, not liking Prescott's raised voice, hissed from nearby.

"Mr. Fleming," Cleopatra said, "no one in my organization is responsible for those photographs."

"Then how do you know of them?" Fleming countered, keeping a steadying hand on Prescott. Now was not the moment for a breakdown.

"Because the police know. Mr. Quick reported to them when the pictures appeared in his mail."

Contacts on the police force? Fleming wondered. It made more sense that this woman—or those who served under her—was behind the murders and the sending of those photos. Surely here were the sought-after voodoo practitioners, and this Cleopatra was their voodooienne, the high priestess. Somehow Faith Ullrich and her paramour Gerard Marquette had become involved with this evidently well-organized group, and two grisly murders had resulted. It was sound, logical. There remained only loose ends. And unfortunately both he and Prescott qualified as such.

Yet . . . the intrigue made no ultimate sense. Why *had* those photos been sent? Angelina Marquette's nearly decapitated body to Prescott, Martin Dours's butchered corpse to Fleming. Why?

And no mention had in fact been made of that second photo, which had found its way to Jamaica.

"You see, Mr. Fleming, your suppositions are crumbling before your eyes." The Queen's voice was so controlled, so fine, that he couldn't say with certainty if it carried an accent. Yet some hint, some nuance between the words, made him think of places tropical, of gleaming Caribbean waters.

The sweat was beginning to make his flesh itch. The chamber's sultriness was only another effect, he knew, meant to add to the sealed-in claustrophobia of the dark space.

Staring straight for where her eyes must be, Fleming said, "I believe you are responsible for the murders of Angelina Marquette and Martin Dours. Do you deny this?"

He heard several sharp intakes of breath throughout the room. Her guards, shocked at his impudence. But now was the time to lay the last bets, before one player or the other raked in the pot.

There was another pantomime of supple movement from the throne, and an object suddenly rattled lightly onto the wood floor at Fleming's feet.

He let go of Prescott and stooped to collect it. He felt what it was before he'd brought it up into the feeble light. A surge of revulsion went through him, and he heard Prescott's appalled gasp. The black feathers were tied to the chicken bone cross by red thread.

"What do you make of that, Mr. Fleming?"

"I imagine you could guess."

"Imagine. Guess. Assume. The ways of the small-minded, the ignorant, the bigot."

"I do not belong to any of those categories," said Fleming.

"You recognize that object?"

"I do. It bears a striking resemblance to the items that were found with the two corpses in question." The thing felt unclean to him, even merely pinched as it was between thumb and fore finger. "But you know that."

"Yes. However, I am curious how you know of Mr. Martin Dours, though. It's been kept out of the newspapers."

The photo he'd received. *Ghost of Christmas Past.* She didn't know about those, thought Fleming.

"Perhaps Mr. Quick's informants in the police department have kept him abreast," Cleopatra continued. "No matter. You believe that object in your hand to be damning evidence in the case of these murders. You believe . . . what exactly, I wonder.

That it has an occult significance? It's the calling card of the killer or killers?"

He waited. Was this to be his cross, after all? Had she waited until now to order one of her minions forward with the axe?

"That," said the Queen, willowy body sliding forward on the flamboyant seat, "was made from the leftovers of the chicken soup my cook prepared two nights ago. The feathers come from a pillow's stuffing."

Fleming's gaze returned automatically to the object. In this new context the thing was . . . almost comical. A Halloween prop.

"It has no significance." The luxuriant purr had left her voice, replaced by cool metallic tones. "It is imbued with nothing. It is a spiritless thing. A hunk of matter. It means *nothing*. Except what imagination might give it."

He tossed it aside. It clattered again faintly on the floorboards. "Why tell us?"

"The police have made assumptions. Two corpses, savagely massacred. A bauble like that one at each scene. The white policemen draw their conclusions. They conjure the Blood Red Devil to assail us."

Fleming frowned at this last non sequitur. Then he realized. "McCorkle, you mean."

"Yes. That heinous little man."

He thought of the inspector's words in that cul-de-sac in City Park, his blatantly racist convictions.

"He is . . . troubling us," Cleopatra said. "This is his excuse to wage a racial and religious war. He is in a position to carry it out. But we are not defenseless."

Fleming didn't doubt this. However, all was hardly clear. "I still do not know who you represent."

"It isn't necessary that you do. We have our interests. The police have theirs. Those interests do not always overlap."

A crime syndicate, then. It certainly had the earmarks, and this pseudo-priestess was apparently its head.

"McCorkle and the police," Fleming said, "they're causing problems for your organization. You are being harassed for crimes you didn't commit. For the murders." If the claim was true, it fit the facts of this scenario. Or nearly so.

"Correct."

"But what do you want of us?"

"Come nearer."

Prescott nearly made to reach for him, perhaps to hold him in place, but he let his hand drop back to his side. Fleming, very aware of the guards who had brought them here and however many others were unseen in this chamber, took slow steps forward. Nearer to the throne, nearer to the woman. Perspiration was hot upon his body.

The white gown was beaded with pearls at the wrists and neckline. The Queen's flesh was dusky dark. The elegant arc of her face was caught by the simmering candlelight, the curve from chin to earlobe. He halted at the foot of the dais.

"You are acting in this matter," she said. "You and Mr. Quick both. Your allegiance isn't with the white devils, with the police. You are your own men. I respect that."

He inclined his head to acknowledge that. He had to will himself to straighten afterward; it felt quite proper to bow in her presence, perhaps even to prostrate oneself. But he was not a worshiper here, he reminded himself.

"We will act against the evil being committed against our kind. We will do what we can. But there is a deeper purpose in all of this, and you two will answer that purpose."

"How so?" Involuntarily his voice had reduced to a whisper barely louder than Hush's.

"Give me your handkerchief."

He didn't have to will his hand to move. It dipped immediately into his pocket. He saw only when he held the handkerchief out to her that it was the one he'd used to stanch his bleeding scalp after the Cajun had shattered that bottle against it. Even in the dim light he could see it was speckled liberally with his dried blood.

Cleopatra's hand floated out and plucked the square of cloth from his fingers.

"You will act as we cannot. Your destiny is marked. We could only fail in the task that has been set aside for you and Mr. Quick."

"And we will not fail?"

A single note of laughter rippled through her svelte form. So near to her, Fleming felt it as a spreading tingle of gooseflesh.

"You may well fail," she said. "But only you might succeed."

She still held the handkerchief before her. Now her other hand rose, gathering the cloth into a fist, hiding it.

"Your fortune is to try," said the Queen.

Her fingers—long and long-nailed—now reached into that closed fist and slowly uncoiled the crumpled handkerchief, drawing it out. She dangled it for him to see.

It was unsoiled, unbloodied.

"It is you, Mr. Fleming, on whom the worst weight of this sits. But without Mr. Quick you'll have no chance at all. You must do this thing together. Do you understand?"

"I hear your words." He reached for the handkerchief, and she released it. There was nothing distinctive about the item; it was not monogrammed. Sleight-of-hand could account for the substitution, particularly in this light. He tucked it back into his jacket without examining it closer.

"Go now, Mr. Fleming, Mr. Quick." The Queen settled back into her seat, hands lolling on the carved arms. "There are forces working in your favor, but you would not believe in them. You are, after all, merely white men. So I will give you words from your own world." A single long nail tapped the armrest. "Good luck."

Chapter 25

OUTSIDE, ONLY the white Studebaker waited. The other was gone, along with the cohort of blacks dressed as laborers. Not even the house's sentinels came past the front door as Fleming and Prescott stepped out onto the porch. Only Hush remained with them.

The large man moved wordlessly down the steps, and they followed.

Fleming drew in long drafts of the night air. The lamplit street was preternaturally bright after the Queen's audience chamber. A part of him was amazed to find himself whole, unharmed, walking away from the scene apparently scot-free. He had been braced for much worse on the journey here, and being in Cleopatra's presence, so close to the woman as she'd handled the handkerchief . . . the moment had been potent and perilous. He knew that a word from her could have meant his life. But she hadn't intended him harm. She had instead informed him of his "destiny."

With the poise of a chauffeur, Hush opened the Studebaker's rear door. Yet this man was no mere driver, no white man's servant.

"Gentlemen, I will drive you home," the black man rasped, no obvious emotion in his voice.

They got in. Prescott was gazing about with almost shell-shocked eyes. He wasn't up to this sort of strain, Fleming thought. He was trying to function under exceptional conditions without the succor of either alcohol or his lover, Martha.

Hush took the wheel. Before starting the engine, he turned about, holding out Fleming's Enfield and Prescott's derringer, butts first. The men reclaimed their weapons. Fleming noted that the revolver was still loaded before slipping it into its holster.

Hush started the auto and guided them smoothly away, unconcerned about the two armed men at his back.

Fleming felt drained. It had been an extraordinary episode.
Among other things it had widened the scope of this affair. Those
two murders were causing even more fallout than he'd suspected.
However, the fact that McCorkle was inconveniencing the work-
ings of a criminal organization didn't concern Fleming overmuch.
Even so, it didn't make the little racist any more admirable.

Cleopatra had pronounced Fleming fated to his role in this.
He was—what?—the champion, the crusader. He and only he
was meant to resolve the matter. Balderdash. Worse, it was
mumbo jumbo dressed up as divinely revealed truth. Cleopatra
wanted him to find the murderers; of course she did. It was
purely self-interest.

But she had also said, *We will do what we can*. What had that
meant?

The Studebaker glided along through the ghetto's streets.
Fleming recognized a few of the landmarks he had noted on the
way in. Hush apparently was indeed driving them home.

The chance to ask a question of this man—or of anyone in the
Queen's organization—might not come again. Fleming put a cigarette to his lips and lit it. Then he offered the open case over the
seats.

"Care for one?"

"Thank you. I don't." Hush slid down his window a few
inches. The thread of gray smoke from the cigarette's tip
streamed toward the gap.

"If Mr. Quick and I are to be responsible for concluding this
business," Fleming said, measuring out the words, "what roles,
may I ask, do you people intend to play? That of mere specta-
tors?"

The flinty eyes didn't shift toward the rearview, staying on
the road. Fleming thought the man simply meant not to answer;
then in his strangled whisper he said, "Inspector McCorkle has

sanctioned widespread arrests in the cases of these two murders. He is employing false charges and will possibly go as far as to order his officers to perjure themselves. Nevertheless, I personally have amassed a body of evidence pointing to the illegality of his methods. I have done this at the Queen's behest. Tomorrow it is my intention to file a civil suit against Inspector McCorkle and the New Orleans Police Department."

"Is that all?" Fleming retorted, somewhat dismayed. "You're going to *sue?*" It seemed almost feeble compared to what the Queen was asking of him.

"We are restricted in our responses, Mr. Fleming. We can't wage outright war against the police. We can't even, under the present circumstances, aid you in your task. McCorkle is more likely to grab up our people." Hush turned the car back onto St. Claude Avenue. "So we fight white law enforcers with white law."

Fleming had to concede the logic, but it made nothing easier for him and Prescott. Presently Prescott was gazing out the window like a daydreamer.

"You're going to file the suit yourself?" Fleming said. "I didn't realize you were a lawyer."

"What white man would assume I was?" said Hush.

FLEMING CHECKED HIS dressing in the bathroom mirror. The cut beneath the bandage over his temple was well scabbed over by now and showed no signs of having become infected. If it left a scar, it would be a small one. The area was still tender to his carefully probing fingertips. He would heal. Yet that didn't detract from what Prescott had pointed out the other night: If chance granted him the opportunity to pay back something of what that massive Cajun had given him, he would not squander it.

He also took a moment to examine the handkerchief that Cleopatra had handed back to him. It *looked* like the original, minus the bloodstains, but that was hardly conclusive. It had been a trick, of course—a nimble-fingered one but a trick nonetheless. He slipped it into his pocket.

He found Prescott in the kitchen, once more sorting through cabinets like a man hoping to stumble upon worthwhile salvage.

"Prescott, I should like to divide whatever fees you are paying to Slim and Chopper."

Prescott waved a dismissing hand. "Oh, that's not really necessary, old boy."

"Necessary or not, it's fair."

"Very well. When all this is done, I shall write up a bill for your half," Prescott said rather indifferently. "Will that suit you?"

"That will be fine."

Prescott rummaged through another cabinet, then closed the door with a sharp bang. "Bloody hell. I've no idea where anything is. I wish Martha . . ." He trailed off.

He had somewhat recovered himself from their strange and frightening visit to the Queen. There seemed little Fleming could do, however, in the way of offering comfort over the absence of his lover.

Prescott of a sudden was eyeing him sharply. Then, seeming to snatch the thought from Fleming's mind, he said, "You know about us, don't you? Yes, of course you do, else I would not ask. Martha and myself."

"I consider it none of my business," Fleming said neutrally.

"That's mannerly of you. Perhaps I should explain, nonetheless."

"Unnecessary."

But Prescott rolled onward. "Martha quite simply rescued me, Ian. Body and soul. I came to this city looking to give my existence some sort of renewed meaning. I had been a military man, I had been a spy, I had been . . . an assassin. Now I needed to redefine myself. You invented yourself afresh as a journalist. It seems to have agreed with you. Had I not found a new niche, I might well have gone the way of our former colleague, Wallace Ullrich. Suicide."

Fleming, standing in front of the glass doors of the silverware cabinet, felt a bit uncomfortable at the unexpected depth of this confession but listened attentively nonetheless. Prescott seemed to be speaking out of a need to unburden himself, and Fleming would oblige his partner.

"Martha," the hazel-eyed man went on, "saw I was foundering. She offered assistance. First in the proper establishing of my practice, connecting me with the right people. But the greater aid she gave me was in helping me to separate myself from the past. I did not—and have never—told her the details of my military history. I didn't need to. She saw the hurt, and that was enough. She . . . she *forgave* me for what I'd done. By accepting me. And later . . . by loving me." He brushed at his eyes.

Fleming could only nod.

"Oh, ours is something of a forbidden passion, to be sure," Prescott continued, voice somewhat strained but remaining steady. "Until this blind bloody species called humanity can see past the trivialities of fleshly pigments, our relationship will have to remain secret. Incidentally, she insists on it. She won't submit either of us to the fuss and bother of the world's idiocy, is what she says. I have had to agree with her." He sighed. "But you see now, Ian, why I responded so vehemently when you suggested that she might be a traitor in our midst. She has already saved my life once. And I love her for it."

"I can appreciate that, Prescott," Fleming acknowledged gently.

Eventually Prescott succeeded in brewing up another pot of coffee, adding to the mess overtaking the kitchen's counters. They went into the dining room. Even to Fleming Martha's absence seemed to resound all about them. The gardenias in the vase on the table of blond wood appeared to be dying.

Fleming sipped his coffee. This time the brew had come out on the watery side. Prescott just didn't have the knack.

"So," said Prescott, "what did you make of that so-called Queen? I found it all quite unsettling."

Fleming settled a frank gaze on his partner. "We may not, in the end, be able to resolve this matter ourselves," he said quietly. "No matter what that Cleopatra character sees in her tea leaves."

Prescott frowned at him across the tabletop. "Not surrendering, are you?"

"Merely stating a fact."

"Well, what choice have we? Ultimately we've nothing to rely upon but our own wits."

Fleming wasn't relishing the broaching of this subject, but it had to be done. Levelly he said, "We do have one final alternative."

"And that is?"

"Whitehall."

Prescott reacted as though bitten, visibly wincing. It took a moment for him to gather his breath. In a tiny voice he breathed, "No . . ." But it was more an exclamation of abhorrence than a negation.

"We must consider it," Fleming said firmly.

"I—I do not wish to."

"That's a poor reason not to do something."

"Ian, don't—"

Fleming cut in, "There are national secrets at stake, Prescott. At least we have very good reason to believe so. We have made efforts—sound, sincere efforts—to resolve this matter ourselves. But we've not yet succeeded, and I fear in my heart that time is running out. You must believe that I find the thought of dealing with Whitehall, with our old masters in the intelligence community, just as distasteful as you obviously do. I fervently wish the past to remain behind me. We don't often find our wishes granted, however." He leaned forward in his chair. "I have contacts among MI-5. Two men, named Davenport and Stahl. I recently had dealings with them. I could ring them today—"

"Oh, God," Prescott muttered. "Can you imagine the inquiries we would be subjected to? Being interrogated by our own British agents. They would likely first suspect that *we* were involved on the wrong side of this. They'd cross-examine, they would grill us about our pasts, unearthing our files, exposing all that—that business to daylight once more. And why should you trust these contacts, Davenport and Stahl? What we did after the war, that operation, was absolutely clandestine. Hardly general knowledge, not even in Whitehall. Only the uppermost echelons knew of it. Do we dare expose the existence of . . . of Churchill's Boys, even to our own people?"

As unpleasant as this proposal was, Fleming had realized from the start the almost assured inevitability of this. If bringing in MI-5 was the only chance of success, so be it. He could only hope to convince Prescott. Convince him of something that he, Fleming, wasn't even entirely sure of.

"Prescott, I'm not saying this is a palatable choice. But with Whitehall's intervention perhaps this can be resolved favorably, and we can return to our lives, our normal lives. I for one don't enjoy playing at being a spy again. I miss my home. I miss the quiet and sanity of it. What of yourself?" He nearly added, *What of Martha?* but it was unnecessary.

They sat in total silence for something near to a full minute. Fleming let Prescott weigh the matter, a secret part of himself hoping that his partner would reject all this utterly, would refuse to go along.

Prescott's hazel eyes were wandering aimlessly across the table's lacquered surface, which glared beneath the room's light. Of a sudden those eyes lifted, focused, with a new purpose.

"I shall make you a counterproposal," he said evenly, hunching forward in a posture similar to Fleming's, so that the two men now faced each other like a pair of gamblers.

Fleming said, "Go ahead."

"We act as you say. Contact Whitehall. Tell them everything

we know. Submit ourselves to being reimmersed in those waters, to having our past deeds spoken of aloud, to being questioned by strangers who will likely look upon us as little better than executioners. We will relinquish the matter. Pass on its responsibility to others. Forfeit our privacy and accept the consequences."

Fleming waited silently for the rest.

Which was this: "We do none of this for the next twenty-four hours."

After a moment, when he saw there was nothing to follow, Fleming asked, "Is that all? Twenty-four hours? What do you imagine we can accomplish in that time?"

"Imagine?" said Prescott, an eerie smile coming to his lips. "I can *imagine* much, Ian. I can imagine fate stepping in. I can imagine a miracle occurring. I can imagine us finding some crucial bit of evidence we've as yet overlooked. I can imagine hope. I should like very much to enjoy the luxury of hope just a while longer. Is it agreed?"

Fleming shrugged. It was hardly an outrageous proposal— rather the opposite, in fact—though he found himself unable to share in any real sense of hope. Fate, in his experience, rarely interceded in positive fashion. And miracles had gone out with the New Testament.

Prescott, still smiling, thrust out his hand across the table. Fleming shook it.

"Done and done," said one, then the other.

Chapter 26

FLEMING STILL had Francis Davenport's contact number in the small black address book he had automatically tossed into his suitcase before leaving Jamaica. He had met the MI-5 agent in London when the man tried to lure him into participating in a bit of intelligence work. Fleming had declined the offer but later ended up embroiled unwillingly in the matter nonetheless. In San Francisco, during that whole sordid business with Oscar Winterberg, he had hooked up with Davenport's aide, Stahl, and had wound up side by side with that man during a gun battle with one of Winterberg's cronies.

Tomorrow night he would dial the number. He would tell Davenport everything that had transpired. He would pass the entire matter into the hands of Whitehall. And, as Prescott had said, he would accept the consequences—the rude unearthing of the past, the full disclosure of his buried yesterdays.

He held out no hope that before the allotted twenty-four hours were up he and Prescott could resolve this affair themselves. They might know who their opponents were—or in the cases of the Cajun and the blond-haired woman, have their descriptions at least—but they were no substantial step nearer to capturing any of them. Faith Ullrich remained at large, as did Gerard Marquette. It was still a hopeless tangle. Without knowing what their adversaries meant to do with the information they had about Churchill's Boys, all the rest was virtually meaningless. The murders, this supposed cabal of warped voodoo practitioners—these were the grisly dressings around the central impenetrable mystery.

"I think," said Prescott, "that standing watch tonight would be a good idea." They were in the office, and the hour was quite late. Slim and Chopper hadn't called, and no other convenient miracle had materialized. "Far too many people seem to know the location of this house. I find I'm having unpleasant visions of that Cajun creature creeping into our bedrooms by night and—" He whacked the flat edge of his hand against the surface of the desk. It was a vivid enough impression of a falling axe blade.

Fleming had dismissed the notion previously, but it was worth reconsidering. He saw no harm in it, and it would keep Prescott occupied. "Perhaps you're right. Four-hour shifts—does that sound agreeable? Who will go first?"

"I will." A bit sheepishly Prescott added, "I wanted to ring Martha at her hotel anyway."

"It's late."

Hazel eyes settled on the telephone atop the desk. "She'll be awake."

Fleming left him there and went upstairs to retire.

FLEMING HAD NEARLY forgotten just how torturously dull guard duty could be. He sipped cold coffee during his stint and smoked enough Players to leave his lungs raw. Nothing had happened. No intruders, no assassins. At about five-thirty a pair of inebriates had gone past along Dauphine Street, slurring out a college fight song, but that was all.

When Prescott arose, Fleming went upstairs for a shave, dousing his face repeatedly with cold water afterward in an attempt to make up for the four hours of sleep he'd lost. A few years ago he would have shrugged it off without a thought. Later in the morning he and Prescott set out.

They were making the rounds through the Quarter yet again, checking in with Prescott's Irregulars, stopping in at diners, grocery stores, hotel lobbies. Fleming acknowledged that this sort of dogged persistence often paid dividends in detective work, but today it only felt like last-minute desperation.

Yet Prescott seemed in an eerily good mood, humming some jaunty tune on into the afternoon. It was as though he were utterly confident that his hoped-for miracle would manifest at any moment.

The hours were ticking steadily away. Fleming mentally reviewed all the facts and speculations and suspicions they had accumulated in the course of this case. He sought—without any true faith in success but with sincere effort nonetheless—anything they might have neglected. But he found no crucial clue that would suddenly break this matter wide open.

Prescott prepared another plain dinner of cold cuts, which Fleming was growing decidedly tired of. It was ironic that in a city famed throughout the world for its cuisine they were reduced to such modest fare, but going out to a restaurant seemed an unnecessary luxury now.

A few minutes past eight o'clock the telephone jangled. Prescott picked up the extension in the kitchen. "Prescott W. Quick speaking. Ah. Good. Yes." He returned the receiver to its cradle.

Fleming was rinsing off plates in the sink and laying them in the drainer. It seemed only proper that he should do his share of the house's domestic chores, now that Martha was absent; even so, the state of the kitchen was scandalous.

By the conversation's brevity he could make a fair guess as to who had called. "Chopper and Slim?"

"Yes. Come, we're meeting them in ten minutes."

"Why not have them come here?" Fleming asked. "Or have them tell you their news over the telephone?"

Prescott was straightening his tie. "We are assuming that this house is under watch by the opposition. I would rather Slim and Chopper were not too closely identified with our present business, out of concern for their safety. They have served well in the past, almost loyally, one might say. As to collecting whatever they have for us this evening over the telephone—I can't very well pay them for their services over the wire. I've always conducted my practice conscientiously. Payments from me are received on time and in full. That is in part how I have earned my favorable reputation. I shan't become derelict now, no matter what the circumstances." He adjusted the right sleeve of the gray jacket he wore; for a moment Fleming saw the outline of the derringer's tiny holster against his inner forearm. Then he added drolly, "If you'd prefer to remain here and read a good book, Ian, I shall go without you."

"Don't be an ass, Prescott. Let's be off."

The rendezvous was at the same Conti Street pub where they had met two nights ago. Frank, the brawny bartender, spied the two of them immediately.

Frank was reaching automatically toward a whiskey bottle set on a shelf behind him when Prescott said, "Not tonight, my friend. Just a soda water, if you would."

The bartender raised a bushy black eyebrow. "Liver ailin' you, Mr. Quick?" he asked in his heavy baritone.

"Merely a practice run for Lent, Frank."

Fleming ordered a gin and tonic, and together they moved past the customary row of carousing laborers, into the bar's rear niche where the pool table sat. Surprisingly Slim and Chopper weren't engaged in a game; were, instead, sitting on stools in the dim corner.

"Gentlemen," said Prescott, "good evening to you."

"Mr. Quick, Mr. Fleming," Chopper said in his usual uninflected speech. Beside him Slim was lighting a cigarette. As his Zippo sparked, Fleming saw that the lad's right hand was wrapped in a bandage. As he put the flame to his cigarette, his skeletal features below the brim of his black cap were clearly illuminated for an instant, revealing a split upper lip and a swelling discolored patch of flesh between his left eye and pronounced cheekbone. Both wounds appeared very fresh.

Slim offered a sort of savage little grimace. "Yeah, how're you guys tonight?" Curiously he looked quite pleased with himself.

Prescott noted the young man's injuries almost blandly. "I see you've indulged in another spate of fisticuffs, Slim. Did you have one of your famed disagreements with some chap over the attentions of a young lady?"

Slim's barbaric grin remained in place. "Naw. Wasn't a skirt this time, Mr. Quick." He dragged on his Lucky Strike. "I bumped into the Baptist."

"Baptist?" asked Prescott. "It was a religious quarrel, then?"

Fleming ignored the lighthearted comment. Obviously whatever had happened was serious. Speaking up, he asked, "Who is the Baptist, Slim?"

The two Irregulars shot him a glance. Fleming normally remained silent during these meetings. Chopper's gaze was flat and cool; Slim's was lit with a mirthful heat.

"Big fella," the lad said. "Real long hair, pulled back in a braid. I didn't see much of his face. But he kinda fit that description you gave us, don't'cha think?" He appeared almost smug now.

"Good Lord," Prescott said, all banter suddenly aside. "Do, if you would, furnish us with the details."

Slim proceeded to.

He and Chopper, wasting no time, had been devoting themselves to their assignment since Prescott had proposed it last night. They had worked well into the small hours. Though Slim worked at the docks during the day, Chopper had no job and so had been free to do a bit more scouting than his younger cohort. Slim didn't provide the specifics of the hunt, likely wishing to keep whatever private or illicit channels the two employed a secret. Fleming couldn't rightfully object to that. These two had evidently produced some rapid results. That was admirable.

By the time Slim had ended his workday on the docks this evening, Chopper had picked up some sort of definite trail. As night fell, they set out together. The Cajun's profile apparently made things fairly easy. The large man was about. The Quarter was spacious in its way, but in the end it was only a single neighborhood, with a finite number of places to hide, and this Cajun evidently wasn't going to extremes to hide himself. What followed was a kind of safari, Slim and Chopper tracking their prey by scent, by spoor, by the snapped branches of this urban veldt. They at last homed in on their quarry at a roughneck tavern far down along Decatur Street.

Chopper sipped docilely at his Kentucky whiskey throughout this tale, occasionally looking Fleming's way with quietly scrutinizing eyes.

Slim continued. He and Chopper entered the bar. It was a treacherous establishment, filled with a seedy brand of riffraff, the sort of men who spoiled for a fight just to break up the monotony of their nights. Luckily neither of the Irregulars appeared especially genteel, and both blended fairly well.

They quickly reconnoitered the place, finding a rear exit that led out onto a trash-strewn patio, which was ringed by a sagging wood fence. Beyond the fence were the yards and outbuildings of neighboring homes and businesses. A fleeing man could easily vault the fence and scramble away in any of a dozen different directions. Chopper stationed himself nearby this exit. Slim went to survey their prey.

The two had, of course, spotted the Cajun shortly after entering the tavern. He stood out quite readily, a Titan-like figure sitting alone in a shadowy corner, silently drinking. Slim edged along the bar until he had a good—and what he thought to be covert—view of the man. Slim was now between him and the front door. Chopper had the rear.

"And you ended up brawling with this fellow?" Prescott cut in, suddenly exasperated. "I only asked you two gentlemen to find this man, *not* engage him. I warned you he was dangerous. Mr. Fleming here received a rather brutal blow to—"

Chopper lifted a hand. "Let him finish, Mr. Quick."

Prescott grumbled into silence. Apparently his concern for these two Irregulars was sincere.

Slim took a swallow of his rum and went on, still wearing that fierce grin. He had eyed the Cajun awhile, waiting to see if anyone approached his table. But the man merely sat and drank, an ugly sneer on his shadowed face.

Slim furtively waved over the bartender and asked if he knew who the man was. "I think I know him from New York," was the lad's explanation for his curiosity, "but I ain't sure. You got any idea who he is?" The bartender chuckled, telling Slim he had the wrong guy, that the Baptist sure wasn't from New York. "Baptist?" Slim asked. "Who's that?" Unfortunately it turned out to be one question too many.

At that moment one of the bar's patrons sitting on an adjacent stool decided to take exception to Slim's curiosity. Perhaps he didn't like the lad's snooping; perhaps he was merely looking for the opportunity to start trouble. At any rate he suddenly turned, fixing Slim with a dangerous stare. "Why you askin' so many questions, kid? You a cop or somethin'?" Not waiting for a reply, the man, in his mid-thirties with a jagged scar above one eyebrow, reached out and seized the front of Slim's leather jacket, yanking him off his barstool and growling in his face.

This, naturally, didn't agree with Slim, who, without ceremony, laid a roundhouse punch across the man's jaw. What followed was a predictable kind of chaos. It would be difficult to sort out the many players who leapt eagerly into what developed swiftly into a classic barroom brawl. Slim fought any and all who came within the sphere of his swinging fists. He bloodied his hand in the process, which explained the bandage, and received a few choice blows in return, which accounted for his split lip and bruised cheek.

"And what of the Baptist during all this?" Fleming asked.

"We lost him," Chopper said mildly.

"*Lost* him?"

Chopper shrugged. "I had to come to my young friend's aid."

"You don't seem to have incurred any injuries in the process." Chopper's bronze-toned face was unmarred.

"I'm a more careful fighter than Slim," he explained.

Slim cackled, drinking off the last of his rum.

Fleming didn't share in the amusement. "So, you mean to tell us you had this man, the Cajun, the Baptist, located—and you neglected to contact us. Damn it, that's what we hired you two for."

Chopper showed no response to Fleming's rather sharp tone.

"Things jus' got outta hand," Slim said.

Prescott said, "Ian, do go easy. These two gentlemen—"

"This Baptist could now be anywhere," Fleming interrupted. The two Irregulars had failed, squandering the opportunity to at last net one of their adversaries.

Chopper was shaking his head. "No, Mr. Fleming. He couldn't be *anywhere*. We know where the Baptist is. After I finally managed to get Slim out of that bar, we picked him up again. Shadowed him. That's one thing about this fellow—he's easy to spot."

"Then where the devil is he?" Fleming asked.

Slim dropped the smoldering butt of his Lucky Strike on the bare boards of the floor and ground the toe of his boot over it. He said, "He's in a house on St. Philip." He recited the address, a familiar one. "He's got company. You guys know who the Red Dwarf is?"

Chapter 27

HE FELT something of a fool. A blind, obtuse fool.

The house on St. Philip Street. Faith Ullrich's former residence, where she and Gerard Marquette had had their lurid trysts. They were using it as a hideaway. Of course. So simple. Who would think to search for one of this case's chief suspects in her *very own home*?

What was genuinely dismaying, though, was hearing that Inspector McCorkle was very evidently a part of this. It was incredible, but it fit, though how the Red Dwarf had come to be involved on both sides of this Fleming had no idea. Of course, this wouldn't be the first double agent he'd known. It explained why McCorkle had paid that visit to Harry Braniff's office, to warn him off the investigation; apparently he'd had the same intention when he had brought Fleming and Prescott out to City Park for that meeting. This great hubbub of arrests the inspector was ordering was a diversion, then, to keep the public's fears allayed.

Since McCorkle had been put in charge of the investigation, he must have declared the house off limits. No other policemen in or out. He had the power to order that. Surely the whole circle was using the house as a retreat—Faith, Marquette, the blond-haired woman, the Cajun. A safe harbor right there in the middle of the French Quarter, a perfect base of operation.

But there were a number of unanswered questions.

Prescott was the one to voice them. "If you saw the Cajun—this Baptist character—go into that house, why have you waited to contact us? Did the Baptist see either of you? Did McCorkle? Was anyone else about? And if we're all wasting our breath here, who is watching the house now to see they don't escape? Good God, what are we waiting for?"

Chopper and Slim remained comfortably slouched on their stools in the dim rear corner of the bar. Fleming, too, was eager for the news, but he put a hand to Prescott's arm.

"Easy there, Prescott. Let's hear what they have to say."

It was Chopper who calmly provided the answers. "We delayed contacting you, Mr. Fleming, Mr. Quick, because Slim here needed his injuries looked at right away. He'd gashed open his hand bad—probably on somebody's teeth—and he was losing blood. We got a buddy who's a sawbones. Lives on Dumaine. We've done him favors. After we tracked the Baptist to that place on St. Philip, we doubled back, and Slim got his mitt stitched up."

Slim waved his bandaged right hand, then tilted his head at Chopper. "He was a real mother hen 'bout it, too."

"And left the house unwatched?" Fleming said. "You should have rung us immediately. You—"

"I wasn't about to let Slim bleed out a couple pints of blood in the street." Chopper's tone grew heavy. His deep-set eyes drilled into Fleming's. "It wasn't an option."

Fleming, still not entirely mollified, started to say, "Yes, of course, but—"

"But," Chopper interrupted, "to answer the rest of your questions. No, the Baptist didn't see us. Neither did the Red Dwarf, who was the one who let him into that house through the front door. Those two shook hands. We've done this stuff before, you know. We know how to put a tail on somebody without them knowing."

"Damned straight we do," averred Slim proudly.

"And," continued Chopper, "we put a spotter on the house. A fellow called the Mouse. He owes us a few favors, too. He's watching the place right this minute."

Fleming let out a breath. Finally he nodded. "Very well. Yes. I see your actions were only correct. I apologize for criticizing."

"Think nothin' of it," Slim said airily.

"You have done fine work, gentlemen," said Prescott, reaching into his gray jacket's inner pocket for his billfold. "I believe I now owe you your fee."

Neither of the Irregulars reached for the offered bills.

"How 'bout double or nothin'?" asked Slim.

Fleming frowned at the non sequitur, then dismissed it. Whatever the lad was gibbering about would have to wait. He and Prescott had to *act* and act now. They had discovered the lair of their adversaries. They had to capitalize on this crucial bit of intelligence. They had to—

But Prescott, money still in hand, asked, "And what do you mean by that, Slim?"

Chopper and the lad exchanged one of their telepathic glances.

"This whole thing's got our curiosity piqued, Mr. Quick," Chopper said, a rare soft smile creasing his face. "What with the Red Dwarf mixed up in whatever's going on. McCorkle's made a bit of a nuisance of himself in the past, when Slim and me have been trying to conduct, uh, business. If he's on the wrong side of whatever this is, we'd like to be in on the caper."

"Be fun watchin' that red-haired pygmy get himself a dose of his own medicine," said Slim. "He got me thrown in the slammer for thirty days once a couple years back. This whole deal sounds big. Big enough that you two guys might need some help on it. We're that help, if you want it. Like I said"—he eyed the money in Prescott's hand—"double or nothin'. If we don't come through, you can keep your dough."

Now it was Fleming and Prescott who traded a glance. Prescott lifted his brows above his hazel eyes. *What do you think?*

Fleming considered logically, momentarily reining in the critical urge to move immediately. Perhaps these two Irregulars could prove useful. He and Prescott hadn't even formulated a plan yet, after all. Just what were they going to do, now that they had at least two members of the opposition waiting unsuspectingly at a single location? Should they storm the house? Should they lie in wait for the other members to appear? Or were Faith, Marquette, and the blond-haired woman already on the premises?

Immediate haste might not, in the end, be the wisest strategy. Having Slim and Chopper in their ranks would even the numbers considerably. Also, some niggling intuition told him that these two were the proper men for the job. His well-trained military mind considered all these facts rapidly.

"Are you gentlemen armed?" Fleming asked. He had his Enfield revolver, and Prescott, of course, was carrying his tiny derringer.

"Well," said Slim, "we don't carry no rods . . ."

"No," Chopper said firmly. "No guns. Bad way to do business. But we're not without other means." While he spoke, his hand had fished around to the back pocket of his dungarees. Now, with a deft flash of his arm, a long bone-handled folding knife appeared, a practiced flick of his thumb producing the blade. Beside him Slim, too, had flourished a knife with an equally sly sleight-of-hand. His was double-edged, bayonet-like, the metal dull but gleaming along its carefully honed edges. It was as long as a maestro's baton. The two men waited.

Prescott turned again to Fleming. "Well, what's your view, old boy? The more the merrier?"

Fleming deliberated silently and coolly. Finally he said, "Do you both understand that this is a hazardous situation?"

At that the knives disappeared, Slim returning his to a long sheath beneath his shabby leather jacket. With a grin stunted only slightly by his split lip the lad said sardonically, "Gee, we've never faced danger before. I'm scared."

Chopper put in, "Don't worry. I'll hold his hand."

Fleming nodded slowly to Prescott, who said, "Very well, gentlemen." He returned the bills to his wallet. "We shall brief you on the enemy's strength and then devise a battle plan."

THEY DIDN'T DAWDLE over the matter. Within the space of roughly five minutes they had made what preparations they could and disbanded their conclave there at the rear nook of the Conti Street tavern.

Prescott's miracle had evidently manifested. Or at least a passing version of one. They knew their enemies' whereabouts. Sometimes that was half the battle. Fleming hoped this was one of those occasions.

They made their way swiftly on foot to St. Philip Street, their quartet cutting neatly through the raucous celebrants littering Bourbon, this time without incident. The night was mild, but clouds loomed once more over the city, obscuring whatever phase of the moon hung above. Soon the house came into view, there on the corner, with its yellow stucco walls and green woodwork. A light was burning behind the curtains of the upstairs bedroom window. Apparently their adversaries weren't taking great pains to stay concealed. Likely they felt smugly assured in their lair, protected as it was by Inspector McCorkle. It was rather insidious that *here*, in this most blatantly obvious place, was their enemies' sanctuary.

"Where is this Mouse character you mentioned earlier?" Fleming whispered to Slim as they skulked toward the corner. "The one who is supposed to be watching the house."

"You're lookin' at him, Mr. Fleming," said Slim.

At that a small grayish shadow detached itself from the corner opposite their target and scuttled rapidly up the sidewalk. He was a diminutive man, shorter even than McCorkle, aged indeterminably somewhere between thirty and fifty. His long coat was a tired faded black. His hair was a graying blond shade that left it almost invisible. His features and bearing were so unassuming, Fleming had the impression this individual could simply evaporate at will.

"Anybody come in or out?" Slim asked the Mouse quietly. Behind, Prescott and Chopper had halted. Their band was still a half block from the corner.

"N-n-n-no-b-b-b-body," the Mouse said through a thick chronic stutter. His eyes were tiny and had an almost yellow cast to them.

Chopper stepped forward and palmed a bill into the man's hand. "Good work, Mouse. See you later." And off the creature scuttled, vanishing up St. Philip toward the river.

Fleming turned to face the others. What a curious assembly we make, he thought fleetingly. Two retired English spies, a former film actor turned mercenary, and a scrappy featherweight dockworker.

Shaking this off, he said, "Here we are. Prescott, Slim, to your places. Be alert. Chopper, you claim to know a thing or two about burglary. You and I shall attempt to gain access to the house from the rear."

Chopper said blandly, "Yeah, I know something about it. Not that I make a habit of it, but you pick up skills in this business."

Fleming wondered in just what terms this man would define his "business" but said nothing.

It was Slim who said, "I still think I oughta go with Chopper." He now wore a somewhat sullen expression on his gaunt features.

Chopper spoke before Fleming could respond. In a calm, placating tone he said, "Now, Slim. We're working for Mr. Fleming and Mr. Quick here. They call the shots. Besides, you shouldn't be hopping fences with that hand. You'll tear those new stitches."

Slim nodded, kicking a stray leaf toward the gutter. "I know, I know. You . . . jus' be careful, all right?"

"I always am," the older man assured his younger cohort.

Prescott said, "If we hear gunshots, Ian, we'll be coming through that front door, like it or not."

"Yes, yes. Enough." Fleming made a shooing gesture. "Away with both of you. Get down to that intersection and watch the street-facing sides of the house. We will wait until you're in place."

The group divided. Slim and Prescott took kitty-cornered positions, crouching into the shadows. Luckily this street was far enough from the hubbub of Bourbon that no stray revelers were likely to blunder by. Equally fortunate was the fact that the intersection was not well lit, allowing the two men to fairly disappear into their surroundings.

Fleming nodded to Chopper. Through his veins tingled that intense alertness that had always preceded combat. It was adrenaline mixed with excitement mixed with a rational dose of apprehension.

Chopper stepped casually across the street, aiming toward a gated alleyway set between the second and third houses from the corner. Fleming moved up behind him, hoping no neighbors were watching from their windows. Chopper's hands set upon the gate's latch. Something metallic glinted briefly in his fingers; then came the *snap* of a lock disengaging. Chopper nudged open the linked metal of the alley's gate and slipped inside. Fleming, on his heels, pushed it shut behind himself.

The alley was dim and quite narrow. It smelled of soil, growing things and garbage.

"Watch out for the trash can." Chopper's whisper was barely audible. Fleming stepped around the barrel that stood just behind the gate. The long sides of the adjacent houses seemed to press in on them, allowing only a thin strip of the cloud-swathed sky above. Chopper moved forward, and Fleming followed. Both men bent low, moving almost noiselessly. Fleming admired Chopper's stealth. Whatever else the man had been or now was, he was no fumbler.

The pinched alley spilled out onto a rear yard where a thick snarl of rose bushes was contesting for space with a wheelbarrow, a rake, a sack of moldering fertilizer, and an array of other gardening supplies lying about haphazardly. Fleming eyed the back screen door of the house. Within a light burned, and tinny laughter bubbled from a radio.

Chopper glanced over his shoulder. Fleming nodded, and they moved once more, hunched and darting, both stepping nimbly through the ill-lit obstacle course of scattered tools. They reached the far fence, roughly six feet high and made of sturdy wood slats. Fleming silently thanked the heavens that whoever owned this home didn't also keep a dog.

Fleming, using quick hand signals, indicated that he would go first. Chopper offered no protest, immediately kneeling and cupping his hands. Fleming set his foot into the makeshift step and vaulted, Chopper—proving himself rather muscular—helping to lift him smoothly upward.

It was even darker in this yard. Fleming remained atop the fence, balancing precariously until he secured his stance by hooking the heel of his shoe along the horizontal brace on the other side. Then he reached downward. Chopper took his hands and bounded silently up onto the fence. Together, groping into the shadows, they dropped onto the patio behind Faith Ullrich's corner house.

Here they lingered a few seconds, listening keenly for any signs that their intrusion had been detected. There was only silence but for the faint normal sounds spilling in from the surrounding Quarter and the dwindling buzz of the radio behind. Fleming's eyes were at last adapting to the dimness. He could make out the small square of the concrete patio, upon which a few sticks of lawn furniture were distributed.

Chopper tapped his arm and pointed. "Drainpipe," he breathed nearby Fleming's ear.

He peered, picking out the stout metal pipe that ran from the roof of the house, passing within fairly easy reach of the unlit upper-story window of what was likely a back bedroom. He considered. There was also a rear ground-level door at the far side of the patio . . . but making their entry from the upstairs might indeed be more advantageous. Surely that door was bolted. And entering on the upper story, if they managed it quietly enough, would give them the element of surprise. It was an edge they might well need.

Again Fleming nodded. Again they moved.

Chopper sized up the drainpipe at close range for a few seconds. It was braced every few feet by bolted struts. Hopefully these would serve well enough as rungs. His inspection done, Chopper grabbed hold of the lowest brace and, locking his knees on either side of the pipe, started shinnying upward.

For a man at least half a decade older than Fleming, he was quite agile. He went skyward as swiftly and effortlessly as a monkey. In less than a minute he was near the top. Anchoring himself with a tight grip on one of the struts, Chopper reached for the window, slithering his fingers into the sill's wedge. It was a terribly awkward angle, and at one point his body swayed precariously away from his target, but after another minute he had levered the window open a crack from the outside and now slowly and noiselessly pushed it upward.

He swung himself off his perch with an acrobat's dexterity and slipped his body through the aperture. A second later he leaned his head out and flashed a thumbs-up signal. Fleming had waited until he was completely off the pipe before he started his climb. No sense in testing the drainpipe's weight tolerance.

It was a chore going up, belying the ease of the older man's ascent. Twice the toes of Fleming's shoes slipped off a brace, leaving him briefly dangling by his hands. He was slowed also by the necessity for stealth. It wouldn't do for the house's occupants to hear someone clattering up the rear of the building.

Eventually he came level with the window. With a stifled grunt he maneuvered himself off the pipe, conscious of the fifteen-foot drop to the concrete patio beneath him, hooked a leg through the open window, and wriggled inside.

The room was dark, without even the muted moonlight to give

it shadows. It smelled unused, thick with long-undisturbed dust. Fleming crouched a moment on the floor, catching his breath, giving his eyes the chance to adjust further. Chopper hunkered silently beside him. Until now Fleming, deferring to the other man's evidently extensive knowledge of cat burglary, had permitted him to lead the operation. Now it was Fleming's turn.

He drew his .38, letting Chopper see it silhouetted against the window. The Portuguese half-breed nodded.

On the far side of the room a glowing yellow outline marked the door. Beyond it were sounds—muffled, nebulous, not voices, more like animal grunts.

Fleming stood and stepped toward the door, moving cautiously in the virtual blackness. Fortunately the room was apparently completely unfurnished. When a floorboard creaked underfoot, he froze, then eased his foot slowly off and continued. Chopper trailed soundlessly.

He felt for the doorknob. Pulling it inward a scant inch, he set his eye to the crack.

The hallway beyond was empty. A bulb burned in an overhead fixture. The strip of carpeting was the color of champagne. Another room stood immediately opposite, closed, no light visible around the door. The forward bedroom would be to the right, a short distance down the corridor. From his angle Fleming couldn't see its door. The animal sounds were louder, rhythmic growls and now high faint breathless cries, sounding for all the world like the bleats of a lost lamb.

He tugged the door wider and peered around the jamb. He held his pistol low, ready to swing it upward at a heartbeat's warning. The remainder of the hallway was vacant as well. Stairs descended further along at the left. At the right was the opened door of the lavatory. Straight ahead was the door into the main bedroom. Shut. Light spilling from beneath, along with the curious and disturbing noises.

Fleming glided out into the corridor, creeping along one edge,

Chopper taking up the opposite side. He hadn't drawn his long bone-handled folding knife but prowled warily, every movement fluid. They neared the door and halted.

The door had no keyhole. No way to spy on the chamber before making an entrance, then. Of course, they could try to gain access to the balcony that wrapped this corner house's outer faces. Surely they could find a way onto it from that room they had already passed. But that would also leave them visible to the street. The curiosity of a passing policeman at this stage would be ruinous.

The grunts were coming louder now, the matching high-pitched whimpers sounding more pained. Fleming drew a silent cool breath. Something dreadful was transpiring in this room. He looked to Chopper, who gave him another thumbs-up. He now had his knife in hand, having flicked open the blade silently.

Fleming raised his Enfield revolver, put his hand to the knob, and turned it sharply.

Chapter 28

THEY MET a tableau.

The actions—the abominable, atrocious, depraved actions—taking place in the forward bedroom ceased abruptly and absolutely as Fleming swept open the door, Enfield Mk II in hand. Chopper was behind, on his right.

Here they were: the Baptist, the blond-haired woman, Everett McCorkle. Only Faith Ullrich and Gerard Marquette were absent, though Fleming would soon revise this appraisal.

The ornate vanity table was to their right, the bed just beyond it. The wallpaper was red and textured. The bed's silky coverlet, currently in disarray, was of the same deep hue. A large trunk of cedar sat along a wall, its lid gaping wide. Across the carpet—the same champagne color as the hallway strip—and across the bed was strewn a confounding assortment of oddities. Though impossible for the eye to sort at a glance, Fleming nonetheless immediately grasped the items' basic similarities to the chicken bone crosses. Here lay a boiled white chicken's claw, there a gleaming gold crucifix to which had been tied scarlet-colored birds' feathers. Atop the matching nightstands at either side of the head of the bed, fat black candles flickered. They were scented, releasing an odor like charring molasses into the room. Each was imprinted with a profane image of the Virgin Mary. Her robes were parted, and she bled from her womb.

Disturbing enough as these props and scenery were, the spectacle would have been nothing without its players.

McCorkle stood rigidly against the wall nearby the head of the bed. His broad-brimmed straw hat with its jaunty orange band lay at his feet, leaving free his bush of dazzlingly red curly hair. His black shoes were scrupulously polished. He wore a natty blue and olive plaid suit, neatly tailored to his five-foot-five stature. His features were as rigid as his body, closely set eyes wide and ringed with white, face flushed, beads of sweat trickling from his full sideburns. His narrow lips were parted, and the tip of his tongue protruded. His left hand was locked in the act of worrying a string of purple and white rosary beads. His right was buried in his trousers.

The blond-haired woman was on the bed, amid the scattered idolatrous trophies. She wore only a harlot's undergarments, some of which had been violently ripped away. She was arranged on her hands and knees, her feet—clad in impractical pencil-heeled black shoes—dangling off the foot of the bed. Her ample blond hair tumbled all about her heavily made-up face, which was presently turned toward the door, her lipstick-thick lips open on a cry of mixed pain and pleasure. She wore no dark glasses now, and her eyes, boldly outlined in mascara, were visible through her cascading locks.

Pressed hard against—and unmistakably coupled to—this woman was the Cajun, the man Chopper and Slim had identified as the Baptist. He towered behind her, bare feet firmly planted on the carpet. Candlelight reflected itself along the smooth muscled pillars of his calves, thighs, and flanks. He was as tall and mighty as Fleming recalled from his brief glimpse before the man had crashed that bottle across his temple. His massive hands were closed tightly over the blond woman's sleek hips, fingers digging reddening furrows into the dainty flesh. He wore only a billowing white shirt—tight across his cannonball shoulders, sleeves drooping—and the black satin highwayman's mask. His single long black braid hung nearly to his waist. Strange chevrons in white and yellow paint were drawn on his cheeks, and his mouth was locked into that malevolent sneer he wore so naturally.

All eyes had shot toward the door. All motion in the chamber had been suspended. Nothing was said.

Fleming stared back at the silent paralyzed scene. A great disgust filled him, but he remained clearheaded. Chopper was a presence behind his right elbow.

McCorkle was armed; Fleming could see the shoulder holster peeking out from beneath his jacket. The blond-haired woman was in no position, literally, to be of any threat; and the Baptist, too, was occupied, hands visible, not wearing enough clothing to easily conceal a weapon.

These facts flitted through Fleming's mind. He was parting his lips to speak when the tableau was broken for him.

"Don't hurt me!"

The shout was shrill, as high-pitched as the pitiable whimpers he had heard from the hallway before entering the room. Yet . . . the voice was masculine. McCorkle, stiff against the wall, hadn't spoken. The sneer was still stamped on the Cajun's face.

The blond head whipped sharply, and the disheveled locks spilled off the slight chin and rounded cheeks and away from the wide inoffensive eyes. Beneath the layering makeup the soft face was now terrified and pleading.

"Please don't hurt me!" shrieked Gerard Marquette again.

Fleming's stance remained firm, his revolver raised. The sight was, however, quite a sickening horror.

The spell of immobility was now broken, and with its sundering events occurred in rapid order.

With a savage grunt and a twist of his hips the Baptist disengaged his most unnatural joining to the creature in the blond wig. Turning further, he leapt forward, long muscled arms lifting, the sneer contorting itself even more beneath the black mask and face paint. As he vaulted, looming hugely, all vestiges of humanity left that face. His mouth opened into a monster's maw, and a speechless cry ripped itself harshly from his throat. His fingers were hooked into talons.

Fleming's .38 barked in his hand. There had been virtually no time for conscious thought, for deciding whether to backpedal into the hallway or engage the Cajun in hand-to-hand fighting. Only the swiftest flicker of instinct told him to try to wound this man, and so the revolver's barrel had twitched minutely up and to the left, looking to put the bullet into his brawny shoulder. But he moved so fast, this giant, and his leap carried him so high; and the slug struck the chest, near its center. Too near.

Fleming scarcely saw this as the enormous half-naked shape came crashing toward him, falling short only owing to the bullet's impact. The shoulder he had been half-aiming for hit his legs, and he tumbled, staggering back out into the corridor, pulling free his feet just as the Cajun slammed to the floor with a thud that actually shook the walls. Fleming reeled backward several steps, groping quickly for balance, managing to hang on to the pistol.

Ahead, Chopper, who had neatly sidestepped the falling Cajun, was entering the room.

His arm drew back, the knife's pommel balanced expertly on his fingertips. Then the arm slashed gracefully downward, and the knife flew, toward the right, toward where McCorkle had stood—

—just as a second gunshot sounded.

Chopper spun like a child's top, arms twirling. And crumpled.

At Fleming's feet the Cajun's enormous body gave a single violent shudder, limbs flailing, then moved no more.

Inside the bedroom Gerard Marquette screamed.

Fleming had caught his balance and now charged forward, leaping nimbly over the Baptist's outstretched body, dark gray smoke trailing from the barrel of his Enfield. Below—far away, unimportant right now—he heard a crash. Wood splintered; a pane of glass shattered; footsteps struck floorboards.

He came into the bedroom. Marquette had rolled over on the bed's red coverlet, one hand pulling the shreds of the lingerie across his delicate body, the other in a fist that was jammed between his teeth to stifle another scream.

Chopper was facedown on the carpeting. The bullet's exit wound, there at nearly the precise center of the rear of his skull, was spewing blood like a punctured water pipe.

McCorkle still stood against the wall. He was now pinned there. Chopper's knife blade had pierced his upper right arm just below the shoulder socket and gone through to spike itself into the wall. McCorkle had evidently wrested his right hand out of his trousers and drawn a snub-nosed revolver from his shoulder holster. As Fleming aimed, that gun dropped from his suddenly nerveless fingers. He gasped sharply, obviously in great pain. His left hand still clutched the rosary beads.

For the blink of an eye Fleming considered pulling his trigger anyway.

There were raised voices now from that distant unimportant place somewhere below; then the hurried footfalls found the staircase.

Seconds later Prescott and Slim reached the top. The lad was brandishing his long knife like a cutlass. Behind, Prescott was laboring to catch his breath, his left hand rubbing his shoulder gingerly, his right holding the ivory-handled derringer. They immediately saw the Cajun lying in the hallway. He too was facedown, blood pooling out around his broad chest. His long braid spilled off one shoulder onto the floor.

Prescott wheezed, "What—"

Slim cut him off sharply. "Where the hell's Chopper?" He took a step toward the bedroom, where Fleming still held his pistol on McCorkle and Marquette, and the question became unnecessary.

It was a terrible thing to watch. The lad's eyes went wide and still. His unshaven jaw clenched itself like a vise. He moved slowly forward. His knuckles above the bandage went bone white around the hilt of his weapon. He entered the bedchamber and knelt with something like reverence beside Chopper's body.

Fleming nearly said he hadn't yet checked for a pulse, but once more it was unnecessary. Slim put his free fingers uselessly to the older man's throat, held them there a moment, then removed them. His wide fixed eyes studied the raw gaping wound where the bullet had erupted from the back of Chopper's head. He did not touch the man again.

Prescott, meanwhile, checked the Baptist in similar fashion, found the same result, then stepped into the bedroom's doorway. His hazel eyes flickered around the scene, alighting on Marquette in the blond wig quivering on the bed and McCorkle pegged neatly to the wall by his upper arm. Blood was flowing generously down the policeman's jacket sleeve. His teeth were now bared in an anguished grimace, but he made no further sounds.

Prescott's face registered something near to abhorrence. Fleming could understand the reaction.

Slim was now standing. He had picked from the floor one of the scattered curios. It appeared to be a dog's skull. Crosses and stars had been painted in luminous red all across its surface. Slim studied it a moment, then dropped it to the carpeting and slowly, deliberately, ground it beneath his boot heel. The snapping bones made a horrid sound in the sudden quiet. The scene smelled of gunpowder, blood, and the charred aroma of the burning candles.

"Which one of 'em was it?"

The question came out like the growl a dog might make deep in its throat in the final seconds before attacking and sinking its teeth into its enemy's vitals. Slim's eyes at last moved. He looked back toward the half-naked Cajun in the hall. Then he swung about and eyed Gerard Marquette, who continued to tremble on the bed, making a further effort to hide his body in a grotesque parody of bashfulness. Then Slim looked at McCorkle, noting the bone-handled knife pinning him against the red wallpaper.

The lad nodded grimly to himself.

Prescott moved an instant before Fleming did. The taller Englishman lunged and caught Slim's leather jacket by its matted fleece collar, at the same time jerking him off balance. The lad had been in the act of launching himself across the room at Mc-Corkle. Fleming caught Slim's knife hand deftly and gave it a hard turn. The long blade landed on the carpet with a dull thump. Fleming kicked it toward the windows, then spun back around to cover their two prisoners. It wasn't especially necessary. Marquette was immobilized by fear; McCorkle, by Chopper's knife. Neither was going anywhere.

"No, Slim, no!" Prescott barked into the young man's murderous features. Showing impressive strength, the Englishman wrestled him as he struggled, lifting him bodily off his feet and crashing him back against a wall.

"We must sort this debacle," said Prescott in a tone of firm command.

We must indeed, thought Fleming.

"Prescott, if you would, go downstairs and secure the front door. If fortune favors us, the neighbors will mistake the gunshots for fireworks or some such."

Prescott looked dubious. Then he shrugged. "It is possible. It's Carnival, after all. The police normally have their hands full during this season. Even if they receive a call, they may not respond with any haste." He rubbed his right shoulder again. Likely he had used it as a battering ram against the house's front door. He lingered a moment, fixing Slim with a fierce warning glare. The lad wrapped his bony arms across his shallow chest and now sank toward the floor, squatting at the baseboard of the wall against which the Englishman had hurled him. He was crouched next to the open cedar trunk from which had come all the pagan accoutrements that littered the room. Slim's eyes were growing glassy, and a dreadful grief was stealing over his features. He looked at Chopper's corpse, looked away, and dropped his forehead onto his knees.

Prescott nodded and went downstairs.

"Please don't hurt me," Gerard Marquette repeated, this time in a frail beseeching whisper. Against the wall near the head of the bed, Everett McCorkle was sucking in sharp steady breaths through clenched teeth; but he made no move to pull the knife from his arm. He was instead waiting to discover his fate.

Fleming surveyed his captive audience.

"Now. You two. Gerard Marquette and Everett McCorkle. You are going to answer some questions, with the sure understanding that the continuance of your lives hangs in the balance. First, where is Faith Ullrich?"

Chapter 29

IT WAS a vile tale that followed. It began with that initial question as to Faith Ullrich's whereabouts, and its answer came from Mc-Corkle, and it was this: "We don't know."

Slim remained huddled at the base of the bedroom wall, his head on his knees. Sporadically his bony shoulders shook, as if he were silently sobbing. Chopper and the Baptist lay where they had fallen, both dead. From downstairs Fleming heard the front door being wrestled closed. He wondered if Prescott had actually knocked it off its hinges when they had burst inside.

Fleming's gaze moved from the pathetic trembling form of Gerard Marquette on the bed to Everett McCorkle standing nailed to the wall.

"I think it likely you do know." He kept the revolver raised.

"Where she *might* be, sure," the Red Dwarf amended. His face was draining of color. The blood from the wound through his upper right arm was flowing unchecked. He spoke through a painful grimace. "Where she is, right this second, none of us knows."

Prescott's footsteps were ascending the stairs again. A moment later he was in the bedroom. "The door is secured. I saw no one out on the street. The rumpus may have gone undetected after all."

Fleming nodded. That was good. He had no clear idea of what they would do if they had to clear the scene immediately. How would they transport these two prisoners they had netted, and where would they hold them? Neither could very well be turned over to the authorities. Police involvement was something they had desperately wished to avoid from the start.

He said, "Inspector McCorkle here is likely to swoon from blood loss at any moment. Prescott, perhaps you'd be good enough to unpin him and do something to stanch that wound."

Prescott had returned his derringer to its sleeve-holster. He strode toward the red-haired policeman in the eccentric but stylish blue and olive plaid suit. Prescott, who loomed over the man by nearly a full foot, first pocketed the snub-nosed revolver that had been dropped to the floor. Then he gripped the bone handle of Chopper's long knife and without any especial delicacy pulled the blade from the wall and McCorkle's arm with a hard jerk. Marquette, cringing on the bed, flinched and emitted a doleful sympathetic whimper.

McCorkle's knees gave immediately. Prescott caught him easily and peeled away his jacket and shirt. From the shirt he tore a long strip, which he wrapped tourniquet-wise about the short man's arm, just inches above the long neat wound the knife had left. Fleming noted the deep, blood-spattered hole in the wall. Chopper's throw had been powerful and accurate. He had surely been attempting to disable the man's gun arm before he could fire. A sound strategy, but McCorkle obviously had been a hair quicker, and the unhappy fact had cost Chopper his life.

Prescott, showing remarkably little concern for his patient, shoved the policeman roughly toward the bed, where he landed next to the wretchedly shivering body of Gerard Marquette.

"You won't hurt me, will you?" whined the dainty-bodied man in the torn remains of his feminine undergarments. Under other circumstances the sight might almost be darkly laughable. Instead, it only added to the general repugnance that Fleming had felt since entering this dreadful boudoir.

"Shut up," he said flatly. No matter what came of this, they didn't have time to dally. He required answers to his questions from these two deviants. The opposition's numbers had shrunk considerably in the past few minutes. The giant Cajun was dead, and Marquette and the blond-haired woman had grotesquely merged to become one and the same person. Only Faith Ullrich remained at large, presuming there were no others in this perverse cabal—which was, he admitted, a large assumption. But it was she they most urgently needed to apprehend. Faith, daughter of Wallace Ullrich, who was himself a former member of Churchill's Boys . . .

Sins of our fathers. The Ghost of Christmas Past.

"You people murdered Angelina Marquette, née Angelina Dours, and her brother Martin Dours. Did you wish to contradict these charges?" Fleming's tone indicated that the course would be unwise. He hadn't lowered his Enfield.

Marquette, however, tried another tack. Pointing to the large corpse in the hallway, he sniveled, "It was *him*! Baptista! H-he used the axe! He—he—he did it—"

"And he has paid his price for the crimes. Which should give you remaining two some concept of how serious we are about this matter. We hold you responsible for those ghastly murders as well, whether or not you committed the actual deeds. Now, returning to my original question. Where is Faith Ullrich, the woman I gather is the leader of this perverse circle of yours?"

Yes, thought Fleming, these three had obviously been a part of it all. But Marquette was plainly too weak to lead anyone or anything; McCorkle seemed more a morbid spectator; and the late Cajun—the Baptist—had likely been brought aboard to serve as muscle, to carry out the brute physical demands of the killings. It was Faith at the pinnacle of everything. Again instinct told him he had it right.

"We've got another hideout," said McCorkle. He spoke mildly, though not without fear, not without clear awareness of the direness of his situation. He was likely only reverting to his natural aplomb as a longtime police detective. His voice carried little trace of a typical southern American dialect. Perhaps he had been educated elsewhere, not that it mattered.

"Where is it?"

"Outside the city. In the bayous. It's Baptista's place. You probably know him as the Baptist. He, Faith, and this one"—he nodded to his right at Marquette—"ducked down there after the first killing. After I took over the case, I secured this house and smuggled them in."

"You will provide me with the precise whereabouts of this secondary hideaway," Fleming said.

Prescott produced a small notebook and pencil and took down McCorkle's directions. The names of the roadways and towns meant nothing to Fleming, but Prescott nodded as his pencil scratched on the pad.

"I don't know if Faith is there or not," McCorkle finished. "She comes and goes as she pleases."

"Was she present for the murder of Angelina Marquette?" Fleming asked.

"Yes."

"And Martin Dours?"

"Yes. She was in charge of everything, Mr. Fleming, as you've surmised."

This was a different scenario, Fleming mused, than when Mc-Corkle had questioned him and Prescott yesterday. Since, the tables had decidedly turned.

"Why did she call for these killings?" he asked.

Gerard Marquette was now tugging compulsively at his lower lip, smearing the bright red lipstick he wore. McCorkle let out a sigh, wincing and cupping his right shoulder as he shifted slightly on the bed.

"That's a long story," he finally said.

"You may abbreviate," said Fleming, aware of the passing minutes, "providing you omit nothing crucial and substitute no falsehoods for absolute fact."

"I wasn't planning on lying at this point. I've got a fair idea that you're wanting to kill me—kill us both." That produced another whimper from Marquette. "I also imagine you'd like to avoid doing so. As I see it, my only hope of living through tonight is to tell you everything you want to know."

"Very sensible," Fleming said coldly.

McCorkle sniffed out a weary little laugh. "Sensible's the last thing any of this is. Frankly, I'm surprised things lasted this long. We all knew it was going to blow up in our faces sooner or later. At least, *I* knew it."

Prescott interjected, "Yet you went ahead with your diabolical deeds nonetheless." His tone was heavy with censure and disgust. "Not the actions of a sane man."

"No," said the policeman flatly, as if finally squarely facing a fact that had haunted him some while. "They weren't."

At that the tale unfolded, the Red Dwarf laying out the details matter-of-factly, as if reciting the cold particulars of some case to his junior officers. But these were like no criminal episodes Fleming had ever heard of before, much less imagined. To call them bizarre or unholy did them precious little justice.

McCorkle's story originated, inevitably enough, with Faith Ullrich. She had arrived in New Orleans some eleven months ago, as Fleming already knew, and had soon rented this house in the French Quarter. She had money but not an unlimited amount; still, enough so that she didn't need to worry about employment. She was unmarried, twenty-six years old—

"We're aware of her basic profile," Fleming interrupted. "How did you come to meet her?"

McCorkle dispassionately altered his narrative to suit his audience. "He met Faith first"—again the nod toward Marquette—"a few months after she'd arrived here from England. I made her acquaintance two months later on, during the summer."

It had been a typically sweltering Louisiana summertime, bubbling humidity, nearly daily downpours that did nothing to cool things. Owing to his commendable record and long service to the police department, McCorkle fairly picked and chose his cases, often opting for those that seemed unresolvable by his learned but not infallible fellow detectives. Occasionally the mayor or some like luminary would personally ask him to intervene in some matter, if it impacted some socially ranking family or city government member. Evidently McCorkle was also known for his discretion. As it happened, that summer he was tapped for just such a special duty.

On the surface it was a simple enough case of prostitution. The patriarch of a wealthy family had been discovered by his children to have been regularly paying for the services of a strumpet. Hardly an earthshaking matter, but the children were threatening to make it one of public record. Apparently the father had been expending exorbitant amounts of money for his carnal hobby and refused utterly to cease his activities. So extravagant were the sums that his offspring feared for their inheritance.

The obvious solution was to locate the woman of the evening in question and send her packing out of town. It wasn't the first time the police had interceded in such a manner when a prominent family's name was at risk; it certainly wouldn't be the last.

The problem lay in the fact that the woman could not be found. The elderly patriarch refused to divulge her whereabouts, and not even the strident threats his children were making would pry the information from him. McCorkle was brought in to find her.

And so he did. Here the wounded detective condensed his tale, assuring Fleming and Prescott in a few brief words that the hunt had been arduous and his quarry immensely skilled in covering her tracks. Nonetheless, after a week and a half he had cornered Faith Ullrich.

He did as he'd been instructed. He handed her a railway ticket and a fifty-dollar bill and told her to disappear permanently. She made him a counteroffer.

"You can't understand without having met her," said McCorkle, voice remaining laudably steady as his ashen features drifted away into a kind of reverent dreaminess. His close-set eyes lost focus and seemed to glaze. "She's a beautiful woman. Yes, she is that. But a beautiful woman, even the most exquisite in the world, couldn't compare to the added allure she possesses. Power. Strength of spirit. A fantastic will. She radiates it. It gushes in her veins. It's unmistakable—and inescapable. If a goddess ever walked the earth, it's her. No, I won't bother you with my unpolished attempts at poetry. I see you're impatient. But I felt what I felt, and I'll never be free of that feeling."

The counteroffer to McCorkle's train ticket, money, and uncompromising invitation to leave the city was to experience firsthand what that venerable patriarch had been shelling out such vast sums for. It was more than a simple offer of sex. McCorkle somehow knew this immediately, sensed that something of incredible power and beauty and dread was about to occur to him—for, before he was scarcely aware of it, he'd accepted her proposition, though it went against every lawful code he'd so far scrupulously obeyed throughout his lifetime.

Faith Ullrich, here in this house, here in this very room, introduced Everett McCorkle to the gods of her creed.

Fleming felt his lips slowly curling in a fresh surge of profound repulsion as the diminutive detective proceeded to describe the belief into which he was initiated that night. It was, in the end, much as Prescott had so cannily speculated it might all be: a bastardized form of voodoo. But how thoroughly warped, how utterly twisted, how hideously dismembered and reattached and mixed and defiled was it! Yes, Faith Ullrich had indeed borrowed arbitrary elements from that pagan brand of worship. Voodoo might be bizarre, yes, even unsettling at times, what with its own borrowed trappings of Christianity. But even its most outrageous aspects—spiritual possession, the laying of curses, the raising of the living dead, and other such macabre follies—didn't compare to what this woman had concocted.

She had, evidently entirely on her own, shaped a complex theology and raised a psychotic pantheon of demon-deities. Each was named; each had its special characteristics; each required appeasing in its own ordained manner. Worshipers, so she assured

McCorkle, would enjoy vast mortal power in this world and a supreme reward in the afterlife.

She had invented rites for every conceivable occasion, events dictated by the movements of the stars and moon, by the whims of the gods—and ultimately by Faith herself, who was the sovereign priestess of this "religion" she had fabricated so convincingly. Her creed even had its own paraphernalia. McCorkle's hand swept over the gruesome baubles and trinkets littering the bed and floor. Each piece had its meaning, its place in the ceremonies.

Then the red-haired detective began to describe, with restrained fervor, the nature of the rites he had first practiced with Faith and later with Marquette, whom she'd already initiated, and later still Baptista. At this Fleming lifted a hand.

"You needn't elucidate the particulars further," he said. Standing beside him, Prescott looked rather dazed by it all. Fleming understood that no matter what justifications McCorkle made, he had in the end been seduced wholly by the promise of sexual fulfillment. No more, no less. Faith's "power" was evidently one to discern, with extraordinary precision, those human individuals who secretly longed to experience the deviant side of carnality. She had formulated this perverse creed of hers merely as set dressing, to ease her victims into the dark waters of unnatural sexual congress. It was a means of allowing her prey the ultimate exoneration for their lewd acts: They did these things in service of their profane deities, which they were only too happy to embrace.

And so she had collected Marquette, then McCorkle, then the Baptist.

"What of this elderly patriarch?" Fleming asked.

"He died," said McCorkle. "A short time after I met Faith. Aneurysm. I think it was all too much for him in the end. He was the only one she ever charged. She wasn't really a call girl, of course. She just wanted some more money, enough to set her up, if not permanently, then for a while. She inherited a tidy bundle from her father when he died, but she needed a bit more."

"Are there any other members in your circle, other than those you're mentioned?"

"None that I ever met or heard of."

Fleming nodded. He shifted his grip on his revolver, which was beginning to grow heavy in his hand. "When and why did Faith Ullrich proclaim that Angelina Marquette was to be murdered?"

McCorkle took up the second part of the question first. "She said we needed a sacrifice. I won't explain which god needed appeasing or why, because you wouldn't understand."

"No. I wouldn't."

"Nor would I," agreed Prescott.

McCorkle showed no response to the statements. "We all knew all along that Angelina was going to be killed. Gerard here knew it before the rest of us. She was still just his fiancée then. He joined up with Faith, oh, four or five months before the wedding."

At this Prescott erupted, "Do you mean to say that you, you degenerate swine, knew that your future wife was slated to be . . . be executed! *Sacrificed.* And you went ahead with the marriage regardless?" The hazel-eyed man directed this stream of invective at the cowering shape of Gerard Marquette.

The man in the blond wig looked to be trying to shrink into himself. He squirmed and fidgeted violently. It was a loathsome display. Even McCorkle seemed vaguely affronted.

Tears left black streaks of mascara along his rounded cheeks as he looked up imploringly at Fleming and Prescott. His voice was a breathy whisper as he sputtered, "F-Faith wanted Angelina and me . . . to be husband and wife. She said—she said the s-sacrifice of my legal wife would—would—would mean *we* were then married! In the eyes of our gods. And . . . I w-w-wanted to be married to Faith! Wanted. Oh, how I—"

Prescott made a revolted noise and turned away. Fleming himself felt no small urge to stride forward and pistol-whip the creature into silence.

Instead he snapped, "Shut up."

Marquette dutifully clapped a hand over his mouth.

As outlandish as it all was, it explained Angelina's murder. Faith had waited . . . waited until Gerard Marquette had lawfully wedded his bride, waited until she had recruited a strong capable man, the Baptist, into their circle, waited for the prime opportunity to dispatch Angelina in a ritual that had involved rape and beheading. Fleming believed the stories of these two despicable men.

"So," he said after a lengthy pause, "Martin Dours was murdered for a similar reason, then? Another sacrifice to your unholy gods? The fact that he was searching for the killers of his sister had no bearing. Is that what you wish us to believe?"

McCorkle met Fleming's heated stare evenly and said in the same mild manner, "Faith told me to shut down their investigation. They'd hired a fellow named Harry Braniff, a PI, to snoop around. I cooled him off. It was no trouble. The man's a pushover. Then Faith said we had to sacrifice Martin Dours."

"I suppose Elliot, his brother, was next?"

McCorkle said simply, "Yes."

"It makes no bloody sense!" Prescott suddenly thundered, turning to face the prisoners again. "I want to know why you bastard sodomites sent me those damned photos of Angelina Marquette's corpse! Why did you involve me? What was the purpose? Why?"

It was Marquette who answered, spreading his fingers over his smeared lips and speaking through them. "S-she wanted you. She knew something about you. Wouldn't s-s-say what it was. Only that . . . only that those photographs would intrigue you."

Prescott's narrow aging face darkened terribly. He stalked toward the bed, lifted a hand, and soundly slapped the quivering creature across the side of his skull, knocking the thick blond wig to the floor. Without it he looked even more wretched and ridiculous. More tears oozed from his fouled eyes.

Prescott whirled back around, eyeing Fleming. "Bloody lunatics, all of them! *Intrigue* me? It's madness, Ian. Sheer madness!"

Fleming nodded. It was that. But what underlay it? The ultimate question was this: Did Faith Ullrich herself believe in this demented religion she had erected? If so, she was only a madwoman, acting on deranged impulses. If not, she had a deeper scheme, one that had required the recruitment of these pathetic men to do her bidding.

"Do you know why my friend here was sent those photos of Angelina?" Fleming asked McCorkle. "And why was I sent the one of Martin Dours? Why did Faith want us to know of these murders?"

The detective seemed to be trying to flex his right hand, but the fingers now barely fluttered. He said evenly, "She didn't say specifically. You don't know how easy it was for her to simply say that something needed doing—and we would do it. The dictates of the gods were impossible to interpret, as complex and caught up in astrological movements as they were. Impossible for us, anyway. Not for Faith. She understood. She had those photos delivered to Mr. Quick. She had us spy on his outgoing mail. That's how we got your location, Mr. Fleming. She sent that photo and message to you."

That torn sheet of notebook paper, the scrawled words.

McCorkle continued, "When you came to the city, she got very worked up. Happy and agitated at the same time. I asked— somehow I found the nerve to actually ask—if the two of you were going to be sacrificed sometime soon. She gave me this stare, this terrible cold and knowing stare. She said the gods would decide."

But why had that warning letter been sent to Jamaica? It seemed now that Faith Ullrich had wanted him to come to New Orleans, surely so that she would then have *two* former Churchill's Boys within easy reach. But again, why? What was her final plan?

It was hopeless, he now saw. These two so-called men knew nothing of ultimate value. They were Faith's foot soldiers. They were her slaves, in her thrall, caught in the intricate web of degenerate carnal fulfillment she had spun about them all. She had told them nothing of substance; had, instead, made their every action a service to their gods, a prescribed ritual, an obligatory ceremony. How easily she must have manipulated them.

"Why did the Baptist attack me on Bourbon Street?" he asked. It was a question they might have a useful answer for.

"Gerard was shadowing you, in disguise, and Baptista was there as backup," said McCorkle. "Faith wanted us to find out what you two were up to. We also did some asking around. That night you spotted Marquette. He was sloppy." He said this with some contempt, eyes flickering toward his confederate. "The Baptist just kept you from following."

Fleming's fingers brushed his left temple.

"Why did you bring us out to that park yesterday?" Fleming asked.

"Same reason. To try to find out what you were up to."

"And your harassment of this city's voodoo practitioners—why bother?"

McCorkle said, "It's something for the newspapers to chew on."

Fleming nodded slowly. A mere smoke screen, then. An unwitting public would think voodoo really was involved, where the ugly truth was that the rituals were purely fabricated. McCorkle's campaign against the city's Negroes was the ultimate hypocrisy.

"Is there anything else you wish to ask?" Fleming said to Prescott in a tone of finality.

That was enough to elicit a terrified gasp from Marquette. McCorkle beside him drew his spine up rigidly but otherwise gave no reaction.

Prescott studied the pair a moment with cold condemning eyes. "I feel we've learned all we can."

"As do I." Holding the revolver steadily on Marquette, he said, "Gag him."

Quickly Prescott tore another strip from McCorkle's shirt,

stuffing a wad of it into Marquette's mouth and wrapping the ends tightly around his skull. The dainty man offered no resistance, did not even make another whimper. The procedure, if those surveillance photos Prescott had taken were any judge, wasn't entirely unfamiliar him.

"Bind him to the bed," Fleming said.

Prescott did so. McCorkle rose to his feet, and Fleming waved him back to his original position against the wall. In moments Gerard Marquette was lashed to the bed's frame by his wrists and ankles. He was quite secured. The shreds of his undergarments had fallen away, exposing more of his soft flesh than Fleming had ever wished to see again. His wide eyes stood out boldly in their rings of blotched mascara. He was breathing sharply and rapidly through his nose. On some perverse level the situation was arousing him. Fleming turned away from the evidence.

McCorkle, standing against his wall, said with some dignity, "I've told you what you wanted. I haven't lied." He was not supplicating himself. He was instead stating a fact, his final defense before he would stoically face his sentencing.

Fleming let silence hold the room a moment. Then he shook his head. "I've no intention of killing you. I would much rather remand you to the authorities. Both of you. Let justice see to you. But the police cannot be involved in this affair, for reasons that do not especially matter at this moment, not to you. That, Inspector, is something you would not understand." Without turning he called, "Slim. Get on your feet, lad."

Behind, on the far wall, he heard the young man rising slowly to his booted feet. Heard him crossing the carpet to retrieve his knife from nearby the bedroom's windows where Fleming had kicked it.

Fleming pointed to Marquette. "This one had nothing to do with your friend's death." To McCorkle he said, "Justice shall have to find its own way."

Prescott stepped forward, billfold in hand. Quickly he snatched bills from it—quite a few, it seemed to Fleming—and held them out toward Slim. "Your fee." His voice was subdued, and his eyes didn't meet Slim's.

The lad acknowledged neither Prescott nor the money. His gaze was fixed to McCorkle, unblinking eyes in a face that at the moment looked colder than ice water. Finally Prescott simply stuffed the wad into a pocket of the leather jacket.

He and Fleming stepped past the corpses of Chopper and the Baptist. Fleming would have liked to close the bedroom door behind them, but the Cajun's giant body lay in the way.

Using handkerchiefs, they spent several minutes wiping their prints from every surface in and outside the house that they had touched. Swiping off the drainpipe proved particularly onerous, but Fleming managed it. He did his best not to listen to the sounds that issued briefly from the upstairs bedroom.

Chapter 30

PRESCOTT MADE the telephone call to Elliot Dours from his office. "I promised to keep you informed of our progress," he began. Prescott's voice was taut but controlled. He explained shortly where the naval man could presently find one of the murderers of his sister and brother. He would discover the perpetrator in the house's forward upstairs bedroom, gagged and bound to the bed frame. In the room he would also find the corpses of three other men. Two of these were the bound man's accomplices, one of whom was Everett McCorkle. The third had been killed in the apprehending of the others. Prescott recommended that Elliot wear gloves to avoid leaving fingerprints if he intended to visit the house, then laid down the receiver without saying farewell.

"How much money did you pay Slim?" Fleming asked, slumped bonelessly in the chair before the desk. He wanted nothing so much this moment as to wring himself clean, expunging tonight's revolting sights from his memory. He drew on a cigarette.

Prescott rubbed his brow. They had both seen unpleasant things tonight. "I gave him . . . I don't know. Everything I had in my wallet. I don't know what the going rate is for when you demolish someone's life so completely."

Slim was now a murderer. He had become such because of his involvement with Prescott and Fleming in this affair that had cost Chopper his life.

Prescott continued, "Slim is likely making for the bus depot as we speak. The lad's too smart to remain in the city." He sighed grimly. "I wish I'd left those two out of this."

Fleming offered a platitude. "It's unfortunate." The truth was that Chopper and Slim had performed admirably. Without them he and Prescott would have been forced into contacting White-hall, an unappealing eventuality. Fleming had led espionage op-erations that had cost men their lives during the war. Such things happened. Chopper was a casualty. What perhaps made his death truly tragic was that he would never know that the cause his life had gone to was a worthy one.

The night had been quite enervating. Now that it was done, Fleming felt limp, within and without.

"Yes. Very unfortunate," Prescott finally said. He dropped himself heavily into the other leather chair. "I cannot say I even knew Chopper terribly well. Still, we shared a drink now and again, engaged in conversation. There was a particular evening, when he was uncharacteristically in his cups, that he told me rather candidly about his years in Hollywood. How he was forever being shunted into minor film parts. He portrayed Mexican ban-dits, Spanish corsairs, Apaches, Mongol warriors, Italian gang-sters. And on one memorable occasion an Eskimo. How sick he had grown of it, being forced into these inglorious roles. He told me he was a fine actor, dedicated to his craft. It had meant every-thing to him, to be on that silver screen. But the machinery of the film business never allowed him to step once from the shadows. He was bitter about it. I cannot say I blame him for the attitude."

The serving cart was still there, the bottle of port atop it. There looked to be just enough to fill two glasses.

Fleming ground out his cigarette in an ashtray on the corner of the desk. "I believe I should like a drink," he said, giving no re-sponse to his partner's impromptu eulogy of Chopper.

"Do help yourself."

"Did you care to join me?" Fleming asked quietly.

Prescott gave a wan imitation of his familiar chuckle. "Taking the side of temptation, are you, Ian?"

"I would judge you've earned a reprieve."

"I pledged to abstain until the conclusion of this affair. In a just world it all would have ended tonight. The villains slain, the crisis averted. But the mother of these vile doings remains at large." From his pocket he removed the small notebook in which he'd written McCorkle's directions to the second hideaway. He tossed it onto the desk. "I've no way to secure a car tonight at this late hour. We'll have to go in the morning, and I believe we both need the sleep. So, no. Do not pour one for me. One glass would be thoroughly insufficient. Likely ten would be as well."

Fleming filled one of the tulip-shaped glasses, swallowing its contents unceremoniously, tasting nothing whatever of the port but feeling its effects immediately. Warmth crawled outward from his chest. The horror of that bedroom . . . it was yet another frozen mental snapshot he would carry with him for some long time. Nearly rivaling any given memory from the catalogue that made up the worst moments of his final days in the service of the British government.

Prescott once again seemed to be tracking his thoughts with preternatural accuracy; or perhaps it was only that they two shared so common a background and thereby followed roughly parallel mental pathways.

"The past, Ian, the past. We distance ourselves. We sprint ever onward, no matter that at the end of all our roads lies death. We want only to shake away the memories, to cleanse our hands. But the past is devious, and it overtakes us at every opportunity, sometimes lying in wait for long periods, waiting on the prime moment of ambush. It reproduces itself in our present. It crouches expectantly in our futures, ready, always ready, to remind us that we are never truly free. We can never be fully purged. The bell has rung, and that shall never be undone."

Fleming realized he had emptied his glass. He refilled it, draining the bottle. This port was too fine to be wasted in this manner, when surely the cheapest of liquors would serve the moment's needs; but it was at hand, and he availed himself of it.

Prescott might well be on the verge of another of his lapses.

He had performed well tonight, but the horrors they had so recently faced could undo nearly anyone.

Fleming drank off his second glass even quicker than the first. He left it atop the cart. He crossed the blue and purple carpet, pausing to press a hand onto Prescott's shoulder. "You did fine work this night. I was honored to serve with you."

Prescott patted his hand. "Well, the sentiment is mutual, Ian. Yes, we are on the side of good in this gruesome affair, aren't we?"

"Of course we are." Fleming exited the office and climbed the steps to the guest bedroom.

He undressed and washed with somewhat sluggish movements in preparation to sleep. He and Prescott, once they had finished erasing any possible traces of their fingerprints, had made a silent stealthy exit from that house on St. Philip Street. He was reasonably assured they had gone unseen by any curious neighbors. He hoped Elliot Dours exercised similar caution. Surely as a career military man, one who had served in the war, he knew how to conduct himself. Those corpses in that upstairs chamber of horrors would be discovered eventually. *Four* dead men—well, four once Elliot had rightfully dispatched Gerard Marquette. It was quite a body count.

There was no good reason to inform Elliot that Faith Ullrich was the ultimate culprit behind the murders of his siblings. He would have to be satisfied in taking his revenge on his former brother-in-law, Marquette, whom Fleming and Prescott had left behind, bound and gagged on the bed . . . stretched out like a sacrificial lamb.

It was a poor choice of words, given the tales they had been told tonight. But it was applicable nonetheless. Fleming had shot and killed the Baptist, but the act had been self-defense. He had been unwilling, however, to murder McCorkle and Marquette in cold blood. That would have cut too hard against the grain. He did not fancy himself an executioner. And so he had given those two over to others, to Slim and Elliot Dours, men who had righteous reasons to claim those unclean lives.

Fleming's conscience might not be entirely satisfied. He was walking the finest of lines between morality and the stigma of dishonor. But, despite it all, he couldn't regret his actions. Those three men had been beasts. They had relinquished all rights to their own humanity. They had fouled themselves irreversibly with their deeds. In the final analysis the world was well shut of them.

He slid a fresh bullet into the empty chamber of his Enfield and laid the pistol and holster on the bedside table. There was little reason to fear intruders tonight, he thought as he laid himself in the bed, drawing its quilts up about his throat. All of Faith's soldiers were dead.

Fleming was asleep almost immediately, but dreams came. Chicken bones and bleached human skulls painted with stars and crosses tumbled chaotically through a veil of gun smoke, which parted here and there to reveal the faces of the men who had died tonight, then cleared further to uncover the disembodied head of Angelina Marquette; it was being clasped between the hands of Martin Dours, whose own face was a butchered ruin; Angelina's mouth worked convulsively, but Fleming could understand nothing of what she said.

HE WOKE JUST after sunrise between sweat-damp sheets. The dreams had been relentless, transmogrifying incessantly, the diabolical near-nonsensical images garbling, distorting, a seemingly endless narrative of surreal visual allusions.

He sat upright, tossing his head to clear it of the final fresh mental imprints. He did not feel remotely rested. It would have been better, he judged, to have remained awake through the night.

He bathed, left off the bandage, then dressed, picking charcoal trousers and a white shirt. He opted for the warm black coat, despite that its collar was badly torn. Whether it suited the day's weather or not, the coat best hid his revolver and so seemed prudent to wear.

Downstairs, Fleming met Prescott, who had set an alarm clock and looked no better rested than he. He said he had arranged for their car. Once more coffee was brewed. Prescott went to the front step to fetch the morning's newspaper.

"It seems that civil suit was no joke," he said.

Fleming had commandeered the stove and was whipping up eggs and rashers of bacon. Prescott folded over the paper and pointed to the article. It was small and had not gotten front-page treatment, but it was there nonetheless. Names weren't mentioned, but someone had filed the suit yesterday, claiming undue harassment and false arrests on the part of the New Orleans Police Department. Cleopatra must have contacts among the press, Fleming mused, and had used them to see that the story saw print.

"I telephoned Martha again last night," said Prescott as they sat down to eat.

"Is she well?"

"I told her she could return to the house this afternoon. Actually I asked her to return. It never does to grant a woman *permission* to do anything. I warned her that we two would be gone by the time she arrived. I didn't specify when we would return. Tonight, I said I hoped. Perhaps tomorrow morning. Do you think that shall be enough time to accomplish what we need to do?"

Fleming shrugged. "I've no means of knowing."

Prescott nodded. "Of course. It is a long drive there and back. We'll be heading southwest, into the wetter regions of the state of Louisiana, lands mostly unclaimed by what we call civilization. Of course, the Cajuns still live in some of those places, hunting, trapping, trading, living lives not dissimilar to some of their long-bygone ancestors. Inspector McCorkle's directions were quite exact. I'm confident I can locate this secondary hideaway. However, if we don't find Faith Ullrich there . . ."

"Then we may be facing a long day indeed," finished Fleming. Prescott drank off the last of his coffee. He was wearing his dark gray suit but hadn't bothered with a necktie. Today was a crucial day. Make or break, as the Yanks said. If they didn't find Faith Ullrich in that country hideaway, Fleming would finally make his call to Francis Davenport in London, and MI-5 would be brought into the matter. It was a last resort and one neither he nor Prescott wanted to employ.

The auto arrived at eight. It was delivered by a freckled young chap in a garage worker's greasy coveralls, who handed Prescott the keys, turned on his heel, and disappeared on foot down Dauphine Street.

The car was a black Lincoln, with heavy chrome trim and an elongated body. Even in the morning's muted sunlight it gleamed. Clouds again hung above the city, these dark gray and rather menacing. The air promised rain, and the temperature was several notches chillier than the past few clement days.

"I fear a parade or two may be spoiled today," said Prescott, eyeing the thick, darkening blanket overhead.

Fleming nodded wordlessly. They were standing in the mahogany-trimmed vestibule. Prescott picked a gray raincoat from the varnished rack in the corner and folded it over his arm. Another, this one black, hung there as well.

"Take that for yourself," Prescott said. Fleming did.

They lingered there in the entryway in silence. The moment was somber yet strangely tranquil.

Eventually Fleming broke it. "Well, let's see this through to the end, shall we?"

Prescott nodded, and together they stepped out the door, making for the automobile parked at the curb.

Chapter 31

LEAVING BEHIND the home and office of Prescott W. Quick, Finder of Lost Fortunes, they made their way from the city of New Orleans.

Fleming finally did catch a glimpse of a parade, or at least the preparations for one, after the Lincoln had slipped from the French Quarter. They were wending the outward city streets, Prescott at the wheel, taking them through morning traffic toward the roadway that would lead them from the city. Cars were bottlenecking at an intersection half a block ahead. The snarl was slowly being sorted by a traffic officer already wearing a long yellow rain slicker.

"What the deuce is that?" Fleming asked in some astonishment, peering beyond their auto's hood ornament. At the junction ahead, a long platform towed by a squat truck was rumbling slowly along the cross street. The bed had tall sides that trailed vibrantly colored paper streamers. Erected upon it was a large, truly bizarre sculpture. A sun disk, with flaming serrated edges and a big white-toothed smile, loomed above the oversized plaster figures of a pair of angels with outspread wings. Between them they held a purple-on-white banner that Fleming couldn't read at this distance. There were robed figures atop the platform as well, these actual people. They wore hoods in addition to their gowns, which themselves sparkled with gold and green piping. They were moving busily about the platform's large centerpiece.

"One of the Mardi Gras floats," Prescott said. "I'm afraid I couldn't tell you which parade it belongs to. There are a number of krewes that sponsor and mount these cavalcades."

"Crews?" asked Fleming, still eyeing the platform as it was towed from view.

Prescott spelled the word for him. "It is a matter of some social standing and import to belong to a krewe. Some of them have quite extensive histories, back into the 1800s. Each Mardi Gras season they put on these lavish parades, wear costumes, throw out beads and other trinkets to those that come to watch the parades. Then they conclude things by hosting a ball, the more elaborate and munificent the better. They even have kings and queens and retainers and whatnot. It's almost a tribal imitation of the royal court in some respects. Frankly, I never took to it. It always seemed a great deal of pretended ado about nothing. Then again, I am not a native of the city."

"It sounds almost like a cult," Fleming said wryly.

"Indeed. However, I am relatively confident that they make no human sacrifices to pagan gods. If that happened, surely I would read about it in the newspaper."

Traffic began flowing steadily again. Overhead the sky was darkening further, bringing on a false dusk to this morning. Some ten minutes later, as Prescott drove the Lincoln onto the road that had delivered Fleming from the airport several days ago, the rain commenced. It started as stray fat droplets that spattered the windshield. The clouds mulled things over for several moments, then decided to unleash a proper torrent.

Prescott snapped on the auto's wipers, which had an arduous job of swiping away the water that was now falling in dense sheets. In short order it had become a full-fledged deluge. Rain pounded the Lincoln's roof and hood. The tires threw up great splashes as water rapidly accumulated on the roadway. The other motorists slowed. Prescott, however, maintained his speed, guiding the long auto with proficient control. Fleming recalled abruptly that the man had been something of a car enthusiast when they had served together. In fact, Prescott had claimed to have even done some professional racing in his youth.

For purely theatrical effect, heavy thunder growled from the sky. Thick forks of lightning appeared on the horizon. It was all shaping up to be quite a storm.

Prescott only seemed to warm to the challenge. He held the steering wheel easily, a smile curling his slightly pruned mouth as they sped and occasionally jounced along the paved roadway. He looked like a man in his element.

The Lincoln's engine thrummed along steadily. It was a fine auto. Fleming asked why Prescott didn't actually own a car.

"In most American cities a car is indeed a necessity, as it is in London. New Orleans is no especial exception. However, I make my home in the French Quarter and have become rather provincial in my habits. I find that weeks often go by without my leaving its confines. I have my restaurants, my taverns. All are easily accessible by foot. Even my practice doesn't often force me to leave, since I conduct much of my business from my home, doing legal research and such. There seems no great motivation for me to go exploring. I imagine that sounds dreadfully slothful of me, but there it is."

The rain kept up for some thirty minutes, not flagging. In the end they escaped it only by outrunning it. The Lincoln nosed from the storm and onto a dry stretch of the two-lane blacktop onto which they had turned. Glancing from the window, however, Fleming saw more clouds building—to the south and the west if he had his bearings right. These appeared quite dark. They lay in the direction in which the men were heading.

The surrounding landscape, now that they had passed the suburbs, was dense with trees and overgrowing wild stretches, interrupted here and there by the buildings of some small township or farm. Much of the land appeared unsettled. There was an abundance of creeks and lakes.

Without preamble Prescott launched into a brief travelogue. "Southern Louisiana peters out into marshes and wetlands well before it reaches its coast. The Gulf of Mexico lies along its rim, which connects, of course, to your beloved Caribbean and eventually to the Atlantic Ocean. When a hurricane bounces into the gulf from that sea, the people of New Orleans have every reason to be afraid. Were a sizable tropical storm to sweep up the Mississippi River, for instance, it would fairly wash away the city. We reside below sea level, as I've mentioned. A single properly placed hurricane could virtually erase the city and all its history from the map."

Fleming said, "I do find it curious that anyone thought it prudent to found a city of such size atop a swamp."

Prescott chuckled as he continued to guide the auto. There was almost no other traffic on the road now. "New Orleans is unconventional in every sense. Perhaps it is in part the very precariousness of its foundation, as it were, that makes its inhabitants live their lives with a bit more zest than might be considered seemly. We never know, you see, when we shall be summarily wiped off the earth."

"Surely every locale lives under its own particular threat of annihilation." Fleming thought of San Francisco, which he had so recently visited, and the constant menace of earthquakes. Early on in the century just such a catastrophe had in fact struck the city, nearly obliterating it. Yet during his stay he had seen no evidence of that not-so-long-ago calamity. The people went about their daily business, lived their lives calmly and productively. He shared these thoughts with Prescott.

He shrugged. "Ah, you're correct, of course. Perhaps the people of New Orleans need no philosophical excuse to behave as they do. More likely they simply enjoy their vices a bit too much. What does that sign say?"

Fleming turned to look at the passing road sign. He read off the name.

Prescott nodded. "We take the next turn. Do take a look at these directions, though, just to make certain I've not muddled them." He extracted the small notebook from his jacket and handed it over.

Fleming flipped to the page and studied the directions the late Inspector Everett McCorkle had so kindly dictated.

"It would be a bit of a fly in the ointment if it turned out the Red Dwarf was prevaricating. We may, of course, be going nowhere." Fleming looked out at the unfolding road.

Prescott said, "I don't believe he was. You'll recall he thought that complete honesty was his last hope of redemption. Men in mortal jeopardy are often admirably truthful."

"Yes, I agree. Let's hope he wasn't simply having a last laugh."

Growing suddenly grave, Prescott said, "If he was, then our hope of keeping this a private affair is lost. We shall have to follow your plan and contact Whitehall." He shook his head grimly. "Bloody Whitehall."

The prospect was equally unappealing to Fleming. He would postpone telephoning Davenport, however, until they had exhausted the possibilities of this outing. If these directions proved false or if Faith wasn't to be found at this secondary hideaway, then they could delay no longer.

On the new road, the countryside about them grew even wilder and wetter. This lane was a narrow one, its center yellow stripe well worn by the elements. Its tarred surface was rather rough, and now Prescott had to slow to negotiate the terrain. The Lincoln bumped forward. So constricted was the road that when the occasional motorist came from the opposite direction, one or the other was required to pull onto the weedy shoulder to allow passage.

To make matters more demanding, the rain reappeared. This fresh batch of thunderheads was as vigorous as the last. Booming thunder broke seemingly directly above the auto. Lightning slashed through the now quite dark sky. Prescott switched on the car's headlights. The downpour slickened the poor road, and even at moderate speeds the Lincoln had a tendency to slide alarmingly. Mounting winds were whipping leaves across the windshield and shaking the branches of overhanging trees wildly.

They were passing through a storm-lashed landscape of marshy lakes and untamed greenery.

Road signs, when they appeared, were not well maintained in these wild reaches and were difficult to read. Prescott would slow the Lincoln nearly to a full stop, and Fleming would swipe at his side window with his palm and peer through the sheeting rain. The signs pointed to oddly named places: Houma, Thibodaux, Bayou Terrebonne, Barataria Bay. He could only guess at the pronunciation of some of these.

They had been on the road for something near to an hour and a half by now. Their progress was necessarily slowing, and Fleming was uncertain how much ground they had covered and how much they had left to go. The Lincoln's interior was beginning to smell clammy. He lit a cigarette out of habit and sat rather rigidly in the passenger seat, tensing further each time the auto slid off the straight track Prescott was trying to maintain. At one point they were nearly dumped entirely off the roadway, as a heavy gust and a particularly bad patch of road surface conspired to strand them in the mire just beyond the shoulder.

The Lincoln's engine didn't stall, but its right front and rear tires had bogged in the pulpy ground. Prescott gunned the motor, slotting the car repeatedly into forward and reverse, attempting to rock them free, but the long auto gained no purchase. Mud flew up in black sheets, spattering Fleming's side window.

"Blast," muttered Prescott.

Fleming reached into the rear seat and grabbed the black raincoat. "I shall see what I can do."

He stepped from the car, his feet sinking immediately into the saturated ground. The ooze at the edge of the road's shoulder rose over his shoes, dampening his socks. He grumbled a curse as the sharp winds pelted needle-like raindrops across his face. The air was bitingly cold.

Visibility was poor. Fleming squinted and saw they were presently beached alongside an open field where numerous junked vehicles were sinking leisurely into the earth. The rusted hulks resembled nothing so much as the plaster skeletons of dinosaurs that one found in museums.

The field was bordered alongside the road by a collapsing fence of rough planks strung together with steel wire. He made his way toward this fence, needing to forcibly wrench his feet free of the sucking ground with every step. The downpour continued to assault him mercilessly. Already the treated raincoat was growing heavy across his shoulders. Water was trickling down his collar, and his hair was soaked. The cold was already in his bones.

Reaching the fence, he set numbing hands to a plank and tugged and tore. The wood's protest was barely audible above the cacophonous drumming of the rain and the punctuating thunder, but eventually the rusting nail holding it to the wire snapped. He staggered back a step, clutching his prize. The fence wire had snapped as well. The howling wind caught a stray end and whipped it smartly across Fleming's right cheek. He winced, then stepped forward to seize another plank.

This one came loose with a slightly less obstinate struggle. Turning about, he trudged back toward the Lincoln, which now looked remarkably inviting, its interior sealed away from this vicious deluge and the exhaust breathing from its tailpipe promising life-giving warmth.

Fumbling a bit for balance, he wedged the planks beneath the marooned tires, angling them back toward the relatively safe ground of the roadway. Then he wrenched open his door and scrambled back inside, icy water drizzling from his hair, his shoes fouled with clinging mud. He had spent less than ten minutes out in the storm and felt ruthlessly drenched. Awkwardly he shucked off the dripping raincoat and pitched it into the back seat.

"This is unseasonable weather," commented Prescott.

"That's a splendid comfort. Do apply that pontoon-like foot of yours to the accelerator, won't you?"

Prescott did as instructed. The Lincoln's tires spun vainly for a second, then the treads grabbed the wood planks. They fishtailed dangerously as they slid back onto the road, and for one troubling instant Fleming thought they were going to go careening off the other side. But Prescott proved again to have sure control over the auto.

Fleming huddled shivering in his black coat, arms crossed and knees together as he tried to keep his teeth from chattering. Prescott switched on the car's heater, and by slow degrees, as they now crept cautiously along, he began to thaw.

"How much farther is it?" Fleming asked.

"Not far, my dear fellow, not far. I find suddenly that I am none too eager to arrive, however. I am filled with a deep foreboding, which I shall attribute to this awful gothic climate. I confess I hope that when we arrive, we discover Faith Ullrich struck dead by an errant bolt of lightning."

"Not before we find out what this has all been about," said Fleming grimly.

"No, I suppose," Prescott sighed. "Not before then."

They drove onward through the mighty rain.

Chapter 32

PRESCOTT GUIDED the Lincoln across a short and narrow concrete bridge that spanned a reed-infested creek whose black waters were rippling madly in the wind. On the far side the tarmac turned abruptly to gravel. They were by now well off the beaten path, in regions of the state that likely received few casual visitors.

Trees closed themselves once more over the road, pressing in thickly, dangling great bundles of Spanish moss from gnarled branches. The lichen danced capriciously in the wind. Prescott appropriated the middle of the graveled lane, as the road's shoulders here appeared even muddier than earlier. Were they to bog themselves in the viscous black grime, it was an even wager they would not get free until the ground hardened—if that ever happened.

Bits of flying moss tangled in the laboring windshield wipers. Since Fleming was still wet from earlier, he volunteered to step out and pick them away.

"I think we would have done better to rent a Land Rover," said Fleming as he slid back into his seat.

Prescott only grunted. Whatever pleasures he had found in piloting this fine automobile at the outset of their journey had by now evaporated. This had never been a joyride, but it had steadily degenerated into a frustrating slogging. The Lincoln was having a difficult time with the road's gravel surface. Whenever Prescott pushed it to speeds above twenty-five miles per hour, the tires showered the tiny pebbles up around the fender, adding a final chaotic note to the general anarchic music of the crashing storm. If anything, the deluge was increasing. The thunder was loud enough to rattle the windows. The beams of the Lincoln's headlamps careened ahead of them as the auto jounced painfully along.

Intermittently there came a break in the enclosing trees, revealing an unmarked lane or another meadow of moldering vehicles. Through one gap Fleming briefly spied a tangled expanse of foliage—more trees hung with more moss, intertwining above a flat bed of almost luminous greenery. It wasn't until they had passed that he realized that the "ground" had in truth been swamp, paved over with moss and lily pads. The scene had looked alien, a landscape that belonged more to a fairy tale.

Under other conditions, he imagined, this countryside could be quite charming. But these weren't relaxing conditions, and this was not a sightseeing venture. Their mission was a grave one. A grueling total of six people had already been slain in the course of this horrid affair. At least one more might be added to that grim sum.

Road signs had by now entirely vanished. The lane remained utterly empty of other vehicles. Prescott asked Fleming to recite the last of the directions again. He did so.

Prescott nodded. "Very well." With a final hail of gravel against the undercarriage, he turned the long auto into a small cul-de-sac that wound out into a stretch of weeds and reeds on their left. Likely it was used as a turnout, since reversing directions on this pinched road would be otherwise impossible.

He unslotted the key from the ignition.

"On foot from here?" asked Fleming, already reaching for the black raincoat that hadn't yet dried from its previous soaking.

"I fear so. The supposed hideaway is a quarter of a mile ahead, recessed from this miserable excuse for a road. I only brought us this close because even a hound's keen ears wouldn't be able to detect our motor above this inclement cacophony." To illustrate, rolling thunder rocked the blackened sky. "I hadn't counted on a storm of this magnitude. Really, it's not the season for it. But perhaps it shall work to our advantage. And if not, we will at least both assuredly contract pneumonia."

From his pocket Prescott lifted a snub-nosed revolver, opening and checking its cylinder.

"Where did you get that?" asked Fleming.

Prescott snapped it closed. "It's McCorkle's."

A better weapon than the derringer, thought Fleming. It took a great mutual effort of will for the two Englishmen to tug their door handles and step out into the turbulent climate. Fleming secured only the top two buttons of his raincoat, leaving the tails to flap and snap about his legs. He wanted to be able to reach the Enfield revolver tucked at the small of his back without any unnecessary fumbling.

Icy raindrops and bits of moss and twig slashed cruelly across his face. The place where that fence's steel wire had whipped his cheek now stung quite painfully. Even with the canopy of the thick-limbed trees he was drenched almost instantly. An errant memory came unbidden to mind, of being caught in a similarly raw downpour in the north of France in the late autumn. During the war? No, after. Prescott had been with him. And yet another of Churchill's Boys, a thickset bowlegged fellow named Hensley. Their auto's front left tire had punctured on a countryside road, and they were on foot. They had—

He shook it all away. This was hardly the proper time to reminisce—and hardly a subject matter he had any desire to recollect. The past had already been prodded sufficiently into wakefulness. He didn't need to aid it in any way. He hoped, in fact, to bury it permanently and absolutely this day. Prescott was fervently nurturing the same ambition. They had come here to perform the last rites.

Prescott was grimacing against the frigid deluge, clutching the collar of his gray raincoat. He glanced back somewhat mournfully at the Lincoln. Mud clung to its front and sides, muting the brightness of the chrome. It looked quite the worse for wear.

They trudged up the road. Fleming could smell the swamp all about them, a scent of eternal organic decay. They stayed near the trees on the right-hand side. Walking the road's gravel was much like drudging along a beach; each step required an extra effort, and one's center of gravity never remained properly fixed. Even though Fleming was quite physically fit, a dull ache came to his calves before they had covered half of the quarter mile.

Prescott, who showed his years more readily, was fairly struggling along, teetering in the gusting wind. He muttered curses and swiped his hand across his wet face repeatedly.

With bleak determination they advanced. Fleming squinted against the rain, searching for the lane that would lead to the house. It was unsafe to act on the presumption that Faith had no other members in her black circle. Because McCorkle had said that he, Gerard Marquette, and the Baptist were the only ones aligned with her didn't mean Faith couldn't have easily drawn in others. She was manifestly a devious and beguiling woman. There might be sentries guarding the house. They would have to be cautious.

Despite the hardships, Prescott appeared to be remaining alert as well. At last they saw what they were looking for, where the row of trees they were following was interrupted by the mouth of a lane. The gap was some twenty yards ahead.

Prescott paused briefly, hunkering, peering ahead, hazel eyes carefully scanning the scenery. Fleming was doing the same. Together they moved onward, crouching. Prescott drew the snubnose, holding it beneath a fold of his raincoat. Fleming reached behind to lay his fingers on the grip of his .38 but didn't slide it from its holster.

They closed on the lane. A long iron stake was driven firmly into the ground, off to one side, where the lane met the road. It leaned at a casual angle, not moving in the wind. If it was meant to hold up a sign of some sort, the placard was gone.

Fleming was momentarily startled by tiny scuttling movements along the bole of the fat brown tree immediately beside him. Then he saw that they were rats—gray-bodied, long, fur beaded with moisture—scampering with unnatural agility up the face of the gnarled wood. He ignored the prickling of automatic revulsion and marched onward.

He bent lower as they reached the last of the trees, creeping up warily on the turn, Prescott now a step behind him. He eased up against the final tree, whose bulky jointed overhanging branches dangled wet moss in his face. He brushed aside the gray-green veil, set his shoulder against the tree and peered around the corner.

The lane wound away to the left, almost immediately disappearing behind more knotted foliage. He studied this wild greenery where someone with a rifle and a camouflaging poncho could so easily be squatting, patiently watching the road.

The chill had returned to his bones, but he did his level best to ignore it. He glanced over his shoulder. Prescott pointed to himself, pointed to the other side of the lane's mouth. Fleming nodded.

The tails of his gray raincoat fluttering wildly, Prescott dashed across the brief patch of open ground, kicking up gravel. He dodged past the curious iron stake and hunched alongside a tree's knotty trunk, scanning the forward terrain from his vantage. He kept his grip on the pistol beneath the coat. After a moment he threw Fleming a nod.

They moved once more, keeping low, stealing up either edge of the lane. Fleming still didn't like how exposed they were, but the surrounding thickets were too tangled to penetrate. He eyed the enclosing trees, his senses heightened. They came up on the bend.

Did this road in fact lead to the promised secondary hideaway, which they had journeyed so far to find? Or had McCorkle been playing games, and the lane would spill out on another of those impromptu auto graveyards that were apparently customary here in the country? They would see.

Moving in tandem, they slipped around the bend. And there it was, some thirty yards distant.

It was a rude house, single-storied, all thick dark lumber, with a canted roof and a wide overhung porch at its front. It was quite weathered, and its angles stood lazily. A brick chimney protruded from the roof, coughing out dark gray smoke that the wind whipped instantly into nonsense. It had glass in the two wide windows Fleming could see from where he had stopped and squatted.

There were two vehicles parked in the weed-ridden plot in front of the house. The first was a red pickup truck, a concentrated rime of rust eating patiently at the edges of the undercarriage. A blue tarp covered the bed, lashed down by rope, and the canvas undulated like the surface of a stormy sea but remained in place.

The second was a white sedan of a make Fleming couldn't identify. It was parked nearby a pair of ragged tree stumps. It had a body nearly as long as the Lincoln's and looked just as out of place in these rustic environs. Its windows were darkly tinged, and it appeared to be in showroom condition, despite the mud that coated it almost to its windows. Evidently whoever had driven it here had met with automotive trials similar to those he and Prescott had experienced.

Fleming now drew his revolver. Light was burning inside the house, the smooth buttery glow of a lantern or two. He saw nothing beyond the windows, but visibility was unreliable. There was no movement in the surrounding plot beyond the rippling greenery at its edges. He carefully studied the scene nonetheless for any signs of sentries.

The two vehicles indicated at least two occupants inside the house. The truck plainly fit the scene; the white sedan was the visitor. Had the pickup belonged to the Baptist, and was the auto Faith's? Or was there some other party involved? Or did none of these characters figure into the matter? Fleming still didn't implicitly trust McCorkle's directions. Who knew whose house this was?

More thunder growled overhead. The storm clouds seemed fixed in the sky, as if this violent weather were stalled stubbornly above the region. He was shivering with the cold again. His shoes and the legs of his trousers were soaked through. More icy water was spilling in around the raincoat's collar. It felt as though his blood were starting to freeze. Prescott's quip about pneumonia might not be so farfetched.

He waved for his partner's attention, and they went onward, using the tangled growth along the boundaries of the lane for cover. Prescott abruptly lost his footing and dropped heavily to one knee. Mouthing unheard oaths, he swayed back to his feet.

They closed on the cleared area before the shabby house. There was still nothing visible beyond the wide windows, no convenient moving shadows, nothing even to mark positively that the place was presently occupied, though that at least was a safe bet. There was an unpainted door on the face of the house that looked out on the front plot, set back among the porch's shadows. Craning his neck as far as he dared, he saw that the truck and sedan were both empty.

He made hand signals at Prescott, who studied them a moment, then nodded. They would each go around the house's sides, avoiding the front door. As tempting as it was to simply charge that door—and thereby bring this situation to an immediate culmination—a more cautious approach was called for.

At another sign from Fleming they darted forward, each crossing a short stretch of the front plot, then slipped quickly out of view of the windows as they ducked around the sides of the house. As he dashed past in a low crouch, Fleming tried to get a look underneath the canvas tarp flapping over the red truck's bed but could make out nothing.

Prescott was now out of sight on the opposite face of the wood house. Fleming would be able to hear a gunshot, no matter what noises the skies made, but it would be difficult to detect the sound of a knife or an axe blade striking a human body. He hoped Prescott hadn't run into any trouble.

He smelled the damp, vaguely rotting scent of the house's

planks. Splinters protruded from the wood nearby him. There were no windows along this side and no gaps or convenient knotholes through which he could peer.

Cobwebs trailed from the sagging eaves above, the strands glistening with raindrops. He was now at least out of the full fury of the downpour, though the wind continued to whip it at him from erratic angles. Gingerly he put an ear to the wall, still gripping his Enfield revolver. He strained and thought he heard intermittent voices, but it might only be the crackling of a fire.

He crept toward the rear of the house and looked around its corner. He was glad to see Prescott just sidling around from the other side. The two men shook their heads at each other. Prescott's side of the dilapidated house must have been without windows as well.

The rear, however, had another door. It stood atop two rickety-looking steps and was inset with a pane of glass. They edged carefully toward this, staying out of sight against the wall. A hand-operated water pump was rusting into ruin a few yards from the back door.

Fleming put his toe to the top step and raised himself, planting his eye against the lower right-hand corner of the door's dust-covered window. He was looking into an unoccupied kitchen of cabinets and cupboards. Mismatched dishes were piled high in the metal tub of the sink, and flies were darting about. If this was the Baptist's place, the Cajun hadn't been much of a housekeeper. There was an open doorway at the kitchen's far end, but he could see nothing helpful from where he stood, just the glow of lantern light from the main room beyond.

He came down off the step and pulled Prescott toward him so he could whisper in the man's ear.

"I am going in this way. You go back, position yourself so that you can watch the front door. If anyone bolts out of it, stop them."

Prescott nodded and whispered tightly, "Do be careful, Ian."

Tension etched his homely-handsome features. Then he turned and glided off in the direction he had come, his pistol stiff at his side.

Fleming eyed the rear door's hinges dubiously. They were, of course, rusted. Staying below the level of the glass, he tested the knob. It turned without protest. A half inch at a time he drew open the door, slowly enough that the hinges' inevitable squeal blended with the general howl of the wind. He squirmed through when there was enough space and spent just as much time and care closing the door behind himself.

The kitchen frankly reeked. It was a stench of aging meat and long-soured milk and several other unpleasantly redolent things. The flies buzzing about the sink swarmed over to investigate him. They were fat-bodied things, black and jade with large red eyes. A sufficient number of them, he judged, could likely lift him bodily and carry him off.

He waved them from his face. The tails of his black raincoat were dripping on the decades-old peeling tiles of the kitchen floor, but there was nothing he could do about that. He stood still a moment, pistol in hand, and listened.

Voices, yes. Not intelligible above the crackling of the fire that was pouring that dark gray smoke from the chimney. The rain drumming the canted roof was no help either. But the tenor of the voices told him it was a man and a woman, and told him further that an argument was in progress.

He stepped toward the kitchen's doorway. No, less an argument—more like an intense negotiation.

"... million ... and I ... if ..."

"... won't ... over ..."

He could make out nothing more useful as he pressed against the jamb. It seemed the male voice was accented, a vaguely Slavic lilt to the few words he could distinguish. The woman, hopefully, was Faith Ullrich. The man might be anybody.

Prescott had had ample time to place himself to watch the front of the house. Fleming drew a long silent breath, then stepped through the doorway, his Enfield Mk II straight out ahead of him. The main room took up the house's remaining space. The sooty stones of the fireplace were against the wall to the left, where yellow tongues of fire were lapping at the chopped bits of a log. The furnishings were unkempt. Most appeared handcrafted but not skillfully so. The ceiling was composed of exposed beams where more cobwebs looked to have been flourishing unchecked for many years. Two vertical wood struts connected to the ceiling's crosspieces. These slouched at indolent angles, and from them two lanterns were hung by nails.

One of these squared braces stood between Fleming and the woman, who was seated on a three-legged stool, her back toward him. He couldn't see her face even as she turned, but her hair was long and shaded mahogany, spilling nearly to the waist of the blue dress she wore. The garment left her shoulders bare.

The man was seated opposite her in an unpainted wood chair with a high back. Fleming had a good view of him. His body was constructed in squares—large flat head, right-angled ruddy face, broad straight shoulders, stocky torso, and short legs. He had thick metal-gray hair that stood in tufts. His brows were dark and peaked into odd points above his wide eyes. He wore a brown suit, double-breasted, with a soft gray tie and large black shoes.

He looked up sharply as Fleming entered the room, his glance alerting the woman. Then he merely stared, his heavy clean-shaven face mild, wearing no particular expression. His hands, resting on his knees, didn't move.

The woman, however, leapt to her feet as Fleming quickly advanced, getting the ceiling strut out of his line of fire.

Her curving jaw was tense, hanging open on whatever words Fleming's sudden presence had interrupted. The nostrils of her sloping nose were flared, and her firm cheekbones stood out prominently in her creamy-skinned face. She had her father's confident eyes, which now drilled into Fleming. Faith Ullrich did not look pleased to see him.

"Do not do anything foolish with your hands," he said. "Leave them in plain view, both of you."

He was passing the fireplace, through the immediate blast of its luscious heat, his .38 aimed at the room's two other occupants. At that moment he wanted only to shuck his raincoat and stand there, thawing himself, returning full feeling to all his chilled extremities.

Also at that moment, however, Faith Ullrich took it upon herself to do something foolish. The results were most unfortunate.

Chapter 33

FAITH ULLRICH'S eyes had a supremely self-assured depth to them. Into them a man might tumble, might willingly plunge. Those eyes held promises, and those promises would be kept.

Fleming, however, had seen what those eyes—this woman, this sorceress—could wreak. He wasn't tempted by her, though she was indeed a beautiful woman. He had seen Prescott's photos of her, had seen that supple sculpted body unclad. But she was an unclean spirit. She had ordered the murders of Angelina Marquette and Martin Dours. She had fouled the souls of Gerard Marquette, Everett McCorkle, and the Baptist. All those individuals were now dead. Only Faith remained.

He closed rapidly on her. The square-bodied man in the brown suit sat motionless in his chair, studying the scene sedately. Faith, as Fleming neared, abruptly bared her teeth in an unsettling grin, stooped, and snatched up the short stool on which she'd been sitting by one of its legs.

She brandished it like a bludgeon.

"Did you wish to shoot me, Fleming?" Her grin broadened across white teeth. Her accent was English. "Did you wish to kill me without uncovering the full facts? Are you still an *assassin?*" This last word she spat viciously.

"No. I will, however, cheerfully put a bullet through your shoulder if you do not lower that stool. You're a multiple murderess, and you've caused me and others a great deal of grief. I suggest you do not afford me the opportunity to return you some of that pain."

Faith continued to bore into him with her eyes.

The foolish thing she did was to make as if she were lowering the stool, then cock it swiftly over her shoulder and hurl it in Fleming's direction. The unfortunate result was that as he easily batted aside the stool, he fired his revolver—not at her but aiming above her head. He might not even have bothered to do that if it weren't for the presence of the unidentified man with the pointed brows. A loud gunshot, Fleming judged, would convince this pair to behave.

The shot, however, alerted Prescott outside. Seconds after it he burst noisily through the house's front door, allowing in a cold blast of wind. His snub-nose was in hand, but Faith was already on the move, pivoting and leaping unexpectedly at the doorway, shoulder lowered.

Fleming aimed again, but Prescott was in his line of fire. Faith Ullrich hit the red-haired Englishman with the point of her shoulder, driving it into his chest and elbowing his right wrist at the same time, hard enough that the revolver came loose in his grip.

Prescott was knocked against the door frame, his hazel eyes wide with surprise. He made a wild grab for Faith as she hurtled past, her flat-heeled shoes striking the porch's planks.

Fleming launched himself after her. He hadn't wanted to go to the bother of shooting her. That would have meant having to deal with a wounded woman, one from whom they still wished to extract information.

"Ian, I'm—" sputtered Prescott, snatching his pistol from the floor.

"Watch him!" Fleming shouted, hooking a thumb back at the man in the chair. Faith was off the porch and sprinting past the muddied white sedan. Her blue dress was already soaked and dark. The damned storm was relentless, thunder snarling mightily, lightning brightening the black sky in disorienting flashes.

She didn't run for the road but turned instead toward the trees. As Fleming leapt from the porch, she struck the dense foliage with the full force of her body, cleaving through branches and greenery, hands held up to protect her eyes. She left a ragged human-sized gap in the growth that ringed the house and yard like a wall.

Fleming pursued, the wind and rain lashing him yet again. He bounded through the breach, the bramble clawing at him. It caught and hung securely to the tails of his raincoat for a heartbeat. It was easier for him to simply allow the coat to be pulled off his arms, and this he did.

Faith was only a few yards ahead, springing madly through the undergrowth beneath the brooding mossy trees. Her dress had torn in several places. There were lines of red across her arms and exposed shoulders.

"Halt!" he yelled after her, but it was wasted breath. He could still only shoot her to stop her. She was not about to surrender willingly. However, wounding her now as she leaped and crashed furiously through the knotted greenery wouldn't be easy. His shot might go astray. He might end up by killing her. While this was an appealing prospect in some respects, they needed her alive, to find out what lay at the root of this terrible puzzle.

He pursued her, smashing through the bramble, feet slipping on the wet tree roots. He was getting well scratched in the process also, tiny painful nicks appearing on his hands and face.

Faith would eventually stumble or hit an impenetrable patch of this wild. Meanwhile Fleming, without even the protection of his raincoat now, was drenched to the flesh.

She slashed her way tenaciously forward, hands tearing aside branches and moss, legs pumping. With deranged will she blazed her trail, still only a few maddening yards out of reach.

Fleming was reconsidering the tactic of bringing her down with a bullet, perhaps shooting out one of her legs, when abruptly she dropped completely out of sight.

She hadn't ducked or dived; she had dropped in one clean sweep straight through the ground.

He charged onward, grabbing an overhanging tree limb to halt himself as he came upon the place of her sudden disappearance. The ground under his feet was oozy, sucking hungrily at his soiled shoes. A step further on, the ground wasn't ground. It was the green-black surface of a swamp, which was still rippling viscously. He went to his knees, holstered the Enfield, and plunged his hands beneath the surface. It had the consistency of drying paint, fouling the sleeves of his jacket. He groped beneath the top layer of moss, leaves, and soil. He saw that he was at the edge of a wide pool of this mire in which stood thick-boled trees and sluggishly drifting logs.

He probed beneath the surface where Faith had vanished, feeling nothing but the slime. Finally he laid himself flat in the mud and swept his arms downward, his movements urgent even as he remained coolheaded. Leaping after her into this quicksand wasn't a viable option. He continued to grapple for her.

Abruptly he touched something solid. Fingers groping, he clutched both hands around the object and drew on it, summoning all his physical reserves. He panted as he pulled against the grimy water.

He saw he had her securely by her left wrist as her hand broke the surface, but the pool didn't wish to let her go. He dug his knees into the mire and tugged, estimating that time was rapidly running out for her. More of her arm came free from the bog. Then her head surfaced. Her long hair was thick with mud, and her head lolled at a boneless angle. Heaving, he yanked her shoulders and torso loose; then, planting a foot, he hauled the last of her body out and onto the ground's dark ooze.

Faith's flat-heeled shoes were gone. She was positively coated with the dark viscous earth. Fleming was unconcerned with these niceties as he laid her on her back and swiftly wiped the grime from her face. He cleared her nostrils and scooped the mud from between her lips. She was, he saw, not breathing.

Fleming stooped, pinched fingers over her nose, and laid his lips to hers, tasting the swamp's foul decaying flavor. He exhaled evenly, blowing a long stream of breath down into her still lungs. He pumped her chest with his other hand, palm between her breasts. Her eyes remained closed, her body unmoving.

The thirty seconds it took to restart her lungs, while the storm continued to crash above the trees, stretched itself into something resembling an eternity. He pulled his mouth away just as her backbone went abruptly rigid, arms flailing outward, head lifting and turning. She vomited hugely on the ground.

He helped her into a sitting position. She was shivering convulsively now, hands clutching her elbows, body drawing into itself. He swiped more of the grime from her face. The fight seemed to have gone entirely out of her.

He scooped her up into his arms, swaying a bit as he got to his feet. His clothes were nearly as soiled as hers. His bones ached with the cold. She huddled against his chest as he retraced the ragged trail through the undergrowth. Keeping his balance was a challenge. By the time he reached the cleared plot surrounding the house, dizziness was whirling through his skull. He didn't bother collecting his raincoat from where he had discarded it. He fairly staggered across the yard with his human bundle, teetering onto the porch and through the open doorway.

"My God!" Prescott yelped at the sight of them. He was holding his gun on the brown-suited man, who apparently hadn't moved an inch in his chair while they were gone.

Prescott fetched a pillow and two blankets from the far end of the room. Fleming laid Faith's shuddering body on a long bench that stretched nearby the fire. Prescott tucked the pillow beneath her head, spread a blanket over her, and handed the other to Fleming.

He gratefully wrapped the musty-smelling cover over himself and stood directly before the fire, basking for several moments, feeling the first tingles of returning circulation. Prescott waited for him silently, keeping an eye on the square-bodied man, who was still watching these proceedings blandly.

"Who is he?" Fleming finally asked, wishing for a hot cup of coffee to further restore himself.

Prescott's hazel eyes flickered to the chair. "He says his name is Vlasta and that he came here to meet her." He glanced at the bench where Faith lay, eyes closed, trembling, occasionally coughing. "That is as far as we had gotten, actually. He was also carrying this." He lifted a short-barreled automatic from the pocket of his raincoat.

Fleming eyed the man. "A Russian?"

It was Vlasta who answered. "Yes, I am Russian." His accent wasn't thick but still unmistakably Slavic. His voice didn't waver, remaining at a calm, even pitch.

"Why did you come to meet her?" Fleming asked.

The Russian was silent a moment—not, Fleming thought, planning to stonewall, rather laying out the order of his words. He was deciding how much to tell and how quickly to tell it.

At last he said, "I came at her invitation." He nodded at Faith's prone form.

"How did she contact you?"

"Through established channels."

Evasive answers. Or replies that only hinted at the full breadth of truth beneath them. This Vlasta required some persuading as to the seriousness of this situation, something to break his poise. He was maintaining an admirably professional aplomb.

"You are a spy, then?" said Fleming, choosing a direct route.

His pointed eyebrows only rose slightly. "I am a servant of the Russian people," he said neutrally. "May I ask in whose employ are you two gentlemen?"

"We are nonaffiliates."

Prescott said, "I think he suspects us of being his competitors."

Fleming nodded. He dug through his wet pockets and came

up with his engraved cigarette case. The Players inside had remained dry. He lit one.

"We're not Hoover's lads, if that is what you're imagining," he said to the Russian.

"No, I did not imagine this."

"Neither are we connected to Whitehall," Fleming finished. "We're private citizens with a vested interest in this matter. I feel certain you've not failed to notice the pistol my partner is holding. We are involved in this affair, and we mean to learn all we can concerning it. You will aid us. Or, I assure you, there will be consequences."

It was a vague enough threat but, he decided, effective. They would play their cards as close to the vest as this Russian agent.

Vlasta continued to gaze mildly, then slowly nodded.

"It is very well then, gentlemen. I concede the superior hand to you."

The fire was drying the damp mud on Fleming's ruined clothes. He ignored the discomfort and drew thoughtfully on his cigarette.

"Why did the woman invite you here?"

Vlasta indulged in another pause, then said, "To bargain."

"Over what?" Fleming was careful to keep the edge of growing impatience out of his voice. If this Russian flatly refused to speak, they could only resort to drastic measures—ones he wasn't enthusiastic to employ.

"Information."

"An elusive commodity," commented Fleming.

"Not, I think. Information in our new world is the ultimate merchandise. Few things have greater solid value."

"And what was she selling?"

He lifted his large hands from his knees, spreading his fingers and lifting his broad shoulders in a shrug. "I do not know this." His tone remained level. His blocky face and wide eyes betrayed nothing.

He wasn't lying. Instinct told Fleming so. Too often in this adventure he had relied on intuition; still, it hadn't yet failed him. "Yet you came some great distance to bargain," he said. Vlasta drew a breath. "She made contact. She offered information. She promised it was of vast value. I came to test the truth of the matter. You gentlemen interrupted our negotiating before it had properly begun." Again he spoke guilelessly.

There was, of course, only one kind of information Faith Ullrich would be trying to sell to the Russians: details on the postwar operation in which Churchill's Boys had engaged. Such data the Russians might indeed find valuable. Releasing it to the world would do much to discredit the British intelligence community.

It was much as Prescott had once said. This bloody undeclared murky war with the Russians. Communists versus capitalists. But no proper battles fought. The contest was made up of posturing, politics, threats, counterthreats, and espionage. The spy business was flourishing once more, only the Germans were no longer the enemy. The Nazis had been so clear-cut a menace, a sinister empire bent on world conquest. How easy they had been to hate, what with the atrocities that had emerged from the war. How easy that war had been to *understand*.

But this conflict with the Russians . . . its battles were fought invisibly, by spies and agents and moles stealing atomic and military secrets from each other. It was purely cloak-and-dagger, a shadow play.

Fleming realized his thoughts were rambling away from him. He was weary. He pitched his cigarette into the fireplace.

If this Vlasta knew nothing of what Faith had meant to sell, then he didn't figure into this. Evidently he and Prescott had arrived in the very nick of time.

"Prescott," he said quietly, "take our Russian friend here out to his car, the white sedan. Put him inside and hold him there." He turned a few degrees, now looking down on Faith reclined on the bench. Some pieces of the puzzle had tumbled into place, but there were many unanswered questions. They would not remain so.

Prescott nodded silently and with his pistol waved Vlasta out the front door, closing it behind them.

Chapter 34

THE LOG shifted in the sooty fireplace, throwing a fistful of sparks up the flue. Fleming shucked away the musty blanket in which he had wrapped himself, letting it drop to the floor's poorly set planks. The fire's heat had sufficiently melted the deep-seated cold from his bones, but already he could feel a sickly congestion accumulating in his chest and throat. Whatever else came of this day, he had surely caught a chill. Even as he thought this, he abruptly sneezed.

From the nearby bench Faith, eyes still closed, murmured, "God bless you."

He looked down on her in her cocooning blanket. The mud was hardening in her hair.

"And which of your gods would that be?" he asked quietly.

Her eyes opened at that. Despite her thoroughly disheveled appearance, those eyes still possessed that remarkably confident cast, a trait inherited from her father. Wallace Ullrich's eyes had burned with the brightness of a full moon, and to stand beneath his gaze had been to feel oneself probed to the core of one's being.

"You do not understand the ways of my gods," Faith enunciated clearly.

"I understand enough to know you fabricated this demented religion of yours out of nothing but a knowledge of the basest perversions of humanity."

"You speak of sacraments."

"I speak of degeneracy of the highest order. I've witnessed one of your rites, you see."

She coughed raggedly a moment, then turned her head and spat on the floor. A tiny smile moved a corner of her mouth. "Did you like what you saw?" A wicked glint came into her eyes.

"I was repulsed," he said darkly.

"Naturally. We are drawn inexorably toward that which we are repelled by. All the universe is based upon the tension between the positive and the negative. Opposite extremes are in fact one and the same. The greater your revulsion, the keener your interest, the sharper your desire to know more, to experience more. Given time I could make you understand and admit to those yearnings you are unwilling to acknowledge."

"Eternity would be too brief. And it would be wasted. What I saw was foul, odious."

Her smile gained strength. "And ultimately alluring," she finished, purring it out. Her voice, Fleming realized uneasily, recalled the provocative tones that Queen Cleopatra had used.

"Believe what you will. Your days as a priestess are at an end." He took a step nearer the bench. Thunder crashed, but for the first time the burst seemed not to be directly overhead. Perhaps the storm was at last moving. "You no longer have adherents. Your disciples are all dead."

Her expression did not change, but something queasy and dark slipped in among the sensual tones she'd adopted. "Did you kill them?"

Fleming said nothing.

"My men," said Faith, and suddenly those penetrating eyes were growing glassy. "My beautiful boys, my children . . ." A tear detached itself from a corner of one eye, slipping over her firm cheekbone, cutting through the dirt.

"You are alone," Fleming said, studying her face, looking for evidence that his assertion was in fact the truth. It seemed so.

With that she sat up on the bench, slowly, smoothly. He had thought her sprint through the woods and dip in the swamp would have spent her thoroughly. She coughed again, then said, "You're still just an assassin, then."

"Believe what you will," he repeated.

She wiped her mouth with the back of her hand, then licked her lips with a venomous tongue. The blanket fell to her waist. The muddy dampness of her dress clung to her upper body, betraying its secrets . . . secrets Fleming had already seen in those photos Prescott had taken.

He studied her a moment longer than he wished he had, then said, "I want answers from you."

"Then ask questions." She pushed the blanket to the floor. The rents in her dress were nearly strategic, offering burlesque glimpses of the body beneath. It was quite implausible, he told himself, that anyone in so frightful a state as this soiled creature could hope to appear enticing. He nearly told her she was wasting her time, as she subtly arched her back to push forward her breasts; but to do so would be to acknowledge that he was even aware of her ploy. She was no longer shivering from the cold.

The log shifted once more in the fireplace. The flames were beginning to die.

"Why did you send those photographs of Angelina Marquette's corpse to Mr. Quick?" Fleming asked.

"To draw him in, of course."

It was something of what Gerard Marquette had claimed during that interrogation on St. Philip Street. "Toward what end?"

"I meant to add him to my ring of—what did you say?—disciples." Her smile simmered. She rolled her head slowly, spilling mud-caked hair across her scratched and bleeding shoulders.

He responded with a frown. "Why did you imagine that Mr. Quick would want anything to do with your corrupt band?"

"He is a weak man. Weak in the right ways. He longs for release, for forgiveness. His crimes are quite heinous. So are yours, Fleming. Under my care he would have found salvation."

His lips curled in disgust. "I have seen what sort of redemption you have to offer."

A kind of dreamy eroticism came to her features. "Those pictures, also that note I wrote him . . . how could they fail to remind him of his past deeds? He was already weak. This I knew from my father. I meant to weaken him further, to send him into a prolonged convulsion of penitence. Then he would be ripe. And I would pluck him."

"Did you send that photo of Martin Dours to me for the same reason?" The very question felt unclean. "To draw me in?"

"Of course." Her tongue tip traced her lips again.

"But your note warned me off. You told me to keep my nose out of it."

"That," said Faith, "was your bait. You're much like Quick, you know, but there are differences. My father told me. Nothing intrigues you so much as being told *not* to do something. I'm a keen reader of character." She punctuated this with a strangely unnerving little-girl giggle.

"You're also a homicidal maniac. You orchestrated the murders of Angelina Marquette and Martin Dours. Why?"

"They were sacrifices."

"I don't believe you. I think you had other purposes in mind."

"They were sacrifices," she repeated with a slinky shrug. "My beautiful boys thought them sacrifices, and so they were. If they believe"—she shifted tense—"believed in the gods they were appeasing, then those gods were made real. Belief creates reality."

Fleming's eyes narrowed slightly. "But you, *you* don't believe." He almost made a question of it.

Again she shrugged. "Those who establish religions on this earth rarely reap their benefits. Moses never made it across the river Jordan, you'll recall."

"How highly you regard yourself," he said with a note of flat contempt; but she had answered well enough, and the question was crucial. Faith Ullrich was not so deranged that she genuinely credited the mishmash of deviant theology she had concocted. It was all a sham, meant to keep her converts in line and under her thrall. The human sacrifices of Angelina and Martin had bound her followers to her permanently. After committing such acts at her behest, they had literally pledged their souls to this diabolical woman.

Her ruined dress had ridden high up her shapely legs. She positioned herself so that this fact wouldn't be overlooked. "Angelina's murder—which I made certain became public knowledge—sealed my boys to me, particularly my sweet Gerard. The killing of Martin Dours had a similar purpose. He was also inconveniently probing about into his sister's death. His brother, Elliot, would have followed."

"Yes. I know." He sorted his facts, ignoring the revulsion he felt as this puzzle was being clarified. To Faith the human lives under discussion were merely gaming pieces that had been swept from a board.

Marshaling his thoughts, he asked, "Did you know that Mr. Quick had been hired by Edmund Dours to investigate the affair between yourself and Gerard Marquette? Did you know that when you sent that first batch of photographs?"

Faith purred out another disturbing giggle. "Gerard was afraid his father-in-law suspected us. Edmund never really liked Gerard, you see. Thought him soft. But Gerard had made a friend of one of Edmund's house servants. The maid learned that the old man had hired a PI. When Gerard mentioned the name of Prescott W. Quick, I recognized it. I was very pleased. I saw how easily I could use him." She pursed her lips. "I know your friend took snapshots of Gerard and me. How often, do you guess, did he think of what he'd seen through his lens? How often did he secretly long to participate?"

Coldly Fleming said, "I can assure you that Mr. Quick was as revolted by those photos as I. You made grave errors in estimating his character and taste. And mine."

The sickly carnal heat of her smile oozed up into her eyes. "Did I, now?"

He continued, "You knew Mr. Quick had made contact with me in Jamaica. Gerard Marquette was spying on the mail. You sent me that message and photo."

"We kept an eye on your friend's mail to see that he did nothing foolish, such as contacting MI-5. When he instead contacted you, I was ecstatic. Now I knew the whereabouts of *two* of my father's old friends. I was determined to bring you in. And I did." She was plainly pleased with the victory. "And if you didn't come . . . I would still have Quick."

"I would not have abandoned Mr. Quick," he said firmly.

"You sound rather like a man trying to convince himself."

In even harder tones he said, "It was a matter of honor."

Her laugh sounded poisonous this time. When she had finished, she said, "Yes, you men of honor. Oh, what honorable, honorable men you are. You, Quick . . . my father."

"You may know something of what we did after the war—"

"I know *all* of it."

He went on as though she hadn't spoken, "—but you obviously know nothing of why we did it. It was our duty. We were pledged to obey our orders, and our orders came from the highest level. An honorable man doesn't need to agree with his commander's orders. But he will do his duty."

"Like the Nazis in those death camps obeyed their orders."

He did his best to ignore his automatic anger at the barb. She was trying to lead him astray, toying with him. But, he told himself, he was too levelheaded to be misdirected.

"You meant only to sell secrets to the Russians, then," he said.

"I saw no reason not to profit from what I knew."

"The Russians would no doubt release the information."

"That didn't matter to me." So carelessly was this said, with such indifference to the disaster that would have resulted, that Fleming—improbable though it was—felt an even deeper loathing for this woman.

Drawing a long breath, he said, "But why did you bother with the rest of it? All of this—your faux pagan gods and rites and recruitment of adherents and your murders disguised as human sacrifices . . . all of this was in service of what? I do not understand. You even played at being a prostitute for a while," he said, referring to the elderly man McCorkle had mentioned who was paying great sums for the services of a strumpet who had turned out to be Faith. "Why?"

She considered. Thunder sounded again from the sky, but now it was definitely at some distance. The rain was easing its drumming of the roof.

"Because I discovered I could," she said, seeming to examine the words as they left her lips. "Theodore was his name, and he was a pruned old man, and I found I could manipulate him any way I wished. I forced money from him. Why not? He was merely an experiment. I was too much for him, of course." Fleming recalled McCorkle saying that the old man had died of an aneurysm. "By then I had met Gerard, and that was where the real fun began."

"Fun," Fleming said. "Is *that* what is was?"

Faith stood slowly from the bench. She made a great effort at perfect poise, but Fleming saw her totter slightly as she gained her feet.

"Look at me," she said. But he already was. "See me . . ." She pressed her hands to herself and slid her palms slowly down her body. "How dirty I am. How . . . foul, you would say. You'd be correct. Foul. Lewd. *Filthy.*" This last was said in a snake's hiss.

"You corrupted those men for amusement?" said Fleming.

"They . . . they were my family. I had none left, you know. Not after Father died." She slid a step nearer him. "He cut his own throat. I was there when he did it. He was weeping like a child, begging for forgiveness. I could have stopped him. Instead I told him to go ahead and do it." That she was saying this in husky seductive tones made it all the more loathsome.

In silent amazement Fleming wondered just how much more sordid this could conceivably become.

When she glided forward another step, he smoothly drew the .38.

"Why did Wallace want forgiveness?" he asked, imagining the man had been nurturing some drastic guilt over the deeds he'd committed as one of Churchill's Boys. Curious, since Wallace Ullrich had always seemed a most stable character, a dedicated career military man. Unlike Fleming and Prescott, he hadn't retired after that postwar operation.

"For what he'd done . . . to me," answered Faith.

Fleming's brow furrowed. "To you?"

Despite the pistol pointed at her, she edged still another half step closer. They stood roughly three yards apart. Fleming didn't believe she had it in her to make the lunge.

Her hands moved to a tear in the blue dress. Her fingers wriggled into the rent and, to Fleming's amazement, started to pull the rip wider, laying bare more of her flesh.

"You cannot conceive, I assure you, how that man used me." The demented carnality that heated her face grew even hotter, taking on a dangerous glow. "The things he made me do. Things Satan himself could not have imagined. Things God should have struck down before they could occur. Things never meant to take place between a man and a woman—and so much less between a father and daughter. From where did you think I gained inspiration for the creed I founded? Did you imagine I created those rites from nothingness? No. No. Father taught me. He taught me well. Being an assassin had changed him, you see. But . . . when I came to New Orleans and began collecting my men and discovered purely by chance that one of my father's old colleagues— Prescott Quick—was there as well, I turned the tables. *I* was the one in charge. I held the whip in hand. I commanded. And my beautiful boys . . . they obeyed me. They crawled. They did my bidding. They were the ones being degraded and debased, not me. They became my new family. Oh . . . oh, how I loved them.

And you and Quick. What could be better than having my father's old friends to do my bidding? I wanted you, too, to join the *family* . . ."

She had torn the dress thoroughly in two. The wet halves fell away. She'd also come several steps closer; he had watched her do it. He aimed the .38 at her bare left shoulder.

Vile. How vile it all was.

He heard the front door. Faith's now deranged gaze didn't waver. Prescott crossed into his line of sight.

"Ian?"

He realized that he had been about to shoot anyway. A bullet in Faith's shoulder would have stopped her from coming any nearer, would have stopped any further words she might say. Would have ended the sickening spell of this terrible scene.

"Ian," Prescott repeated. He, too, had a gun in hand. He stepped between Fleming and Faith, and now she did halt.

"Did you hear any of it?" Fleming asked. His chest felt even heavier now, the congestion building.

"I heard it," Prescott said solemnly. He held up a set of car keys. "Vlasta asked for you. I think you should go speak to him." Fleming glanced through the open door. The large man was visible past the porch sitting in the auto's backseat. Prescott had McCorkle's snub-nose. "I'll watch her."

Fleming turned, glad to be relieved of the sight of the filthy disrobed woman. He went through the door, stepping numbly off the porch, barely feeling the rain, which was definitely slowing now.

Faith remained an enormous problem, he thought dully. That critical information was still in her head. She was still dangerous, even divested of her disciples. She had been casually willing to sell her knowledge to a Russian agent, with no thought but for monetary profit. If Fleming and Prescott turned her over to the police, she would surely blather what she knew to any and all, merely as revenge. Diabolical she might be, but she was also insane. No, he would have to contact Davenport as soon as possible, make arrangements with MI-5, somehow—

Fleming was two steps from the sedan when the scream followed by the single shot rang from the house.

Chapter 35

HE HAD thought Prescott a faulty copy of himself. He had thought him the weaker man. He'd had the presumptuousness to think that all along.

"She tried to wrest away the pistol," said Prescott eventually, voice utterly empty. "I had no choice."

Fleming went back into the shabby house to wipe it of all possible fingerprints. He didn't need to confirm Faith's death by seeking a pulse. Her mad heart had beat its last. The bullet had entered her temple, at extreme close range.

By now the rain had stopped, but the heavy clouds allowed no glimpse of the sun.

THE PHLEGM WAS building in Fleming's chest, and his nose had started to drip. What spare clothes there had been at that backwoods house had belonged to the Baptist and so wouldn't have fit; and anyway he was reluctant to remove anything from the premises. So here he sat in the Lincoln's passenger seat, in his horridly soiled clothing, wrapped in Prescott's relatively dry raincoat. He'd retrieved his own damp one and tossed it into the backseat.

Prescott's hazel eyes stayed fixed on the road ahead. They had crossed the short concrete bridge and were back on the narrow, poorly tarred road, on a course back to civilization. They had encountered none of this swampy region's indigenous inhabitants during all of this. Inside the car was a paralyzed silence. What had happened hung heavily.

Fleming didn't try to imagine the particulars of the horrors

Faith had suffered under her father. Wallace Ullrich must have been a madman, a sadist. His facade of self-assurance and stability, which he'd worn all the time that Fleming knew him, had been impressively deceptive. It seemed unlikely that his duties as one of Churchill's Boys were the sole root cause of his derangement. Perhaps as a child he had experienced similar atrocities. Perhaps taking on the role of an assassin had been the final nudge over the brink, enough to transform him beyond all human recognition, enough to make him use his own daughter—

Fleming abandoned the pointless thoughts.

They had left Faith where she lay inside the house. No final words spoken over her corpse, certainly no burial. The marshy ground would doubtlessly not hold a body indefinitely, and regardless, digging and laying her in a grave was impractical. She would be discovered eventually. If the authorities found her lying on that floor, a bullet in her skull and the pistol in her hand where Prescott had put it, they might think nothing beyond suicide. The snubnose would ultimately be traced back to Inspector McCorkle, who, also being dead, would shed little light on the matter.

What to do about the Russian agent, Vlasta, had been a cause of some concern.

Prescott had emerged from the house, the deed done, Faith dead. Fleming, realizing what had happened, realizing that Prescott had taken the ultimate necessary step, stood mute, stilled by shock.

Prescott approached, nodding toward Vlasta in the sedan, and asked, "What shall we do with him?" His face was as impassive as slate.

Fleming found his voice. "Do? Nothing. I'll return him his keys, and we go our separate ways."

"But he can identify us." Prescott's words were as inexpressive as his features.

The chill Fleming felt had little to do with the local temperature. "By sight, yes. But he doesn't know who we are. And he won't be inclined to go running to the nearest sheriff's office. He will drive to the airport and board a plane for home. He came here to buy information, and that information is no longer available. His mission is done. We can't hand him over to the police or Hoover's lads. How would we explain ourselves? That Russian, I assure you, has unimpeachable travel documents and a perfectly plausible reason to be visiting United States soil. He is a spy, but we are no longer in the business of dueling with foreign spies. The game goes on without us, Prescott. Let the mighty intelligence agencies of the world wrangle among themselves. I for one am tired."

Faith had obviously learned much from her father about the inner workings of the British Secret Service and the spy business in general. She had known what covert channels to employ when she had announced to the Russians that she had valuable information to sell. Just as obviously she had made her offer an enticing one, enough to tempt a foreign buyer to come to investigate.

But the transaction—most fortunately—had been interrupted by Fleming and Prescott. The information remained unsold. The past, which of late had risen so disturbingly to life, was again securely dead.

Fleming sneezed wetly. He reached for his handkerchief, the same one Queen Cleopatra had handled.

"That sounds a wretched cold," Prescott said, breaking the long silence.

"It's shaping up to be," Fleming said in resignation. He lit a cigarette, choking slightly on the smoke. His throat was already growing raw. He felt his forehead for a temperature.

"You must get yourself into a hot bath and then some dry clothing when we return. Martha will make you some soup. She becomes rather maternal whenever someone is ill."

"I expect you are looking forward to seeing her."

"More so than I can adequately describe, old boy."

Fleming returned the handkerchief to his pocket. "She said I would carry the worse weight," he murmured.

"What?"

"Cleopatra. When she spoke of destiny."

"I recall she said we would act together. So we did."

"But," said Fleming slowly, "you were the one who took the worst of it."

He didn't say aloud that he hadn't been prepared to kill Faith in cold blood, no matter that her crimes warranted it, no matter that she *couldn't* be left alive, not if anything they had done was to have any meaning. But Prescott had done what he wouldn't do.

"That was . . . strong of you," he finally added.

Prescott slowed the Lincoln, then stopped it. The Russian had gone ahead of them by a few minutes.

Hazel eyes turned to Fleming. They looked as tired as he felt, brimming with fatigue. As he watched, they grew glassy.

"Strong?" said Prescott, emotion—raw and powerful—at last creeping into his voice. "Perhaps. I did what had to be done. Just as we did in the old days. That's it, Ian, finally. That is the ultimate judgment. As Churchill's Boys we were called upon to do service. Today we completed the final mission of that operation. Our past need never trouble us again, except as memory . . . and perhaps not even as that anymore. Perhaps."

Only a single tear finally spilled. Prescott didn't wipe it away.

The muddied Lincoln made it back to New Orleans in the waning afternoon. The sky remained gray, but the rain was long gone.

Chapter 36

As IT happened, there was no available flight to connect him to Miami—and from there to Jamaica—for two days. So Fleming stayed on at Prescott's house on Dauphine Street. It was just as well, actually. Martha's soup hadn't quite neutralized the severe cold he had contracted, and travel in his condition would only have aggravated the illness.

"WAS THE CONSULTATION successful?" Fleming asked, knocking on the office door, then entering. A fire crackled in the fireplace, and the room was warm. Prescott had spent an hour in here with his new client this afternoon. She had been, from the glimpse Fleming had caught, a rather withered elderly lady. Before Prescott even had the office door closed, she was making incensed hen-like noises about the ownership of an oak tree that stood on the boundary between her and her neighbor's property.

Prescott chortled. "Oh, indeed. I believe a calamitous tragedy has been narrowly averted. Mrs. Gilyot may sleep peacefully this night in the sure knowledge that I shall establish beyond reasonable doubt her rightful proprietorship over the stately oak her grandfather planted. Ah, I am decidedly back in familiar territory."

Fleming could only chuckle in turn.

Prescott stood and crossed to the serving cart. The empty port bottle was gone. In fact, the entire house, particularly the kitchen, had been cleaned and tidied. Prescott poured respectably aged whiskey into a tumbler.

"I see your alcoholic fast is at an end."

Prescott took a sip. "Ah, yes. Oddly, it doesn't taste as fine as I'd remembered. Oh, well. Care for one?"

"Your Martha warned me not to drink. It would offset the medicinal powers of her soup, she said."

"I won't tell," said Prescott, pouring two fingers into another tumbler and bringing it over. Having Martha back in the house obviously agreed with him.

Fleming's limbs still felt mildly weak, but several long baths had cleared the last of his congestion. He would be well enough for his flight tomorrow morning.

"It's time to settle my bill, Prescott."

Prescott looked at him blankly. "What do you mean?"

"The expenses." Fleming took out his billfold. "For Slim and Chopper's services and for the rented auto. We were going to divide the costs, remember?"

Prescott tried tut-tutting it all away, but Fleming eventually made clear his seriousness on the issue by threatening to empty his entire wallet atop Prescott's desk.

"Oh, very well, Ian," he grumbled, mock-pouting. "You're dashedly stubborn, you know."

"It is only fair. We were partners in this, Prescott."

The lanky Englishman nodded. "Yes, we were that, weren't we?"

After some quick tallying a figure was named, and Fleming counted out the appropriate bills.

"I hope Slim made good his flight from the city," Fleming said. Once the corpse of the scrappy lad's well-known confederate, Chopper, was identified, suspicion would surely fall upon him.

"Slim is doubtlessly in Minneapolis or Flagstaff by now." Prescott took another sip of his whiskey, wincing slightly and frowning at the glass. "The hullabaloo that shall arise when that passel of corpses is found, however, shall be extraordinary. That is, if the police do not decide to bury it all—literally."

Fleming hoped, not for the first time, that his and Prescott's movements in and out of that house had gone unobserved that night. Prescott nodded as he voiced this thought.

"I shall have no difficulties, I should think, in concocting a perfectly suitable alibi for my whereabouts on the night in question—presuming, of course, that the coroner is able to establish a reasonably accurate time of death for our murdered quartet."

Fleming said, "I shouldn't make your alibi too airtight. That tends to appear suspicious in and of itself."

No doubt the inevitable discovery of those bodies would make *very* dramatic headlines. No further arrests had been made in the Angelina Marquette case, at least so far as had been reported in the newspaper. Fleming didn't know if this was due to Mc-Corkle's demise or to the civil suit that man named Hush had filed. At any rate, the "war" against Queen Cleopatra's people appeared to be at an end.

Prescott set down his drink and reached into a drawer of his desk. He carried a handful of papers to the fire and tossed them in.

"What were those?" Fleming asked.

"The dossiers we made on Gerard Marquette and Faith Ull-rich."

"A sound precaution. If suspicion falls your way when those corpses surface, you would do well to have no damning evidence lying conveniently about your office."

"I was thinking it was almost a shame. This is the most complex and exciting case I've ever been involved in, and I can't breathe a word about it to any soul but you. If I've fancied myself a minor Sherlock Holmes, then this was surely my *Hound of the Baskervilles*. Sadly, I have had no John Watson to keep scrupulous notes of these exploits. I say, you wouldn't be inclined to write all this up, would you? Add a bit of fiction here and there, alter the names? I feel it would make fine reading. You, as I recollect, had something of a flair for prose."

Fleming sipped his whiskey. Its smooth flavor and warming flush were welcome. "Which often caused my knuckles to be rapped when I wrote up reports for our superiors. And to answer your question, no. I should not care to commit this adventure to paper or even to know that someone else had done so."

HUSH SNAPPED SHUT the tome in his lap and picked up the jangling telephone. The instrument might ring anytime, day or night, and so he was never startled by it.

However, the voice that came to him now through the earpiece caused the big man to launch himself up out of his chair, the thick volume of white law thumping the floor.

"Hush." The pronunciation of his name was sensually languid.

"My Queen . . ." he breathed. There in his room he automatically bowed his hairless head. He waited through the faint electrical hum of the wire. Queen Cleopatra, so far as he knew, had *never* spoken into a telephone in her life.

At last she resumed, her voice no less mesmerizing for being rendered into electronic impulses. "A measure of evil has been removed from the world," she pronounced. "It is concluded."

"I am glad, my Queen." How strange it was, hearing her words here in the neat but less than elegant confines of his room. Suddenly the water stains marring his ceiling seemed quite offensive.

"You are to be congratulated on your performance during this," Cleopatra added.

A thick heat crept over his large body at that, as if he stood now in the Queen's clammy parlor. "I . . . am humbled," he rasped.

The line clicked dead, but it was a long moment before Hush let go of the instrument. Something odd was happening to his face. The permanent steely cast of his features was being undermined, and eventually something approximating a smile contorted the grim stripe of his mouth.

THE TAXI, DRIVEN by a chunky man in dark glasses who appeared to have enjoyed the previous evening a bit too much, pulled to a stop before the terminal. As the cabdriver swayed out of his seat to collect Fleming's luggage from the trunk, Prescott made to follow Fleming out of the cab.

"I'll see you properly off," he explained to Fleming's puzzled glance.

Together they entered the terminal building. The scene was quite a flurry. More people arriving for Mardi Gras, Fleming figured.

"Ah, indeed," Prescott said when he mentioned it. "Each year it seems we receive a greater influx of tourists. One day the city—or at least the French Quarter—will simply burst at its seams during Carnival."

Fleming waited awhile in a queue before he could collect and pay for the ticket he had reserved. The fetching young woman with the bobbed red hair at the counter told him the flight was quite underbooked; he would have plenty of room to stretch out.

"What's taking you away?" she asked. "Business?"

"Pleasure." He smiled.

"Can't think of many more places in the world where there's more pleasure to be found than New Orleans." Her local accent crept out as she phrased the city's name; it came out as "N'awlins."

"Then I've had my fill of its pleasures. Cheerio."

Prescott, wearing his black suit and spruce red vest, came with Fleming into the spacious departure lounge. He slipped his gold pocket watch from the fob and checked his time against the large clock on the wall.

"Fifteen minutes," Fleming said, eyeing the busy airfield through the broad lounge windows. His suitcase at his feet, he remained standing, ignoring the ranks of seats and listening for the call for his flight to board.

"So anxious to be away, are you?"

"I've my own sanctuary to return to. Just as you have this city, I have Jamaica. I should like to while away what precious little remains of my winter in unabashedly slothful fashion."

"Yes, you've quite earned it, dear chap."

Fleming laughed a bit dryly. "Earned or not, I desire it."

"Earned, I should think," Prescott said, tone growing serious. "I found myself reading Homer late last night. A dream disturbed me, and I woke. I wrote down a portion of it." From his suit jacket's inner pocket he suddenly produced a folded sheet of his stationery.

Curious, Fleming opened it. Prescott, in his tidy penmanship, had written: *Of men who have a sense of honor, more come through alive than are slain, but from those who flee comes neither glory nor any help.* He reread the lines, then raised quizzical eyes.

"You did not flee when you could have," Prescott said somberly. "Rather, you could have chosen not to arrive at all. You could have remained safe in your Jamaican retreat, and none of this would ever have touched you. Instead, you came to my aid, whether that was your initial motivation for involving yourself or not. The facts stand. You did the honorable thing."

Fleming absorbed this slowly. "And you regained your honor during all this horror. Didn't you?"

The hazel-eyed man drew himself up to his full impressive height. "I did," he said firmly.

Fleming nodded and extended his hand. "Then may that honor carry us through the remainder of our days."

Their handshake was long and firm, and neither man was eager to break it.

Less than a half hour later Ian Fleming was in the sky, homeward bound.